The GHOST HUNTERS

The GHOST HUNTERS

NEIL SPRING

Quercus

First published in Great Britain in 2013 by Quercus

Quercus Editions Ltd
55 Baker Street,
South Block, 7th Floor
London W1U 8EW

A CIP catalogue record for this book is available from the British Library.

ISBN 978 1 78087 975 8
EBOOK 978 1 78087 976 5

10 9 8 7 6 5 4 3 2

Typeset by Ellipsis Digital Limited, Glasgow
Printed and bound in Great Britain
by Clays Ltd, St Ives Plc.

This novel is dedicated to Mum and Dad,
and my brother James

'Of all ghosts, the ghosts of our old loves are the worst.'

SIR ARTHUR CONAN DOYLE
The Memoirs of Sherlock Holmes

THE FINDING

OF MISS SARAH GREY'S MANUSCRIPT

1977

There had always been rumours about the eighth floor. According to the curator, John Wesley, the other librarians said there was something about it that made them uncomfortable. The braver of his colleagues who had ventured up there alone reported that shadows stalked its dusty stacks and secrets lingered in the air. The only way up, I learned the day we met, was via a small lift the same size and shape as a telephone box. The librarians called it the coffin.

I should say, to begin with, that before this I was never inclined to take such stories literally. Though I have always held a deep, theoretical – and private – interest in matters of the peculiar, tales of haunted libraries and similar legends have never represented anything more to me than fascinating insights into the way people think and form their beliefs. An appropriate subject for a university lecturer with a doctorate in psychology.

It was late one miserable afternoon in October when I arrived at Paddington, weary and agitated from a delayed train journey from Oxford. I promptly made my way to Senate House Library in Bloomsbury, north London, stepping out briskly against the windy weather that snagged at my spirits, squinting into the rain and still clutching, in my overcoat pocket, the curious letter I had received on the preceding day from Mr Wesley. 'Dr Caxton, your assistance with an urgent matter is required. Come at once.'

I'm not at all the sort of man who responds quickly to such vague last-minute requests. My many commitments to the undergraduates – marking essays, preparing and giving lectures – simply wouldn't allow the indulgence of such distractions, and the fact that this note had been hand-delivered to my home address made me all the more suspicious that someone was having a game with me: a disaffected student perhaps or a fresh-man put up to the joke by his friends. That was certainly the opinion of my wife, Julia. But then a familiar name within the letter made me think there was probably more to the mystery than a mere prank – and I was right.

Turning on to the slippery cobbles of Malet Street, I paused for some moments at the entrance to Senate House, admiring with quiet appreciation its notorious architectural character – an enormous tower of glittering Portland stone in the heart of London. It looked serene, dignified.

Though of course I regard the place somewhat differently now.

Once inside, glad of the refuge from the raw afternoon, I hastily sought out Miss Christine Eastoe, Head of Historic Collections, whom the letter had instructed me to ask for, and was instructed to wait by a young receptionist. I did so, wiping my spectacles clean and taking my place on a small bench at the end of a vast, marble-floored corridor. Alone.

I was hardly surprised by the emptiness of the library; it was the end of term and most of the students would have left for the holidays. Nonetheless, just then I felt . . . what was it? Uneasy. Unsettled. And I was aware suddenly of an uncomfortable chill.

'Robert Caxton?'

The sharp voice made me turn to see a neat, precise-looking woman with a beehive of white hair.

'You're late,' she said impatiently, ignoring my proffered hand. 'Now then, if you would care to follow me.'

I waited with Miss Christine Eastoe in uncomfortable silence at the door to the rickety old elevator which was to take me up. It was her name I had recognised in Wesley's note. Although I didn't care for her cold manner I had dealt with her, years earlier, on a bespoke research project concerned with the religious revival of 1903, and she had impressed me by her diligent attention to detail. I wasn't sure if she recognised me now – I hoped she didn't. Eventually she said in a taut voice: 'You know, there's an old story that in July 1929 the Principal of the University of London, Sir Edwin Deller, fell to his death in this lift shaft.'

'What an awful tale,' I remarked. 'How did he fall?'

'When they were constructing the Senate House Tower, apparently. A skip fell from the top and struck him. Some of the librarians here think that's why it's so cold on the eighth floor.'

'Do you believe the story?'

'Not a word! John does, of course. But then' – the corners of her mouth twitched – 'he'd believe anything.'

'Where is Mr Wesley?'

'You'll find him up there,' she said coldly, looking up. 'But please, I'll thank you not to indulge his fantasies, Dr Caxton. He's due to retire soon. And that suits the rest of us well enough. The eighth floor, that odd collection' – she shook her head disapprovingly – 'it fascinates him. Fascinates a lot of people – the lunatics!'

'Why? What's up there?'

Her flinty eyes darted a critical and surprised glance that stirred my discomfort. 'You don't know?'

'To be quite honest with you, I'm not even sure why I'm here.'

'Upstairs is the Harry Price Magical Library,' she said beneath her breath, as if the mere utterance of the phrase was a crime. 'Harry Price was a maverick,' she said sharply, 'who devoted his life to the exposure of fraud and the proving of truth in the field of psychical research, of all things. In 1948, after his death, he bequeathed his collection to this university to assist students of the subject of phenomenological happenings.'

'Phenomenological . . . ?'

She rolled her eyes. 'What some people call the "paranormal", Dr Caxton. The library upstairs contains some twelve thousand volumes dealing with magic, astrology, spiritualism, leger-demain, charlatanism, witchcraft and psychical research. I'm surprised you haven't heard of it.'

But of course I had. It was impossible to work, even secretly, in the fields that had long fascinated me and not to know the name Harry Price, or be aware of the vast collection of books he had given to the University of London. For some years, I had been quietly conducting research into the esoteric fringes of psychology, more normally disparaged and dismissed by the orthodox mainstream as parapsychology. I had even published articles on the subject under assumed names. 'It sounds fascinating.'

Her jaw clenched. 'It's an embarrassment. To academia and to the reputation of this university. In truth, we would like to be rid of it, sell it off. Perhaps we'll soon have our chance.' She glanced away from me. 'Mr Wesley is not at all well. He has become deeply paranoid – delusional, in my opinion.'

Just then the lift arrived with a thud and my eye happened

upon a small wooden framed sign displayed on the wall next to it: '*If the above alarm bell rings please telephone the engineer – No. 3344. The alarm indicates that passengers in the lift are unable to get out.*'

'Well, here we are,' said Miss Eastoe, unlocking the lift's wooden door with an ancient-looking key she produced from her cardigan pocket. 'You'll have to go up unaccompanied. There's only room for one.'

As I stepped into the lift and drew the door to behind me I felt my pulse quicken.

The narrow box creaked up slowly, and as the seconds ticked by a nagging voice at the back of my mind willed me to go back down. When the lift eventually stopped it did so with a jolting thud, and with mounting trepidation I dragged the old cage door to one side, stepping out into the semi-darkness. Lamps overhead slammed on and the sight before me took my breath away.

Cardboard boxes fought for space amid tables and shelves piled high with photographs and artefacts, scrapbooks, cuttings, pamphlets and ancient volumes: George Melville's '*Bones and I*': or, *The Skeleton at Home*, as well as books on snake taming, *The Physiology of Evening Parties*, *Memory in Animals* and *The Enigma of the Mind*. I was relieved to note some order in the chaos: a glance at a nearby shelf revealed that the calfskin-bound tomes collected there were concerned with the subject of stigmata, with unsettling, curious titles such as *Blood Prodigies* and *The Edge of the Unknown*.

I trod over creaking floorboards into the thickening, mysterious smell of wood and old paper, and among the records of lost lives and lost souls – sundry letters, press cuttings and photographs – I soon lost all sense of time. It was growing dark. As I passed a small window and tried to peer out I saw nothing but my own reflection in the opaque surface of the rattling glass. Pinned to the wall was an tattered illustration of the prophet Nostradamus predicting the future of the sovereigns of France in the reflection of a great mirror. Outside, the wind was whining as it whipped around the towering building and rattled the glass. Otherwise, the place was as silent as a tomb. Where, I wondered, was John Wesley?

As I crossed to the south side of the building my route took me past a stack of shelves cluttered with dirty test tubes and wires and, finally, into a small area where I was confronted with a stone bust staring back at me, its eyes hollow and vacant. An inscription engraved on a brass plate beneath informed me that this was the man to whom all of these intriguing items had once belonged – Harry Price.

Behind the bust was a long corridor framed by ancient-looking bookshelves and at the end I could make out, in the shadows, a great wooden chair, its arms and legs tangled with wires. I was reminded instantly of the electric chairs used for executions in America. Unlike those chairs, however, this one was used not to inflict death but to understand it, for this, I knew, was a seance chair, once used to secure and control spiritualist mediums as they communicated with 'the other side'.

As I looked upon the contraption, reassured by the fact that I was some distance away from it, I was startled by a short, quick movement at the far end of the corridor, close to the the chair, and by a shuffling sound, faint but discernible. Footfalls.

I stood, holding my breath, listening hard, squinting into my dim surroundings, and my eye was caught once again by a slight movement next to the seance chair. It was so quick, I might easily have missed it. I approached hesitantly, thinking it might not have been wise to come up here alone. But when I stood immediately adjacent to the chair, looking quickly about me, I saw nothing, heard nothing, and reminded myself that I was tired. My imagination was playing tricks with me. Still, I was unable to shake the uneasiness and I resolved to leave immediately.

Then, as I turned to walk away, I heard it – something behind me, moving.

I spun round just in time to see a figure shifting in the shadows.

'Who's there?' I called, noticing, to my embarrassment, a tremble in my voice.

An elderly gentleman with half-moon spectacles stepped forward timidly, his sallow face showing an expression somewhere between relief and anxiety. 'At last,' he rasped, extending a bony hand to welcome me, 'you have come.'

So this was John Wesley. 'How long have you been watching me?' I asked, thinly disguising my displeasure.

'Too long, my friend, too long.' He gave a sad nod, his hands clasped together in nervous expectation. 'I apologise for startling you but you seemed so intrigued with the collection. Most people are, you know – when it takes hold of you it doesn't let go.'

'Tell me why you asked me here,' I demanded, producing the note he had sent.

A dark expression slid on to his face. 'This is a sensitive matter but I have something to show you, a manuscript which I would like you to read. If you are willing.'

'That depends,' I replied drily. 'What is it?'

He hesitated. 'I've read your work, Dr Caxton . . .' He listed two of my books on his fingers: '*Belief and Reason. Trauma in Childhood.* All appropriate subjects.'

His smile was making me nervous, and as he stared at me in contemplative silence a thousand little thoughts seemed to flow into his craggy face. I sensed an inner restlessness stirring. Then: 'Dr Caxton, have you heard of a place called Borley Rectory?'

The name sounded familiar, no more than that. I told him so.

'Well, you *do* surprise me,' he continued, beckoning me over to a nearby desk. 'Borley is an isolated hamlet some sixty-five miles from here. A *troubled* place, to say the least.'

We sat down opposite one another and the curator produced from his cardigan pocket a small black-and-white photograph, which he laid before me. The image was of a gloomy, rambling old mansion from the Victorian era.

'Borley Rectory,' he said again, almost under his breath, before his rheumatic hand swept the image aside. 'Harry Price called this building the most haunted house in England. The things that happened there . . . Dr Caxton, such terrible things – spectacular events – captivated the nation after the Great War.' He nodded thoughtfully. 'People needed something to believe in.'

Though open-minded on matters of the soul and undiscovered abilities of the human mind, I certainly didn't believe in ghost stories. I had studied too many folk tales for that, had been to led to them by odd yearnings after arcane knowledge; and although I certainly knew of Harry Price's reputation, I was not especially familiar with the intricacies of his work – his sensational investigations into ghosts.

I watched with rising curiosity as Wesley opened a drawer in the ancient desk, from which he produced a thick leather wallet of the sort used to contain manuscripts, fastened with a small lock. 'Twenty-two years ago this manuscript was left here with me for safe keeping, the most important document in this collection. No one knows it exists. The archives and manuscripts catalogue contains no mention of it, nor does it appear in the wider catalogue. In fact you will find no trace, anywhere, of its existence.'

I couldn't help but feel intrigued by this old man's tale, his furtive manner. 'What is it?' I enquired. 'A work of fiction?'

'A confession.' Wesley smiled mistily and leaned back so that his face was shouded in darkness.

Naturally, I wanted to know how he came by the manuscript. Was it genuine? Why was it important? For reasons clear to me now, the old man did not address my first question. But the issue of its authenticity and significance made his eyes widen and caused him to speak with increased passion.

'The 12th of June, 1929 – that was the night when the *Daily Mirror* dispatched Harry Price to Borley Rectory so that he could assist their reporter in an investigation. There are various accounts of what happened that night and afterwards, most famously from Harry himself. But this' – he hesitated, resting his hand on the smooth brown wallet – 'this is the most extraordinary account of all: the story of what happened at Borley Rectory as experienced by Harry's secretary and personal assistant, Miss Sarah Grey.'

He flicked a quick glance across the table, as if afraid that someone was listening. 'Her account, Dr Caxton, is incredible. Terrifying. Tragic. And now I am retiring, the future of this entire collection could be in doubt. I promised to look after this manuscript, but I no longer can. You must take it,' he insisted, pushing the heavy wallet towards me.

'Mr Wesley, are you all right?' I asked. His face was ashen and I sensed there was more he wanted to tell me. 'You seem troubled.'

He nodded and replied, unconvincingly, that he was fine. 'Nevertheless,' he added, 'you are to have this and tell no one.

I see the future in your eyes – I have followed your work, your clandestine research in folklore and mythology and matters of the mind. You are trustworthy and I have carried the burden long enough. Please, take it.'

And so I did. The wallet felt weighty, important. Although I wanted to open it immediately I had no wish to do so there, under the curator's melancholy scrutiny. It seems odd admitting this, for I am not an anxious man and I certainly don't scare easily, but something in Wesley's tone had affected me. So much so that I wanted suddenly to escape the suffocation of the eighth floor.

'Excuse me,' I said, rising, 'but I must go now. Thank you. I promise I will read this.'

I headed back towards the elevator, trying not to look again at the stone bust or the seance chair, choked with its wires.

'Doctor Caxton,' Wesley called after me. 'Please, read it immediately. Time is short. Sarah . . . Miss Grey . . . she would want you to understand. And if you can, try to forgive . . .'

But I was quickening my pace now, unsettled, confused. Forgive what?

The curator's icy eyes bored into me.

And the elevator door closed.

Academic curiosity compelled me to open the wallet the instant I arrived home in Oxford. The small lock that had kept the papers safe within for so long broke surprisingly easily. I reached inside and slid the bundle of musty handwritten pages onto my desk. There were drawings too: one of a tall, balding man and a photograph of an attractive young woman with elegant bobbed hair. Her gaze pierced me.

The hour was late. My two little girls were already asleep. When I had made a sandwich and mug of coffee, I told Julia to go up to bed without me. Then I went into my study where the manuscript was waiting on my desk, and closed the door.

As I read, I was hardly aware of the hours passing, the faded pages seeming to turn themselves; and by the time I was done, the fire beside me had long since died down, its embers glowing like eyes somewhere in the distant past, watching me.

I hope my readers will understand that I have kept this manuscript secret until now because the personal implications of making it public frightened me. I have many reasons for not wanting to delve deeper into a mystery that has already bemused so many and which, I realise now, helps answer so many questions about my own past: why, since a child, I have felt so lost, so out of step with the rest of life. Perhaps I would have kept the document secret always, as John Wesley requested, had he not shown me a particular letter afterwards – a plea for help on which my own future now depends.

I have left the narrative exactly as I discovered it. The only additions I have made are the footnotes, which provide further useful background information to the central events of Miss Sarah Grey's story and occasional commentary on the author's observations.

Ultimately, it is for the reader to decide the veracity of Miss Grey's tale and the significance of its events. But for reasons that will become apparent, I am as certain as I can be that this story is true.

Dr Robert Caxton
London, 1977

EX LIBRIS

ABOMINATION DES SORCIERS

Est il rien qui soit plus damnable,
Noy plus digne du feu denter,
se cette engeance abominable
Des ministres de Lucifer?

Ils tirent de leurs noirs mysteres
L'horreur, la hayne le debat,
Et font de sanglans caracteres
Dans leur execrable Sabat.

C'est la que ces maudites ame
Se vont preparer leur tourment,
Et quelles attisent les flames
Qui bruslent eternellement.

HARRY PRICE

Miss Sarah Grey's Manuscript

CONTENTS

PART III – THE BAD DEATH OF HARRY PRICE

BORLEY RECTORY ORIGINAL FLOOR PLANS

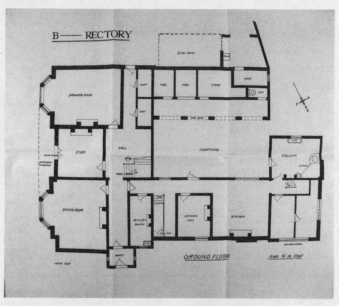

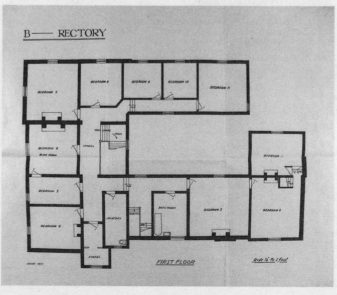

Part I

The Midnight Inquirer

'An extraordinary man, Price – a most extraordinary man.'
Sir Albion Richardson

'Yes indeed. Look, no strings, no wires attached.'
Harry Price (April 1944)

– 1 –

HARRY

November 1955, London

A wise man once told me that for every moment that passes, there is another that might have been – moments we lose through the misfortune of circumstance that slip like sand through our fingers and scatter to the past. Only now, with fear in my heart, do I properly understand what he meant. For now I know what it means to feel the pain of regret, and to wish it gone.

My name is Sarah Grey. For five years I was the confidential secretary to the late Mr Harry Price, honorary chairman of the National Laboratory for Psychical Research, an organisation that ceased to exist, shortly after the Second World War.

My duties, in the main, were common enough, but I like to think that Price relied on me. He was a restless man, impatient and sometimes disorganised. The way his mind jumped about like a skipping record meant that he needed someone to manage his affairs, make appointments and, especially, keep his well-thumbed files in order. He was a prolific writer of letters, articles for journals and no fewer than twenty books. But these books were nothing compared to the vast collection in his private library – the most rare, valuable and peculiar sorts of volumes that anyone is ever likely to come across. Building that library was a life's work for Price. He cherished it. And so I tended to it most carefully indeed. I kept it safe.

I kept his secrets too.

In the years after his death I was often asked to divulge all I knew of the man behind the carefully cultivated facade that Price presented in his lectures, writings and broadcasts. But I did not speak. Even after the affair – after the burning of that peculiar old rectory that preoccupied him so and became a personal obsession for me, after the hurtful allegations that followed, I did my duty. I held my silence.

I was twenty-two years old when I entered Harry Price's employment. He was forty-five, and his reputation was the envy of every fashionable household in London. From the smoky gentlemen's clubs in Mayfair to the finest upstanding dinner parties of Chelsea, his name could always be relied upon to tempt a smile, raise an eyebrow and ignite an impassioned, even aggressive, debate. None of this was accidental for, as is commonly the way with gentlemen who possess a different point of view, the fact that he wanted to be noticed was a distinguishing characteristic of Price.

Was he powerful? No. Wealthy, even? Not especially. In fact, he did not possess any of the qualities that usually attend the famous and influential. But he was, certainly, a noteworthy man for one very particular reason.

Harry Price was a ghost hunter.

As I sit here alone, listening to the wind hiss at my window, I can look back and remember every detail of Harry's old town house in South Kensington, buried in the London fog. In this 'ghost factory' I passed many an hour at the side of the world's foremost paranormal detective, the two of us plotting thrilling adventures with the uncanny and the macabre: our investigation of the Cottingley Fairy photograph that the world never saw, our excursion to Loch Ness, the eleven-day disappearance of a certain famous British crime writer. Harry Price and his mysteries – volumes could be written about the investigations into the supernatural which were the focus of his immense energy and magpie mind during our five years together.

I remember it all: the case of the wild man with the X-ray eyes, the exorcism at the Grand Hotel in Brighton, the spiritualist whose criminal conviction we helped secure, the mythical wildcat we hunted on Bodmin Moor. Such wild memories! If I find the strength, perhaps I will write about them. An ageing woman who has witnessed such horrors must somehow find a way to bleach the stains they leave behind.

I was reminded of Harry – as if I could ever forget him – by a recent article in *The Times*. It announced that members of the Society for Psychical Research are to reinvestigate his most famous work, a case widely regarded as the most critical inquiry into the supernatural ever conducted. It saddened and alarmed me to read this.

In 1940, when Price published his first conclusions on the matter, Richard King of *Tatler* described the case as 'one of the most extraordinary stories imaginable'. It was championed by Sir Albion Richardson, KC, CBE – one of the most distinguished jurists of the day – as a case that stood 'by itself in the literature of psychical research'.

I speak, of course, of Price's twenty-year investigation into the haunting of Borley Rectory. Some said tribute should be paid to him for the entirely unbiased way in which he chronicled the happenings. And when his book on the case was published, it was among the events of the year. But was it quite right to describe the Rectory as 'most haunted' – or even as haunted at all?

After Price's death, some years ago, many complained that too much about the way he presented the case was – much like the man himself – vague and inconclusive. His critics attacked him in their droves, branding him 'spiteful', 'deceitful', 'possessive' and 'self-seeking'.

He was, I confess, all of these things. He was also my friend. I miss him, even now, in spite of the terrible things he did. And sometimes, in the small hours, I fancy I can still hear his deep voice announcing a new day's work: '*Come, Sarah – let's begin!*'

And now the Society for Psychical Research also has its doubts due to the discovery of yet more inconsistencies in the evidence Price amassed: missing details, ill-substantiated facts and accusations. They are certain their investigation will bring them to the 'truth'.

Well, let them look, if they dare. They already know that at the moment of his death Price was writing the opening chapters of a third book on the haunted Borley Rectory. What they don't know is that Price died in very mysterious circumstances and that in the months leading up to his death he was troubled with the worst nightmares imaginable: he thought he was being followed and he received something rather mysterious, rather dangerous, in the post.

The world would be astonished to hear it, but I know that these events – his greatest investigation and his death – were connected.

I know that his pursuers will find me. They will want my story.

They will insist I reveal what I know. But they will never read this document, because the story it contains is for me – and for one other, should he ever find it

– 2 –
FAMILY SECRETS

January 1926

It was a blustery Saturday evening, two weeks before my twenty-second birthday, when I first met the man known as the Midnight Inquirer.

'I'm not coming.'

That was selfish of me, I know, which was silly, because the last thing I wanted to do was hurt my mother's feelings. From my position before a mirror hanging in the hallway I had a direct view of her as she sat in a deep armchair beside the fire in the drawing room, looking at that day's edition of the *Morning Post*. And although she had lapsed into crestfallen silence, I knew she would repeat the question.

'You're quite sure you don't want to accompany me, Sarah? Mr Price will be there in person! He is something of a phenomenon himself, a scientist who believes. They say he's wonderfully eccentric.'

'I dare say they do,' I muttered, moving to the drawing-room window to peer out on to the raw evening. An omnibus clattered out of the fog, full of passengers swaddled in scarves, hats and overcoats, and across Westminster Big Ben chimed the hour.

'But it's a rough night,' I said with deliberate misgiving, rubbing my arms as a chill shuddered through me. The house was far too large for just the two of us. We could never get it warm. There were perhaps twenty other town houses on our road in Pimlico, behind Victoria Station, but they were all nicer than ours. Our situation meant we could no longer afford to keep the house looking as we would wish.

'Well, the newspapers say the laboratory is a marvel.' I felt Mother's pleading gaze pressing into my back. 'Sarah, tonight's the gala opening. Everyone's talking about it. There will be tours. Also, it's not all about the work, you realise – plenty of young men for you to meet, I'm sure of it.'

I turned away from the faded red curtains to face her earnest expression. She was dark and tall with an oval face which was carved with lines that had come too early. The gold bracelet on her wrist reminded me of the woman she had once been: proud and confident, always immaculately presented in flowing dresses and wide feathered hats. Now I couldn't help but feel sorry for her. Her elegance had been eroded by the weight of her troubles.

From her armchair she inclined her head and arched her eyebrows, sending me a hopeful look that caught my conscience. I was so proud of her. Even my friends, who knew her simply as Frances, would comment on her gentility and grace. With or without her refined background, she would still have been a lady. In her sleek fitted jacket with matching skirt, she looked as though she were meeting a gentleman friend for supper. Of course, I knew that couldn't be true.

There had been no one since Father.

We left our house in Pimlico together a little after six o'clock. By that time the winter darkness had drawn in, bringing with it a stale fog which coiled around buildings and street corners. I pulled my furs tightly around me, sheltering from the cold that snapped at our faces as we walked past the rows of handsome Victorian town houses on Eccleston Square, where the Labour Party kept their offices.

'Poor souls,' Mother murmured, and I followed her pitiful glance to a row of ex-servicemen busking for money with a barrel organ, shabby overcoats decorated with war medals. She knew these men deserved better than to stand out here in the biting air selling bootlaces and matches and copies of the *Daily Worker*. During the war, she had belonged to the Voluntary Aid Detachment. 'Every woman has to do her bit, Sarah,' I remember her saying when I was at school. Now of course the factories shunned those men who had been so badly injured fighting in Europe to protect the Empire. So many men lost. The 'roaring twenties'? That phrase still rang hollow to me. The only roaring which seemed significant was the roaring of the guns. Women like my mother went regularly to the memorial in Whitehall, and no amount of jazz or frenetic dancing would banish their loss.

'I could sign up with the Labour movement,' I suggested. 'Work in an office.'

My comment turned her head. 'That's quite a departure from your last job!' She seemed concerned. It was a curious reaction for one who had seen firsthand how brave and essential women were to the world. 'You've been terribly agitated since you returned from Paris. You seem . . . *changed* somehow.'

Unfulfilled, lost – that's what she meant. I tried to ignite some passion for the work I had taken as a model in Paris in the summer, but I felt nothing inside. The job was far too shallow for my liking. In truth, I was more interested in the cameras than the photo shoots. The idea of pausing a moment in time and capturing it forever struck me as not only technically brilliant, but wonderfully romantic. Ironic, I suppose, given that it was romance that had led me to Paris – that and Peter Lewin's limitless charm. But our flirtation and my taste of the high life proved short-lived, and when I returned to London without the promise of further work it was with the realisation that my medium complexion, brown hair, hazel eyes and slim figure would carry me only so far in life.

'I need to find employment soon,' I said, 'or we will have to account for ourselves to the Poor Law Guardians. Your war pension isn't enough any more.'

The truth in my remark cut Mother's forehead into a deep frown and she sighed. 'You must do whatever makes you happy, dear.'

But that wasn't what she wanted to say. I could tell by the way her eyes slid away from me. No, what she meant to say, I was sure, was that most young girls looked forward to having a home of their own, a family, a husband. By the time we had reached the underground station at Victoria, I was already wishing I had stayed at home.

At the end of the last tube carriage I spotted three remaining empty seats and we settled down next to each other, Mother holding my arm as our train rattled and wound its way through the darkness. The fingers of her right hand drummed with agitation, and her yearning, absent gaze settled on the last remaining vacant seat opposite. Then I knew: the memory of my father, Harold Robert Grey, was with her once more.

It was nine years since he had been taken from us, eight years since Armistice Day. I was thirteen when it happened. She had knelt for half an hour on the kitchen floor, clutching the dreaded telegram against her heart, sobbing uncontrollably. Although I never read that telegram, in my own small way I thought I had made peace with the knowledge that he was gone. I thought Mother had too. During the many years we'd had to adjust, I'd watched with pride as she tutored children at home on Father's old piano. Her social life had improved and she had continued giving many hours each week in voluntary work with the Women's Institute at the Chelsea and Westminster Hospital.

And then, a year previously, something had changed within her. Without explanation, she had regressed into severe, unnatural grieving. Something had undone all the progress she had made recovering from Father's death.

Now she sought out spiritualist mediums who claimed to converse with the dead.

*

As we emerged from the underground station at South Kensington, I cursed myself to think that I was adding fuel to Mother's strange interest. Attending seances was her "hobby", but that didn't seem right to me. Hobbies should enrich lives, not replace them, and this interest was fast becoming an obsession.

I wondered what surprises awaited us behind the doors of number 16 Queensberry Place. Spooks, poltergeists, mediums – for me such notions were at best a bit of fun, possibilities to be lightly entertained among friends maybe, but then laughed off and forgotten. But for a whole year Mother had been frozen in an insidious cycle of fraud and disappointment imposed on her by false hopes cooked up by charlatan mediums and served up to her on a plate.

If Harry Price had similar intentions then I wanted no part of it.

Mother, who had been lost in her own thoughts, seemed to read mine.

'I know you disapprove, Sarah,' she remarked suddenly, throwing me a disappointed glance.

Was it any wonder? Why should I have had any concern for what came after life when I had yet to live mine?

'Darling, I appreciate this must be hard for you to understand,' she said, 'but all I ask is that you remain patient.'

I attempted to suppress my annoyance as we continued walking. 'I *am* coming, aren't I?'

'Yes,' she acknowledged, 'but reluctantly. Sarah, I need you there in heart too.' She came to a sudden halt next to a flower stall at the roadside, fixing me with eyes that were serious and sad.

'Well, I'm sorry, but you have to admit these practices are in rather poor taste,' I said solemnly. 'The war has consumed far too many lives already. So many tragedies . . . But Mother, the guns are silent now. It's done. It's over. The world needs to move on – *we* need to move on.'

I couldn't help the exasperation that had trickled into my voice. She was shaking her head, secure in the certainty of parental wisdom. 'To move on, you have to have something to move on *from*. I know your father wasn't always around when you were younger, and that when he was his moods changed like the weather. He was far from perfect, believe you me. But Sarah' – she frowned – 'he went to his grave loving you.'

'Just because I haven't put my life on hold, it doesn't mean I never mourned for him.'

My father had meant the world to me. He was a terrifically busy man, one of the most highly respected barristers in west London. Work, for him, had been a matter of survival. I remembered him telling me, 'Sarah, a wage in your pocket gives you freedom.' It was he who empowered me with the confidence and self-esteem I had needed even to consider glamour modelling as a career. He had given the ultimate sacrifice to make us safe, and now, without him, the world was a far lonelier place.

'I've mourned him twice,' Mother said quietly. I looped my arm around her waist and squeezed tightly, reassuring her that we weren't arguing. These conversations were becoming more and more difficult to negotiate without that happening.

'I know you miss him,' I said, watching her bottom lip tremble. It made me sad to see her looking suddenly so vulnerable. 'But you're living on your nerves, consulting with these quacks.'

She wasn't a gullible woman. Indeed, I had always thought of her as reasonable and wise. So naturally I wanted to know why she persisted. Why now, after all these years?

'What do you honestly hope to achieve? You know Father wouldn't want you to live in sorrow, don't you?'

'Your father kept secrets.'

'You mean during the war?'

'I mean before the war. And I have a question for him – something I must know.' Her voice juddered with the effort of holding back her tears.

I didn't understand, just as I couldn't understand why she had put so many of his photographs away, but I could pinpoint the day her obsession with the supernatural had begun. Just before the previous Christmas, late one evening, a stranger had appeared on our doorstep. I only caught a glimpse of him from the top of the stairs: his black hat and coat, his face, half shadowed, red raw from the cold. Whatever he said to Mother had driven her to slam the door in his face and then shut herself away in her bedroom. Since then, as often as two or three times a month, I would hear her through my bedroom wall – and in the dead of night – rummaging through the old boxes of letters and photographs she kept in the wardrobe, hear the snap of buckles as a trunk was opened then closed again once whatever had been removed and inspected was meticulously replaced.

'You're not to go in there,' she had instructed. 'Not under any circumstances. Understand?'

I had agreed, reluctantly, my puzzlement deepening until it bordered on suspicion. But I never disobeyed her injunction. Sometimes I saw Father in my memory, kneeling on the floor of his bedroom, examining something I couldn't quite make out. Sometimes it seemed to me that he was crying. The image was too unsettling. I always pushed it away. Perhaps Mother was right. Perhaps I hadn't acknowledged the pain of his passing.

Then a thought struck me, pulling me out of my reminiscence. She had said that Harry Price was a scientist. Given everything else I had learned about him, I had grave doubts that he would prove a rational man. But still . . . there was a chance, a very slim chance, that he might be – that this man of science might shine a light on her misplaced beliefs.

The hope prompted me to squeeze her hand with my support. 'All right, Mother, I suppose this once it can't do any harm.'

She smiled her gratitude and I consoled myself with the thought that I could not have dissuaded her from this. At least by coming with her I could ensure she was not drawn any deeper into the absurd practices of Spiritualism.

'But one day,' I added, 'I'd like to you to tell me who it was who came to the house last Christmas. It's important that I know what he said to you.'

She nodded. Smiled, but said nothing.

Arm in arm, we turned right into a short road lined on both sides by gleaming stucco Georgian townhouses with pillared entrances and wide, tall windows.

'There it is,' said Mother.

Just up ahead, the entrance to the Laboratory loomed into view, orange light pouring from the opening front door.

I drew in a breath as we joined the throng of other visitors.

There was no turning back now.

– 3 –

THE MAN WHO DID NOT BELIEVE IN GHOSTS

'Nobody try to stop me!' cried Harry Price from the front of the lecture room. And to the astonishment of all of us in the audience, he threw up his long arms, brandishing a glass beaker that flashed as it caught the beam of a spotlight.

I suppose, given his reputation, I had expected Price to be conventionally handsome, but the man before me was balding and rather stocky, his large ears balanced by bushy dark eyebrows curving towards a pronounced nose. And yet his eyes, wide and icy blue, twinkled with charisma and something about the way he held himself, straight and smart, exuded a commanding integrity that made a flush creep to my cheeks.

'Ladies and gentlemen, I recovered this viscous substance less than a day ago from the body of a medium under my scrutiny. It quite literally oozed from her nose while she sat upstairs in my laboratory, in a deep, trance-like state.'

Sitting with Mother in the front row, my stomach turned at whatever was contained in the beaker: a gluey white substance which seemed to glow under the lights. It reminded me of mucous.

And then, to the amazement of everyone in the room, Price,

with his white lab coat covering a poorly fitted brown flannel suit, raised the container to his wide mouth.

'He's going to drink it!' someone behind us cried.

'Wait!' someone else exclaimed. 'Mr Price, don't!'

I looked back over my shoulder to see that the order had come from an elderly gentleman in a dusty tweed jacket sitting a few rows back. 'You mustn't drink that, sir, you simply mustn't!'

'What I am about to do is *not* dangerous,' Price boomed back, his eyebrows shooting up, 'but merely . . . experimental. True students of science must surely put their faith in open-mindedness?'

'But that's . . . ectoplasm!' his critic retaliated. 'No one has ever before attempted to ingest a spectral manifestation. Anything could happen!'

Price grinned. 'Anything usually does.'

Horrified, I turned to Mother in disgust and complained, 'What in heaven's name have you brought us to – a freak show?' And the fleeting look of worry in her face suggested that even she was out of her depth.

'Hush, Sarah!' she mumbled. 'I'm sure Mr Price knows what he is doing.'

'Do you know *anything* about this man?' I demanded.

'I know he hunts spirits,' she answered. 'That *is* why we came.'

'Mr Price, I insist!' continued his challenger. 'Consider the consequences!'

'The *con-se-quen-ces* . . .' Price echoed. Up on the stage he had become as still as a cat, his domed head glistening with sweat under the heat of the stage lamps. His gaze settled on me – only for a second – before fluttering away and moving over my shoulder to the man who had dared challenge him. 'My dear sir, since the day I founded this institution, the first laboratory in

Britain dedicated to the investigation of spiritualist phenomena, I have done nothing else *but* consider consequences . . . the effect of the astonishing claims that spiritualist mediums so wilfully drip into the ears of the recently bereaved.'

Moving to the centre of the stage he asked, 'What comes *after* death? The Spiritualists, good men like Sir Arthur Conan Doyle, will tell us that the human personality can survive death in this world and continue living in the next. And many gathered here this evening think that the evidence from seances, mediums and other such supernormal phenomena constitutes proof for this survival theory. That what we call 'ghosts' are in fact spiritual embodiments of the human personality.'

'Yes, but what do *you* believe, Mr Price?'

'I believe we must be careful not to let our emotions swamp our reason. These theories are entirely at odds with our under-standing of the world. And science has ignored these issues.' He flashed a sudden grin. 'Until now.'

'Mr Price – no!'

With horrified amazement I watched as Harry Price raised the beaker and its gelatinous substance to his lips.

And drank.

*

All those present were holding their breath and though we exchanged many questioning glances, no one spoke.

Price's body had become perfectly still. Rigid. His eyes were firmly closed.

We waited. And he was *worth* waiting for, really he was – for here, I realised, was a man who had learned ways to intrigue and mystify, who in that brief moment in the cavernous rooms beneath number 16 Queensberry Place had quite captured our attention.

Suddenly his eyes blinked open. He lifted his head into the glow of the stage lamps and wiped the sleeve of his lab coat across his mouth. 'You see?' he said in a low voice. 'I'm completely fine. And the medium who produced the substance I just ingested is here with us tonight!'

Dashing to the back of the stage, he hastily drew back a dark velvet curtain to reveal an enormously fat woman who was sitting motionless in what resembled an instrument of torture: a high-backed armchair with a wooden table on each side. She was around fifty, I guessed, but the blindfold wrapped around her wide face made this difficult to judge with certainty. Her hands were strapped to the arms of the chair and her slippered feet attached to wires which led to a single light bulb on the table to her right.

'I call this contraption the electric chair,' Price thundered, an untamed energy burning in his eyes. 'Believe me when I say it is perfectly safe. The armchair to which Mrs Tandsworth is fastened is fitted with electrical contacts that cover her entire body. Should she attempt even the slightest movement to produce fraudulent phenomena, it will be indicated by the light bulb you see here.'

With practised purpose, he approached the table on the medium's left side and retrieved two objects from a box on the floor – a trumpet and a tambourine. He held both instruments above his head for us to see before placing them far from the medium's reach, at the opposite end of the table.

'I've spent years learning mediums' tricks and secrets,' Price declared, 'and I can assure you that in the hands of a trained magician, the man of science can become as impressionable as salt dough. That is why I decided in the first place that there ought to be a laboratory, equipped with the necessary scientific equipment, where men and women with open minds can test the mediums unhindered by preconceived prejudices, or' – he paused, throwing the elderly gentleman a disapproving look – 'emotional and religious influences. I must ask all of you now for silence, please.'

Drawing the curtain closed again, Price concealed the medium and the table with the instruments on her left side. The remaining table, with the light bulb on it, was left uncovered. A flick of a switch and we were plunged into near total darkness. A dim red light shone from the side of the stage, faintly illuminating the black curtain at the back. In the eerie gloom, Price's form was just visible. As we waited for something to happen, I felt a chill in the air and shivered. Mother, whose face was pale and attentive, shifted nervously. Then the promised spectacle began.

*

The noise that signified the beginning of the demonstration was so unexpected I almost leapt out of my seat, as did many of the men sitting around me. We were, I might add, justifiably surprised, for despite the fact that the woman sitting behind the curtain was securely bound – we had all witnessed as much – and despite there being a clear distance between her and the inanimate musical instruments, it was the sound of a tambourine we now heard, jangling violently, urgently in the darkness. It was as if some unseen agency were in the room with us. An intelligence. Then came another sound, more alarming than the first.

'The trumpet!' someone behind me cried. 'By Jove, something is playing the trumpet!'

But how could that be? And why wasn't the light bulb to

which the medium was connected lighting up? Surely she was doing this, wasn't she?

Aglow in the dim red light, Price was smiling to himself, as if savouring a private joke. 'Ladies and gentlemen,' he cried, sweeping back the curtain, 'observe!'

The lights in the main hall slammed back on and more human sounds surrounded us: sharp intakes of breath, gasps of surprise.

To everyone's audible amazement, the heavy-featured Mrs Tandsworth was still sitting motionless on the small stage just where Price had left her, her arms and hands still bound, her feet still visibly concealed by the slippers which were connected via wires to the light bulb. As for the tambourine and trumpet, the instruments lay undisturbed on the table just where Price had left them.

It's a trick, I thought. *Got to be a trick.*

I looked around me to see rows of confused, transfixed faces staring back at Price. Turning his back, He concealed the medium for a second time, but no sooner had he done so than the tambourine hurled itself over the railed curtain, landing with a loud clang at the front of the stage. Mother jolted sharply in surprise, and one of the gentleman in the front row reeled backwards.

When Price drew the curtain again Mrs Tandsworth was still sitting limply, her face quite vacant, her hands and feet still apparently secure.

Mother's mouth dropped open in astonishment. 'See, Sarah,' she whispered, 'I told you.'

'Spirits?' Price cried incredulously. 'Demons? Not a bit of it! Indeed the very same trick is performed almost nightly by the Great Houdini on the opposite side of the Atlantic. All Mrs Tandsworth had to do was slip free her left hand – which is not connected to the electrical wiring system – and reach for the instruments you observed. A sharp tug on the bandage would restore the ties to their original place.

He beamed at us. 'Isn't that marvellous? Such a simple illusion. As so many illusions are. Which partly explains why . . . ladies and gentlemen I do not believe in ghosts!'

Sitting back in my chair I glanced from Mother, whose eyes were overflowing with disappointment, across to the row of gentlemen next to me. Their faces were shocked, some horrified. No wonder. These eminent paranormal researchers had, I imagined, witnessed many strange disorders of nature: encroachment of the supernatural into the ordered world, spirits that walked the earth, telepathy and the ability to move objects with the power of thought alone. But I doubted that many of them had anticipated that the great and enigmatic Harry Price, who had made the world of psychical research his own, would declare so publicly that *he* did not believe in ghosts.

Still centre stage, the man of the hour was smiling fully now – a wry, self-satisfied sort of smile that belied the stark simplicity of the statement he had just issued, as if he were privy to secret knowledge.

'That is to say, ladies and gentlemen, I do not believe in ghosts . . . as the term is commonly understood.'

With the grandiloquence of a politician tipped for great things, he leaned forward, letting a moment pass as he gripped either side of the lectern. 'When we speak of ghosts, we think of ephemeral and intangible figures that flit across the ill-lit stages of haunted houses, graveyards and suchlike. Of course I accept that people have reported seeing such things.' He proceeded cautiously, moderating ever so subtly the tone of his voice. 'The evidence comes to us from countries poles apart, from races civilised and savage, and from every period of history. Consider the legendary Spring Heeled Jack, once known as the Terror of London. One hundred years ago, sightings of the ghost were common all over our capital. People said he vaulted over walls and attacked young women with his claws. But what do these ghost stories actually mean?' he continued, creasing his brow and raising his hands. 'What exactly do they *represent*?' He rapped his knuckles sharply on the lectern in front of him. 'Ladies and gentlemen, what is the *truth*?'

Surprise and relief washed over me. So he wasn't a charlatan after all. Far from it. He was asking us to be critical, to pay closer attention to the meaning of the term 'ghost'.

'I think it was Goethe who wanted "light, more light". Let light shine upon that question – the greatest question – of our era. Let light bring us out of ignorance and furnish us with proof conclusive. My science, psychical research, has the capacity to do just that: to leave behind the cheap mummery of the seance room. This laboratory represents the beginning of a new age of discovery. On these premises the miracle-mongers can be tested and the genuine mediums – should we find any – encouraged. My Laboratory will answer, once and for all, the ancient question of immortality.'

There followed an uncomfortable silence. As I surveyed the audience of eager believers, I wondered if he had gone too far; whether his propensity towards showmanship betrayed an ego that might provide fodder for his critics. The thought hadn't passed through my mind before suddenly, from the back of the room, an authoritative voice turned everyone's heads.

'Mr Price, I am sorry to say that you have let down the side of Spiritualism. And you have let down yourself.'

The accuser was an elderly gentleman, tall and distinguished-looking, with a great bristling moustache. His face, thoughtful and tenacious, was heavy and lined – but not unkind. To me he seemed familiar somehow.

'And who might you be?' Price strained his eyes under the stage lights.

'Sir Arthur Conan Doyle.'

I had not expected that!

A brief pause. 'How wonderful of you to join us, Sir Arthur,' Price said, his courtesy an obvious pretence, watching warily as the great author rose to his feet. 'I didn't recognise you there in the dark.' He recovered his confidence quickly. 'But surely even you, Sir Arthur, don't believe that every medium is honest, every phenomenon genuine? What you just saw was nothing but an illusion, albeit an illusion of which the great Houdini himself would be proud.'

In the poor light I could barely make out Conan Doyle, but his gruff Scottish accent was unmistakable. 'We cannot allow rare instances of fakery to derail our search for the truth.' He was speaking now not only to Price but to the entire room. 'We owe it to future generations, and generations past who are waiting for us in the next life, to keep looking with our minds fully open, to hear and understand the vital message of Spiritualism.' He directed the full force of his anger at Price. 'But you! What has your "precautionary scepticism" achieved? Tell us that. Indeed, is there *any* evidence capable of convincing you?' He snorted his disdain. 'Frankly, sir, I doubt it.'

The scornful question seemed to bother Price, for he hesitated briefly and shook his head.

I wondered then, as his eyes darted around the room, if he had sensed what I sensed – the beginnings of a distant cynicism amongst his peers, a certain reluctance to understand the processes of trickery and illusion that the mediums had mastered.

'I have found nothing yet,' Price answered eventually.

'And in all your travels,' Sir Arthur challenged him, 'your observations of fortune tellers, quacks, thought readers and the like, have you ever encountered *any* person capable of predicting the future?'

'I have had my fortune read many times,' Price answered, 'albeit with consistently variable results.'

'Then I fear you have wasted your time,' said Conan Doyle. 'Your mind is closed.'

'Perhaps your mind is too open,' Price retaliated. 'You have suffered a loss, sir?'

Conan Doyle pursed his lips, as if struggling to contain a considerable internal burden, and then said softly, 'As you well know, I lost my son and my brother to the influenza, and before that countless friends, my nephew and my brothers-in-law to the war. I was too old to serve.'

Mother lowered her eyes sadly to the floor.

'But that didn't stop me,' Conan Doyle pursued. 'I offered up my services to the War Office. I even visited the trenches in Ypres, saw with my own eyes the devastation, the rivers of blood. Those poor men, cut down with bullets through their brains. And now their souls reach out to us. Look around you, Mr Price! This is an agonised world. Your contemptible belief that everything is reducible to animistic causes, can be intercepted with wires or bottled in test tubes, is an insult to God. What a wretched outlook to have on life!'

Despite this bombardment of hostility Harry Price remained not only calm but, it seemed to me, inwardly sympathetic to his attacker's view. His mouth curved down with genuine sensitivity. 'I have put my faith in science, sir – rational enquiry. These psychic traders – mediums – their smug advertisements appear almost weekly in the newspapers. What does that tell you? That they make a very handsome living feeding on wilful, gullible dupes! I tell you, it is immoral and I will see the deceivers prosecuted!'

'Shameless medium-baiting,' Conan Doyle's voice trembled with anger. 'You are a perfect paradox, Mr Price. I remember your pledge that this great institution of yours would develop psychics' powers. You believed! And now you have the audacity to stand before us and proclaim that you do not? Well, you can rest assured that your strident and shrill and polemical denials will not convince me. If you do not cease your exhibitions of showmanship, Mr Price, then I will *fight* you and I will stop you – by God I will!'

Mother had said Harry Price was a phenomenon but I hadn't expected anything like this! Nor, I could see, had she. I looked away from her disappointed and surprised face to drink in my surroundings – the expensively furnished lecture room, the tense atmosphere, the sea of discontented expressions – and with some alarm it occurred to me that I was impressed by Harry Price. Intrigued. Watching him standing alone on his stage, surveying his audience as they filed out of the room, I almost felt sorry for him for it was clear to me, notwithstanding all his hard work to popularise psychical research and despite his tireless investigations into the supernatural, that this man had yet to secure the professional recognition and respect he needed to complete him. And this, I believe, was his greatest dilemma. In the truest sense of the word Harry Price was alone, searching hopelessly for ghosts he needed but could not find.

– 4 –
WHEN WORLDS COLLIDE

'One has to admire the gall of the man,' said a voice from behind me, 'joining forces with the Spiritualist Alliance. Who would have thought it? He promised them he was coming here to help psychics, not humiliate them!'

We were standing in the hall of the converted town house, caught up in a throng of excited visitors: journalists with notepads rushing up and down the grand staircase, curious bystanders like myself and, most obviously, elderly gentlemen – all starched collars, waistcoats covering white shirt fronts – from a rival organisation, the Society for Psychical Research.

'I say, Mr Salter,' the voice continued, 'you don't suppose he is plotting *against* us, do you?'

'Plotting is exactly right,' said a new voice belonging to a short, barrel chested man with a huge moustache. 'And it's our attention he wants, not our scrutiny. Any corroboration from us will simply take the limelight away from him.'

Mother was silent beside me, and a quick glance confirmed that she was hanging on to their every word.

'What do you suppose is his plan?' asked the first gentleman, whose name was Fogarty.

Salter lowered his voice, and I leant back a little to catch his words. 'It is my firm opinion that Mr Price intends to recast British psychical research in his own mould, to challenge our own great society. Why, it's an outrage!'

'Ahem . . . Ladies?'

I started and Mother flushed with embarrassment as a tall, gaunt gentlemen with thick glasses appeared at our side, catching us eavesdropping. Behind us, the unremitting rhythm of conversation continued as I focused on this wiry man with a crop of grey hair that was beginning to turn white. He seemed flustered and kept stealing glances over my shoulder at the group of chattering men.

'Ladies, my apologies. I should have been here to welcome you when you came up from downstairs.' He smiled. 'I am Joseph Radley, Mr Price's assistant. Did you enjoy his inaugural lecture?'

'It wasn't exactly what I had expected' – Mother started, but my warning glance quickly silenced her.

'Mr Radley,' I said, turning to our host, 'we're very keen indeed to witness the marvels of the house. Perhaps you might show us around.'

'But of course,' he said with a smile, pointing through the crowds to a doorway leading off the main hall. 'Over there is the reading room and tea room.'

Over the heads of the other visitors I glimpsed plush curtains, warm carpets and panelled walls.

'I imagine this is rather like a gentleman's club,' I said briskly.

'I think you'll have a rather different view of the main laboratory, upstairs. A short tour is about to begin. Won't you follow me?'

Steering us through the throng of other guests, Radley led us up the ornate staircase to the top floor of the house where several men were waiting for the tour. I turned to Mother and asked sternly, 'What's the real reason we're here?'

She tilted her head away from me.

'You were invited, weren't you?' I went on.

She nodded her head slowly, lips pursed.

'By whom?'

'An old associate of your father's.' Her voice had a quiet, disapproving tone. 'Professor McDougall – a psychiatrist.'

'But why?' I wanted to know. 'Where is he?'

Before she could answer, Mr Radley called for our attention. I looked around me. Up here the atmosphere was markedly different from downstairs: modern, clinical and brightly lit, the air filled with a thick, chemical smell. We passed down a long corridor with doors leading off it into rooms whose functions were indicated by enamelled nameplates. All, that is, except for one. The closed door at the far end of the corridor had no nameplate at all. Before I could remark upon it I was led hastily, along with the rest of our party, into the room where we were told Harry Price spent most of his time.

'Welcome to the workshop,' said Radley grandly, ushering us in.

I stopped with amazement as a new world of modernity unfurled before me.

'Goodness me!' Mother gasped. 'This must have cost a small fortune.'

I don't know what I was expecting. I suppose I had had in mind one or two dimly lit poky rooms reminiscent of the Edwardian seance parlours so popular at that time. Instead I found myself in a gleaming cavern of wonders, surrounded by wires, cables and chemicals. A huge glass cabinet dominated one wall, filled with stopwatches, dictaphones, luminous clocks and paints. In one corner steam hissed from a valve, in another an automatic camera flashed, catching us in its glare as we stepped forward past rows of shelves, all crammed with test tubes, scales and beakers. I ran my hand along the smooth surface of a glazed porcelain sink, while Mother, who had wandered to the opposite side of the room, looked with puzzlement at a Bunsen burner on top of a sturdy workbench.

It wasn't only the expense of this equipment that impressed me, but the sheer amount of it. So many cameras! Even video-cameras. I loved the cinema and had always been curious about how films were made, which might explain why, at that moment, I found myself becoming even more fascinated by the man who had created this place.

'What's that?' I asked Radley, pointing at a large machine in another corner.

'That's an X-ray machine, Miss Grey. We use it to see into the stomachs of mediums.'

The Laboratory seemed complete, except for one curious absence.

'Everything in this room is designed to help us detect alleged psychic forces or impressions of spirit intervention. The rest of the Laboratory, which you will see shortly, includes a seance room, baffle chamber and dark room.'

'Is there an office too?' I asked.

'That's out of bounds,' Radley replied curtly. 'But as you can see, we do everything we can to control the environments in which the deceivers perform for us.'

'What did he say?' Mother asked, in a flutter of alarm. 'Decei-vers? *Impressions* of spirit intervention?'

'Now, if you would please follow me.'

We were led back out into the corridor and into the adjoining room.

'In here, ladies, is where the true thrills happen. The electric lights in this room are temporary and have been installed for your benefit this evening.'

'Look,' Mother exclaimed. I tracked her gaze to a tall wooden cabinet lined with a black curtain. I stepped forward, but as I did so something else struck me as unusual – the floor.

'It's made of cork,' I remarked. 'Why?'

'Cork and linoleum,' our guide corrected. 'This is the seance room. In here we control all conditions, including temperature. Cork is a bad conductor of heat. In this room we invite mediums to enter trance-like states and attempt to channel messages from souls of the dead.'

'What about physical seances?' Mother asked sharply.

'Yes,' Radley nodded, 'we control those as well, requesting spirits to communicate via knockings or by levitating tables or objects.'

It was a gloomy space, not clinical at all. Sadness lay heavily on the air.

'How can you possibly see what's going on in darkness?' I asked, noticing the wide mahogany shutter which covered the window. And then I remembered the luminous paint.

'We miss nothing, monitor everything with state-of-the-art equipment. And we normally catch our culprit.'

I caught an expression of profound disappointment on Mother's face. Then she sent me a look that was muddled and somehow distressing: *What happened, Sarah? I brought you here to find your father.*

My thoughts quickly turned to the enigmatic person whose name and work had drawn disparate crowds from across London on this freezing, murky night. This was his big opportunity. His lecture was over. Why wasn't he up here, with us?

After only a moment of irresolution I decided I would seek him out, and waited while Radley demonstrated the ways in which mediums concealed items about their clothing, moved objects in the dark and produced ghostly rapping noises with their feet. Mother was watching, shaking her head in stark disagreement. And at last, when I was confident I would not be missed, I slipped quietly away.

✳

The corridor outside was deserted. I walked back down it and came to the door I had noticed earlier: the one without a nameplate. I tried the handle; it clicked and the door creaked open.

The only light came from a log fire crackling in the hearth and there was an overpowering scent of tobacco. As I stepped forward, my eyes moved from the sash windows to a hatstand before settling on an enormous desk strewn with papers, journals and unopened letters that overflowed from its surface onto a chair and the floor.

Harry Price's private study. But my goodness, what a mess! My sympathy went out to any secretary who had to contend with such chaos. But perhaps I was over-hasty, for as I looked more carefully at my shadowy surroundings – the tea table spread with scones from Fortnum's, jam, clotted cream and pastries, the well-stacked bookcase, the vast array of fountain pens and sharpened pencils, the filing cabinet – it occurred to me that this was a peculiar, ordered chaos: a faint clue to the man I was destined to know.

My attention was drawn to a substantial glass cabinet secured with a heavy lock. I pressed my palm against the surface of the cold glass and peered in at the intriguing collection of items inside – a bunch of roses, a trumpet, strings of pearls, decks of

cards and various other items of bric-a-brac. Especially interesting were the photographs, black and white images of men and
women huddled tightly together around seance tables, heads
lowered in semi-darkness as ghostly forms and faces of the dead
floated in the void surrounding them. Yet more faces stared out
from the other photographs: once-popular mediums, exposed
and disgraced by Harry Price, together with the signed confessions in which they admitted their trickery. Above these, placed
neatly on top of the cabinet, a single wooden frame displayed a
photograph of Price himself standing proudly in a black frock
coat, high-collared shirt and black necktie. A handkerchief in
his breast pocket completed the look.

'Young lady, what the devil are you doing in here?'

The voice, deep and commanding, made me jump.

I turned with alarm to see the man I had sought.

Harry Price was standing in the open doorway, looking straight
at me with an expression that was deeply hostile. I did my best
to look as though I had a right to be there, extending my hand,
which he ignored.

'Mr Price,' I said awkwardly, feeling my face flush, 'it's a
genuine pleasure to meet you. Your lecture just now was truly—'

He began to take slow, deliberate steps towards me. 'I'll ask
you again, what are you doing in here? Are you with *them*?'

I felt helpless, as though I were trapped in a cage. Then a new,
more alarming realisation: *No one knows I am in here.*

'Are you with them?' he asked again, louder this time.

'Them?'

'*Them*. The rival camp. The Society for Psychical Research.'
He was so close now that I could see the dark cigarette stains
on his teeth.

'Oh. No, no I'm not with them,' I managed in a somewhat tremulous voice. 'I'm Sarah Grey. Hello.' I offered him what I hoped was a genuine smile. 'Sorry – I'm afraid I wandered away from the rest of the group. I'm not sure how I—'

'Afraid?' He stopped just a stride's length before me, and now I had to look up to meet his piercing gaze. 'Why are you afraid, Miss Grey?' he said with quiet menace. 'A woman who is not an intruder, a thief, a spy – a woman who has nothing to hide – has no need to be afraid, surely?'

'I am certainly not a thief, Mr Price! As I was saying, I . . .'

But he had looked away from my face and was surveying me slowly from top to toe. I suddenly felt like a guilty child caught in a wayward act of disobedience. A distant memory jumped into my head: my best friend Amy and I sneaking into a late-night showing at a cinema on Leicester Square. We couldn't have been much older than fifteen. The usherette had caught us crouching in the flickering glow behind the seats in the back row. There was something reassuringly familiar about this memory as I stared at Price. It reminded me of a time when daring to take risks could be both thrilling and safe, like getting on a fairground ride you knew would eventually end.

Finally, he said, 'Then could it be that – by some wonderfully convenient coincidence – you are merely fond of books which do not belong to you?'

I realised I was still holding the tattered volume I had only moments before removed from the shelf. 'Yes!' I exclaimed with great relief. 'Yes, that's it.'

'So you wandered in here merely by *accident*?'

'By no means.'

'Then you are . . . curious?'

'Yes! I am curious – about books especially. And may I say, Mr

Price, you have quite a collection here,' I went on, deciding that flattery was the best course of action. 'I don't think I've ever seen so many books.'

He beamed at me suddenly, with great energy, and I watched the curve of his lips as he spoke. 'Well, there are many more downstairs. Four thousand, three hundred and seventy-six books, to be exact, not to mention the five thousand, three hundred and forty-three pamphlets and seven hundred and twenty-five columns of periodicals. The books in this room are the oldest in our collection.' His eyes twinkled as they moving lovingly over the volumes, then returned to me. 'The title you hold in your hands is a first edition of 1762, one of Oliver Goldsmith's finest. It contains the first recorded account of a seance.'

He let a moment pass and once more I was subjected to his trenchant stare. 'But yes, of course you would have known all of that if you *were* a spy, wouldn't you? And from the expression on your face, it is very quickly becoming clear to me that you did *not* know that – which means, Miss Grey' – he pointed at me in triumph – 'that I can *trust* you!' He squinted. 'Possibly.'

His cologne was too strong, his suit crumpled, but I found myself moved by his passion and by my memories of Mother's suffering down the years at the hands of tricksters. My initial intimidation had quite left me, replaced by an unexpected desire – I might almost say a need – to impress him.

'This building,' I remarked, 'it's beautiful. How does one afford to keep such grand premises dedicated to such an ... alternative ... subject?'

My curiosity seemed to please him for he smiled and said with little modesty, 'I am a fortunate man of some means who has enjoyed success in business, Miss Grey – this much is true.'

He sighed heavily. 'But this building does not belong to me.'

'To whom does it belong?'

'The Laboratory is held on lease from the London Spiritualists' Alliance. I persuaded them to let me have it for a time to see if I could shed some light on their mysteries. I told them I would use the Laboratory to help develop mediums' powers in communicating with the dead.'

So that was why Mother had been so keen to attend.

'You lied to them?'

He hesitated and said with boyish charm, 'I was perhaps a little hazy with the truth.'

'And what is the truth?' I asked him. 'Even I was under the impression that you were a believer.'

'I did believe. A long time ago.' His eyes slid to a small framed photograph on his desk: the picture of a young man with dark hair and sideburns joining a moustache.

'What made you change your mind?'

'The fear of all reason falling out of it, my dear.' His answer came so swiftly it sounded rehearsed. His eyes flicked back to me and he smiled, the gesture tempering his introspection. 'You're very fond of asking questions, aren't you?'

'It helps me learn,' I said, shrugging, taking in the room's curiosities: an ancient typewriter with some missing keys and next to this, resting on his desk, a china human hand that served as a paperweight.

'Isn't there another group – a rival group – the Society for Psychical Research?' I asked carefully. 'I shouldn't think they're terribly pleased with the rival institution.'

Price gave a thin smile. 'So – you *do* know something about the subject?'

'I wouldn't say that, exactly. I'm . . . well, I'm a good listener.'

'Both organisations are important to my work as regards my reputation, and financially, but they are also rivals.'

'So you're rather caught in the middle?'

He nodded and flashed me a smile as charming as it was sudden. 'The Spiritualists think I'm a paranoid witch finder; the scientists think I'm a crank with unconventional methods.'

'*Aren't* your methods unconventional?'

'Observe the masses and do their opposite,' he quipped, loosening his black necktie. 'I like unconventional.' He saw my concerned expression. 'Oh, I wouldn't worry too much, Miss Grey. I don't. Life's too short. And being a man who spends every hour of every day delving into the possibility of the afterlife, I should know!'

I nodded my agreement, beguiled by his strange presence, and said airily, 'This must be a fascinating place to work.'

Price's eyes gleamed with interest. 'Is that really what you think, Miss Grey?'

'I wouldn't have said so otherwise.'

'Well, why don't you?'

'I beg your pardon?'

'Why don't you come to work here? You can see I need help.' He nodded self-consciously towards his desk and the pile of papers and unopened letters on top of it.

Letters.

The sight of them grounded a lightning flash of memory to a miserable night in early 1914: my father as I had never seen him before, crying as he crouched furtively in the darkness next to his bed. He was holding something I couldn't see.

What was it?

'Miss Grey?'

I snapped back and saw that Price was smiling at me. The

rapidity with which his mood had softened was astonishing.

'The position will be well paid, of course.'

'I'm . . . hardly an expert in these matters,' I protested, struggling to find my words.

'You can learn, can't you? I need an astute assistant.'

'But you already have an assistant.'

'Why don't you let me worry about him?' Price cut in, his eyes never leaving my face. 'My, I sense in you so much doubt.' He nodded and said with a confidence that made my neck tingle, 'I can make that doubt go away.'

I didn't know how to respond, so instead I asked him what the role would entail.

'That's the best part,' he breathed. 'In this line of work, one never quite knows . . .'

For a moment I felt as though all the air had been sucked out of the room, taking all rational sense with it. Of course I was tempted, yet a large part of me was floundering for an excuse to say no.

'Can you drive?' he asked hopefully.

'I have no intention of becoming your chauffeur!' I said sternly, and from the way he cowered immediately behind outstretched arms, smiling broadly, I could tell he was only half serious. 'Anyway,' I added, 'if it's a secretary you want, I don't do shorthand.'

'I don't want shorthand. Can you type?'

It so happened that I could type, rather well in fact, and I told him so. During the school holidays my father had occasionally taken me with him to his chambers on Fleet Street and instructed some of his lovely secretaries to sit with me and teach me.

'Very well, then it's settled!' he said confidently.

'But Mr Price – you know nothing about me!'

'No.'

'I could be anyone.'

'Yes.' His hand brushed mine. 'But are you the sort of woman who likes to take risks?'

What was I doing? This peculiar stranger, this loner, was asking me to follow him into something I knew nothing about. And what about Mother? Now she knew Price was a sceptic, she would hate the idea of me working for him, surely?

'I need to go,' I said abruptly, stepping back from the heat of his gaze.

He took a slight step towards me and immediately I felt a warmth rising in my throat and an uncomfortable feeling of self-consciousness came upon me. I glanced at his left hand. No wedding ring.

'Leaving? So soon?' He looked so surprised that I had an immediate impression that 'no' wasn't a word he often heard. 'But you didn't say what you thought of my lecture.'

'That's because you interrupted me!'

He gave me a smile which seemed to say 'touché' before looking away thoughtfully. 'Perhaps just as well,' he sighed. 'I require total loyalty from anyone who works with me.' His stern eyes flicked back up at me. 'Total and unconditional loyalty, Miss Grey.'

I was about to tell him that I was not the sort of woman who takes orders blindly, when Mr Radley burst into the room.

'Mr Price, here you are! It's time, I'm afraid. Our guests are leaving. You really should be thanking them for coming.'

In the corridor behind him, a swell of other visitors was advancing towards the sweeping stairwell. 'Excuse me,' I said politely, stepping out of the room, 'but I must go.'

Suddenly, out of the throng of guests, my mother appeared at my side. 'Sarah, where have you been?' She sent a furtive glance towards a tall gentleman in a long black coat who was approaching from down the corridor. Then, as she raised her left wrist, I saw that her favourite piece of jewellery was missing. 'I must have lost it on the tour.'

'Then we must search for it,' I insisted. She loved that bracelet. It had belonged to my grandmother.

'No, no,' said Mother, giving another flustered glance to the man who was coming our way. 'We must leave. Now, please.'

– 5 –

PIERCING THE VEIL

It had been almost a week since I met Harry Price. His job offer had hijacked my thoughts.

'Sarah, you're not going to say yes – are you?'

'I'm thinking about it.'

I was strolling past the statue of Peter Pan in Hyde Park with my best friend Amy, whom I had known since we met as girls in Sunday School. I wanted to enjoy the splendour of that crisp afternoon, but my mind wouldn't allow it. Images of Harry Price – cool gaze, mechanic's hands – raced through my head.

'Well, stop thinking about it!' Amy insisted. Her yellow hair fell forward as she turned her soft round face towards me. She had bright, adventurous eyes and a lightness of spirit that never failed to relax me. 'Anyway, there are more exciting matters to attend to now, and I'm not going to manage without your full attention.' She meant her wedding, which was to take place the following year – 1927. All afternoon we had traipsed the streets of Mayfair to find a suitable printer for her wedding invitations, but I didn't mind. Although I adored Amy, our shopping trips did sometimes feel like entering a competition I couldn't win. Her family was incredibly wealthy.

'The wage will be handsome. Perhaps I should say yes.'

Amy looked at me with something close to shock. 'Have you lost your senses? Working for someone so divisive – a spookologist?' She laughed at the phrase. 'You'll be about as fashionable as a horse and buggy!'

She was being sarcastic. Most of our friends would prefer a motor car as a mode of transport if they could afford one. Amy obviously could.

She asked me another question.

'Do you really want to work in a place like that?' Her tone and the expression on her face told me she didn't think this was a good idea. I, however, thought it might be exciting to meet new and interesting people, whatever their class. I imagined myself greeting these men of the scientific age, working alongside them. This was my chance for a proper career, more fulfilling than modelling, a chance to develop myself. What good was an education if I couldn't put it to some use?

'It is a worthy position,' I said.

'Don't you think office jobs are generally more suited to the man of the house?'

But this wasn't 'just an office job', was it? And I wondered how to explain to a dear friend who would never need to work, a girl whose biggest concern was her wedding seating plans, that I already felt like 'the man of the house'.

'What was he like anyway – Harry Price?'

'Intense,' I said, remembering the way his gaze had held mine, how he had made me feel as though I was the most important person in the world. 'And his passion was . . . electric.' I pondered the matter. 'I suppose I believe in what he stands for – justice, truth.'

'Oh Sarah, he's obviously a crank. Keep your distance. You've a family name to uphold. And you need to consider how a job like this will reflect on you, too.'

I saw she had a point. I could get a respectable job – take a position in a children's charity perhaps, or with the Women's Institute. Mother would like that. Or apply to one of the new film companies that were establishing offices in Soho. I had an eye for visual representation. The photographers in Paris had said so.

'Here's an idea, Sarah!' said Amy suddenly. 'Come out with me tomorrow night. There's a party at the Café de Paris. Jazz and men and cocktails!'

'I'd love that!' I exclaimed. Then with sudden disappointment I remembered that Mother had asked me to accompany her to a dinner party hosted by one of the neighbours.

'How is Frances?' asked Amy.

'Not good. She was at it again last night, rummaging through the wardrobe at two in the morning.'

'I'm sorry, Sarah. Do you know what's she looking for?'

'I wish I did.'

'Sarah, forget about the dinner party – your mother can do without you for one night. And forget about all this darkness, for heaven's sake! Otherwise you'll only drag yourself down. Tell you what,' she continued, 'go and see Mr Price now. Tell him, thank you, but no thank you. All right?'

I hesitated.

'Sarah, Sam Merrifield is single again.' She dangled the comment as an incentive. I was familiar with the mischievous gleam in her eye; I remembered it from when she had first mentioned her now-fiancé, Andrew Hampshire, over fourteen months earlier. She had known from the outset then he would belong to her, and now it seemed that she wanted Sam Merrifield for me.

'All right,' I replied. 'Yes, all right.' Immediately I felt lighter in spirit.

'Tomorrow night then?'

I felt a smile spreading across my face as I pictured myself laughing and dancing with Amy and other bright young things.

'Tomorrow night,' I agreed.

As I hugged her goodbye I thought: *This is what good friends are for: they take us out of ourselves.*

But it was to be many months before I saw Amy again.

*

'I wasn't expecting an answer so soon,' said Harry Price, throwing an anxious glance back over his shoulder into the depths of number 16, Queensberry Place. 'Yes, yes, I'll be back in a moment!' His eyes flipped back at me, flustered. 'My apologies. We were in the middle of an experiment. Not going exactly according to plan.'

'An experiment?' I chanced a discreet peek over his shoulder, into the darkened hallway, but saw nothing past the great staircase but an eerie glowing light.

'Miss Grey?' Price focused on my face again. 'It's getting late.'

'Um . . . yes.' Now it was my turn to be flustered. *Try to concentrate*, I told myself. 'I wanted to give you an answer in person.'

'Well, of course.'

'And I don't want you to think me ungrateful . . .' I hesitated.

'But . . . ?' He arched an eyebrow.

'But the position you offered me, it's just not for me, I'm sorry. But thank you.'

Suddenly, from somewhere within the house, a woman screamed. 'What on earth is going on in there?' I demanded, trying to see past Price, but his sturdy frame blocked the doorway.

'Have you made your final decision, Miss Grey?'

'Yes . . . yes, I think so—'

'You *think* so?' His eyes were sharp in their scrutiny as he studied me. 'And there was me thinking you were a woman who knew what she wanted.' He pursed his lips. 'I should have known.'

'How dare you!' I exclaimed, feeling my temper flare. 'I'll have you know, Mr Price, that women helped pick this country up when it was on its knees. And they didn't just do their bit, they carried us over the finishing line. Women like my mother were remarkable and brilliant and brave, and they showed everyone what we can do!'

I hesitated, caught my tongue. I had made my point.

'Thank you,' he said, smiling suddenly. I thought he would be angry, but a strange look of satisfaction had come over his face, as if he had intended to rile me. 'Good day to you, Miss Grey.'

'Wait! My mother lost a—'

The huge door slammed shut and for a moment, stranded there, shivering on the doorstep in the gathering darkness, I had no idea what to do. Would he come back? Yes, of course he would. A person didn't just slam a door in your face without intending the gesture as a joke, did they? And I wanted to ask him if he had found the bracelet. So I waited. One, two, perhaps three minutes. Nothing. Something inside me snapped.

'Well, it was nice to meet you too!' I bellowed sarcastically at the door, turning on my heel.

*

It was shortly before eight o'clock when I arrived home, welcomed by the crackling wireless announcing that the first woman was planning to swim the English Channel. Mother was in the drawing room, reading. The fire had burned low and there were no fresh logs. No sign of any supper either. It made complete sense to me, then, to try lifting her spirits by telling her that I had declined Price's job offer. I knew she would be relieved. Since Price had shocked her on the opening night of his Laboratory she hadn't had a good thing to say about him, and of course the loss of her bracelet hardly helped matters. The only problem was, I didn't feel able to tell her what I was thinking: had I made the wrong decision?

A sensation of guilt began taking me over, and that was silly. No one had high expectations of me, but perhaps that was the point. Perhaps I wanted them to believe that I could succeed. That I wasn't content just to sew and stitch or be an object of admiration. My mind was alive with images of Price's modern equipment – cameras and X-ray machines – which automatically made me think of other impressive new types of technology: television sets, radio and the hand-held hairdryer. The world was striding forwards in so many wonderful and interesting ways and yet I felt cut adrift.

It occurred to me then that if I let this opportunity pass I'd never know where it might have led, and I'd always look back and ask myself what I might have learned. The idea was somehow alarming.

And that was how it happened. That was how a young woman who didn't believe in table-levitators, healers and prophets returned to a place nicknamed 'the ghost factory' and looked into the eyes of its owner.

Determined, this time, to say yes.

– 6 –

FIRST DAY AT THE GHOST FACTORY

'What on earth—?'

A terrifying woman lunged at me as she stumbled out of the doorway of number 16 Queensberry Place. My goodness, what a sight she was! Short and stout, with hard features and limp brown hair hanging in curtains around her face, she was dressed in a flowing black gown.

Worst of all, a sticky white substance, which smelt revolting, was bubbling out of her mouth and dripping onto her chest.

She stared straight at me, her bloodshot eyes wide and ferocious. I felt helpless, wanting both to help her and to run away, but before I could do either an urgent voice from inside the hallway beyond called out, 'Helen, come back here!'

Pushing me aside, she hurtled into the road, screaming, retching and spitting that disgusting substance from her mouth.

'Come back, I say!'

Two men were emerging from the doorway, the first a stranger to me. This was the man who had shouted and he seemed so genuinely concerned for the woman that I assumed he was her husband. The other man I recognised instantly. It was Harry Price.

He saw me at once. 'Ah, Miss Grey,' he said, beaming. 'We'll deal with this!' he added, ordering me to stay exactly where I was.

As he bolted into the road, his white lab coat flying out behind him, he looked very much as if he were enjoying himself, but it took both men to tackle the medium and drag her to safety, their feet sliding as she kicked wildly, punching and shrieking into the wind. Her cries echoed up the street: 'Let me go, I say! Let me GO!'

'Please, my dear, just allow Mr Price to X-ray you,' her husband insisted as he struggled to contain her. 'Then we can go!'

'No!' she bellowed, promptly dealing him an almighty blow to the side of his head.

I watched in shock as Price stood back and observed the couple's squabble with a look of great consternation. When they had eventually calmed themselves, he said quietly, 'I think we're done here for today, Mrs Tyler. I was hoping to inspect the contents of your stomach via my equipment,' he frowned, 'but I see now that won't be possible.'

To my disgust, the formidable woman drew her head back and spat on to Price's black leather shoes, covering them with the disgusting white mess. The repellence in his face showed so clearly I thought he was about to fly into an uncontrollable rage, but instead he merely stared, curling his lip before turning his back on the woman.

'All this is fiercely disappointing,' he said to her husband. 'However, I must thank you, Mr Tyler, for behaving with some modicum of dignity. I see no point in carrying on here. In any event, I have little doubt that an X-ray would reveal little else than cheesecloth.'

'Cheesecloth?' said the other man incredulously.

'Yes,' Price snapped. 'Cheesecloth. Regurgitated cheesecloth, to be exact. Your wife thought, no doubt, that she could dupe us all into believing that the substance emanating from her body was some sort of ectoplasm.' He heightened his voice grandly. 'Oh yes, I've seen it all before!'

He wheeled round to face me. 'You see, Miss Grey, our guest – Mrs Tyler here – makes a very profitable living from conducting seances the length and breadth of this country. The "ectoplasm" which comes from her mouth during her trances is supposed to give form to spirits and allow them to communicate, whereas in fact she is regurgitating – in a rather overly dramatic fashion, I must say, Mrs Tyler – cheese-cloth and other substances she has previously swallowed. Egg white and toothpaste are both popular ingredients. Yes, it's a common enough trick.' He smiled warmly and looked me in the eye. 'But on to more important matters! Miss Grey – you came back!'

'I did.'

'Splendid! Quite splendid.'

'Sorry about the other day,' I said quickly, looking away.

'No you're not.' He smiled. Our eyes met again and he raised his voice, lifting us both out of an awkward moment. 'You look very much as if you need a cup of tea. Shall we go inside?'

✳

When we had reached the top floor of the building, he led me down the long corridor and into his modern workshop. In the far corner was the electric chair I had seen him demon-strate on the night of the Laboratory's opening. The thing gave me a chill.

'Ah, you have not forgotten this, I see,' Price said, catching my gaze. He scuttled over to the chair, tending it carefully, adjusting this wire and that. 'The old girl needs a few improvements before I can put her to the test on him.'

'Him?'

'Schneider,' he said shortly. 'Rudi Schneider.'

'Oh,' I muttered, not having the faintest idea to whom he was referring.

A troubled, almost accusatory look, settled on his features. 'Rudi Schneider,' he prompted. 'Come on, woman, surely you've heard of him?'

Woman?

I hadn't expected such further abruptness so soon, to be made to feel so uncomfortable, so I said flatly, 'I'm sorry, Mr Price, but I never claimed to be psychic.'

He stared at me blankly and blinked.

'In fact,' I continued with rising confidence, 'I never claimed *any* expertise in your particular field of research. I merely claimed that I could type. This Mr Schneider might be very important to you, but I am afraid his name means nothing to me!'

I puffed up my chest and, for a second, held my breath.

His stern expression gradually softened before finally dissolving into a satisfied smile.

'You have some spirit about you, Miss Grey. I like that. Helps keep me in check. I need that sometimes.'

It was then that I remembered Mother's lost bracelet and asked Price if he or his assistant, Mr Radley, had found it. 'No, no, I don't think so,' said Price absently.

'Where is Mr Radley?' I enquired.

'I got rid of him,' Price said coolly. 'Mr Radley's time was up. Regrettable, really. He was a hard worker, intelligent with it.' A dark expression had settled on his features, which belied his complimentary description. 'No matter. You're here now, aren't you?' Smiling, he grasped my shoulders gently with both hands, looking me up and down as one might marvel at some rare and important possession. 'Sarah Grey, the ghost hunter's assistant.'

'Let's not get ahead of ourselves,' I began, but before I could say another word Price had released me and suggested I join him in his private study where a pile of his written correspondence was waiting to be sorted and answered.

As we walked, he returned to the subject of Mr Schneider. 'Now, he's a most interesting medium from Australia. My own dealings with him go back a few years. To be frank, I am rather surprised you haven't heard of him.'

'Why?'

'Somehow he has managed to cultivate quite a reputation for himself here and on the Continent. You see, Sarah, his mediumship gives the impression, at least, that he possesses some quite spectacular psychic abilities.'

'What's so remarkable about him?'

'Well, for a start,' said Price, 'he very recently managed to impress Dr Lamb of the Engineering College of Cambridge, as well as a professional magician during a seance held at Tavistock Square. And every precaution, I am assured, was taken to rule out the possibility of trickery. His ankles and wrists were bound with luminous straps; they even held his hands.'

'And what happened?'

Price came to an abrupt standstill on the threshold of the room into which he was leading me. He made no sound, his face drained of expression.

'Mr Price, are you all right?'

Nothing. Just an absent stare.

I reached out and touched his hand. It was rigid. 'Mr Price?'

'Hmm?'

Accustomed as I would become to Price's curious faculties, I always found his ability to mentally detach himself and disappear to a private, secluded part of his mind most disconcerting. I was about to shake his arm when, in an instant, he snapped back to normal, as though nothing out of the ordinary had happened.

'Where did you go? You were somewhere else entirely.'

He raised his eyebrows, unconcerned. 'Was I?'

'Well . . . yes, you were. Are you quite all right?'

'I have dark moments, Miss Grey. Black days sometimes.' He gave a half smile. 'It's nothing to worry about. Now, where was I?'

'You were telling me about Schneider.'

'Yes, I was,' he whispered. 'According to the witnesses' testimonies, the young medium levitated himself in perfect light. Just imagine that, Sarah. He hung stationary in the air, his feet just above the heads of the observers, before floating across the room.'

A man who could fly? I thought Price was joking – he had to be – until the outrageous thought came into my mind, as I looked upon his cool eyes and saturnine features, that he was deadly serious. Perhaps Amy was right; perhaps he was crazy. I felt my self-doubt about the job creeping upon me once again, remembered the strained conversation with my mother that morning as she urged me to reconsider, and remarked, 'People don't just float into the air. That was a gift reserved only for the saints.'

My words drew from him an obvious curiosity. 'You know something of religion?'

'My father was a devout Catholic,' I explained. 'I was taught by nuns.'

'You look doubtful, Miss Grey . . .'

'If you mean do I carry the faith, the answer is no. A loving

God would never have allowed the war. Saints levitating' – I shook my head – 'they're just stories. Like these tales about Mr Schneider.'

Price nodded briskly. 'Well, indeed, and who knows what a clever man can do nowadays, with some mirrors and ropes and the power of suggestion?'

'But I imagine the scientists who tested Schneider were frightened.'

'Possibly. For some, I am sure, such wonders must be the fabric of nightmares.'

'Then what,' I mused, 'are mediums afraid of?'

'Ah, well, that's easy,' Price proclaimed, sweeping past. 'They're afraid of me!'

I hurriedly caught up with him.

'I always have my doubts, Miss Grey. I call them my evil demons. Remember, the possibility of doubt can be a very useful thing indeed.' Price jerked round to face me, his eyes sharp with interest. 'And Mr Schneider hasn't been properly tested yet.' He released a startling laugh. 'But he will be, oh yes. Just you wait! My letter requesting his participation in a series of seances here, under this roof, is already with his family awaiting a reply.'

As I followed Price into his private study he looked at me shrewdly and said, 'Now, you remember this room, of course.' His eyes narrowed, tracking me warily as I moved towards his desk where I glimpsed an open letter. At the top of the page were the words 'Concerning B— Rectory', but before I could read any more, Price had quickly covered the note with his hand. 'Take a seat please, Miss Grey.'

I did so, feeling somewhat nervous as he took the chair opposite me and rolled a cigarette.

'You gave up an initially promising career in glamour modelling. Why was that?'

That was odd. I didn't recall telling him about my previous vocation. And he was looking at me differently, sitting as motionless as a cat, drawing smoke into his lungs.

I thought about his question for a moment. I was trying to decide how much to tell him, about Paris and my relationship with Peter Lewin.

Price repeated his question in a heavy tone. 'Was it stability you craved?'

'Partly,' I said eventually. 'Times are changing. I want to be part of new ideas that help us see the world differently. I want to be a part of something special.'

'And you think that working for me will be . . . special?'

'It will certainly be different.'

'What made you decide to come back?'

Picturing Mother's melancholy face, I explained that I was intrigued to know how and why humans can be tricked into believing what is not there. 'Life is precious, Mr Price. It's the living we need to look out for, not the dead. Working here, helping you combat fraud, will help me do that.' My eyes looked past him and fell on an expensive-looking camera set on a tripod at the back of the room. 'Besides, I might learn something.'

He was smiling at me. 'The idea of working here doesn't scare you?'

I thought of the war years, when the German Zeppelins had appeared in the skies above London like huge glowing cigars, and the battle planes that sometimes came during the day. At my school we were told to shelter under our desks.

'No, Mr Price. It takes a lot to scare me.'

'But you must worry, surely, about what people will think.'

'Why?' I leaned forward. 'Why should I worry?'

He shrugged. 'You bright young things are more concerned with having a good time – dancing, enjoying the company of young men – than pursuing a career.'

It was a sweeping generalisation and one to which I could feel myself wanting to react. I remembered what Amy had said: '*Sarah, working for him, you'll be about as fashionable as a horse and buggy.*'

'I'm not concerned with what people think, Mr Price. I think those on the side of truth owe you a great deal of gratitude. Your work is exceptionally original. It has nobility.'

'You think so?' he asked softly.

'Yes. But then,' I reflected, 'I suppose we can never be sure of anything, can we?'

'No,' Price said curtly. 'Not anything. Not anyone.'

He smiled and I shifted uncomfortably in my seat. For some reason it was suddenly important to me that he didn't see me as a workaholic. So I told him that I often visited jazz clubs. It was only when I mentioned my love of cinema that his face lifted with genuine delight. 'What a splendid interest for us to have in common,' he said, clapping his hands together. 'I plan, one day, to form a National Film Library if I can secure the appropriate backers. You could help me with that.'

I have to say, the idea sounded thrilling and only served to forge a greater unity between us. Then he lowered his voice suddenly, as though he had just remembered why I was there. 'Now, to business. Tell me this: how do you view the performance of my Laboratory?'

This was rather an unfair question. 'It is a little early for me to judge. But' – I cast my mind back to Conan Doyle's vented frustrations – 'the way I see it, people are looking to you to answer their hopes. That's a dangerous position to be in – it makes you vulnerable. Believe me,' I continued, thinking of Mother, 'hope is a passion that burns the brightest. Extinguish that hope and you'll devastate millions. Validate it, and you'll become their saviour.'

'I have never thought of myself as saviour.' He arched an eyebrow. 'Is that how you see me?'

'Let's not get ahead of ourselves, Mr Price. But I suppose in some ways you are the answer to an extremely vexatious question that has been troubling me for some time now.'

'Oh really? And what is that?'

'Whether it can ever be reasonable to believe that a genuinely paranormal event has occurred.' I leaned in to demonstrate my interest. 'Mr Price, what got you interested in this subject?'

I surprised myself by my candour; something about the man sitting opposite me invited a frank response.

He drew in a great lungful of smoke, leaning back in his chair. 'Ah, Sarah, for now you must allow me the indulgence of my own mysteries.'

'You mean secrets.'

'If you like.' It never occurred to me that he might not want to discuss the catalyst of his interest.

'There will be plenty of time to learn about me. We are talking about you now. Is there a personal reason why you want to work for me?'

'No,' I answered quickly. 'But you seem to me such a sceptical man. After your lecture the other night, I was left wondering whether there is any evidence that *could* persuade you. Surely, there must be? Otherwise, how would science ever make new discoveries, if it wasn't prepared to reject old, established theories under the weight of new evidence?'

I was pleased to see that I had piqued Price's interest. 'Very good. Go on, please.'

'Well – theoretically, if a case were to cross your desk which involved enough witnesses, enough incontrovertible evidence, physical trace marks, photographs and the like – well, then one would have to accept that a genuinely paranormal event had occurred.'

Price considered this for a moment. 'Tell me, how many times have you watched the sun set?'

'I'm sorry . . . ?'

'How many times have you watched the sun set?' he repeated with a hint of impatience.

'Why, too many to count, of course.'

'And how many humans in the history of the earth do you imagine have witnessed the very same thing?'

I shook my head. 'An unfathomable number. But I don't see—'

'What, then, if I were to inform you that the time is now past twenty-one hundred hours, that it is not morning but night time, and that the sun has not yet set?'

'I . . . well, I would say you were lying.'

'I never lie, Miss Grey.'

'Then I would say you were mistaken.'

'Very well.' He stood quickly, came around the desk, placed a gentle hand on my shoulder and led me over to the window before rolling up the blind. 'Then what if I could *show* you too?' His voice, I noticed, had a propensity to drift between registers. Low and soft, it rolled over me with beguiling influence. He gestured at the view out of the window over rooftops set against a grey sky. 'And what if you could see with your own eyes that the sun was still as high in the sky as it is now? What then?'

He was so close to me that I could feel the warmth of his

breath on my cheek. 'Then I would say the event was a violation of a law of nature. A miracle.'

'Exactly.'

'But what does that have to do with my question?'

'It has *everything* to do with your question,' he snapped so abruptly that I gave a slight start. 'Indeed, it goes to the heart of the matter.'

He returned to his chair. I followed suit.

'Your understanding of possibilities in this world is governed by the totality of your experiences, Sarah. You hold certain principles sacred about what is physically *possible* and physically *impossible*, and it is from these that you construct a world view – a consistent theory of all phenomena observed within nature. A law of nature, if you will.'

'Correct.'

'A paranormal event is one which, by definition, would contravene any or all of these basic principles whether it's the sighting of a ghost, the imparting of information from a spiritual source, or even the ability to read someone's mind. Experience tells us such an event is hugely unlikely, totally outside the basic principles of common sense, in the same way as it would be contrary to common sense for this pencil you see here to rise from my desk, float into the air and write on my office wall.'

'So that would mean . . .'

He anticipated my thought and nodded. 'That if one – just one – genuine paranormal event is proven, everything that modern science believes would be wrong! And so it follows that we would need an overwhelming quantity of evidence to show that such events are possible – to show that the sun, in my example, really had not set at twenty-one hundred hours; we would need, Miss Grey, repeatable, successful scientific experiments.' He leaned forward, his face projecting intent seriousness. 'And that is why our work here is vital; that is why we must *never* give up. You and I, Sarah, we are the guardians of the modern world view.'

The harmony and logic of his argument flowed into me. And his passion, his piercing conviction, sent an instant thrill down my spine. But something about the way his eyes flittered from side to side told me there was an inner torment working away at him. A deep longing, perhaps, that it could all be true. I wanted to know.

'You said before that there was a time when you believed in Spiritualism. Tell me why you changed your mind. Why is all this so important to you?'

He saw in my face enough determination, I think, to be convinced that I was not going to drop the matter. His expression became sullen, clouded with a memory.

'There was a man, a spirit photographer called William Hope. The Society of Psychical Research suspected a hoax, but had no proof.'

'So they sent you to investigate?'

Price nodded. 'They wanted someone new, someone fresh on the case. And I went with my mind fully open. More than that, actually. I went *wanting* to believe, for personal reasons.' He shook his head, dropping his gaze to the photograph on his desk of the man with the dark hair, sideburns and moustache. 'But William Hope was a fraud. I proved that he had switched the photographic plates. And from that day, I became the enemy of every medium with skeletons in their closets.'

We hadn't yet come to the original source of his interest. This man had his secrets, his boundaries, and I already sensed that we breached one too many for his comfort. After a long moment he found his voice again. 'Do you know how it feels, Miss Grey, to have your wildest hopes, your deepest beliefs shredded?'

Without waiting for my answer he eased himself out of his chair and came around the desk to stand beside me with seductive authority. Although he wasn't a conventionally handsome man, his words and mannerisms exuded a magnetic curiosity. His eyes floated down to meet mine.

'The day I exposed Hope, I learned that if you break a man's beliefs you can break his spirit. I'm still hurting, Miss Grey. My mission is to stop these charlatans, to bring the deceivers to justice. Every case will stand or fall on its own merits. We owe that much to the fallen.'

He extended his right hand, curling his fingers. 'Are you with me?'

Suddenly everything about his curious world had assumed a greater relevance than the fact that this was a good, stable job, and I realised that my decision to return to the Laboratory now went far beyond my personal motivations – a desire to answer questions about my family or a need to prove my ability. This was bigger than my personal doubt, bigger than everything.

'Yes!' The word almost flew out of my mouth. 'Yes, I am with you.'

The rough warmth of his touch as he took my hand hinted at unimagined possibilities.

'Then, Sarah, let us begin!'

– 7 –

A HINT OF
MENACE

'You said you wanted to help. You can start in here.'

'Now? Today?'

He nodded. 'No time like the present. I want you to catalogue and cross-reference all the books in the collection.' He saw my jaw drop, and laughed. 'Don't worry. It's not an exercise I expect you to complete any time soon, not with all your other duties to attend to.' He gestured to the large desk in the corner of the room and the pile of unopened letters that had been left to build up on top of it. 'But it must be done. I wish to compile a short-title catalogue to assist the serious investigator in detecting psychical imposters, but at the same time enable him to recognise a genuine phenomenon if and when he sees it,' he explained. 'It is crucial that I don't alienate the Spiritualists. My supporters – like your own mother, Sarah – won't tolerate that. A good many of them have put up money for this establishment, and although I may not agree with all of their methods and beliefs, it is important now that I am seen to be working in their best interests wherever possible. Every one of my investors expects answers and it's up to us to see that they get them, all right? Otherwise, all this could be gone.' A thought struck him. 'You're available to work late this evening?'

I remembered I was supposed to be seeing Amy at the Café de Paris. 'Actually—'

'Good,' he cut me off. 'We may have one or two further experiments to run.'

'All right, Mr Price,' I said. It was the only answer I could give, really. Having changed my mind once about the job I would have to show him now that I was committed.

'And that's another thing,' he said curtly. 'This isn't the stuffy, stiff-collared Society for Psychical Research. We're a lot less formal here. From now on, call me Harry. All right?'

'Of course,' I said, nodding politely. 'I understand.'

Satisfied, he declared he would return in an hour or so to see how I was coping. 'I'm sure by then you'll be full of questions for me.'

'Yes,' I said confidently, 'I am quite certain that I will.'

When he had gone, my eyes fell on the alarming tower of letters. There must have been a hundred or more. They looked far more interesting than working on a library catalogue! All would need to be opened and answered, so I did that instead.

The notes – some handwritten, some typed – ranged from the vague and theoretical to the very strangest practical problems. It baffled me how Price was able to move through the world contending with so many absurd claims. I wondered where he found the energy, and was about to tackle another stack of untidy papers when the open letter I had glimpsed earlier caught my eye.

I picked it up and read it:

Dear Mr Price,

I was surprised and disappointed to attend your lecture, two weeks ago, at the gala opening of your National Laboratory. Truthfully, I found what you had to say somewhat at odds with my own experiences; and it is for this reason that I am writing to you.

I am the Headmaster of Winchester Grammar School, and soon to retire; but between the years of 1879 and 1881 I was an undergraduate at Exeter College, Oxford. My subject was History, and one of my tutorial partners – a most studious fellow – was a puckish, amiable man by the name of Harry Bull, whose father was at that time the rector of a small hamlet near Sudbury.

Harry and I soon became friends and he would sometimes regale me and the other men with dark tales and eerie legends of mystery, murder and passion which were common in his part of the world. One night, after we had listened to the college choir, we retired to Harry's wood-panelled rooms and, with brandies in hand, planted ourselves in comfortable armchairs beneath mullioned windows. We all knew it was a night for one of Harry's tales. One of the men asked him what it was like living in a rambling country house – and were there ghosts? My old friend became rather quiet, and sat gazing for some time into the crackling fire. 'You know,' he said eventually, nodding to himself, 'I do believe there might be such things as ghosts.'

He offered no elaboration and nor was any sought by the rest of us, for he was clearly troubled and so we quickly dropped the matter.

I thought little else of the exchange until a few days later when Harry asked me if I should care to visit him that weekend at the family home, in order to celebrate the end of our first term. I said I would be delighted, and I was. The village – it was hardly that, just a scattering of houses – lay at the end of a long lane at the top of a hill commanding some spectacular views. As for the house – my goodness, it was fine indeed, with two wings and high turrets. Cedars of Lebanon and thick hedges screened it from the world.

The weekend passed carelessly in the delightful company of the Misses Bull, Harry's four sisters, with many hours laughed away over light refreshments and games of cards which we enjoyed in the library. The servants of the house kept themselves to themselves and at night many of them left the house altogether. I thought nothing of this then. On reflection, however, their unwillingness to remain during the hours after dark makes a great deal of sense.

It was on the last day of my stay, after Evensong in the ancient small church across the road, when I detected a subtle – but unsettling – change in the mood of the place. A certain stillness seemed to inhabit it, and as we crossed the narrow lane which separated the grounds of the house from the church, and entered the wide driveway, I felt the first chills of the evening and couldn't help noticing that Harry's mood had become uneasy, his eyes darting furtively this way and that until they settled and fixed upon a narrow, overgrown path on the opposite side of the lawn. 'Shall we head on inside?' he ventured, with a distinct edge to his voice. And so we did, his sisters, who were normally so light-hearted, lifting their skirts and leading the retreat.

Then came the second surprising element of the evening. Dinner was not to be taken in the dining room but in the library. No explanation was forthcoming, and as we waited for the servants to bring the food and wine the atmosphere grew strained, as though the entire family was afraid that our meals would arrive cold or that the glasses we were passed might, at any moment, shatter in our hands. In such circumstances, I confess, it was difficult to relax, but my curiosity was awakened and, try as I might to dispel it and to enjoy what little remained of my stay, it did not leave me.

After dinner, I chanced a discreet peek around the dining-room door. The only remarkable sight was the great Italian fireplace which featured the prominent marble heads of two monks, one cowled the other not, leaning out, their faces glowing eerily in the moonlight which shone through a large Gothic window opposite.

'Come away,' urged a sharp voice from behind me, and I turned to see one of the Misses Bull who was already closing the door on the room. Her gaze – I will never forget it – was wide-eyed, fearful, and fixed on the window. 'It's to be bricked up,' she whispered, leading me back towards the library where my host was waiting. 'Father insists.'

The family kept a dog – a retriever, Juvenal – who was normally, I was told, impeccably behaved. On that last night, however, the creature refused to settle. Eventually, after padding the corridors, it lay down with its head between its paws just over the entrance to the basement, periodically whining.

When the others had retired to bed and we were sitting next to the spitting fire, I asked Harry to tell me whatever was troubling him. He seemed to sink back into his chair, the shadows enveloping him, and for a time remained silent, until gradually he raised his glass, examining it wistfully by the warm glow of the fire, before muttering something under his breath.

'Say that again?' I asked.

'I said, you hear of things going bump in the night. Well, let me tell you, David, they don't bump, they scream . . .'

We spoke for perhaps an hour about matters concerning the unexplained, and I could tell that my friend was in awe of the subject of spiritualism. 'The problem,' he proclaimed, 'is that when communing with spirits through ambiguous rappings, one can never be sure of the identity of the entities speaking. When I die I will come back by doing something distinctive, so people will know it is me. I will throw mothballs.'

It was long after midnight when I retired to bed. I locked my door, from the inside, and removed my shirt, which I dropped on the floor beneath the window. But in the morning, to my puzzlement, I found the shirt pinned up by its sleeves, with some drawing pins, on my bedroom door!

And that wasn't all.

I had with me, on this visit, a French dictionary, which I had misplaced. During the night I was awaked by a loud 'thump', which came from the floor of my bedroom. You can quite imagine my surprise when, turning up my oil lamp, I saw it there on the floor, returned to me.

I heard afterwards, from one of the servants of the house, that the room allocated to me was haunted.

Some years later, after we graduated, Harry confessed that one afternoon he had looked out of his study window to see a darkly clad figure go by and disappear into the shrubbery next to the house. His description of the apparition was vivid: it began, he said, as a vague shape which solidified as he kept his eyes on it until it had formed the appearance of a woman in black robes. A nun. He went out quickly with his spaniel, and the dog stood on the spot where the figure had disappeared, howling.

Another time, he told me, one summer afternoon, he had heard knocking and scratching noises coming from inside the church, though the building was locked up and empty.

I know you will be highly sceptical of my account. I am a rational man, Mr Price, much like yourself; so whenever I experience an odd or 'unnatural' experience I always seek, and usually locate, a satisfactory explanation. However, in all my years I have been unable to explain these disquieting events.

I leave the tale for your consideration anyway, in the hope that it might prove to be of some use to your ongoing investigations.

Of my visit to this old house, there is little else to tell. Only its name, which even now makes me uneasy:
Borley Rectory.
Perhaps you should visit the place.

Yours sincerely,

David Chipp

Winchester Grammar School, January 1926

To my bemusement, Price was distinctly uninterested in the content of this letter, saying it was 'no different' to the plethora of other rantings he received. 'Our work here with the mediums is far more important than trekking out to some remote house on some wild goose chase.'

I thought this a peculiar reaction from a man who presented himself as a ghost hunter, and pressed him on the point.

'Do you think I haven't been seduced by such stories before now?' he protested, still facing away from me. 'I've been investigating so-called haunted houses for nigh on twenty years. All of them nonsense!'

I myself, however, felt certain that this story was different – the witness sounded reliable, well-educated. At the very least he deserved a respectful reply.

This is the letter I wrote:

Dear Mr Chipp,

I am afraid that, owing to significant restraints upon his time, Mr Price is presently unable to take up an investigation of the house you mention. However, he has asked me to thank you for writing. I found your tale intriguing, not least because of the objects you mention – the French dictionary and shirt – that were found moved, without any obvious explanation. Mr Price has asked me to tell you that such events, although rare, are usually explained through the interference of mischievous pranksters, in this case possibly a maid employed at the old house. He has also enquired whether the house is located in a district known for interesting legends . . .

I should like to remain in contact and will write to you should the need arise.

Yours sincerely,

Sarah Grey

*

From the windows of my office on the top floor I had a perfect view over the rooftops of South Kensington to the spires of the Natural History Museum, but it wasn't a view I ever had much time to enjoy. When we weren't out on field investigations, my mornings were preoccupied mostly with librarian duties, which I carried out on the ground floor in a large, comfortable reading room located to the left of the main hallway. The lofty walls of this carpeted room were lined with grand portraits of famous psychologists, philosophers and scientists, each splendidly show-cased with ornate frames.

After two months working with Price, he still possessed a frus-trating ability to defy my expectations and to keep me guessing at every turn. Like the dreary afternoon in February – Valen-tine's Day – when I made the mistake of asking him whether he had any arrangements for that evening. He looked awkward.

'Arrangements?'

'Yes . . . umm, you know, dinner arrangements perhaps.'

'Why would you ask that?'

'Why?' My mind started racing. 'I . . . well, I don't know why . . . I suppose I was just interested, that's all.'

He stared. 'Interested?'

'Yes.'

'This evening I have a meeting,' he said somewhat petulantly.

'With whom?' I wasn't aware of any meetings. I certainly hadn't cleared any space in his diary for meetings that day.

'A meeting. With my wife, if you must know.'

'Your wife!' I exclaimed. 'But – I mean, you never *said*.'

'Am I obliged to tell you everything about my personal life?'

'Well, no, obviously not. But—'

'Then kindly rein in your indignation every time you see

or hear something about me that you didn't know already.'

I felt my face flush with embarrassment, but of course I couldn't stop myself asking the obvious question: 'How long have you been married?'

The question was met with an immediate glower of resentment. 'Twenty-one years.'

'Oh.'

'Is there something the matter, Sarah?'

'No,' I said tersely. 'Of course not. I suppose I just assumed you were . . . well, a bachelor.'

'A *bachelor!*' He looked gravely offended. 'Good grief, woman, no! I wouldn't wish that upon anyone.'

My embarrassment heightened still further. He thought I meant homosexual. 'No, no,' I said quickly, 'I didn't mean *that!* I just . . .' I paused to collect myself, then continued in a firmer voice, 'What is your wife's name, may I ask?'

'Constance.' The name rolled from his lips without any trace of affection.

'And what is her occupation? What does she do?'

'Do?' Price issued an abrupt laugh. 'As little as possible. Her late father was Robert Knight, the jeweller.' He frowned and looked away. 'Ours is, as I say, a fortunate predicament, and she is an excellent woman in most respects. She adores her charity work . . .'

'But . . . ?'

He gestured towards the seance room. 'Sad to say her interests do not stray quite as far as this Laboratory. Not nearly as far.'

I relaxed slightly, my gaze returning to his naked ring finger. He caught my glance and quickly clenched his hand. 'Anyway,' he continued, 'what's next on our agenda today?' Conversation on the matter, at least for the moment, was closed.

But that did not stop me thinking about the singular oddness of this exchange during the weeks and months that passed, nor wondering why he never mentioned his life at home with his wife, why he never involved her in any of his social engagements, why he never mentioned her at all.

*

Much to my annoyance, it had become part of Mother's routine to rise early and open the post – even letters addressed to me. On the first day of May, over breakfast in our kitchen, she presented me with the invitation to Amy's wedding.

'She's planned it precisely twelve months from now,' she said with delight.

The invitation card was exquisite: elegantly printed and tied with lace. As I stared at it over the breakfast table it made me think of another more innocent time, long before I had taken the job with Price.

'And in Chelsea Town Hall, Sarah. How splendid! A spring wedding. We must go shopping for hats.'

I agreed to meet her that afternoon at three o'clock in the pleasure garden at the top of Selfridges on Oxford Street. I don't know what I was expecting when I arrived: air vents and piping perhaps, certainly not stone-flagged floors and a gazebo covered in climbing clematis!

'Quite something, isn't it?' said Mother, as I joined her under the flagpoles, near the entrance to the secret garden. Close by, pigeons nested in ornate dovecots. Linking arms, we looked north to Hampstead Heath in silence.

'I used to come up here with your father,' said Mother quietly. A smile covered the sadness of her memory and she said nothing else. Now, thanks to Harry Price, our lives were becoming easier. We could afford to visit places like this.

We took the escalator down to Ladies' Wear and I watched Mother's eyes moving lovingly over the new streamlined fashions. Her gaze settled on a wide pink hat with an upturned brim before she looked away, discouraged by its obvious expense.

'Have it,' I said.

She gave me a quick look of surprise.

'Please,' I urged, 'treat yourself. What good is it me working such long hours if I can't make our lives a little easier?'

As the shop assistant boxed and wrapped the hat, Mother squeezed gentle thanks into my hand.

One morning in August I was at work in the library on the ground floor of the laboratory when a loud bang from Price's office upstairs disturbed me and I heard my employer raise his voice in a cry of anger. A door slammed, and seconds later an elderly, sturdy-looking man dashed down the main staircase. As he reached the hall he saw me and entered the library, projecting the full force of his anger. 'I say, young lady, do you work here?'

I introduced myself as Price's new assistant.

'His assistant? Whatever happened to Mr Radley? He was a gentleman with whom I could do business.'

'You can do business with me,' I said shortly.

My inquisitor was tall and distinguished-looking, with a great bristling moustache. His face carried the traces of a hard life but was not unkind. Beneath his discontented gaze I stood firm in my resolve to defend my employer. Something about him was familiar.

'Would you like to tell me what the matter is?' I asked.

'The problem is Mr Price! His tests are going too far. If he carries on like this, there isn't a medium in London who will want to be tested!'

I leapt to my employer's defence, almost without a second

thought. 'You must appreciate that his work has some merit, surely?'

'Of course I recognise that these claims of spiritualism need to be most carefully put to the test. There are many dishonest and clever people who would wilfully take advantage of those who believe in an afterlife.'

I wanted instinctively to tell this stranger that I agreed with him, because I now realized who he was. It wasn't just his light Scottish accent that had given him away. I recognised him from Price's opening night. I decided to take the heat out of our exchange.

'May I say, Sir Arthur, it's a great pleasure to meet you. I adore your writings.'

He seemed warmed by the comment and his face softened. 'In truth,' he sighed, 'I was glad to remove Holmes before the public became tired of him, but I am pleased, at least, to have entertained you.'

'Shall we start again?' I smiled, leading him to a leather sofa where we sat by a huge window overlooking Queensberry Place.

He apologised for what he called his 'rough temper'. 'But I feel my frustration with Mr Price grows daily. My efforts now,' he continued, 'must be to promote the great movement of Spiritualism and to defend it from the activities of your infernal employer.'

'You know him well?'

'I'm not sure that anyone can truthfully claim to know Mr Price well. I have always felt there was something not quite right about him.'

'Not right . . . ?'

'Something dangerous.' Sir Arthur nodded. 'When I watch him tie up mediums, I think he is the sort of man who is lacking in all boundaries. The fellow's a showman. We all know what they do – shock, my dear lady! As old Harry indeed shocked us all at that lecture of his.' As he spoke he was shaking his head. 'He fails to realise that the biggest mystery awaits us all: that of the Great Beyond.'

'So you actually believe—'

'That when the body dissolves, the spirit endures.' He nodded and smiled kindly. 'Yes, that is what I believe.'

'But how can you believe that? A man of your medical background.'

'You think it foolish of me?'

I chose my words carefully. 'I'm surprised that a man of your shrewd intellect would be taken in by stories of mental projection, automatic writing and the like. You have to admit it all sounds rather far-fetched.'

'When you have eliminated the probable, whatever remains, no matter how improbable, has to be the truth.' He smiled. I did too, recognising the comment from one of his novels. It created a greater familiarity between us, and he immediately elaborated. 'To be very clear, young lady. I have arrived at my position through treading the stepping stones of empiricism and logic. It might surprise you to learn this, Miss Grey, but Harry Price isn't the first man to set out on a sceptical quest. The chief judge of the French Colony of Crandenagur in India, Monsieur Jacolliot, travelled a very similar path. His legal mind was against spiritualism. Using a series of complicated experiments designed to root out fraud, Monsieur Jacolliot studied native fakirs who claimed the same abilities as today's mediums. What he found changed his mind: the movement of objects with the power of the mind, levitation, the handling of fire. He concluded that spirits are very real.' He paused, reflecting. 'Afterwards I read countless books on the subject, met hordes of witnesses. They impressed me greatly. The most famous medium of all, Mr. D. D. Home, demonstrated his powers in the cold light of day, and was willing to undergo whatever test was put to him. Of course the occasional scandal is to be expected, but that shouldn't mean we dismiss the rest of the evidence as easily as Mr Price would. Haven't you seen any evidence of the supernatural?'

'Not a scrap.' I looked into his eyes, which shimmered with hope. Then a memory slammed back: the letter mentioning a haunted rectory.

'Except . . .'

'Except what?'

Borley Rectory. I held in my mind a romanticised conception of the place: a rambling mansion set on a desolate hill beneath scudding clouds and wind-tossed trees. The letter I had opened, and which Price had so quickly disregarded, still provoked within me a latent sense of purpose. 'It's nothing, really – *probably* nothing. Harry thinks so.'

He let out a hearty laugh. 'Now, why doesn't that surprise me? You listen to me, Miss Grey: he can teach you everything, I'm sure, except how to recognise a real ghost when you see it.'

Though I didn't share his faith, I couldn't help admiring Conan Doyle's passion.

'Detection and deception . . . those are two subjects you know a great deal about, sir – both opposed, yet both giving meaning to the other. Like you and Harry.'

The author smiled gently, keeping his eyes on mine as I spoke. 'You're clearly a very intelligent woman, Miss Grey. What led you to work here? Have you, like me, lost anyone close to you?'

'We all lose people,' I said shortly, 'in the end.'

'But are you not curious?'

'Curious, yes. Foolish, no.' The words came out rather too quickly. 'I'm sorry, sir – I didn't mean . . .'

To my relief, Sir Arthur broke into laughter. 'Oh, it's quite all right, Miss Grey.' But he saw I was mortified with embarrassment and rested one hand on mine. 'Please, don't worry. Your remarks are nothing compared to Mr Price's bullish attitude.'

'Yes,' I acknowledged, remembering the door he had slammed in my face.

'The man is ruthless, Miss Grey, utterly ruthless; there's nothing he wouldn't do in order to get what he wants. Harry Price needs someone to balance him, soften his edges. Someone rational but open-minded.' He nodded at me. 'Someone in your position could be very useful to me.'

'You want me to spy on him for you?'

'Oh no, no. I meant someone to help me better understand the man. That's all.'

But something in his expression told me that wasn't all he had meant.

'Perhaps you might remind your employer that this build-ing is owned by the Spiritualist Alliance, and that his tenure depends on his good behaviour.'

The suggestion was made perfectly politely, but that didn't make it any less of a threat – one that Price was certain to resent bitterly.

As Conan Doyle rose to his feet, wishing me good day and good luck, I had a sense that I might need that luck. Because now I had no doubt: these men were at war and I was caught on their battlefield.

8

VELMA'S WARNING

'Well? Where is he?'

I looked up from my desk, where I was typing one of Price's recent manuscripts, to see a tall blonde woman framed in the office doorway.

'Well?' she demanded again, fixing me with an expectant glare. 'Where is he?'

She was in her mid-thirties, I guessed, with a straight nose and sensual lips; almost pretty, but her square jaw and masculine frame mitigated against such a description. She looked like a woman who had spent too many nights on the town and she possessed that most unattractive of qualities in a woman: she was loud.

'I assume that you're referring to Mr Price,' I said politely.

'Yes, I mean Harry!' she said, releasing a startling, raucous laugh. 'Now, where is the old buzzard?'

And before I could utter another word she had shoved past me and was heading for the main corridor and Price's office.

'Excuse me!' I called after her. 'You can't just barge in here like this! Now, just hold on a moment!'

I bolted after her, catching the scent of her sweet, cheap

perfume, and skidded to a halt at the door to Price's study. 'Stop right there,' I said, striding into the room. 'I demand that you—'

'It's all right, Sarah,' said Price softly but with ill-concealed embarrassment.

The woman was standing at his side, nail-bitten hand resting on his shoulder. There was something not right about her: her hair looked limp, not quite clean, and her faded black dress might have been smart but was too tight, too revealing for someone of her age. I wasn't impressed with this woman's disdainful attitude, and as her eyes narrowed, I felt her harsh judgement. 'Miss Grey,' she said in the lightest of voices, 'what a pleasure it is to meet you at last. Why, I've heard *so* much about you.'

'I've heard nothing whatsoever about you.'

'Oh Harry, you complete ass, didn't you tell her I was expected?'

'No,' I interjected, hating the way this woman with her loud jewellery was looking me up and down. 'He did not!'

'Now, now, ladies, please settle down.'

'Don't tell me to settle down,' I said firmly. I felt my face flush with anger. 'Who *is* this . . . this woman?'

Price sprang to his feet, clapping his hands together with gusto. 'Sarah, meet Velma Crawshaw. Velma is a medium.'

I was annoyed with myself. I knew I'd overreacted – perhaps even appeared too possessive and opinionated. It wasn't just because this woman personified everything that angered me about Spiritualism, it was the fact that Price seemed closer to her than he was to me. And that somehow didn't seem fair when she supposedly represented everything he disliked.

The interloper rolled her eyes. 'Oh, you've hired a right one here, Harry.' Then, turning to me, 'You really don't seem to know very much at all, do you, poor thing! I can't say I'm surprised; after all, you are so new in your position. Still,' – she gave me a saccharine smile – 'Harry tells me you're settling in . . . finally.'

'I've asked Velma to attempt to tell us what is inside the locked box,' Price said. 'A perfect test of psychic ability, don't you agree?' He was referring to the bulky walnut casket that had arrived in the post just one week earlier. It had come with an anonymous note claiming the sealed box was a 'Spiritual Ark' containing spiritual prophecies that had once belonged to the famous religious visionary Joanna Southcott. The note's instruction was compelling: 'This box is only to be opened at a time of national crisis.'

Well, national crisis or not, Price had instructed me to arrange a grand public meeting that week at which he would break open the box and reveal its contents to the world.

'If you wouldn't mind preparing the seance room, Sarah? I think we can begin after lunch.'

Velma pinched a smile. 'Yes, Sarah, there's a good girl. Run along now.'

When I had done as Price had instructed – ensured that no daylight could enter the seance room and laid out the locked casket on a table in the centre – I sat for a while in the glow of a small lamp, waiting for him and Velma to return from their lunch. I couldn't resist imagining the two of them together now, without me. Were they talking about me? I thought of the ease with which I had frequently heard Price speak disparagingly of old colleagues, other members of the private Mayfair clubs to which he belonged. If he spoke in such a way about them to me, then how, I wondered, did he speak of me to them? To Velma.

I was probably just being paranoid. My friend Amy's wedding was approaching; perhaps that's why I was jittery. Or maybe I was just tired. My workload, since starting at the Laboratory sixteen months earlier, had been strenuous; each day preparing cuttings, answering letters, organising our field trips – some of which took us abroad, tending to the library, typing Price's numerous articles and, most interestingly, observing and documenting the proceedings of the numerous seances he held after dark when the Laboratory had closed for the day.

The crowds of people who filed through our doors, volunteering to be tested, included individuals of marked eccentricity; indeed, none of them could have been described as 'normal'.

Price and I had worked with women long before Velma's arrival. So why did I now feel so prickly? Waiting here, alone in the dark, for him to return from lunch, the thought of him spending so much time with another woman was almost unbearable.

Abruptly, the door opened and a shaft of light fell upon me.

'Ah, Sarah, here you are.'

I straightened my back but did not stand.

Entering the room with Velma at his side, Price closed the door firmly. Their forms were dim in the shadows cast by the table lamp. 'Very good,' said Price, scouring the room with his usual keen attention, 'everything seems to be in order. Shall we make a start? Velma, you take a seat here, between Sarah and me. Sarah, I'm going to ask Velma to place her hands on the box and attempt to tell us what might be inside.'

She hovered for a moment near the door, staring uncertainly at the puzzling box as though it were a rare breed of dangerous animal. It looked dusty and old and was bound with tight leather straps.

'What's the matter?' Price asked. 'Velma, are you all right?'

She was swaying, clenching her hands into tight little fists. 'I ... I'm not entirely well, Harry.'

Here we go, I thought I had anticipated this: some cheap attempt to distract us.

Price, eyeing the rough surface of the casket, looked crestfallen. 'Won't you please continue, if only for a little while? Thousands of people have debated the importance of this box and what it might contain. It is said that the contents will reveal to the nation a means of saving the country, but no one has produced it ... until now.' He lowered his eyes to the casket and added, 'If, indeed, this *is* the real box.'

Velma nodded reluctantly, then joined us at the table. Seeing her closer now, I felt a pang of self-doubt. Her face was gaunt and horribly pale. With the black cloak she was wearing, she might have passed for the grim reaper. Perhaps she really was unwell.

Placing her left hand on Joanna Southcott's locked casket, Velma closed her eyes. Slowly, she bowed her head.

'Sarah,' Price whispered, 'I want you to observe very carefully and take notes on everything that Velma tells us – all right?'

I nodded, attempting a smile, then asked Velma, 'What are you going to do? Communicate with the dead?'

'The dead and the living,' she said in a low and tremulous voice. 'We are all connected, Miss Grey. Our souls bind us together. Those with the ability – the gift – can know the present, the future and the past.'

Her head was now resting on her chest and her breathing had become short and spasmodic. She seemed to be concentrating very hard.

'Tell us, please, what you see, Velma. What is inside the box?'

'I see many little objects . . .' she said slowly, her eyelids fluttering. 'Dates . . . something metal . . . a book . . . written in French . . . I get a tremendous warmth; also dread.'

It was as I suspected – vague and ridiculous.

'Three documents . . . one bound as a book . . . drawings . . . something long . . . symbols . . . a crest . . . a medal.'

'What sort of medal?' Price queried. 'Can you describe it?'

'Old . . . so old . . . it carries the face of a saint.'

Her eyes snapped open suddenly and she reached forward, taking up a spare pencil and stabbing it into the desk with short, violent motions. 'The force!' she cried. 'It has taken hold of me. It has never been as strong!'

'Let the record show that Miss Crawshaw does not appear to be in full control of her actions,' said Price, clearly a little alarmed. 'Write it down, Sarah.'

This is absurd, I told myself. But in truth I was less than certain. 'Harry, she's putting it on! Stop this nonsense, Velma, for pity's sake – stop it at once!'

But the woman did not stop. Angrily, Price banged his hand down onto the table. I thought he had done it to calm her. It was only when I glanced up from my notes and caught his expression that I realised he was addressing me. 'Write. It. DOWN!' he ordered.

I wanted to retaliate, to protest, but suddenly Velma was stabbing the table so energetically that her hand did indeed appear possessed. Only when Price asked whether she could get spirits to help her did she appear to regain some control.

'I . . . I have a message,' she said slowly, becoming still, her voice quiet. 'A message from the other side.' It might have been my imagination, but that at instant I detected a faint smell of lavender in the air and a chill which brought gooseflesh to my arms.

Seeing my reaction, Price spread his arms out by his sides and patted the air, cautioning silence in the manner of a schoolmaster. 'Go on,' he prompted Velma. 'Tell us, what is the message?'

'I'm sorry,' I interrupted, 'but I think this is totally ridiculous.'

'You're not paid to think,' Price said sharply. 'Now be quiet!'

I swallowed my anger, appalled by his rudeness.

And then I saw Velma staring straight into me, her eyes radiating fire. I flinched away from her gaze. 'What . . . what is it?'

'Oh my, Miss Grey,' she breathed. 'You are such a very old soul.'

'What are you talking about? Harry, what does she mean?'

'You are a wise old soul on her last journey in this life.' Her eyes floated down to my neckline. And an expression of alarm flashed across her face.

'Oh!' Her hand flew to her mouth. 'Oh no!'

'What?' I demanded.

'No more, please, no more!' she exclaimed, her eyes suddenly clear and penetrating. 'There is a mark upon you. Sarah Grey, the woman with two paths and one regret. You must not go!' Velma commanded me. 'Do you understand? You must not agree to go back, not ever!'

'What do you see?' Price asked softly.

'No, please, no more today!' She rose quickly from the table, tipping it over. The locked casket crashed to the floor.

I leapt up.

'Sarah . . .' The warning was implicit in Price's tone. But I was adamant I would speak.

'Miss Crawshaw – I don't know what that little spectacle was all about, but I have a question for you.'

'Sarah!'

Ignoring Price's interruption, I demanded, 'Why don't you tell us about your *own* future?'

Velma's mouth fell slightly open and she backed away. 'I . . . I . . . *what*? This isn't about me, Miss Grey. You have to understand. You have to be careful. Are you listening to me?'

'No,' I replied. 'Now it's your turn. Tell us about *you*. *Your* future.' I raised my eyebrows. 'If you can.'

'You sound as if you don't believe me.'

'That's right, I don't believe you. If you could see the future – well then, you could change your life! But here you are, traipsing all over London, earning pennies to give advice to strangers. If I were psychic, I would want to know everything I could about my future.'

Velma regarded me with the darkest of expressions. 'Are you *sure* about that, Miss Grey?'

'Sarah has asked a perfectly legitimate question, Velma,' Price said calmly and to my relief. 'Aren't you going to answer it?'

Velma nodded and crossed to the window where she stood motionless, silent, for some ten, perhaps twenty seconds, wringing her hands and twisting one of the cheap rings she wore. Finally she said, 'The truth of the matter is, I see nothing of my own future.'

'Nothing?' I queried. Now it was my turn to be sarcastic, though I was also intrigued now, more so, certainly, than I would have admitted. If Velma was an actress, she was a good one. 'Surely that's a little odd for a psychic of your . . . ability?'

She flinched, turned her head away. 'I have tried, Miss Grey; of course I have tried to see my own fate.' She looked back at us from the window, on her face a pallid, frozen expression of fear. 'But I see nothing of my own future. That's the truth of it. I see nothing at all.'

*

Amy's big day had arrived. I usually relished the prospect of a wedding, but the knowledge that I hadn't spoken to my oldest friend for sixteen months tempered my excitement with anxiety as I went with Mother to Chelsea Town Hall.

As the ceremony commenced, my gaze roamed over the ornate vaulted ceiling, brass chandeliers, a marble fireplace adorned with shimmering white flowers.

I imagined Amy would be fraught with bridal worries: her hair, her make-up, every detail. I pondered on her choice of bridesmaid until fleeting envy chased the question away.

'Doesn't she look beautiful?' Mother whispered.

All eyes were on the bride, resplendent in white lace and satin, as she made her way down the aisle. Her face glowed golden, her smile glittered red. By the time she breathed 'I do', my feelings were alternating between pride and embarrassment. Why hadn't I kept in touch?

The question dogged me until ceremony gave way to celebration. The table plan surprised me. We weren't seated at the back of the room, but neither were we at the front.

'You should think about finding your own husband,' I heard Mother say. Irritation displaced guilt for an instant, but even that was washed away by flowing champagne and rising jubilation. Until Amy targeted me with a precisely calibrated smile all the way from the top table, skewering my conscience. I could only smile falteringly back, painfully aware of my dereliction of friendly duty.

Throughout the meal, beneath the laughter and tinkling cutlery, unspoken questions bubbled through my mind: how much had this lavish affair cost? Where had she planned the honeymoon?

My ignorance of these details underlined the distance between us. Was this what I had become – an interloper at my best friend's wedding?

'Sarah!'

Halfway through dessert Amy approached, laying a gentle hand upon my shoulder.

'And Mrs Grey! How wonderful of you to come.'

I studied my friend's smile for insincerity, then stood quickly, folded her in a hug and kissed her cheek. She looked more beautiful than I could have imagined, and I told her so.

'How's the new job?'

'It's good, it's good,' I said quietly, cautious of being overheard. I was deeply reluctant to talk spooks in front of a crowd of new acquaintances.

It wasn't just my odd reticence that marked the change between us. I saw now the fault-lines in her expression, the puzzled scrutiny that glimmered through her hostess smile.

I thought about this as she led me to a table nearer the front of the room and introduced me to some people I didn't recognise. New friends – all smiles and shrill voices, feathers and rhinestones. After long introductions, we settled into a private moment near the fireplace.

'Where have you been hiding?' Amy demanded.

I gave a bright smile. 'Oh, you know, it's been a nightmare really. We have this case at the moment – a locked casket. Harry's kept me tremendously busy preparing for the public opening next week. So much to do!'

Amy nodded awkwardly and said finally, 'Planning a wedding takes time too.'

At once I felt both defensive and ashamed for not having helped with the preparations. Then I tried diversion: 'You've done such a wonderful job! The cake is simply perfect. Is it for eating or just for show?'

I groaned inwardly at my clumsiness.

Amy looked surprised; clearly she suspected sarcasm. Did she think I was jealous? 'Amy, please, I never meant to neglect our friendship,' I hurried to assure her. 'I've just been so frightfully busy.'

At last my friend dropped the pretence and spoke in a sharper tone. 'I don't understand! Why say you'll do something, and then disappear completely? It wasn't just the wedding invitations, Sarah – I haven't seen anything of you! What's been so important to have kept you away?'

My gaze faltered and I felt my cheeks colour. There was no excuse I could offer. She was right, yet I was lost for words. How could I explain that for sixteen months I had been driven to distraction with locked caskets and people who communed with the dead?

'I am sorry, Amy. And I'm so, so proud of you.'

She nodded and smiled, seeing clearly now my sincere contrition. 'Are you finding it interesting?' A brief pause. 'Is *he* interesting?'

Recollections of the past sixteen months at Price's side flicked through my mind, a montage of uncanny memories: the sun glaring on us at the Colosseum in Rome; damp, frigid mornings on the banks of Loch Ness; the teenage girl we encountered in Berlin who made knives and forks stick to her flesh as magnets grip metal. I doubted anyone in London had experienced a more thrilling, more adventurous or more peculiar year. There was no one more mysterious than Harry Price.

I nodded slowly, not wanting to appear too eager. 'He's taking me to Vienna next year, to a conference. And he's teaching me to drive. Sometimes he even lets me bring the saloon home.'

She took my hand and squeezed it gently. 'Is he worth it, Harry Price?'

Before I could answer, laughter erupted at the next table as another champagne cork popped.

'Don't be a stranger, Sarah.'

I wondered: was my life so empty before Price that it had come to this – hunting the dead when I should have been caring for the living?

'I won't,' I promised.

And I meant it too. But by the following week, I was already wondering if this was a promise Price would allow me to keep.

Seven days later, some of Britain's greatest scientists and historians and a crowd of eager newspaper reporters arrived at Church House, Westminster. On all their lips was the same question: what was inside the locked box? Nothing, not even the violent thunderstorm that evening, could keep them away.

Mother and I took our places in the stalls to the left. Glancing to my right, I caught sight of Velma Crawshaw at the end of the opposite aisle. Her hair had been restyled for the occasion, cut closer to her face in a more modern fashion, and she was wearing a long-sleeved pale grey dress so surprisingly elegant that I wondered cynically where she had found the money to pay for it.

At the top of the room, in the centre of a wide stage, was the mysterious locked casket, picked out by a bright spotlight from above.

'What do you suppose is inside it?' Mother asked with a thrill in her voice. 'They say it contains the salvation for any nation in crisis.'

'That is what they say,' I replied doubtfully, glancing over at Velma again.

And then Price was marching down the centre aisle, his black frock coat flapping behind him. From the front of the stage he looked out with severity, his eyes steady, set firm ahead. He didn't look once at Velma. He didn't even look at me.

'Ladies and gentlemen,' his voice boomed in the crowded hall, 'we are gathered here tonight for a momentous occasion.' He proudly took up his place next to the locked box as a wave of excitement rippled through the sea of onlookers. 'Many of you will be wondering why I decided to conduct this investigation in public. You will have heard that I intend to solve the myth surrounding the contents of this box, which once belonged to a great seeress. Let me tell you now that I am here tonight not to verify this myth but to explode it!'

There came from the audience a hurried exchange of whispers.

'In the last few days I took the liberty of asking one of this country's most talented mediums, who is here among us this evening, to tell me by psychic means what this curious chest contains.'

Surely, I thought, he isn't going to tell them all now, here, like this? What if Velma were mistaken? She would be ruined. I didn't care for the woman, but the idea that I was about to witness her public humiliation made me feel extremely uncomfortable.

From his jacket pocket Price produced a slip of paper and held it aloft. 'I can now reveal what was predicted.'

Velma looked totally dejected. And when Price had completed reading aloud the poor woman's vague list of predictions he raised his eyebrows and said, 'Well then, we shall see, shan't we, how accurate the means of the modern psychic really are?'

The great moment had arrived.

Picking up a pair of heavy metal shears from the table, he cut the seals that had secured the box before prising the lid open. From somewhere at the back of the room someone – probably a follower from one of the Southcott societies – cried, 'Sacrilege!'

But of course that didn't stop him.

As he reached inside the casket, his fingers trembling, you could have heard a pin drop. Each curious item was produced slowly, carefully, with wonderful drama for the benefit of the cameras: a horse pistol, some coins, a pair of earrings, two religious pamphlets and a booklet entitled *The Remarkable Prophecies and Predictions for the Year 1796*. Just a curious assortment of worthless bric-a-brac that was clearly never going to be of any use to anyone whatsoever, let alone a nation in a crisis!

'Well then,' said Price, his sarcasm obvious, 'imagine that!'

The affair was a well-staged sensation. It was not, however, a performance to be relished by Velma Crawshaw, whose face, I could see, was flushed with embarrassment. She must have cared for him dearly to have trusted him so. And now she had been vilified.

When the audience finally saw the objects inside the box they burst into hysterical laughter, enthusiastically thanking Price for arranging such an entertaining evening, many of them grateful for the opportunity he had given them to witness close up the results of his method of applying precautionary scepticism to psychic matters.

But not everyone was as satisfied with the night's proceedings. Mother never returned to the Laboratory after that. For her, and hundreds of other ardent spiritualists, it was just too much. 'He has no respect,' she complained to me afterwards, 'no class or nobility. You would do well to get away from him, Sarah.'

In the end, of course, she was right; mothers usually are.

*

'It's about last night,' I said flatly, eyeing his desk, which was covered with newspaper cuttings.

'Yes, it went well very well, didn't it?' Price said cheerfully. 'The public has always been fascinated by mysterious boxes. Pandora's box, the Ark of the Covenant – one has only to possess a box with history and one immediately becomes a headliner. But a locked box! That's much more exciting. Thank you so much for your wonderful efforts, Sarah.' He glanced down at his newspaper cuttings. 'Really, there's hardly a journalist in London who isn't talking about our little show!'

The way he was revelling in this attention made me feel somewhat nauseous.

'Sarah, what's the matter? You seem displeased.'

'You didn't seem surprised,' I remarked, remembering his reaction to the objects he had drawn out of the casket. 'It was as if you already knew.'

'*Was* it?'

'Yes,' I said sternly. 'It was.'

Price held my gaze with a steady concentration, as though he were expecting me to look away. I didn't.

'Well, *did* you already know?'

'Of course I knew,' he snapped. 'I had to know! Did you really imagine I wouldn't have taken the precaution of checking in advance?'

'But why? *How?*'

'By applying the weapons of secular science, of course.' He grinned. 'The X-ray.'

'Then you *wanted* to humiliate her?' I asked.

'You call it humiliation; I call it making a point. By X-raying the box I was taking no chances.'

'But I thought that you and she . . .'

Price's face was blank. 'You thought . . . ?'

'I thought you were friends.'

'It was vital that I control the proceedings in the manner which people have come to expect from me.'

'Yes, but—'

Price stood up and moved to the front of his desk. 'Sarah, you know your work means the world to me, but I am in charge. I decide what we investigate and what we don't, like that house you told me about – that rectory.' He shook his head. 'I decide. That is the way it has to be. Always. All right?' He left an expectant pause, searching my face carefully. Perhaps he could see that I wasn't convinced, that I was about to challenge him still further, because he continued: 'So, why are you really here?'

'I . . . I don't understand.'

'Oh? I think you understand very well.' His tone stung, and it took me a few seconds to realise, with some surprise, that the expression on his face wasn't anger or even dissatisfaction but distrust. 'I'm beginning to think that perhaps you have not been entirely honest with me, perhaps not even honest with yourself.'

'Not this again!' I said quickly, recalling his initial doubts about me. 'I'm not a spy!'

'Is it true that your father was killed in the last war and that your mother is an avid believer in the Spiritualist cause?'

'Who told you that?'

'*Is it true?*'

'Yes . . .'

'Then would you care to enlighten me as to how these facts are connected with your presence here?'

A hazy memory flickered: me next to Father at home in front of his piano. That was the night he told me that very soon he would be gone. 'Where?' I had asked, and his answer had haunted me:

'There is a war coming, my darling. But I will come back, I promise, and you will see me again.'

I felt my despondency rising in my throat.

'Do you imagine, Sarah, that your being here with me is – in some small way – a means of coping with your loss?'

Was that it? I blinked away an unexpected tear. Working here at the Laboratory, on the outer limits of everyday experience, constantly probing the question of an afterlife, did not dispel my feelings of my loss, but it helped me to understand them better, to see with greater clarity why Mother had enveloped herself in these mysteries. It helped me to understand that she was mistaken and my father would never be coming back and to put right what the mediums had made wrong. Lastly – if only in a small way – it allowed me to tease myself with the very same mysteries and possibilities of hope.

Price was waiting for my answer.

'I think you may be right,' I said quietly. 'I loved him so much.'

'The memory of love is as immutable and as radiant as fire, Sarah, and it burns just as fiercely.' They were touchingly warm words from a man whose fits of depression could leave him so cold.

He sat down again and leaned back, resting his fingertips on the edge of his desk. 'You know, I sensed a secret within you, and secrets are always revealed eventually; like worms, they tunnel and twist their way to the surface. No matter! I feel, at least, that now I know you a little better.'

Our conversation seemed to be at an end, so I rose, but before I could leave a question occurred to me. 'What about you, Harry?'

His expression flickered. 'What about me?'

I had wanted to ask him many times why the need for approval burned within him so ferociously and why he had chosen the paranormal as his subject of study. I had a sense that his work in this building was fired by something deep within his troubled soul. But every time he detected signs of curiosity on my part he would either deflect my questions or change the subject. He gave nothing away.

'With one hand you offer people hope,' I ventured, 'and with the other you destroy that hope. What do you believe? Have you lost someone too?'

He pursed his lips for a long moment until finally, in a low voice, he said, 'Loss is the inevitable consequence of life.'

'And now you have lost a friend,' I said sadly. 'You have lost Velma.'

'London can be such a solitary place sometimes. She is a spirited woman, and in more ways than one.'

'If you weren't convinced of her abilities, why did you continue to see her?' I asked.

He gave a shrug. 'I suppose every psychical investigator wants to find a new medium, to develop and test them and to unveil them to the world.'

'Harry, did you always intend to expose her as a fraud?'

'Oh yes,' he answered coldly. 'From day one.'

∗

The months rushed by as quickly as a fevered dream. The conference in Vienna came and went, but Price's mood swings – his occasional bouts of melancholy – showed no signs of improvement.

'Well?' I asked, twirling into the office one morning in my new fur coat. 'Do you like it?'

He looked up sharply from his desk, 'No, I don't. The taking of life, either for fashion or for pleasure, displeases me immensely.'

He returned his attention to his frantic scribbling.

'Harry?' I ventured. 'What is it? What's wrong?'

'They want rid of us, Sarah. They want us out!' he thundered, banging his fist on the desk. 'They've had enough of us, would you believe it? We've outstayed our welcome!'

I had never seen him so angry. Dark patches had formed under his eyes and he looked as if he hadn't slept in days.

'Who has—?'

'That awful meddler Conan Doyle. He and his dreadful, credulous Spiritualist friends! Who else? Just listen to this!' And he began reading from a letter from the pages of *Light*.[1]

'"Among other things, Harry Price repeats a story against me which he knows to be a lie, for I have already contradicted it when he told it before. The object of a page or so of the article is to hold me up to clumsy ridicule. I suggest that every possible means be adopted to get rid of Mr Price as a tenant. The very fact that he acts in such a way would, I should think, offer a legal reason. I feel strongly upon the subject – indeed my own position as President demands such an action!"'[2]

'Conan Doyle wrote that? Harry, what on earth did you do to provoke such a scathing attack?'

Some weeks earlier, he explained, he had impulsively penned an article for the *Psychic Review*, claiming that Conan Doyle had been hoodwinked at a private seance into believing he had witnessed the materialised form of his dead mother.

'Harry, I warned you – you can't keep doing this! You're making a bitter enemy of him.'

From that day, I think he knew that change was coming to Queensberry Place.

With every fraudulent act we exposed his spirits sank yet lower, pulling him down to a place where his dark moods festered. Trouble was brewing. If the cherished Laboratory was to have any hope of a long-term future, if my relationship with Price was to continue, then something needed to change.

And then, in the dusty summer of 1929, quite without warning, everything did.

Notes

1   A journal devoted to psychic and spiritual knowledge and research. Originally published in 1881 by the Eclectic Publishing Company, *Light* was later published by the London Spiritualist Alliance, which became the College of Psychic Studies in 1955 and still publishes it today.
2   Sir Arthur Conan Doyle to Mercy Phillimore, 5 September 1928.

GHOST VISITS TO A RECTORY

TALES OF HEADLESS COACHMEN AND A LONELY NUN

From Our Special Correspondent, Long Melford, Sunday

Ghostly figures of headless coachmen and a nun, an old-fashioned coach drawn by two bay horses which appears and vanishes mysteriously, and dragging footsteps in an empty room.

All these ingredients of a first-class ghost story are awaiting investigation by psychic experts near Long Melford, Suffolk.

The scene of the ghostly visitations is the Rectory at Borley, a few miles from Long Melford.

It is a building erected on the site of a great monastery which, in the Middle Ages, was the scene of a gruesome tragedy.

The present rector, the Revd G.E. Smith, and his wife made the Rectory their residence in the face of warnings by previous occupants.

Since their arrival they have been puzzled and startled by a series of peculiar happenings which cannot be explained and which confirm the rumours they heard before moving in.

The first untoward happening was the sound of slow, dragging footsteps moving across the floor of an unoccupied room.

One night Mr Smith sat in the room, armed with a hockey stick, and waited for the noise. Hearing the sound of feet in some kind of slippers treading on the bare boards Mr Smith lashed out with his stick at the spot where the footsteps seemed to be, but the stick whistled through the empty air and the steps continued across the room.

Then a servant girl, brought from London, suddenly gave notice after two days' work, insisting that she had seen a nun walking in the woods behind the Rectory.

Lastly, an old-fashioned coach has been seen twice on the lawn by a servant, remaining in sight long enough for the girl to observe the colour of the horses' coats.

This same servant also declares that she has seen a nun leaning over a gate near the house. The villagers fear the neighbourhood of the rectory after dark and will not pass it.

All these 'visitations' match elements of a tragedy which, according to legend, occurred at the monastery which once stood on this spot.

A groom at the monastery fell in love with a nun at a nearby convent, runs the legend, and they used to hold clandestine meetings in the woods on to which the Rectory now backs.

One day they arranged to elope and another groom had a coach waiting in the road outside the woods so that they could escape.

From this point the legend varies. Some say that the nun and her lover quarrelled and that he strangled her in the woods and was caught and beheaded, along with the other man, for his villainy.

The other version is that all three were caught in the act by the monks, and that the two men were beheaded and the nun buried alive in the walls of the monastery.

The previous Rector of Borley, now dead, often spoke of the remarkable experience he had one night when, walking along the road outside the Rectory, he heard the clatter of hoofs. Looking around, he saw to his horror an old-fashioned coach lumbering along the road, driven by two headless men.[1]

I had not seen the newspaper article, but it was clear from the look of annoyance on Price's face when I returned from lunch that summer afternoon that he most certainly had. 'Why didn't you show me this?' he demanded, brandishing the newspaper at me like a weapon.

'What?' I said defensively. But when I saw the headline staring back at me, my heart sank. This was important, the sort of news I was employed to notice. 'I'm sorry, Harry,' I said hurriedly, 'I haven't had time yet to prepare today's cuttings, but I did tell you about this house – the letter! We discussed—'

He silenced me with an expression of fierce reproach. 'Honestly, Sarah, with all the pressures we're under at the moment and you miss a thing like this. It's unforgivable, really it is.'

'Harry, I most certainly did tell you about the rectory in Essex and—'

From behind me came the sound of a gentleman clearing his throat. Surprised, I spun round to see a young man of average height and no more than twenty-four standing in the corner of the room. I didn't know whether to feel relieved or humiliated. He was classically handsome, with thick dark hair and a strong jaw. And he was looking straight at me.

'Sarah, this is Vernon Wall,' Price said, mellowing towards me but still sounding very stern. 'Mr Wall is a reporter with the *Daily Mirror*.'

'Pleased to meet you,' I said, noticing how steadily he met my gaze and feeling a flutter of excitement within me.

'The pleasure's all mine. I apologise for dropping in on you unannounced.' He smiled warmly.

The young man with the lean face couldn't have been standing there long, as I had only been out at lunch for an hour. But from the tense atmosphere in the room I had the strongest impression that I had interrupted something – an argument perhaps.

Price turned to our guest. 'Now, let me be clear about this, Mr Wall. You have some acquaintance with my work, my theories, and yet you still believe I am the man to assist you?'

'My editor said you were the only man for the job, said I was to call on you straight away. He had a jolly old name for you – the Midnight Inquirer!'

I was drawn to this stranger immediately. He had a youthful

confidence and an air of good humour that suggested he was someone I could enjoy spending time with.

'Did he now?' Price replied crisply. 'Did he indeed?'

'Yes, sir – he said this whole business sounded right up your street.'

'Right up my street?' Price was glaring at him.

'Yes . . . umm, your work. Ghost laying, I mean.'

'Ghost laying? Good heavens, young man, is *that* what you think I do?'

'Well, of course! Haunted houses and all that,' said Wall through a cheery grin. Then, seeing Price's horrified reaction, he added, 'That is to say, I know you're a scientist and that you take this seriously.'

'Yes, extremely seriously.'

'Oh, and I have read your paper on William Hope. That was quite a case. I must say, Mr Price, I have never seen a man's reputation ruined so quickly. How long did you work on the investigation?'

'Months.'

'It must all be terribly exhausting.'

'If the answers came easily they would hardly be worth looking for, would they?'

'And you always catch your man, do you?'

'Actually, they're usually women,' said Price. 'Forgive me for being more than a little sceptical about your newspaper story, Mr Wall, but I have never seen any evidence that would persuade me to believe in what you would call a ghost.'

'Well, that may be, Mr Price. But shouldn't we approach every new case with an open mind? Frankly, until I am satisfied that the peculiar events at Borley Rectory have been investigated thoroughly, and by an expert, I refuse to submit to the fashionable assumption which condemns such experiences out of hand.

Absence of evidence is not evidence of absence. And given your speciality in this area, I'm surprised to find you so certain of your conclusions. Am I to understand that you don't find at least some of this believable?'

'No, you are to understand that I find *none* of it believable,' Price scoffed. He scanned the newspaper article again, running his finger down the column. 'This tale about a phantom death coach, for example. You find this report credible, sir?'

Wall shrugged. 'That is what has been reported.'

Price eyed him haughtily. 'The legend you mention in your article – the event concerning the monk and the nun – when did that occur?'

'People say the murders were carried out in the fourteenth century, I believe.'

'Then tell me, in what century were coaches first used?'

The young reporter fidgeted beneath Price's gaze. 'I haven't the foggiest idea,' he admitted. 'And I'd be surprised if you knew the answer.'

'But I *do* know the answer,' Price shot back. 'The first coach to be seen in England was made by Walter Rippon for the Earl of Rutland in 1599, during the reign of Elizabeth. The sixteenth century. So unless the good Earl was capable of travelling back in time in his vehicle, perhaps you can explain how exactly a nun was able to elope in a coach in the fourteenth century?'

A lengthy silence ensued, during which an expression of doubt crept across Wall's face.

'It's quite ridiculous, Mr Wall. You must have your facts if you're to be a reporter of any substance.'

'The house is haunted,' Wall insisted in an even more serious voice.

'An extraordinary claim.' Price glared at Wall. 'Naturally, you have extraordinary evidence to back it up?'

'I am happy to tell you, sir, that everything I witnessed in that house was extraordinary by *my* standards, if not your own.'

'My standards, Mr Wall, are the standards of science. They are universal. I deal in facts.'

'Then you shall have them all,' Wall said gravely. 'The facts of the affair.'

I watched as the young reporter reached into his coat pocket and produced some folded sheets of paper. 'This letter reached our newspaper a few days ago from the Reverend Eric Smith, the Rector of Borley. After reading it, my editor rushed me out there to get the full story – to speak to the rector and his wife and to find out what I could from the locals.'

Price scrutinised our visitor moodily with perhaps with a trace of envy.

'My full report on what I observed there will appear in tomorrow's edition. It's a quiet, mournful little place perched on a small hill at the top of the Stour Valley, just on the border between Suffolk and Essex.'

'Sounds perfectly lovely,' I said.

Regarding me darkly from beneath gathered brows, Wall said in a low voice, 'Believe me, Miss Grey, there is nothing lovely about it.'

'That part of England is steeped in superstition,' Price interrupted him. 'The border between Essex and Suffolk has a long history of ghost stories: anachronistic legends of phantom horse-drawn carriages and the like.'

'And take my word for it, they are apt to the location,' said Wall. 'I found the Rectory in a neglected garden choked with weeds, a rambling red-brick monstrosity of a house full of shadows. The place was so quiet, so still.' He paused and I swear I glimpsed a shudder run through him. 'So utterly cold.'

'Cold?' I asked, puzzled, 'But it's summertime!'

Wall looked at me. 'Yes, I know that, Miss Grey.' His gaze fell on the paper in his hand. 'I had read this letter,' he continued, 'but I did not think for a moment any word of it could be true. Not until I saw it myself.' His alert gaze slackened, roaming the middle distance. Whatever 'it' was, he was seeing it again now.

It was clearly unwelcome news to Price that he was not the sole repository of unusual stories, but as he leaned back against the nearest workbench, watching the reporter carefully, he did at least seem interested. He produced some tobacco paper and proceeded to roll and light a cigarette, before eventually pointing at the letter in Wall's hand and saying, 'Let's hear it then!'

'Very well,' said Wall. He snapped out of his reverie and I watched, intrigued, as the journalist unfolded the letter and began to read.

Note

1   The first of V.C. Wall's articles in the *Daily Mirror*, 10 June 1929.

– 10 –
A PLEA FOR HELP

Borley Rectory
Hall Road
Borley
Suffolk, England
8 June 1929

Sir,

It is not without some hesitation that I write to request the assistance of your newspaper in connection with a series of troubling occurrences that have recently been observed in and about our residence, Borley Rectory, in East Anglia.

My wife and I arrived in England last year, having travelled here from India in pursuit of a quieter life on account of my wife's poor health. After receiving my Holy Orders, I was duly offered the living at Borley, following the death of the previous rector, Harry Bull, whose family has lived in these parts, I am told, for some sixty years or more.

We were delighted to have found a suitable home so soon, in a quiet parish, in a beautiful setting. But then we learned that we were not the first to have been offered the living at Borley. No less than twelve rectors before us had come, looked over the place and left with no explanation as to why.

It was then, to our dismay, that we heard the troubling stories that went with the house and its history. The surviving members of the Bull family, the sisters of the late rector, informed us that the Rectory has a macabre history. And those villagers who are willing to talk (and they are few) speak of a phantom coach and the spectre of a woman appearing in the grounds of the Rectory and near the churchyard.

Under normal circumstances we would dismiss such 'sightings' as superstitious nonsense. I am not a man who has ever believed in ghosts. But the weight of our experience in the short time that we have lived here, combined with stories imparted to us in confidence, compels us to entertain, reluctantly, a different view. Though we have not witnessed these phenomena ourselves, we have been privy to other, less dramatic but no less queer occurrences. There have been unusual happenings here; events quite beyond our understanding.

We had not occupied the Rectory some three months before the troubles began. Noises in empty rooms, loud thumps, the sound of footsteps in hallways where no one was present. Voices, bells ringing, whisperings on the first-floor landing, objects that vanish only to be found in the most unusual of places in and about the house. And then there is a light seen regularly by passersby from outside the Rectory shining in the window of one of the unoccupied rooms on the first floor of the house; the very room where the Reverend Bull, my predecessor, and his father before him passed from this world into the next.

I would add that my wife is of a very nervous disposition and I would be grateful, therefore, for your timely assistance with the matter. Perhaps you might be so kind as to provide us with the address for the Society for Psychical Research so that it may dispatch an expert in these matters to help us. For I am certain what is happening to us demands professional attention.

Yours

Reverend Guy Eric Smith

Rector of Borley

Beams of sunlight slanted through the shuttered window, catching particles of dust and the wisps of smoke that drifted up from Price's cigarette and wreathed around his head. He was lost in thought, perhaps wishing he had listened when I first mentioned the story of a haunted rectory in the northernmost tip of Essex.

'Well?' Wall said, as he folded the letter and tapped it back into his jacket pocket.

'I agree it is interesting,' said Price, gazing intently at the handsome young man. 'You said that you have spent time with this rector?'

Wall nodded.

'Did he appear sincere?'

'Yes, sir, most sincere; charming and gracious too. He and his wife are from Calcutta.'

'And this peculiar light that appears in the window of the upstairs room – did you witness that during your visit?'

'I did, sir.'

'Some anomaly of optics and illumination, perhaps—'

'No,' insisted Wall. 'I saw the thing clearly, Mr Price. An orange globe of phosphorescent light. It was swinging back and forth behind the glass. Not regularly, and yet not randomly, either. It pulsed, Mr Price. Do you see? It was trying to catch our attention! The rector went to investigate.'

'And . . . ?'

'When he reached the bedroom in question, the Blue Room they call it, he found it in complete darkness – and yet from outside my observation of the light persisted. I could see it, Mr Price, as clearly as I see you now! And there was something else. The area immediately outside this room, on the landing, was icy cold, sir – cold enough to make you gasp. You stepped into it like plunging into a river.'

'Weren't you frightened?' I broke in. All this time I had been making detailed notes.

Wall smiled at me thoughtfully. 'Frightened . . . no. But it alarmed me, Miss Grey. The whole experience confounded all reason. In my occupation one is accustomed to discovering facts and reporting them – accepting them. But when I remember what happened at that house I am unable to explain it to my satisfaction. Either what I saw wasn't real, or the bedrock of modern science is entirely inaccurate.' He shrugged. 'I can't see how it can be otherwise.'

The comment had its effect on Price, who was leaning forward, his eyes alive with curiosity. 'You're quite certain of everything you have told us?' he asked, his voice serious.

'But of course!' Wall answered. 'How puzzling and extraordinary the world is, Mr Price; so beautiful and painful. Who are we to deny its magic?' He shook his head. 'I cannot deny the possibility of these events. I can ignore hearsay, I can resist legends, but I cannot deny the proof of my eyes.' He shook his head, raising his voice with passion. 'Surely you can appreciate the reason for my excitement?'

Price nodded, lips pursed.

'And in any event, Mr Price, how many hauntings have you investigated in your career? I mean real hauntings, the genuine article?'

There was a slight pause. 'You know the answer to that question.'

'Then come with me to Borley,' Wall urged, 'and you will have your chance.'

I watched as Price considered the proposal, inhaling deeply on his cigarette stub.

'Just think, Mr Price, we both have a role in this affair: I scoop the story, you catch the ghosts! Isn't that what you're looking for? What you've promised your backers?'

I was certain that my companion's reluctance to help the reporter sprang from envy. The story of Borley Rectory was undeniably Vernon Wall's story; he had already published one article about it in the *Daily Mirror*, and he clearly had plans to publish more. But I could tell, from subtle changes in Price's poise and demeanour, that curiosity was taking hold. I think we both sensed further mysteries.

'Of course if you are too busy, Mr Price, I could always approach the Society for Psychical Research.'

'Wait!' Price stretched out an arm, then regained his self-control and lowered it. 'Yes, all right. I will take the case.' It was as though the decision somehow transformed him. Mobilised him. He snapped off orders. 'Sarah, kindly send a telegram to the Reverend Eric Smith and Mrs Smith requesting an appointment to visit this Rectory as soon as possible. And prepare a bag. We'll need cotton, sealing wax, three electric torches, batteries, matches . . . oh, and steel tape. And flour!'

'You are sure you want to come, Mr Price?' the reporter asked him.

An expression of resolve settled on Price's face. 'Yes, my boy, I am sure. I'll come. And I'll show you, the rector and his wife just how easy it is to be duped by the mundane. You will have to do your level best to keep up. Ghost-hunting is a gruelling test of reason, accuracy and will!'

Reverend Smith's response to our telegram came back within the hour. Its tone was urgent: 'Thank God. We are in your debt. Come quickly, tomorrow. Will expect you . . .'

Later that evening Price reminded me to pack a night bag for the trip. 'We will set off from here first thing in the morning.'

'How long do you suppose the investigation will last?'

'As long as it takes. Why?'

'I'll have to explain to Mother, that's all.'

His eyes narrowed. 'There's nothing wrong, I hope?'

'It's awkward,' I admitted, rising from my chair.

'What's her name, please?'

'Frances. Frances Helen Grey.'

'A lovely name. Doesn't she trust me?' He covered his eyes, making me think of a naughty schoolboy: a little reckless but impossibly endearing.

'Harry, like so many people she thought you were a believer.' I drew close to him, standing beside the glass cabinet which housed props seized from offending mediums. 'She hoped your work would serve as a connection to Father in the after-life.'

'Whatever for?'

I didn't want to tell him about the secrets she believed

Father had kept back, so I shrugged. 'She finds your methods unconventional, in poor taste. She thinks her friends will consider me odd, working for someone whose beliefs contradict their own.'

'Well, we must give your mother the reassurance she deserves,' said Price. His smile was open and bright and confident. 'Tonight I shall escort you home. If you're anything like your mother, then I can't wait to make her acquaintance.'

'Harry, no—'

His finger flew to my lips. 'My enemies are legion. We must keep them at bay by keeping them close.'

By the time we reached my house on Gloucester Street I was excited about the next morning's trip and eager to go indoors, out of the thickening dark, but I couldn't shake off my growing discomfort. I hadn't felt this nervous since Price had found me poking around in his study. How would Mother react to his unexpected arrival?

The answer was obvious on her face the instant she opened the front door, and as we entered the drawing room I felt myself close up with embarrassment. The fire was dead, the room as cold as Mother's mood.

'Well,' said Price, dropping into my father's old armchair beside the window. His eyes roamed the room, moving between the faded red curtains and the wallpaper peeling at the corners. 'What a lovely home you have here, Mrs Grey.'

He spoke without a hint of sarcasm, but his compliment failed to have any effect on Mother, who had selected my favourite deep red armchair in the far corner of the room. She perched in it rigidly, her back straight as a gentleman's cane.

'These town houses are quite splendid. Such a shame so many are being converted into flats.' Price scowled. 'Noisy things, flats! Not private.'

'Mr Price . . . Why did you say you were here?'

'I didn't.' His face lifted into a wide smile. 'But hello!'

'What . . .'

'I came to say hello! Sarah's told me so much about you, madam.'

We told her then about our planned investigation at Borley Rectory.

'With Sarah helping me, I can be sure of a thorough investigation. Your daughter is so helpful. If anything's out of place, I can rely on her to put it in order. Even my tie.' He smiled. 'She's wonderful.'

'She *is* wonderful.' Mother's tone was sharp. She raised her chin. 'But tell me this, Mr Price: will she be safe?'

It amazed me that Mother should have taken against Price just because he wasn't the believer she had hoped he would be. Price, too, looked taken aback at her frank approach and he adopted an expression of wounded concern.

'Sarah isn't just my employee, Mrs Grey, she is my friend.'

'Your friend. I see.' An awkward silence stretched out. Then: 'Are you married, Mr Price?'

He nodded, folding his arms.

'Then, forgive me for asking, but where is your wedding ring?'

I found myself dropping my gaze to Price's lap where his large, rough hands were resting.

'I leave it at home to keep it safe, especially when I'm using the forge in my workshop.'

'Oh, he's always tampering with some gadget or other,' I cut in. I tried to laugh, but my embarrassment made the attempt sound forced. 'You're practically on first-name terms with every hammer, aren't you?'

'Any other hobbies?'

'I collect coins.'

'Oh, so you *profit* from your ventures too?' Mother said in a thin voice. 'And tell me, do you find pleasure in picking apart other people's beliefs?'

'Well, really!' My reaction was quick, untempered, but clearly had an effect on Mother, who looked aside quickly with self-conscious reproach.

'No, no, Sarah, it's quite all right,' said Price. His gaze fell on the telephone by the door. Then he gave Mother a bright, reassuring smile. 'Madam, I quite understand your position, but we owe it to the fallen, and to the those mourn them, to show that there are no hot-lines to the other side.'

'Your experiments make that very clear. But such sensationalist demonstrations, Mr Price – why?'

'The public is hungry for wonders. You might say I have a thirst for answers, madam. Nothing else matters to me.' Leaning forward a little, he smiled and added, 'I'm sure that *you* can understand.'

The loaded comment made Mother flinch and as she caught my eye I felt heat rising in my face.

'Now that is a wonderful photograph!' Price remarked suddenly. 'Such flattering lighting.' He was pointing towards a delicate silver frame on the mantelpiece: a photograph of our family before the fracture. Father was smart in his uniform; I sat at his knee, in a floral dress; Mother stood tall next to him, in a dress that had bunched sleeves and wide shoulders. Her oval face was smooth and untroubled. 'It must be very difficult for you both, two women all on your own.'

'We get by,' said Mother. It was an unfair response to such genuine concern. 'But tell me, Mr Price: how did you spend your time in the war?'

'I worked as a manager in a munitions factory. Our weapons were used by the troops in the very last battles of the conflict.'

'I see. And which battles were those?'

He paused, but before he could provide an answer, Mother asked him if he would care for a drink. It seemed a peculiar intervention, but one that Price accepted with grace.

'That would be marvellous, thank you. Brandy, please, if you have any?'

Mother nodded.

'You will join me, I hope?'

'Oh . . . It's a little early for me, Mr Price.'

She seemed to relish this moment of moral superiority, and as she rose from her chair I mouthed a silent apology to Price before joining her at the dusty drinks cabinet next to Father's old piano.

'Really, Sarah!' Mother said quietly. 'Bringing that man to my house.'

'That man is my employer,' I reminded her, clinking the decanter and brandy glasses slightly louder than was necessary. I needed a drink too. 'Because of Harry, our lives are about to change for the better. Just think, we could have a maid again.'

'He has misled so many people.'

I didn't want to get drawn into an argument, but I had to wonder whether Mother realised her conversion to Spiritualism was just as fervent as Price's devotion to scepticism. 'People change their minds, Mother. You did.'

'On second thoughts, ladies, I should leave.' Price was behind us suddenly, placing his battered hat on his head. In the heat of our conversation I hadn't notice him rise to retrieve his belongings from the hall. 'It was presumptuous of me to come here unannounced. Forgive me. Sarah, I shall see you in the morning, bright and early. We have quite a trip ahead of us. I'll be counting on you to keep an eye on that silly reporter from the *Mirror* too.' He gave a gallant bow. 'But, oh! I almost forgot . . .' And now he was rummaging in the deepest recesses of his overcoat pocket, picking something out and handing it to Mother. 'This belongs to you, I believe.'

Mother's face lit up with relief. 'Yes, oh, yes! Wherever did you find it?'

'At the Laboratory, in the seance room. You must have dropped it during your tour.'

'Sarah, look – my bracelet!'

Strange. I was sure I had asked Price about Mother's bracelet . . . Why had he never mentioned it?

'You must trust me,' Price said to Mother with compelling authority. 'Like you, madam, I am jaded by the cruelty of war. While you have rushed towards the charms of the mediums I have moved away from them, if only that I may spare the living any further suffering. I am here to help. Mrs Grey – Frances – if there is anything you need, all you have to do is ask.'

I don't know if Mother sensed in him, then, the mystery and possibility that was so attractive to me, or whether it was his open smile, infused with charm as he touched her arm, but something in his response made her nod and smile with a modicum of acceptance. I let out a quiet sigh of relief as Price turned and headed for the hallway. His parting words left Mother hanging in hope:

'And you can tell your spiritualist friends that if there is anyone destined to discover a genuine ghost, have no doubt – it's going to be me!'

HAUNTED ROOM IN A RECTORY!

Old Servant's Story of a Midnight Visitor

LAYING THE 'GHOST' – by V.C. Wall

Psychic Expert to Investigate a Suffolk Mystery

One of the leading British psychological experts is to investigate the mystery of the 'ghost' of Borley Rectory, Suffolk, described in the Daily Mirror.

In an effort to lay the ghost by the heels, and either prove or disprove its existence, Mr Harry Price, honorary director of the National Laboratory of Psychic Research, is to conduct the investigation.

Mr Price is famous in this country and in America for his research work and his exposures of exhibitions of psychic 'phenomena'.

Striking confirmation of the weird experiences of the present and past occupants of the Rectory is forthcoming from Mrs E. Myford of Newport, Essex.

In a letter to the Daily Mirror, Mrs Myford reveals that forty-three years ago, when she was a maid at the Rectory, similar phenomena were quite openly discussed in the Rectory and neighbourhood.

'Much of my youth was spent in Borley and district, with my grandparents,' writes Mrs Myford, 'and it was common talk that the Rectory was haunted.

'Many people declared that they had seen figures walking at the bottom of the garden.

'I once worked at the Rectory forty-three years ago, as an under maid, but I only stayed there a month, because the place was so weird.

'The other servants told me my bedroom was haunted, but I took little notice of them because I knew two of the ladies of the house had been sleeping there before me.

'But when I had been there a fortnight, something awakened me in the dead of night.

'Someone was walking down the passage towards the door of my room and the sound they made suggested they were wearing slippers.

'As the head nurse always called me at six o'clock, I thought it must be she, but nobody entered the room, and I suddenly thought of the "ghost".

'The next morning I asked the other four maids if they had come to my room, and they all said they had not and tried to laugh me out of it.

'But I was convinced that somebody or something in slippers had been along that corridor, and finally I became so nervous that I left.

'My grandparents would never let me pass the building after dark, and I would never venture into the garden or the wood at dusk.'[1]

Note

1   Article from the *Daily Mirror*, 12 June 1929.

– 11 –
THE JOURNEY EAST

The warm summer breeze blew through the open window of the saloon as it chugged along the country road. I was at the wheel – Price had insisted – and my spirits were high. Out here on the broad flat lands of Suffolk, on the outskirts of Sudbury, the problems waiting for us back at the Laboratory were forgotten, and I was relishing my freedom from the incessant grind and bustle of London.

The hedgerows and green fields rushed by on both sides, bringing a calming sense of ease. I needed this: a break from the routine to which I had become accustomed in recent months, forever following Price, jumping to carry out his orders and worrying about him. At least with him sitting beside me in the passenger seat I could be certain he wasn't barricaded in his study, tormenting himself with self-criticism or writing letters to critics like Conan Doyle, further invoking their wrath. Here, thankfully, my companion seemed at peace, and as I looked across at him I saw he was smiling as he turned his head to the open window to catch the fresh air.

'Sarah!' he said suddenly. 'Which turning is it?'

'How should I know? You're supposed to be reading the map!'

If Price heard my response, he made no acknowledgement of it.

'Any idea, Mr Wall?' I called back to our companion, who was bundled up uncomfortably among our cases on the back seat. I looked up into the rear-view mirror to catch his reflection, and was surprised when our eyes connected instantly; his gaze had been waiting for me. The expression on his face caught me off guard: that wonderful smile of his might have conveyed any number of feelings – fondness perhaps, admiration or respect – but his eyes revealed everything I needed to know. No one had ever looked at me the way he was looking at me now. Or if they had, I hadn't noticed.

Breaking the connection, I put the car into gear and glanced furtively at Price, whose eyes were fixed on the road ahead. But Wall answered me regardless, raising his voice to make himself heard above the rumble of the engine. 'Afraid I haven't the foggiest! First time I came here it was already dark. I stayed at the Bull Inn and took a taxi up to Borley. But we can't be far away – this looks like Sudbury.'

Price was clearly less than impressed with our companion; when Wall had suggested that we make the journey together, he had been reluctant to agree and I had had to persuade him. The truth was, I rather liked Mr Wall.

'Sudbury itself has a somewhat macabre history,' Price said suddenly. 'It dates back to the time of the Saxons.' He turned his head towards me. 'Did you know, Sarah, that Thomas Gainsborough, the eighteenth-century painter, was born in this part of Suffolk, and in 1381 Simon of Sudbury, Archbishop of Canterbury, was beheaded on Tower Hill?'

'I did not,' I replied, wondering how he knew all this. He had clearly done his homework.

Price nodded. 'Yes indeed! The poor fellow's head was brought back here to Sudbury and installed in the vestry of Saint Gregory's Church. If we get time we should stop and take a look.' He glared at Wall in the rear-view mirror. 'Mr Wall here might learn something.'

Twenty minutes later we were still off course and Price was rapidly losing his patience. As I turned the saloon into yet another winding country lane that looked just like the one before, I had to admit that we had lost our way. The area was quite desolate, the road ahead empty, and we had travelled perhaps four miles and passed no houses at all. I was just about to suggest that Price take the wheel, when I spotted a farmer emerging onto the lane from the entrance to a nearby field.

'Thank goodness! We can ask him,' I said. Stopping the car, I rolled down my window. 'Excuse me, hello there . . .'

The man ambled closer, an expression of wary cooperation on his weathered face. I had a sense that he knew what was coming next.

'I'm afraid we've taken a wrong turn somewhere,' I began. I wonder if you could—'

He cut me off before I could finish. 'It's directions that you'll be after then, I suppose?'

'Yes, yes please. If it's not too much trouble.'

He grinned, showing crowded yellow teeth. Prediction confirmed.

'You from London?' he grunted, casting an inquisitive glance over the saloon. He seemed intent on extracting either some amusement or some interesting diversion in exchange for directing us on our way.

'Yes, indeed we are, but—'

'Thought so. You can always tell. Even before the accent. It's the cars, see? Not enough mud on 'em to be from round 'ere. You don't bother tryin' to keep a tractor clean, do you?' He chuckled as if he had said something deeply witty and I gripped the wheel, forcing a polite smile to cover my mounting impatience. Price wouldn't keep silent through much more of this, and I didn't want to risk offending the man and being sent off with no directions or, worse, deliberately incorrect ones. But he persisted in his rambling monologue, peering at Wall in the back seat. 'And then there's the clothes, a course. You can tell a lot from a person's clothes, I always say.'

'I'm terribly sorry, sir,' I interrupted, 'but we're in the most dreadful hurry.'

'You people always are, aincha?' he said, talking over me, but I pressed on, resolute, noticing gratefully that he had yielded to me, lips pursed in resigned disappointment.

'We have an urgent appointment in Borley, and I fear that our awful map-reading has delayed us too long already.'

As I gave the name of our destination I saw the man's eyes narrow with unmistakable suspicion. We were lost, true, but not in the wrong place altogether. A place like Borley Rectory casts a long shadow, and those living under it felt its chill. He had heard the stories. I could read them in his face.

'Borley? Now, why you be wanting Borley?' the man enquired, peering into the saloon with pointed interest even as he took a cautious step back. He glared past me and across to Price. 'Don't get many folk going up to Borley. Not unless they want their head seen to.'

I glanced sideways, exchanging the briefest look with Price, who was muttering under his breath, a sound that increasingly made me visualise a burning fuse. I could tell that he too knew where this was going but, unlike me, wasn't at all worried about offending this man. It was never in Price's nature to shy away from an argument.

'I don't mean to be rude, my good man, but we simply don't have time for conversation,' he said, leaning forward so he could see the farmer through my window. 'We want the Rectory; we're expected for lunch. We're late enough already, so could you indicate the route?'

'The Rectory, you call it?' The man's face was distorted by fear, and he raised his hands to pat the air between him and the car. He shook his head and said slowly, 'What you mean is – the most haunted house in England.'

'What?'

The man was nodding. 'Aye, sir, that's what they call it down in the village.' He looked away from Price then fixed his gaze on mine. 'Now then, miss, you listen here: anyone in these parts will tell you to steer clear of Borley. If you've some sense about you, you'll do exactly that.'

'But why?'

'Why?' he cried, as if the reason were obvious. 'Her, that's why!'

'Her?' Price sneered. His tone made it clear to me that he did not consider this fellow very bright. I hoped his condescension was not as obvious to this uncomplicated man who was obviously mired in a swamp of superstition.

'She's been seen near the churchyard in Borley, on the corner of the road, and at the end of the driveway leading up to the Rectory.'

'Forgive me, but to whom are you referring?' asked Price.

'The Dark Woman, sir; that's what they call her in the bar at the Bull Inn.'

'I assume you mean this legendary ghostly nun we've read about?'

The farmer nodded gravely. 'But she's no legend, sir, as any right-minded person round here will tell you. Watch yourselves. These lanes are lonely places at night. No one in the village will come near.'

Perhaps it was because of our beautiful and peaceful surroundings, but I was struggling to take the farmer's words seriously. It sounded like superstitious nonsense. Quite amusing, actually.

Price had also heard enough, but he was less than amused. Scowling, he slapped his hand on the dashboard. 'For the love of sense, man, do you really expect me to swallow this routine? Has someone put you up to it? Do you recognise me from the papers or something? Well, I don't take kindly to being mocked, sir!'

The farmer assumed a look somewhere between mystified incomprehension and wounded humour. 'I got no idea who you are, mister. What you on about? I'm just tryin' to do a good turn.' He prattled on, more to himself than to Price, 'Well, I suppose no good deed goes unpunished, as they say.'

I put my hand on Price's arm and made a face at him, trying to restrain him. Visions of spending all afternoon scouring the countryside made the farmer's stories seem suddenly less funny.

My employer turned to me and snapped, 'No, Sarah, it's too much, really it is.' He waved a hand in the man's direction. 'I'm surprised he hasn't crossed himself or made the sign of the evil bloody eye yet! Every time we tackle a new case we find ourselves beset by credulous nincompoops who want to scare us off.'

He checked himself, visibly reining in his temper so that his face took on a mask of polite formality. Then, turning to the farmer, he said smoothly, 'Sir, please, be a good fellow and tell us which road to take.' He checked his wristwatch and looked up again, the picture of reasonable patience.

'Very well, your choice,' said the farmer reluctantly. 'You want

Hall Road; that's first to the left, carry on for half a mile till you see the disused railway tracks, then take the next right at Rodbridge Corner, over the bridge. You'll see some cottages and the old school. Carry on up the hill. You won't miss it.'

Price turned to me, raised his eyebrows and said, 'I hope you got that!'

In the rear-view mirror I saw Wall's expression of surprise echo my own. 'Actually, Harry, you're the one who's supposed to be navigating.' Swinging open the heavy door, I climbed down out of the saloon, went round to his side and opened the door. 'Come along, you can take us the rest of the way.'

His jaw dropped open. 'Sarah . . . ?'

'Hop it!' I instructed with a gesture of my thumb, and as he gave up his seat in the manner of a grumpy child, I stifled a laugh. Climbing up into the passenger's side I caught Wall's wide, nodding smile through the back window. Inwardly I was glowing: his smile seemed to say, 'Well done.'

It took twenty minutes to travel the last three or four miles to Borley, picking our way through the narrow lanes and contending with wrong turnings and dead ends. But my high spirits never wavered. Passing by open meadows and low hedgerows sprinkled with honeysuckle, the smells of the season were beguiling. I had quite detached myself from the idea that we were supposed to be visiting somewhere reputed to be threatening and sinister.

Eventually, and to the great relief of everyone in the car, we came to a small junction where a battered wooden sign indicated that the uneven mud track to our left was Hall Road. At last! The lane ran upwards on a gentle trajectory and was bordered on either side by low hedgerows and high trees. As we drove we saw no one, not even a house, just wide open fields and, beyond, the Essex marshes sparkling in the sun. I began to imagine what it must be like to live out here, somewhere so remote and breathtakingly beautiful.

At the roadside another small sign, with peeling paint and barely legible letters, informed us that we had arrived in Borley. Someone, probably a youth, had attempted to add the word 'haunted'. But there was nothing to see at first, only a solitary church spire reaching out of a cluster of trees. The road ahead veered to the right and brought us to a clearing. I stopped the car and we all climbed out. 'Well, this is the place,' said Wall.

To my right I saw Borley church, a small, pretty twelfth-century building approached by a narrow path and surrounded on all sides by crumbling gravestones, clipped yews and mature chestnut trees. In front of us a crooked centuries-old building was identified by a plaque on its side as the Tithe Barn. But there was little else beyond the three small cottages visible further down the road.

Just the Rectory.

*

Borley Rectory was the perfect manifestation of a haunted house. Standing in the shadow of tall cedars, the place had a decayed and neglected air and was startlingly large. Its windows – I counted twelve on one wall alone – were narrow and covered with iron bars, giving the impression of a prison or asylum.[1]

The immediate area, from the quiet lane that ran from the spot where we now stood to the little churchyard on the opposite side of the road, had an air of utter isolation. I had never been anywhere that felt so remote. As I glanced around, taking in the sweeping views of the countryside, I felt oddly calmed by the quietness – the complete absence of any noise, not even a singing bird – and thought it peculiar that anyone could come here and feel afraid. What was there to fear? Surely nothing as mundane as a foreboding red-brick house and a neglected garden.

Only Wall seemed uneasy, his eyes darting this way and that. I moved to his side and said gently, 'Are you all right?'

He shot me a defensive look. 'Yes, Miss Grey. Quite all right, thank you.' And then he added, rather quietly, 'Listen, are you sure you want to do this?'

'Yes, of course.' I glanced back at Price. 'He hasn't been well recently. This is good for him.'

'Very well. This is where the mysterious light appeared the other night.' He pointed to a window in the centre of the house, immediately above the glass verandah that opened on to the wide garden. 'And down there' – pointing to a path in the tangled garden – 'is the summerhouse, where the family that lived here before used to watch for the nun.'

'Have a look at this!' Price interjected. He was pointing to the wall immediately to the left of the Rectory's turreted entrance. 'The stonework here seems oddly discoloured.' He ran his hands over the area. 'Yes, I do believe these are new bricks. There was a window here once. It's been bricked up.'

'Perhaps because of the window tax?' I suggested.

'No, I don't think so. The window tax was a long, long time before this building.' His eyes roamed the high walls of the house. 'And there are a great many windows – more than twenty, I would say. Why brick up just this one? It's curious because—'

'Good afternoon!'

The sudden interruption caused us all to turn around. A kindly looking bespectacled man wearing a shirt and cardigan was emerging from the Rectory's open front door. 'Hello again,

Vernon. Glad you could come. Ah now, and this must be the enigmatic Harry Price. I have read about your exploits, sir, of course. An honour to meet you.'

The two men shook hands as Price apologised for our lateness, gesturing towards the saloon which I had parked at the end of the gravel driveway. For such a grand vehicle, the tyres looked woefully small. 'You see, it's this infernal contraption of Miss Grey's here!'

Ignoring the remark, I extended a warm handshake to the rector. He was a portly man with an open, friendly face, his dark skin confirming his Indian descent. 'What a beautiful plot you have here,' I said, 'tucked away behind these trees, away from the road. So perfectly private and quiet.'

'You think so?' There followed a brief silence before the rector turned to Price and said, 'You found Borley without too much trouble, I trust?'

'I rather think this place has found me, sir. Strange events and places have a habit of doing so.'

'Yes, I have heard as much. I have read a great deal about your work in London, Mr Price, and I can't tell you what a relief it is that you are here. The house is peaceful now, but these last few days have been rather . . . unsettling for my wife and me.'

Price raised his eyebrows at this. 'You're referring to the hauntings, I assume?'

'We prefer to regard them as highly inconvenient disturbances, Mr Price. I'm not certain that I believe in . . . well . . .' He looked embarrassed.

'I understand entirely,' said Price, giving the rector a reassuring smile. 'Ghouls are for the gullible!'

'Indeed! And believe me, before coming here we did not pay very much attention to the stories about this house. We didn't for a moment think there could be any hint of truth to them.'

Price leaned forward. '*Is* there truth to them?'

'I think you had all better come inside,' said Reverend Smith. 'I'm afraid what you have heard so far is only the beginning of the story.'

Note

1   The Rectory seems to have left an unfavourable impression on anyone who visited it. William Crocker, lawyer for the insurance company which covered the building, described it as being 'as ugly as the bad taste of 1863 could make it'.

Part II

'The Most Haunted House in England'

'I am engaged in investigating one of the most extraordinary cases of poltergeist disturbance and alleged haunting that has come under my notice for years.'

– Harry Price, *Journal of the American Society for Psychical Research*, August 1929, pp. 435–36

– 12 –

LUNCH AT THE RECTORY

We had enjoyed a good lunch of ham and potatoes accompanied by a fine wine and were now sitting in the spacious dining room among the slanting shadows cast by the grimy French windows. As the conversation flowed and coffee was poured, I tried to imagine this part of the house as it had once been: elegant and well-furnished, a place of comfort where the Bull family would have taken breakfast, dined and entertained. But I could not. There was only a sad, neglected air, the same that I had noticed in the dark hallway on our arrival and remarked upon to our delightful journalist friend.

I wanted to be outside in the glorious sunshine, but having heard from our hosts of their life in India before moving to these shores, the conversation was now turning to darker matters and I knew that we would be sitting here a while longer.

'Rudi Schneider? I regret I haven't yet had the opportunity to meet the man,' said Price, answering the question put to him by the rector. 'Although I confess I would very much like to.'

Reverend Smith nodded. His character and faith inspired confidence; but although he was welcoming and friendly, I thought I detected a slight wariness in his eyes. 'My wife and I have read in the newspapers that Mr Schneider is a very respectable and talented young man, a medium of some promise.'

I couldn't tell whether he was hoping for a positive response or not.

Mabel Smith, who was sitting next to her husband, reached for his hand. Like him, she struck me as sensible, intelligent and articulate, and her gracious nature was evident in her efforts to make us feel at ease. She must have been no more than thirty-five, but the Rectory seemed to have aged her prematurely and she struggled to disguise her agitation.

'You see, Mr Price,' she began, 'when we discovered that Sir Conan Doyle himself was convinced of this man's abilities . . . well, naturally we questioned ourselves about the goings-on in this house.'

'Sir Conan Doyle is convinced of many things,' said Price with a smile, 'but that doesn't make them true. Reverend Smith, Mrs Smith – like you, we have heard much of Mr Schneider's purported abilities and I am confident we will come upon the truth very shortly. I have invited him to my rooms in London later this year, and I hope to judge for myself.'

Reverend Smith was looking at Price with an expression of deep professional interest. 'If you don't mind my saying so, you are an intensely active man, Mr Price – so very enthusiastic.'

Price smiled, clearly warmed by the flattery.

'You understand, sir, that Mr Price is a sceptic,' interjected Wall.

The rector searched my employer's face. 'Is this true, Mr Price? You do not believe?'

'I am intensely sceptical, yes, but scrupulously impartial, I assure you.'

Reverend Smith raised his chin with interest. 'Tell me, are you a religious man?'

'Certainly, I am a Christian.'

'Indeed?'

'You sound surprised, sir.'

'I am a little.'

'Why ever so?' asked Price.

'Spirit entities, communication with the dead – these aren't subjects that sit well with Christian teachings, are they?'

Price shrugged. 'I believe that both this world and the next are centred in God. I believe in Jesus Christ.'

Reverend Smith was frowning now, concerned for the implications of these phenomena on his faith. 'Yes but, philosophically, how can a Christian such as you deny the existence of spirits and the supernatural power of mediums like Mr Schneider? One could argue that the soul, being immortal, naturally survives, surely?'

'What I question is whether that soul can return to earth and demonstrate its power.'

'And what if you're wrong and Conan Doyle is correct? What then?'

'I see no contradiction,' said Price, but I saw that he was also troubled by the idea. 'Why should a scientific worker in the field of psychical research have any greater difficulty in accepting Christian teachings than, say, a scientific worker in the field of physics?'

For a moment no one said anything. Wall, who fascinated me, simply stared at the tablecloth and Mabel Smith had turned her face away. Only Price and the rector maintained eye contact, but it was with a strained regard for one another.

'I am sure,' Price said suddenly, 'that if survival were proven it would not make me one whit less of an orthodox Christian, as I am pleased to consider myself. Prophecy, healing, miracles – the early Christian Church was drenched in spiritualism.'

'I'm afraid I don't regard the problem as being as easily reconcilable as you do,' said Reverend Smith. 'I'll remind you that this is a rectory, a house of refuge. These intrusions, or whatever we choose to call them, have no place here.'

'Yes, but—'

'The Bible speaks of a spiritual realm inhabited by spiritual beings,' the rector continued. 'But it also tells us precisely what these spiritual beings actually are.'

Price's face grew serious. 'Demons.'

Reverend Smith nodded solemnly. 'Yes, Mr Price, demons. "In later times some will fall away from the faith, paying attention to deceitful spirits and doctrines of demons." The Bible tells us that even Satan disguises himself as an angel of light, does it not? And unusual lights are precisely the sort of thing we have witnessed in and about this house.'

'Now, that is true,' Wall said eagerly. 'I witnessed the light myself, in the window of the Blue Room.'

'The previous rector, the Reverend Harry Bull, and his father before him died in that very same room.'

'And now you're here,' I said lightly, trying to lift the mood. 'It must have been a challenge for you both, coming to work in this parish after the Bull family had served the community for so long.'

Reverend Smith nodded and smiled at his wife, but with a hint of sadness. 'It has been difficult, Miss Grey, because we're different. The colour of our skin marks us apart. It shouldn't, but it does. My chief concern is that we do all we can to prevent these stories from spreading yet further and alarming the parishioners.'

'I imagine you'll be a good deal more unsettled by the time this weekend is through,' said Price.

'Why so?'

'Reverend Smith!' Price cried, clapping his hands together. 'What an excellent question! And for your answer, you need look no further than Mr Wall here. Didn't you think his article in this morning's *Mirror* was even more dramatic than the first?'

'I haven't seen today's edition.'

'No?' said Price, with mock surprise. 'Well then, let us examine it.' He reached down to his bag, which he had left beside his chair, and produced a copy of the newspaper I had seen him devouring during our journey. He read aloud from the relevant article:

MYSTERY LIGHT IN HAUNTED WOOD — RECTOR JOINS IN QUEST FOR RECTORY 'GHOSTS'

'Ghost laying', to amateurs, is a nerve racking business.

'With a *Daily Mirror* photographer, I have just completed a vigil of several hours in the 'haunted' wood at the back of Borley Rectory, a few miles from Long Melford.

'This wood, and the whole neighbourhood of the Rectory, is supposed to be haunted by the ghosts of a groom and a nun who attempted to elope one night several hundred years ago but were apparently caught in the act.

'Although we saw only one of the manifestations which have, according to residents, occurred frequently in recent years, this by itself was peculiar enough.

'It was the appearance of a mysterious light in a disused part of the building – an appearance which simply cannot be explained, because on investigation of the deserted wing it was ascertained that there was no light inside – although the watchers outside could still see it shining through a window.

'When we saw the mysterious light shining through the trees we suggested that somebody should go into the empty wing and place a light in another window for the sake of comparison.

'You go,' we said to each other, and finally the Reverend G.E. Smith, the rector, who does not believe in ghosts, volunteered to do it.

Sure enough, the second light appeared and was visible next to the other, although on approaching close to the building, this disappeared, while the rector's lamp still burned.

Then we were left alone to probe the mysteries of the haunted wood.'[1]

When Price had finished reading I saw the rector glance disapprovingly at Wall, who shifted in his chair. The poor young man! He was only doing his job.

Price continued in a less cordial tone, 'You've drawn attention to yourself, Mr Smith; or, to be more accurate, Mr Wall has. Congratulations. Frankly, I'd be surprised if your garden and the lanes outside weren't overrun by people in a day or so, perhaps sooner.'

Wall's face was cold with resentment as he looked away. As for the rector and his wife, the pair of them had turned pale with alarm. 'Can you help us, Mr Price? Please, say that you can!'

'I want to help you both, very much. I also want to get to the truth. And to do that, we need to return to the beginning.' Price reached into his jacket pocket for his pipe. 'I want you to tell us the sum of your experiences in this house. Be attentive to detail. Cover everything.'

Uncertainly, Reverend Smith put down his wine glass and rested his hands on the table in front of him.

'What's the matter?' Price asked. 'Something is troubling you, sir.'

The rector's gaze moved to the furthest recesses of the room, his mouth turned downwards. 'It's the stillness of this house – its quietness. Sometimes – and this will sound odd – I feel as though it knows us, as though it's listening to us.'

'Is that how you feel now?'

He paused. 'I do, sir; but nevertheless' – he pulled himself upright in his chair – 'I shall continue.

'On the night these disturbances began, Mabel and I were discussing the cats' cemetery at the bottom of the garden and how to clear it away. The time was shortly after midnight and we were looking forward to a good night's rest. But as Mabel climbed into bed, a tremendous clanging rang through the house. The main door bell – it was so loud, so urgent, we thought someone needed our help. Immediately I rushed downstairs to answer the door, but there was no one out there, Mr Price. Not a soul. A fierce wind was picking up and it was raining so heavily that the flower beds were turning to mud, but I stepped out regardless and, in just my slippers and gown, ventured to the end of the driveway. I could feel someone watching me from across the road, in the churchyard. So convinced was I that there had to be someone out there that I called out to them, "Hello, hello there!"' He shook his head, bemused. 'But no one answered.'

'And it wasn't an isolated occurrence,' added Mrs Smith. 'On too many occasions to mention, our maid, Mary, has answered the front door only to find no one out there; and the bell in the courtyard behind the house has been known to ring as well. We hear angry thuds, too, against the door and against other objects. Once, I swear, I heard someone kick the back of my chair as I sat in drawing room.'

'Somebody kicked your chair?' Price smiled. 'Tell me, did the Reverend Bull enjoy the theatre?'

'I have no idea,' said Mrs Smith. She sounded puzzled. 'Why do you ask?'

'In Victorian times theatregoers would make their disapproval known to the performers on stage by kicking the seats in front of them.' He smiled. 'You mentioned in your letter that the bells inside the house ring too?'

'Indeed they do,' said Mrs Smith. 'There is a row of two dozen of them in the kitchen corridor, suspended on springs and all connected to the various rooms in the house. We only use six rooms. The empty rooms are always kept locked. Yet during the night, and sometimes during the day, we hear these bells ringing. And loudly. Sometimes they all ring together.'

'Ringing bells?' Price scoffed. 'I wonder . . . If you were dead and could exert influence on this world, wouldn't you pick a better way to communicate? Pick up a pencil perhaps? Write something down?'

'Oh, I don't know,' Wall cut in. 'The telephone bell is a rather simple device, but it still rings with vital messages.'

'Now you sound like Conan Doyle!' Price retorted. My employer had lit his pipe and was inhaling deeply on it. Finally, after a few moments' thought, he nodded and continued, 'Although I don't want to influence anyone's interpretation of what is happening in this house, I can tell you that bell-ringing is commonly associated with poltergeists.'

'Poltergeists?' The word seemed to alarm Mrs Smith, who flinched and blinked rapidly.

'Correct. The word is deserved from the German *poltern*, meaning noisy, and *Geist*, meaning spirit.'

'Noisy ghost?' Wall recorded the term in his notepad.

'Reports of poltergeist infestations have existed for centuries,' Price continued. 'They have been noted in many cultures and on every continent. In your own country, Mr Smith, they are known as a *mumai*. Usually, when people report a poltergeist, they complain of spirits wreaking havoc in their homes: the throwing of stones and bricks, scratching on walls, doors opening of their own volition, the smashing of furniture, bottles and household ornaments flying about.'

'You have investigated such cases?' asked Mrs Smith.

'Yes, madam. At a mystery house in Battersea.'

'So you are convinced that such manifestations are real?'

'No. Normally a young child is involved or a teenager; sometimes the culprit is an unhappy servant with an axe to grind. In the Battersea case I could never quite be certain that a human agency was to blame.' He paused and then added, mostly to himself, 'But then I find it difficult to be sure of anything.'

The Reverend Smith spoke up. 'Whatever, or whoever, is responsible I am sure that it is an intelligent force. You would think that by now we might have caught someone in the act – but no, I have seen door keys shoot from their locks and skim across the floor. At night we hear footsteps in the passages on the landing and downstairs. Voices in empty rooms, strange scratching on the walls. When we investigate inside the rooms we see great numbers of flies on the windows and the walls. Sometimes one can actually *feel* a presence.'

'A presence?' Price sounded puzzled.

'Something dangerous. Something vengeful. By my word, Mr Price, on more than one occasion I have waited in the passage outside our bedroom armed with my golf club. Once, I was sure I heard a man's voice. It was low and deep and came from just beside me. I swung out, and I swung hard. But of course there was no one there.'

'It's the pebbles that bother me the most,' said Mrs Smith. Her hands were gripped tightly together on the table in front of her. 'We see handfuls of the things come tumbling down the stairs. Sometimes they fly at the windows, though we've never seen anyone throwing them. One morning, while collecting the milk, Mary found small piles of them in the hall and outside the main door. They were warm to the touch.'

'Have these stones appeared anywhere else?' I asked.

'Yes, I once found a small pile of them next to the bed.'

A chill passed over me at the idea. I recorded the detail on my pad, underlining it twice.

'Tell them about the coach,' said Wall.

'Ah yes, one of the most enduring legends of the house. Just after we came here, perhaps two or three days into our tenure, our London maid admitted to us that she had seen a large black coach moving across the lawn towards the house.'

'Across the lawn?' said Price with surprise. 'I didn't appreciate that ghosts made such careless drivers.'

The rector nodded. 'It sounded quite absurd to me too until I saw the fear in the poor girl's face. I could deny the story but I could not deny her tears. She said it came within yards of the building and then, as quickly as it had appeared, it vanished. That was the word she used. The thing just disappeared!'

Mrs Smith caught my cynical expression and said quickly, 'Please do understand, Miss Grey, that our former maid was an honest girl, someone we relied on.'

'Then she wasn't a drunk?' Price asked. He could be terribly brusque sometimes.

'Mr Price! No, to my knowledge she didn't drink at all. And after she saw that – well, she returned to London soon after. Anyway, our new maid, Mary, has seen the coach too.'

'Old Fred Cooper insists that he saw it as well,' the rector said. 'There is a cottage in the grounds, behind the house, where Fred has lived some ten years. He told us that one night, walking back through the lanes from Sudbury, he heard galloping horses on the road and saw lights coming towards him. He moved quickly out of the road to allow the carriage to pass. And as it raced pass he saw it clearly: two brown horses pulling a black coach driven by two men, all in black, with tall black hats.'

'A death coach,' Wall said eagerly. 'Can you imagine such a thing?'

'I don't suppose you have seen this coach yourselves?' asked Price drily.

Mrs Smith hesitated before answering. 'Possibly,' she said. 'I did have an unusual experience.'

'Tell us,' commanded Price, leaning back in his chair.

'I was alone in the house late one evening when I heard the main gates scrape open. Normally you hear people or vehicles on the gravel driveway, but I heard nothing, so I took a lantern and went to look out of a window. I saw two bright lights, Mr Price, like headlamps. Then' – she snapped her fingers – 'they blinked out, and as they did so I caught the outline of dark shape, some sort of vehicle. Possibly a car, but I think not.'

The rector nodded his agreement. 'I went out to look when I came home. The driveway was empty. It was another in a long list of inexplicable events.'

Price raised his chin in defiance. 'Not inexplicable, my good man, just unexplained.' For now. I have heard many such tales of phantom death coaches and the like. I'm sure you could hear many similar stories yourselves in any of the neighbouring villages. Such legends are common in rural hamlets like this one, especially hamlets controlled by ecclesiastical dynasties such as the Bull family.' He smiled. 'These are modern myths, nothing more.'

'Oh, but there *is* more,' said Reverend Smith, a touch desperately, I thought. 'I have witnessed an apparition: the tall, dark figure of a man which appeared in one of the passageways on the ground floor. And once, late one night outside the Blue Room, I heard a woman's voice cry out, "Don't, Carlos – don't!" And then, of course, there is the matter of the nun.'

I leaned forward: at last, the centrepiece of the drama.

'As long as there has been a house on this site she has been seen – the solitary figure of a nun, telling her beads and pacing the garden, down towards the stream.'

Wall raised his eyebrows. Price smiled softly and said, 'I don't believe it. If there was such a thing then surely by now someone would have proof of the apparition – a photograph perhaps?'

Reverend Smith fixed him with an unwavering stare. 'I cannot blame you for being sceptical. We did not believe it either.' He paused then, pondering the matter as he leaned back in his chair and drummed his fingers lightly on the dining-room table. Perhaps, I thought, he is not the sceptic he claimed to be. 'But consider the facts: since 1863 the spectre has been seen by three successive rectors and their wives and families. Ethel and Freda were the first, the sisters of the late Harry Bull. They saw the dark figure of a holy sister crossing the garden in the summer of the year 1900, in the plain light of day.'

'And don't forget what Mr Chipp said in his letter,' I broke in, addressing Price. 'Harry, you can't deny it. He mentioned a nun. And he was here, in this same house, decades ago!'

'Well then, perhaps it was a woman,' Price suggested. 'Someone in fancy dress. A *living* woman!'

'No, sir,' said Mrs Smith, shaking her head. 'The apparition vanished into thin air right in front of the Bull sisters. You understand, the whole Bull family was fascinated by ghosts. The church organist tells us that Harry Bull spoke about the happenings often, as if they were normal to him. There was no doubt in the old rector's mind that the phenomena were real.

We have heard that Mr Bull was a pragmatic man, not given to flights of fancy. Yet apparently he once distinctly heard knocking outside the church, starting from the south side and continuing the whole way round the building.'

'Yes, yes,' I said, remembering yet more details from the letter in Price's Laboratory. 'Harry, the story tallies.'

'It is said that he locked the church one night only to find that the nun had followed him back to the house. Afterwards, it became his custom to watch for the apparition at dusk, from the summerhouse.'

'And the Bull sisters – they stick to their story, do they?' asked Price.

'Yes, indeed they do. They have pointed out to me themselves the area of the garden where the nun first walked. They accepted that as plain fact. And they are very down-to-earth, practical women.'

'And what about you, Mrs Smith?' said Price. 'Have you seen this mythical nun?'

'No, not yet.'

'Nor I,' said Reverend Smith, taking his wife's hand. 'But the maid, Mary, has. I can only hope that we do not suffer the same misfortune. There is a bad air about this house; I believe that whatever awful events once happened here have left their mark in more ways than one. You see, over there . . .' He gestured to the wall opposite and we all turned to look. 'There was a large window there once, but it was bricked up.'

'Yes, we did wonder about that outside,' said Price. 'Well, to be more specific, I wondered about it. I'm not sure Mr Wall here even noticed.'

Wall resented this comment, his eyes telling me so in a furtive glance across the table. I looked away immediately and returned my attention to the rector.

'Legend records that the Dark Woman would appear at that window and peer in through the glass as the Bull family took their meals in here. So regular were her visits that Mr Bull decided the only course of action was to remove the window. As you can see, he did so.'

'Now, that is an entertaining story,' Price said lightly. He leaned back in his chair, arched his fingertips together and sat like this for some time, frowning as he stared through the dirty French windows out to the garden beyond.

Listening to this tale of a spectral holy sister, I couldn't help but think of my old school in Pimlico, St Mary's – and its nuns. They walked quickly and quietly, but we always heard them coming. It was the rustling of their habits and the clink of the rosary beads which hung from their waists which warned of their arrival. Those women were remote and severe – incapable, I believed, of enjoying a close relationship with anyone at all.

One nun in particular frightened me: Sister Regis, a towering, gaunt woman with hunched shoulders, a fierce grey face and eyes that hinted at suppressed resentment. By the time she advanced into the classroom you had already prepared yourself for the sound of chalk striking and scraping at the blackboard, or for the way her searching gaze would find you and attack with the possibility of punishment.

If she asked you a question, then you made sure you knew the answer.

The rector's wife said suddenly, 'Mr Price, whatever these forces might be, wherever they come from, I have the strongest feeling that they resent us living in this house.'

'I doubt that very much, Mrs Smith,' Price said evenly. 'This is a very large house, isn't it? Have you counted the rooms?'

'I think there are twenty-eight. We are strict in ensuring they are always kept locked. The place is too draughty for us to bother with all of it.'

Price nodded. 'I hardly need remind you that in rambling old country houses like this, the slightest disturbances can play havoc with the imagination. Most of the troubling sounds you have described might be caused by any number of things.'

'Such as?'

'Normal sources,' said Price. 'Rats, wood shrinking, birds in the chimney stack or between double walls, or the wind perhaps. In the spring I'll wager that the north-east wind must sweep right down the Stour Valley. The simplest explanation is always the most likely.'

'Can you be sure of that?' Wall challenged him. 'You speak of simplicity as if it means the same thing to different people. What if the forces in this house are beyond our understanding, Mr Price? Intelligent forces.'

'People are intelligent,' Price replied, looking not at Wall but at the rector. 'And don't forget, there are the locals. Perhaps the culprit is someone from the village out to cause mischief – a dissatisfied member of your congregation maybe? Someone who wishes to drive you away from this place.' He nodded, warming to his own hypothesis. 'Yes, that's possible, isn't it? Why, anyone could be hiding in a house this size!'

But Reverend Smith was shaking his head in disagreement. 'I find that idea most implausible. You can hear now, Mr Price, the Rectory is quiet. I know it is empty.'

'Houses may be quiet, sir. It does not mean that they are empty.'

'But surely we would have seen the intruders by now? As

we have told you, most of the rooms are inaccessible and kept locked.'

Price looked blank, and then demanded, 'How many staircases are there?'

'Three: the main one in the hall, the service stairs and another for the staff at the back of the kitchen passage.'

'I see. And any attics or cellars?'

'We have both.'

'Excellent!' Price cried. 'Then that's where we'll begin. I find cellars to be such curious places, don't you? Full of interesting odds and ends – there's no telling what might turn up in a cellar.'

Mr Smith looked at his wife uncertainly. 'Er . . . yes. What are you proposing, Mr Price?'

'That we seal them up. We'll seal them all up, every single entrance or possible hiding place. Then we'll know what we're dealing with.'

'Mr Price, wait a moment . . .'

'My dear people,' Price continued, quickening his speech, 'the scenario you have just described is fascinating – no, it's more than fascinating, it's *incredible* – and there's the problem! It is far more likely that there is a natural explanation for all of the events you have described.' He smiled at the rector. 'I do not think you need fear for your faith.'

'I appreciate your reassurance, Mr Price, but—'

Already Price had sprung to his feet and was striding now to the French windows overlooking the lawn. As he opened them wide what remained of the afternoon sun streamed into the dining room. He turned to face us all, his broad form starkly outlined against the daylight beyond. 'Here's what we're going to do,' he announced. 'First, Sarah and I will conduct a meticulous examination of the Rectory, the courtyard, the schoolroom and bedrooms – every passageway, every staircase. Above and below we will go, up into the attics and down into the cellars, behind pictures and under carpets. All doors will be sealed, all entrances blocked. No one comes in and no one leaves. From this moment on, the Rectory is in lockdown.'

'And then?' asked Wall.

Price's eyes glistened. 'We wait.'

'For what?'

'For whatever might happen,' he said with a grin, his eyes now wide and bright. 'But you may rest assured, if there is anyone concealed in this house I will find the intruder, and one way or the other we will come upon the truth.'

He marched towards the main hallway, crying out as he passed Wall, 'What are you waiting for, man? Come along, come along!'

I felt sorry for the journalist as he seemed startled by Price's sudden and forthright attempts to dominate the proceedings, but he rose obediently from his chair and I did the same.

'All right, Sarah?' asked Price cheerfully.

I nodded at him and followed the two men as they headed into the hallway, feeling within me the first stirrings of excitement for the exploration ahead.

Note

1 The second of V. C. Wall's articles in the *Daily Mirror*, 11 June 1929.

– 13 –
EXPLORING THE HOUSE

We were standing in the central hallway. A more dispiriting atmosphere could hardly be imagined: an unpleasant, musky odour pervaded the air, the walls were covered with dirty oak panelling, and the sky visible through the arched window above the stairs was streaked with brooding clouds. But there was at least one redeeming feature: a wide and intricately carved wooden staircase that dominated the hall and pulled the gaze up to the first floor, where the infamous 'haunted bedroom' awaited our inspection.

'There are ten rooms on the ground floor alone,' said Reverend Smith. 'The living room, dining room, library, kitchen, scullery—'

'Where's the entrance to the cellar?' Price broke in abruptly.

'Down there, by the kitchen,' said the rector, pointing to a dark passageway that stretched to the back of the house. 'The cellars are vast though, Mr Price. Must you go down?'

'We have no choice. Most likely they're full of rats and mice – the cause, I have no doubt, of your unusual noises.'

Vernon Wall looked embarrassed and the rector seemed less than impressed with the idea that his house was infested with rodents, but when he saw Price's cynical glower he nodded his agreement, sighed and asked us to follow him. We did so, passing down a narrow lamp lit corridor where the windows were barred with iron. 'These bars were fitted, we're told, during the Bull residency to keep burglars out, and to keep maids from slipping out into the night when they should have been in bed.'

'And to prevent gentlemen callers from getting in, I imagine,' said Price.

'I'm afraid there is very little in this house that actually works,' explained Reverend Smith as he led the way. 'We have no running water, no electricity and no heating.'

No wonder Mrs Smith had been unwell. I tried to imagine what a dismal place the Rectory must be during the depths of winter: they would heat only the living rooms and bedrooms to conserve coal, and would use icy water from the well outside for washing. The thought gave me the shivers.

'These are the servant bells you mentioned?' asked Price, stopping under a row of bells suspended on wires that ran above our heads. 'The ones that ring apparently of their own volition?'

The rector nodded.

'How do they work, exactly?' asked Wall.

Price gave him a scathing look for his ignorance. 'The invention of a non-electrical internal bell system was first advertised – I think I am correct in saying – in London in 1744, as an invention that would enhance privacy. What we have here is a more up-to-date example. With this bell system, servants didn't need to be an unwelcome presence in the main rooms of the house. They were simply called up from the kitchen level as and when the need arose.' He smiled. 'I imagine the Bulls had endured quite enough unwelcome presences in this house. But wait . . .'

He leaned closer to the bells, his eyes narrowing, his mouth dropping slightly open.

'What is it?' I asked.

'These wires have been cut.'

'Indeed,' said the rector, 'I cut them myself; I had to. When they all ring at the same time they make the most infernal racket.'

What surprised me most about this statement was the matter-of-fact way in which it was uttered, as if it were the most normal thing in the world that more than twenty bells, disconnected from their wires and touched by no one should ring of their own accord.

'I do believe you are serious.'

Reverend Smith nodded. 'I've never been more serious, Mr Price.'

Ringing bells. Any sober and rational adult should have laughed at this, but for some reason none of us did.

We stopped at a small wooden door which was beginning to rot. The thought of descending into the bowels of the house filled me with dread, for I have always hated dark and enclosed spaces. I said so then, but Price insisted I follow him down to take notes.

'Watch your step,' said the rector with some kindness as he handed each of us an electric torch, which he had taken from hooks on the wall. 'It could be slippery.'

He pushed the door and it creaked slowly open.

*

I peered into the gloom in fearful expectation, and shuddered. It was pitch black below and the air that crept up to greet us was thick with the odour of damp. The staircase leading down was half-rotten with age, and as I stepped forward my foot snagged on a piece of the structure that had come loose. I stumbled, almost fell and cried out. Suddenly, to my relief, Vernon Wall was beside me. I melted into his embrace as he said gently, 'Here, Sarah, let me help you.' Then he stepped in front, guiding my way, his hand wrapped tightly around mine. It was a sweet gesture, but I did not dwell on it for long, my attention now focused on scouring the darkness for any recognisable objects.

From the moment we reached the ground, some ten or fifteen feet below, I had the impression that this cellar was vast. Here and there the light from my torch picked out the remnants of lost and forgotten domesticity: broken furniture, boxes covered in mould, wine bottles, packets of documents wrapped in ageing brown paper tied with string, and a rocking horse, the matted mane of which had once been stroked by a child's loving hand. There was very little light, apart from that which broke in through a grate in the ceiling, illuminating a small patch of earth.

'Hello, and what have we here?' asked Price, advancing to this area. He knelt and pointed to what appeared to be exposed brickwork jutting out of the earthy floor.

'They're bricks,' said Wall with a shrug. 'So what?'

Price glowered at him. 'Bricks, yes,' he said shortly, running his fingers across them. 'But more specifically, foundations. And not the foundations of this house, but some earlier building, I suspect.'

'How can you tell?' asked Reverend Smith, surprised.

'These bricks are incredibly old, much older than this dwelling. Fascinating things, bricks. They used to come in all shapes and sizes and colours.'

'Used to?' said the rector.

'Yes, until 1625, when a new law was passed to standardise

their size. From then on, all bricks needed to measure exactly nine inches by four inches by three.'

'How on earth do you know all this?' I asked.

Price smiled and gave a slight shrug. 'I am quite well read, Sarah. These bricks are much smaller, two inches deep at most, which means we can be certain that these are the footings of a building that stood here prior to 1625.' He glanced up at the rector, who now appeared impressed and very much intrigued. 'Reverend Smith, why did you never mention that there were previous buildings on this site?'

'Because I couldn't be sure there were any.' He hesitated. 'Certainly there is a legend that a monastery once stood somewhere in these parts, but it has never been confirmed. And Old Fred Cooper thinks that a manor house once stood on the site.'

'And that would have belonged to the Bull family also, I presume?' asked Price.

The rector shook his head. 'The Bulls weren't the first influential family to live in Borley. For three hundred years the Waldegraves were the Lords of the Manor.'

'What can you tell us of them?'

Wall smiled with private satisfaction. It seemed that Price's historical knowledge wasn't perfect after all.

'The Waldegrave family tree includes a great many influential ambassadors and confidants to royalty. Sir Richard Waldegrave was Speaker of the House of Commons during the reign of Richard II. Edward Waldegrave was one of his descendants and the first of the family to be associated with Borley, when Henry VIII gave it to him.'

'Fascinating. Then he was a Catholic?'

'Yes, an ardent one. History tells that he made frequent visits to Rome and to France, where the family had associations with convents, and many of the Waldegrave women took holy orders. In 1561 Edward was arrested for holding Mass at Borley Hall and for refusing to take the oath of supremacy making Elizabeth sole head of the Church of England. After his arrest, he was sent to the Tower where he died later that year.'

'He was buried there, I presume?'

'Some believe so,' said the rector.

'Is that what you believe?' Price asked gently.

Mr Smith shook his head modestly. 'Who am I to say? Another, more romantic, legend is that his body was returned here to Borley and interred beneath the Waldegrave monument in our church across the road. The history of the family is recorded in detail there.'

'And there was I thinking you were a perfect historian,' Price smiled. 'I should rather like to see this monument, if I may.'

Reverend Smith nodded. 'It is a grand monument indeed, far too large for our little church. It stands about fourteen feet high, with lifelike effigies of Sir Edward and his wife lying side by side, he attired in armour, his head resting on his helmet, his wife wearing a large ruff and flat cap on her head.'

'It sounds almost as spendid as the monk's fireplace we saw in the dining room,' said Price.

'It is indeed. We have many historians who come to see it. The monument bears inscriptions in Latin together with the Waldegrave family crest, which I have examined many times; it bears a striking similarity to the Prince of Wales feathers.'[1]

'The Waldegraves must have been very well admired,' I suggested.

'Yes indeed,' the rector agreed, 'although there are persistent tales in the parish that the descendants of Edward were beastly and violent men, particularly Henry Waldegrave, who lived after

1600.' He shrugged. 'Who can know for sure? The family records I have examined are confusing. But then' – a brief hesitation – 'there are stories that go with the church also. And the monument itself.'

'Stories?'

'The last rector reportedly heard three loud, distinct knockings emanating from the monument as he was giving a talk on confirmation. We ourselves have found objects displaced around the church after the building has been locked up for the night.'

Crack!

We all jumped at the sudden sound.

'What was that?' asked Wall, looking about him, the beam from his torch cutting fitfully through the dark.

Price gestured to us all to be quiet and we listened alertly and in silence for about a minute. At this moment we were positioned, I estimated, immediately beneath the main hallway and the landing above where the Smiths had experienced a 'cold spot' and heard 'sibilant whispering'. To my relief there came no further sounds and eventually I felt a sense of calm returning. I was about to suggest that we go back upstairs when my eye was drawn by something moving in a beam of torchlight. It was quick, barely noticeable, but I was certain I had seen it, and Price had too, for he immediately pointed in its direction and cried, 'There! You see? Rats! I told you so. And frogs and toads – look!'

I relaxed. I have never been frightened of such creatures. Reverend Smith also straightened up and said in a low voice, 'I'm sure that frogs, toads and rats are most bothersome, Mr Price, but I've yet to encounter a frog that can throw stones.'

'And I have yet to meet a rat that can shine lights in windows,' Wall added. The young journalist was smiling to himself. He seemed entertained to see my companion, normally so self-assured, defeated in an exercise of the simplest reasoning.

We followed the rector to the bottom of the staircase and were about to ascend when there came from behind me a startled cry. I turned and, to my alarm, saw that half of Wall's right leg had disappeared into the floor. 'Help me!' he cried.

I rushed over to assist, quickly followed by Reverend Smith. 'There are wooden boards here,' he said. 'I think it's an old well shaft. His foot's gone straight through! Here my boy, let me help you out.'

We hauled Wall out of the earth, I admit with some amusement, and having satisfied ourselves that no injury was incurred retreated to the passageway above where the kindly Mrs Smith was waiting for us. 'My dears, are you quite all right? I heard a commotion.'

'Not to worry, it wasn't a ghost,' said Wall, brushing himself down. 'I'm fine, thank you.'

'I don't care for it down there,' said Mrs Smith. 'Only went down once, and on that occasion I found something less than pleasant.'

'Oh? And what was that?' asked Price with an enquiring stare.

In the brief hesitation that followed I registered an expression of reluctance on the Reverend Smith's face, which he directed, ever so subtly, in his wife's direction.

There was something she hadn't told us.

'I'm sure it's nothing,' said Mrs Smith hesitantly, 'but when we first occupied the Rectory I found a half-full bottle of sugar of lead in the cellar.'

'Poison?' cried Wall, his eyes gleaming. He produced his notepad and pen.

But Reverend Smith stepped forward. 'Mr Wall, I implore you not to mention this in any of your newspaper articles.'

'Why the devil not?'

'Because this is an intensely private matter,' the rector explained. 'We have been aware for some time now that the sisters of the late rector, Mr Bull, believe that this poison was connected to their brother's death. He left a lifetime interest in his estate to his wife instead of his sisters. It wasn't a happy marriage. The sisters think he intended to change his will before he died but never did.'

'Then so much the better!' cried Wall eagerly. 'This is wonderful!'

'No.' Price fixed Wall with his sternest of expressions. 'That is a very serious and slanderous accusation and we have no business prying into it. We came to investigate the happenings here, Mr Wall, not for you to play Hercule Poirot.'

Reverend Smith nodded in agreement and said, 'In any event, Mr Wall, it is not a theory that my wife or I endorse. In fact, the whole silly notion has inspired Mabel to write a novel to help her relax; that's right, isn't it, dear?'

Mrs Smith was smiling. 'Nowadays I have the liberty of leisure to preoccupy myself with writing. It's my hobby, it calms my nerves. When this piece is finished I will call it *Murder at the Rectory*. Mr Price, perhaps when it is completed you might be so kind as to show it to your publisher?'

'I'm sure Harry would be delighted to help you,' I began, but was quickly silenced by Price, who sliced the air with his hand, instructing my silence and shot me a disapproving glare. I hated him showing me such disrespect in public. I was about to raise my voice against him in protest when it occurred to me that perhaps he was intentionally trying to impose a distance between himself and these witnesses. I hoped so.

Mrs Smith smiled and looked to my employer for an answer to her question.

'There will be plenty of time to talk about books and publishing contracts later,' he said quickly, leaving a brief, awkward silence. Then he turned his back on the woman and fixed his eyes firmly on the grand hallway awaiting us at the end of the kitchen passage. 'But for the time being, we have a ghost to hunt!'

*

That evening, under the rector's kindly supervision, Price and I drew a detailed plan of Borley Rectory. It wasn't easy to measure every dark passageway, but we managed it eventually with the help of our red and black pencils, a sketching block, our torches and trusty yardstick – and, of course, the tasty ham sandwiches prepared by Mrs Smith.

As we worked, I listened to Mr Wall fire question after question at Price about the finer details of ghost hunting: 'What motivates you, Mr Price? What are your aspirations?' and so on. I knew it was Wall's professional obligation to ask questions – after all, he had come here to write a story for his newspaper – but at times I almost forgot he was a journalist and saw only the man.

One of his questions in particular seemed to resonate with Price. 'You seem to know so much about ghost hunting; is it true you want to help establish a university chair in psychical research?'

'But of course,' said Price, contentedly swallowing a last bite from his sandwich. 'I only wish that I'd had someone to learn from – I had to teach myself.'

Price, I think, relished the idea that one day he could claim credit for spearheading a new and potentially world-changing academic science at a reputable university. At that stage, however, I had no idea just how far he was prepared to go to live out this dream.

'The entire house feels uneasy to me,' Wall said ponderously to Price. 'It has an air about it, a disturbing resonance. Do you not feel it too?'

'No I don't, and neither do you.' He turned sharply to face us. 'And if you should see any apparitions, then rest assured they will be nothing but spectres of your imagination. Now tell me' – he hesitated – 'what *don't* you notice in this house? What's missing?'

Wall hesitated, his eyes roaming. He shook his head.

'Sarah?'

My gaze went to the wallpaper peeling away from the walls. Then it hit me. 'Photographs – there aren't any.'

'That's right,' said Price, his lips curving into a smile. 'Photographs make houses come alive. Which is probably the reason, Mr Wall, why this house feels so dead to you.'

Questions over, and keen to eliminate the possibility that someone was hiding in the house and playing tricks on the Smiths, Price insisted that Wall and I conduct a thorough inspection of the walls in the hallways and passages on the ground floor, searching for any secret compartments or potential hiding places. I acquiesced reluctantly; the more I saw of the Rectory, the less I wanted to be there. The saddest resonance pervaded the place. Decades of dust had gathered in these corridors, settling between the floorboards and pressed between the walls of every room. And now, as we opened up the house, I felt very much the intruder. I had not felt this way since Price had caught me trespassing in his study the night we met.

When we returned to the gloomy hallway, I was surprised to notice that the grandfather clock showed the hour fast approaching seven o'clock, and we had not yet moved upstairs to inspect the bedrooms or the attic. As Mr Wall and I turned our attention to the compartments under the main staircase, Price announced he was going outside to the car to fetch his 'ghost-hunter's toolkit', which he had brought up from London. 'But Harry,' I said, 'your pockets are stuffed full already.'

'You can never be too prepared, Sarah.' He grinned.

As Price left us, I caught Wall looking at me.

'You're very close to Mr Price, aren't you?' he said suddenly. 'Only I couldn't help noticing the way you look at him.'

'We work well together,' I said, shining my torch into the cavity under the stairs.

'Yes, I've noticed.' He spoke quietly, calmly.

A brief silence ensued. Then Wall said, quite suddenly, 'Is he a good man, do you suppose?'

The question made me start. 'What? What do you mean "a good man"? He's a brave, brilliant man! A thinker and a worker.'

'How well do you know him, Sarah?'

I tried not to think of the change that came over my employer every time he uncovered another fraud. The change that began with a vacant expression in his eyes and quickly gave way to a violent and dramatic temper. On those occasions, it was as if two men inhabited his being: one fashionable and entirely pre-dictable with a penchant for good cigars, an organised nature and an obsession with recording and filing the most meticu-lously detailed notes, and another of quite a different nature, a man with a socially awkward disposition whose behaviour was impossible to predict; a man who was elusive but charming, brilliant and ambitious, but selfish, too, and unreliable. His eagerness was matched only by his secrecy and his bitter rivalries with others.

'He's full of contradictions,' I said thoughtfully, 'but that makes for an exciting job.'

'But is he, I wonder, a *good* man. A noble man. Please, I mean no offence, Miss Grey, but in my career I am trained to see every angle of a story. And in Mr Price, well . . .'

'What?' I urged.

'I fear he has many dark corners. And to be entirely honest, I can't help but wonder how anybody who is as thoughtful and as sensitive as you can tolerate spending so much time with someone who is as short-tempered, irascible and restless as Mr Price. One never knows what he's about to say or do next! I've met people like him before, and they all have one thing in common: they become blind to the consequences of their own actions.' He looked sharply across at me through the dust and the darkness. 'As others become blinded too.'

'You don't like him?'

'It's not necessarily *him* I don't like,' he said slowly.

'Then what?'

'It's the way he speaks to you, the way he put you down in front of me – a stranger – like he did the other day in your office, and just now outside the cellar. In parts of east London they say that the Midnight Inquirer is a gentleman.' He raised his eyebrows. 'But to be frank, I see little evidence of that. He has an enlivened sensitivity to any matter that directly bene-fits him.'

I smiled my appreciation to be polite, but in truth I had no wish for Price and myself to be analysed in this way. 'I appreciate your concern, Mr Wall, but—'

'But why?' he interrupted. 'Why do you put up with it? Don't you see it? Or do you pretend *not* to see it?'

I pondered this for a moment before a memory of something I had witnessed just a few weeks before at the Laboratory came to me: a touching exchange of letters between Price and someone to whom he had extended a wonderful kindness. 'You shouldn't

rush to judgement,' I said. 'I have seen his better side, his generosity, his modesty.'

'Then tell me.'

'Some weeks ago we received a letter from a Mrs Helen Bobby,
who had written to Price thanking him for his work and his
books which her daughter, Joan, was fascinated by. Poor Joan
was terribly unwell and in hospital in Germany, so the books
made a wonderful distraction. I wasn't going to show the letter
to Price – he had enough on his plate handling the demands of
the Spiritualists – but when he saw me writing out a thank-you
note he asked me more about the matter.'

'And you told him?'

'I did. I assumed that would be the end of it.'

'So what happened?'

'Well, Harry did everything he could to help, of course. Joan
Bobby wanted nothing more than flowers and fruit and someone
to talk to, but he continued to write and to send copies of his
books and articles. Oh Vernon, they were such beautiful letters,
about art and birds and the country! It was as if he was reading
her thoughts.

'Then news came that Joan was going to die. Harry was
propelled into action, convinced he could help. He wrote
letter after letter to the family insisting they accept his help –
he even offered to fly out the best surgeon in London to treat
her. But of course there was no one who could help, not even
Harry.'

'Such passionate concern for a stranger?' The young journalist was clearly struggling with the concept. 'It's as though he
can't have real relationships, so he conducts them anonymously
by letter.'

'The possibility of altruism isn't just a possibility, Vernon, it's very real. I know because I have seen it in him. His friendship with Joan was something unique – beautiful.'

'And you envy that?'

'I do, in a small way, because I have had to work hard at getting it right.'

'You're still working hard at it.' His voice, his eyes, his smile – the kindness in each was sincere.

'Sarah, friendships, relationships – the ones that matter, the ones that last – they're not supposed to be difficult.'

'Yes, they are,' I said simply. 'Whatever we fight for, in the end, we value the most.' I looked straight at him then and said politely, 'Harry needs assistance. Yours and mine. Every day throws up new challenges. Spiritualists like Conan Doyle are baying for his blood. His nerves are so highly strung and his brain is so agile it's always two jumps ahead of him. He never stops working. If he did, his thoughts would be free to wander; he'd have to face the way life is, not how he wants it to be. I don't tolerate any nonsense, Mr Wall – I speak my mind. But Harry needs me and I see good in him.'

'And you . . . what do you need, Miss Grey?'

'Excuse me?'

He took my hand with warm affection. 'Sarah, please do me this favour,' he said slowly. 'Please remember that there are always choices, and always people who care who will help you make those choices. Remember that for every moment in your life that passes, there is always another that might have been.'

'What on earth is that supposed to mean?'

He stared at me intently. 'Don't waste your life living his. That's all.'

I blinked and for a few short moments said nothing at all. It was as if someone had placed a mirror before me and was forcing me to stare at a reflection I had no desire to see.

I can admit now that my feelings for Price went beyond those of a secretary for her employer and they were more than platonic, but up to that point I had denied myself any conscious recognition of this frailty. The realisation caused my heart to quicken and I felt suddenly wary of Mr Wall and whatever else he was about to say. And as I stared into his handsome face, inwardly deciphering his expression, it struck me that, apart from Price, I had never felt so intrigued by a man. Before Wall could speak again the front door banged open and he let go of my hand. Relieved, I allowed it to drop to my side.

'It's really clouded over out there,' I heard Price say as he approached, 'and the wind is picking up. It's muggy. I think there's a storm coming.' He dropped the substantial suitcase he had retrieved from the saloon at his feet, then stooped down and peered in at us under the stairs. 'Now then, you two, how are we getting on down here?'

'Goodness!' exclaimed Wall. 'Mr Price – whatever are you wearing on your feet? Why, they look like slippers!'

And his shoes weren't the only aspect of Price's attire to have changed. A long black coat, which fell to his ankles, now concealed most of his favourite tweed suit and the pockets looked stuffed full.

'Mr Wall, your talents in observation are really something to behold, I must say,' said Price. 'Of course they're slippers – essential accessories for creeping about in big old houses like this one! Young man, take off your shoes. You too, Sarah. Can't have you both clumping around this house making suspicious noises.'

Once we had come out from under the stairs we dutifully removed our shoes, Wall lending me his arm for support. As he did so, the journalist's gaze fell upon the suitcase at Price's feet. 'I say, what have you got in there?'

'My ghost-hunter's toolbox,' said Price proudly as he flipped open the lid. 'I have packed everything we will need for our little adventure tonight.'

I was actually the one who had packed the case, but I decided this wasn't the appropriate moment to make the point.

'Steel screw eyes, fine thread and adhesive surgical tape. I'll use this to seal up the windows and doors – anything on a hinge.'

Wall nodded. 'And what's that?'

'A bowl of mercury.'

'Why do we need that?'

'Why do you think? For detecting tremors in rooms or passages. I can make silent electrical mercury switches too.'

'Of course,' said Wall. 'How silly of me. And this?' He pointed to a small leather case.

'Cinematograph camera with remote electrical control, and films. And next to it, a packet of graphite and a soft brush for developing fingerprints.' His speech was rapid now. 'Mr Wall, you might wish to record the details of these items for your next article. I don't want to tell you how to do your job, of course, but I really think such detail would give your readers a richer insight into the practical techniques of the ghost hunter.'

'Do you indeed?'

'Yes,' Price insisted, 'I do. And because I'm usually correct, you would be well advised to listen to me. Now then, what have we got here?' He delved into the depths of his bulging pockets before producing several items: a ball of string, a stick of chalk, matches, a torch and candle, wires, nails, electric flex, dry batteries and switches, pencils, bandages, even a hairbrush – the oddest item of all, given that Price was bald! 'See here, Vernon

– a steel tape for measuring the rooms and corridors and calculating the thickness of walls. If there is a hiding place or secret compartment anywhere, I expect us to find it.' He peered under the stairs, his eyes wide with fascination. 'Now then, what about under here? Did you find anything while you were poking around?'

Of course we had found nothing suspicious under the stairs, and I quickly told him so, though I felt my cheeks flush as I spoke.

'Then we shall progress to the attic,' Price replied, giving me a searching look. 'Plenty of room for someone to hide up there, I'm sure!'

'Righty-ho,' said Wall with unconvincing cheer. 'Lead on, Mr Price!'

He did.

And I followed.

Note

1　In April 1942, Reverend Alfred Henning, the then rector of Borley, wrote to Harry Price relating the peculiar way in which objects had been displaced in Borley church after the building had been locked up: 'I thought you might be interested to know of . . . matters connected with Borley Rectory. The first is the sanctuary lamp, which is kept burning near the Tabernacle on the altar, where the Sacrament is reserved. Mrs Pearson looks after this, lighting the small wick each morning and putting it out at night. For about a fortnight the wick was frequently moved. She told me this, and I suggested putting a book or cover over the lamp glass. She put a psalter over it, after putting the light out, and then locked up for the night. She was very surprised the next morning to find the book on the floor, especially as both doors were locked and no one could possibly have got in during the night. She next put a book-cover over the lamp, and this was removed on two occasions' (*The End of Borley Rectory*, p.78).

− 14 −
'ALL OF THIS CAN BE ACHIEVED BY A CLEVER MAN'

If I had known that our excursion to Borley Rectory would require me to dress in unflattering overalls and crawl through cobwebs and grime along the joists under the eaves of the rambling house, I might have thought twice about going in the first place, but of course with ghost hunting anything can happen and mostly never does.

We were up in the attic inspecting the bell wires, the light from Price's torch throwing shadows across the rafters. Up ahead of me, Mr Wall was saying something about how annoyed he would be if Mrs Smith published any account of the Rectory's alleged macabre history, and I was sure Price felt the same, for both men had a vested interest in making the story of the Rectory their own, and each would have their own particular versions of the tale. But my mind was on other matters, in particular Wall's stirring words to me. Their meaning was clear: he was interested in me in a way that went beyond professional regard, and he had forced me to see myself properly for the first time in my life.

Was I to resent him or thank him? In truth I wanted to do both, for I was now preoccupied with the very same question that had invoked Wall's emotional confrontation downstairs: why was I so irresistibly drawn to Price? Why was I now thinking not about the peculiar mysteries of Borley Rectory but about my employer and where he would be sleeping that night? And where I would be sleeping.

As we had yet to find anything of much interest in the attic, I was about to suggest we go downstairs when I heard Price announce excitedly that he had discovered something. Scrambling up next to him, I watched as he shone his torch on to one of the rafters. 'There's something written here.' I duly recorded the faint inscription in my notepad: *Bells hung by S. Cracknell and Mercur, 1863.*

'This confirms it,' said Price. 'The Rectory has stood for only sixty-six years.'

'Surely haunted houses are far older than that,' I remarked.

Price smiled. 'Precisely, Sarah. You would think so, wouldn't you? Now then, move back and watch out for any bats.'

We made our way cautiously out of the attic, sealing the entrance behind us, before continuing down to the first floor of the house. Here everything was unnaturally quiet and permeated by a frigid air that reached along the corridors, filling every corner of the vault-like rooms, the chill and the bleak bedrooms inspiring little confidence in the possibility of a peaceful night's sleep. Everywhere about us were the scents and sights of neglect with damp patches blackening the walls and broken furniture lying about like firewood. I wondered how any house that was occupied could possibly feel so abandoned. No wonder so many rectors had refused to live here.

When we had examined the fireplaces and chimneys in all of the ten rooms on the first floor we came, finally, to the Blue Room at the top of the main staircase – the source of the house's most disturbing influences. But before we could even enter the room, Price came to a sudden standstill and motioned at us to halt.

'What's the matter?' I asked.

He remained quite still for long seconds before his fingers gradually came to life, gently caressing the air as if testing its quality or temperature. Then he said, 'I fancy it is much colder in this spot. What do you think?'

'I'm not sure—'

'I wasn't addressing you, Sarah.' He turned his challenging gaze on Wall. 'I was talking to you.'

The growing tension between the two men was making me anxious, but Wall, who gave Price a disarmingly cheerful smile, seemed perfectly relaxed. 'You're the expert, sir – you tell me. Or consult one of your many instruments.'

Price stared. 'You find my methods disagreeable, sir?'

I kept my gaze on the young man as he stepped forward, his chin raised against my employer. 'Your scientific instruments are attuned to the physical world, Mr Price. Physical, not spiritual. Why assume they should be any use at all in detecting corporeal presences? By your logic, I might as well hunt for a shark in the desert!'

Price looked down at the floor. 'A loose board perhaps,' he said quietly, almost to himself, 'allowing cold air to enter from somewhere else. By my estimation this spot is almost immediately above the area we inspected in the cellar.'

At that moment the Reverend Smith appeared on the main staircase. 'Ah, so you've found where you'll be sleeping this evening, Mr Price? I took the liberty of asking the maid to make the room up for you earlier.' The rector looked at me and smiled. 'Your room, Miss Grey, is just a few doors down the corridor. I hope you don't mind but I hung some holy pictures on the walls and prayed to God to send His angels to watch over you tonight.'

I was greatly relieved that the room that was allegedly the source of so many supernormal happenings had not been reserved for me, and thanked the rector for his kindness.

'No prayers for me then?' Price muttered under his breath.

Reverend Smith gave a half smile. 'Ah yes, your room. Let me show you, Mr Price.'

I hated the Blue Room from the moment we entered it. The space had a disturbing atmosphere, as though it had witnessed the worst domestic horrors. In my notepad I sketched its layout, noting its contents: a dressing table with a tilting mirror, a wardrobe, an armchair, a washstand, a single bed and a large marble fireplace on whose mantelpiece stood two red glass candlesticks. As I paced around the perimeter of the room the flinty gaze of the late rector, the Reverend Harry Bull, followed my every move from the enormous oil painting above the mantelpiece. The man in the picture had occupied this Rectory for nigh on sixty years and his father before him and, like his father, he had died in this very bedroom. How the Bull family must have loved Borley to have remained here for so long in a rectory they had not only designed and built but extended on two separate occasions! I was sure that this house had once been loved. How sad then that it should have fallen into such neglect, a shadow of its former self, consumed by time and the elements.

Reverend Smith was showing Price the window. 'It is here that the mysterious light has appeared.'

Price scrutinised the black glass, and when he was satisfied that there had been no interference with the window frame he crossed to the far end of the room and knocked on the wall here and there, checking for concealed compartments.

'Wait a moment,' Wall said suddenly, his voice low. 'Can you smell something?'

I couldn't smell anything, but Price was nodding insistently. 'Yes. It's very faint, but I do believe that's the scent of lavender.'

Odd that he should say so, for I had not seen any flowers in the room.

'And look,' he continued, bending down to retrieve an object from the floor.

'What is it?' I asked.

'A mothball.' He turned to the rector. 'Did you bring these into the house?'

Shaking his head, Reverend Smith said with a sigh, 'We did not. This isn't the first time they have appeared either; these, and little scraps of paper. I'm afraid it's just another of this house's many mysteries.' Then his mood lightened, and he invited us downstairs for some supper.

Before leaving, Price asked us all to wait while he secured the room by stretching fine lengths of thread across the door, knotting them and securing both ends. It was wonderful to see him working again with the same infectious passion I had observed when we first met, three years previously. I wondered whether this improved mood of his was sustainable. So much had happened since that January evening in 1926. We had learned to trust one another and a bond had formed between us (though it was, I suspect, stronger on my part than his). He was no longer solitary; he didn't need to be, for when the critics attacked, I was there. In his blackest moments, it was I who consoled him. And notwithstanding the jealous warnings I had received from Wall, I was adamant I would to continue to do so. Vernon Wall might have disapproved, but if Price fell, I would be there to catch him.

*

As Price was securing the door to the Blue Room, Wall observed the process with the keenest attention. As a journalist it was his duty to ask questions, so perhaps I ought not to have been surprised by the curiosity he had exhibited since our arrival at the Rectory. But it was the nature of his questions, and the way he asked them as we had explored the house, that had drawn my attention. Wherever Price went, Wall followed, all the time firing questions at him, taking notes and watching him with the same careful scrutiny my employer applied to dubious mediums.

Beneath the heavy ticking of the grandfather clock our group assembled in the dining room where we sat again at the table. It was darker now than before, the only light coming from glowing candlesticks above the grotesque fireplace and a paraffin lamp in the middle of the table.

Looking very much intrigued, Reverend Smith leaned forward and addressed Price. 'Well then, sir, your inspection of the house has been most thorough. Please tell me you have reached some conclusions?'

Price lit his pipe and said evenly, 'I am happy to confirm that your suspicions were correct: there are no intruders in your home, no prowler playing tricks on you. I have discovered nothing that leads me to that supposition.'

'Then the matter is settled,' said Wall with triumph. 'The place is haunted.'

'If I believed that,' said Price, 'then by now I would have summoned the rest of Fleet Street to the door!' He laughed gently, as I wondered if he were serious. 'No, no. Although the Rectory is fairly new, it is extremely rundown, with loose floorboards everywhere and rotting window frames wherever I look. All of these faults cause draughts, chills and light breezes. And like every country house, the place creaks and groans. All perfectly natural. It's the villagers' fertile imaginations and the legends of Borley that make the place feel eerie.'

'Ah,' said Wall, 'so you admit the house *does* feel uncomfortable.'

Price smiled. 'I always feel uncomfortable in the company of rodents.'[1]

'All right then; what about the voices in the passages?' Wall demanded.

'Echoes rebounding from the courtyard walls, I should think. The lane outside runs almost immediately adjacent to the property.'

'And the scent of lavender in the bedrooms?'

'Simple! On our journey here we passed a turning for Stafford Allen, the largest lavender factory in the country. It's just across the valley, two miles away, in Long Melford.'

'Mr Price, your habit for debunking is unceasingly agitating,' said Wall. 'Explain to us, if you can, the globe of light that Mrs and Mrs Smith and I as well as countless locals observed in the window of the room upstairs.'

'Reflections from lights inside the Rectory, from the landing over the kitchen, or indeed from outside.'

And there it was. The simplest, most obvious explanation, yet only Price had deduced it. There was a cottage adjoining the Rectory and beyond this a farm, with a block of piggeries and farm buildings. It was quite possible that the mysterious light in the window of the 'haunted bedroom' was in fact the reflection of duplex lamps carried outside by the cottage's tenants after dark when drawing water from the well.

But Mr Wall, who sat opposite Price, protested loudly: 'How can you proclaim so conclusively on happenings you haven't even witnessed, Mr Price? I suggest that you—'

'Look!' the rector cut in. And as I tracked his amazed gaze, alarm rose within me.

*

The pepper pot, which stood on the table before us, was trembling. I had never seen anything so peculiar. And as if this were not enough to startle us, a glass of white wine that had been poured for Price just minutes earlier turned an inky black.

'Good God,' said Reverend Smith. He quickly made the sign of the cross.

All of us but Price got up sharply and backed away from the table, our eyes fixed firmly on the pepper pot. It shot along the table and stopped at the opposite end, immediately in front of Mr Wall. He jumped back, startled. 'There! You see now, Mr Price!' he cried. 'These things *do* happen.'

For a few baffling seconds no one said anything. Only Price remained calm, sitting motionless and smiling. 'I see very well indeed, Mr Wall – and so hopefully do you – how easy it is to be fooled by the trickery of man. As Sarah will verify, I am trained in the ways of conjuring. You approve of my abilities?'

I still don't know how the trick was accomplished, but nevertheless it was wonderful to watch. Wall looked angrily at Price when he realised he had been fooled, but the others, myself included, relaxed and saw the humorous side.

'So you see,' Price continued, 'all of the goings-on in this Rectory can be achieved by a clever man – or woman.'

'Like yourself?' Wall asked pointedly.

'Indeed,' said Price. 'Now, after dinner I suggest that you and I, Mr Wall, keep watch from the summerhouse in the garden for this legendary nun. After that we can retire to bed and put this little business to rest.'

'Agreed,' said Wall as he resumed his place at the table, still glowering at Price. 'But aren't you going to tell us how you did it? Your little trick? Invisible thread, I suppose? Or magnets?'

But it was clear from Price's hardened expression that he had no intention of disclosing how his trick was accomplished.

I thought Wall was about to say something else when suddenly Reverend Smith said, 'Mary, where are you going?'

I looked up and followed the rector's gaze to the hallway beyond the dining-room door where I saw a young woman, no older than nineteen. She was a plain girl with large spectacles and a bob of brown hair, and she was halfway through putting on her coat. Upon hearing the rector she came towards us, but stopped short on the threshold of the room.

'Please, sir, I'm sorry, but . . .' She was fumbling with the buttons on her coat.

'What is it, child?'

'I'm sorry, sir, but I'd rather not stay here tonight. I dare not.'

Observing the girl's agitated state, Price got to his feet and beckoned her over. She stepped into the dining room, looking cautiously around her. 'How can I assist you, sir?'

'By answering a couple of questions,' said Price kindly. 'Just a few, all right?'

She nodded.

'Very good,' Price smiled. 'Come and sit here beside me.'

She did so.

'Now then, Mary, where are you off to in such a hurry?'

Mary hesitated. 'Into the village, sir, to Sudbury, to see some friends at the Bull Inn.'

'Don't be daft, child,' Reverend Smith interrupted. 'It's dark out there, and there's a thunderstorm coming most likely.'

Price ignored the rector. 'Mary, your employers have told me that since you came to this house you have witnessed many strange events here, events beyond explanation, if you will: the coach and horses in the driveway, the spectre of a woman in the garden.'

A prolonged pause ensued.

'Mary, is that correct?'

She nodded slowly, fidgeting beneath his fierce scrutiny. 'Yes, sir, I have seen them, and more besides.'

'More?' Price leaned in so that his face was near hers.

'Yes, sir. Once, outside in the shrubbery near the road, I saw a man. I thought he was a poacher but when I went near – well, he wasn't there any more.'

'You're saying that this figure just vanished?' asked Wall, who was busily taking notes. 'Like the coach on the lawn?'

'Will you please refrain from leading the witness,' Price instructed, glaring at the journalist. He turned back to the maid and said gently, 'Now then, what else, Mary?'

But she was nodding at Wall. 'No, sir, the gentleman is right – he did vanish into the air, into the night, I swear it! And . . .'

'Go on. What is it?'

'Well – I know you will think this crazy. It is crazy. But . . . well.' She swallowed her nervousness. 'His head was missing!'

Wall said nothing this time but was grinning widely as he scribbled the incredible details down in his notepad. It was just the sort of colourful detail his story needed.

Price was silent for a moment, then: 'Interesting. But continue. Tell us of the nun, please, Mary.'

She pursed her lips.

'Don't be alarmed,' said Price comfortingly. 'I promise that whatever you saw cannot harm you.'

I wondered how he could possibly know such a thing.

'Now tell me, where precisely did you see her?'

The young woman fidgeted in her chair, her eyes drifting away from Price to the window behind him. 'Near the trees at the bottom of the garden, opposite the summerhouse.'

'The garden is a horrid place,' Mrs Smith interrupted. 'The more we see of the grounds, the less we like them. The belt of trees surrounding the house cuts it off completely from the rest of the world – takes our sunshine, too; and we're forever finding animal bones outside among the weeds and flower beds.'

Price seemed to register the remark. 'Borley,' he said thoughtfully, musing on the meaning of the word. 'Boar's pasture . . .' Then snapping back to attention, he fixed the maid with an intense stare. 'Now then, Mary, I'm going to ask you another question and it's very important you answer it honestly for me, all right?'

She nodded reluctantly.

'Are you making any of this up?'

'Mr Price!' cried the rector, slapping his hand down on the table.

'Please, I must be certain, sir.'

Mary spoke in an agitated tone. 'No, sir. I saw her as clear as day – a woman dressed head to toe in black robes, her head hooded and bowed. She was in the garden, telling her beads. I saw her face, haggard and pale like the moon – she looked so very sad. And there was something else, something hanging around her neck. It was bright, as though it was catching the light from the sun – metallic-looking, like a coin on a long chain.'

Seeing the maid's distress, Price gave her a reassuring smile; I saw it and thought it conveyed the caring, sensitive side to his character that so few knew he possessed.

'Just one last question: what time of day was this, please?'

'Early evening, I think; it had not long got dark.'

Smiling his appreciation, Price thanked the young woman for her trouble and indicated that she could go. She looked relieved, but while walking to the door she stopped, turned, looked directly at me and said, 'Miss, you're a braver soul than me, staying here tonight.'

I can remember very clearly laughing at that remark. I should not have done so.

'Mark my words,' said Mary, 'there will be doings here tonight. Let no lies be told. Spirits feed on lies. Lies give them power.'

We watched her go. Price looked thoughtful, Wall agitated, Mr and Mrs Smith nervous; as for me, I was intrigued – not just by the possibility of ghosts in this house, for I did not truly believe at that point there were any, but by the idea that such normal, apparently honest, people could be so gravely mistaken over so many years.

'Well,' said Price at last, 'I think it's perfectly clear what we should do now.'

'Oh?' asked Wall.

'Or at least it is clear to *some* of us,' said Price under his breath. Then, loudly, 'You and I must take up our posts in the summerhouse and hold a vigil for the nun, just as the late rector used to do.' He rose. 'But we must go quickly. Sarah, I suggest you stay inside and keep watch with Reverend and Mrs Smith.'

I agreed, relieved to escape the awkwardness dividing the two men. But then I remembered the cold and draughty corridors that ran throughout the house like a rabbit warren and wondered where I would rather be: outside or in.

I said to the rector, 'Mary did look very unsettled, sir.'

He nodded. 'Sweet girl. My utmost concern is to ensure she is happy with us; Mabel and I have rather come to rely on her.'

I considered this and went on, 'She said she feared there would be "doings" here tonight. What on earth does she think is going to happen?'

The rector looked at me coolly. 'I think, Miss Grey, that by now you have heard enough that you might hazard a guess. These things, whatever their cause' – he hesitated – 'do happen.'

I stared into the rector's wide, haunted eyes and believed him.

Before either of us could utter another word, the faint tinkle of a bell sounded from the depths of the house. Everyone heard it. Mrs Smith drew an anxious breath, her husband's eyes caught mine and Price turned his head slowly towards the open door. 'But that's . . . impossible,' he said in a low voice, his eyes narrowing. 'The bell wires are disconnected. I inspected them myself.'

Vernon Wall got quickly to his feet. 'It's beginning,' he said, the alarm in his voice unmistakable.

I gripped Reverend Smith's arm urgently. 'What did Mary mean, sir? What did she think is going to happen here?'

Another bell rang, louder this time.

'Sarah,' Price muttered, 'I think we're about to find out.'

Note

1 That there were bats in the house cannot be disputed; for although Sarah's manuscript informs us that the Smiths flatly denied the presence of any vermin in the Rectory, this information is contradicted by Mrs Smith herself, in the following signed statement provided to investigators of the affair: 'I have gone upstairs in the dark at Borley and watched in the supposed Haunted Room and looked from the windows, and the result has been always "nil" – only bats and the scratching sometimes of rats.' In a separate, later

statement, Mrs Smith states: 'I saw enormous rats in the place, and am sure these were responsible for bell-ringing and many noises attributed to the supernatural; they would scratch the boards. The house had been empty for a long time, and rats had taken up abode in kitchens and cupboards' (signed statement from Mrs Smith, published in *The Haunting of Borley Rectory*, p.47).

– 15 –

A QUESTION
OF FAITH

We arrived in the kitchen passage just in time to see the spring
and clapper attached to the bell that had rung still moving. It
was the bell connected to the Blue Room.

Price was silent for a moment, an expression of utter bemusement on his face as he shone his torch along the row of brass
bells. 'But that room is secure,' he said. 'You all saw me close
and double-seal it.'

The look of satisfaction on Wall's face as he turned to face
Price was palpable. 'Now you have finally seen for yourself. I shall
write this up for my newspaper.'

'Will you indeed?'

'It is abundantly clear that this house is haunted, sir. What
other explanation is there?'

'We saw bats in the attics,' said Price. 'Perhaps one found its
way down here and brushed against the bell.'

'That is your theory?'

'Do you have a better one?'

'No, but—'

'Then if it is all the same to you, Mr Wall, might I propose that
you leave the business of this investigation to me?'

'If you insist, but I really do think—'

'What you think is irrelevant!' Price snapped. 'What's important now is that we gather as many facts as we can.' He looked at
me and said, 'Facts are all we have. That's right, isn't it, Sarah?'

'Absolutely,' I said with a grin, delighted to see him still on
form.

Wall looked exasperated. 'Then what do you propose?'

'That like the old rector before us, we head down to the
bottom of the garden, install ourselves in the old summerhouse
and watch for the nun. Together.'

'Don't forget the globe of light which appears in the window
of the Blue Room.'

'Thank you, Mrs Smith. I will keep my eyes peeled.'

Mr Wall glanced at me. 'What about Miss Grey? You're happy
to leave her here, all on her own?'

'She isn't on her own,' said Price.

I nodded and said I would remain in the house. As the two
men turned to leave I felt a tap on my arm and heard a low voice
whisper in my ear, 'Stay here, and don't take your eyes off them.'
It was Price. I followed his eyes and saw that he was staring at
the Smiths, who were standing now at one of the windows in
the passage, checking it was secure.

'You don't suspect them, surely?' I whispered. But he said
nothing and so, to satisfy him, I nodded to show I had understood.

Watching Price and Wall go, the rector said gravely, 'I warned
him. I warned you both, Miss Grey. Demons, vengeful spirits,
fallen angels . . . they have but one mission: to wreak havoc, to
bring consistent ill luck, to break down a person's will so that
they can take over.'

And with a sharp turn he marched away, ignoring me as

I called after him. I was left alone with his wife and could see from the way she clasped and unclasped her hands that the poor woman was nervous, so I took her hand in mine and told her everything would be all right. 'Perhaps a cup of tea is in order?' I suggested.

She smiled. 'Thank you, Miss Grey. That sounds like a very sensible idea.'

As we made our way to the kitchen, the distant rumble of thunder made me think of Mother, at home on her own in London. Only the night before, she had asked Price if I would be safe with him, here at Borley Rectory.

And now I couldn't help asking myself the very same question.

*

Almost an hour had passed since Price and Wall had commenced their vigil in the summerhouse, and in that time there had been no further disturbances. The Rectory was quiet now, but it was a fragile silence and brought little comfort.

'What first attracted you to the Rectory?' I asked Mrs Smith.

She stood with her back to a wide window barred with iron. It was pitch black outside; anyone could be out there, I thought, looking in at us, and we'd know nothing about it. The idea made me shiver.

'I suppose it was the quietness of the place. We lived very busy lives in India, you see, employed in the civil service. My husband has told you that I have suffered with my heart?'

'Indeed, and I am sorry to hear it.'

'You're very kind, Miss Grey. Thankfully the condition isn't too serious, but it was enough for us to decide that a quieter life was in order. And on first inspection Borley seemed ideal, tucked away up here at the top of the valley.'

'Oh, it's a splendid spot,' I agreed, a little half-heartedly.

Mrs Smith's expression had darkened and her eyes were moving slowly around the room. 'How could we have got a place so wrong? Living here, Miss Grey . . . it is troubling and most unpleasant. The Rectory, its quietness – it holds mysteries, and memories not our own. You can sense it too, can't you? I've been watching you, my dear; I can see you're frightened.'

My stomach fluttered. 'It must get lonely for you, up here.'

'Oh, it certainly does.'

'Do you go down into the town often?'

'No, only when necessary. To be honest, the looks we get deter us from doing so. Mary runs our errands there twice a week, and when we have guests they prefer to stay there. Mr Wall, for example.'

'Really? I was under the impression that he was staying here with us tonight.'

'No, we did offer to prepare a room for him, but he insisted that he would be staying at the Bull Inn tonight, when his business here is completed. It's a lovely old place, said to be haunted itself.'

'I see.'

'You look disappointed, Miss Grey.'

'Do I?'

'Yes, you do,' she said, smiling. 'I do believe you might have an admirer in Mr Wall.'

'Oh, I don't think so,' I said awkwardly. 'He's a little earnest, don't you think?'

'He is rather. I just hope his articles don't attract too much unwelcome attention to the house. The last thing we would want is to upset the locals.'

'I'm sure it won't come to that,' I lied, 'and I'm sure it's not intentional on Mr Wall's part. He doesn't want to make life difficult for you; it's his job to report these things. In some ways I think he is very similar to Harry – he can be a little earnest too; he likes to shake things up a bit.'

We were both startled by an unexpected rumble of thunder. 'It's getting nearer,' said Mrs Smith, flinching. She drew up a chair next to me at the kitchen table. 'I wonder how the men are getting on outside?'

I had been thinking the same, hoping that by now Price and Wall might have resolved their differences. It was unlikely. Their professional ambitions knew no limits. If either man could, they'd drop the other like a stone. I said quietly, 'I'm sure we would have heard if they had seen anything.'

'For all his complexities, Mr Price seems to me such a committed man,' commented Mrs Smith.

'Certainly, he has given his life to this subject.'

'And what about you, Miss Grey?'

'What do you mean?'

She smiled. 'Well, if I may say so, you're a very glamorous young woman and clearly intelligent. There must be any number of secretarial roles you could perform, yet you've chosen to work for Mr Price helping the likes of us, scrambling around in dirty cellars and attics and heaven knows what else. What on earth led you into such a thing?'

'The irony is I never wanted to be a secretary,' I explained. 'I was going to be a model; I *was* a model, for a short time. But then . . .'

'You met Mr Price.'

I nodded. 'Our worlds collided and everything changed. Life does lead us to the strangest places, doesn't it?'

'Well, it certainly has in your case. Do you know why exactly?'

Having no definite answer, I shrugged and said, 'Why do any of us do the things we do? I did it out of love, I suppose.'

'Love? I didn't realise you and Mr Price were—'

'Oh, no, no,' I said quickly, 'I mean my love for my mother.' I explained the impact of fraudulent mediums on her emotions since the year before I met Price, and how I had arrived at this stage in my life through my sympathy for the living, my respect for the dead and the anger I felt towards those who exploited both so callously. 'I'd have done anything to protect her from that,' I explained. 'But you see, Harry offered me a solution. I could relate to him; his perspective on the problem was unique. No one else has done what he has done: developed a science out of psychical research, tested mediums under laboratory conditions.'

'Is Mr Price making progress with his work?'

'He was,' I said ruefully. 'In its early days the Laboratory seemed capable of explaining mysteries, perhaps even confirming the existence of supernormal phenomena and bringing them in line with science.'

'But you have made no such confirmation?'

I nodded. 'Only one long list of disappointments.' I explained then about the numerous instances of trickery I had witnessed in the seance room: the teenage girl with red skin and a swollen face who could make cutlery stick to her limbs, the child who barked with 'the voice of the Devil', Mrs Tyler and the regurgitated cheesecloth. 'She'll be prosecuted before long under the Witchcraft Act. Harry is going to give evidence against her.'

'But why you?' Mrs Smith enquired. 'Why does he need a woman to help him with all this?'

'Well, most of the mediums are females,' I explained, hoping she would understand.

'So . . . ?'

'Well, I'm able to assist with all those awkward tasks that he can't perform.'

'Such as?'

I gave a slight cough, embarrassed, and lowered my voice to a whisper. 'Umm, examinations.'

'You don't mean . . .'

'Internal examinations. Yes.'

Mrs Smith's mouth dropped open.

'It saddens me that his work isn't achieving the recognition it should; it saddens him too. The people who helped fund his Laboratory are now the very people who are trying to destroy it: the Spiritualists, people like Conan Doyle. They disagree with his scientific approach. They see it as disrespectful, incompatible with their faith.'

'But *is* it compatible?' asked Mrs Smith. 'Spiritualism, though unconventional, is ultimately a faith. Whether or not you agree with the principles of that faith, I'm not sure I agree that faith requires scientific validation.'

'But why not?' I asked. 'Isn't it reasonable to ask for some evidence to support our beliefs?'

'On certain matters, yes,' she agreed, 'but surely it is not so with faith?' Another rumble of thunder drew her eyes nervously to the window. 'We need some certainties in this world, Miss Grey. Faith never changes but scientific principles do. All the time.'

For a moment not a word passed between us; she was analysing me, inwardly determining the reasons why she believed I had agreed to work for a man who fashioned himself on Sherlock Holmes and at the same time hunted ghosts.

'If you don't mind my asking, how old were you when your father died?'

'It was just before the end of the war. I was thirteen.'

She sighed and said sadly, 'So young. I'm sorry. It was a bad, bad time for so many people. I suppose the only solace is knowing we're unlikely to see another war like it, at least not in our lifetimes.'

'Perhaps.'

'You must miss your father terribly,' she said kindly.

'We all lose people in the end,' I said shortly, though I was conscious of nodding, for I had to acknowledge that I did miss him but only on the rare occasions when I permitted myself to recall the memories of the short time we had enjoyed together. I didn't do that often, couldn't. Occasionally, of course, fragments of the past drifted through my mind – Father teaching me piano, trips to the music hall – but time had stripped the memories of their colour. And yet, for me, they were enough; easier to endure than the consequences of opening up the recesses of my mind and becoming like Mother, consumed with sadness and grief and the darker side of life.

It seems extraordinary to me now that I should have shared all this with Mrs Smith, a stranger. I suppose I needed someone to listen, and I was glad that she had done so. But I saw now that she was looking at me intently and the natural curiosity of this aspiring novelist was suddenly obvious.

'*Aren't* you consumed with the darker side of life?' she asked delicately. 'It's inevitable, isn't it, when you work with a ghost hunter. You can't avoid the shadows when your job is to chase them, surely?'

I had to confess that she had a point. 'Is that how it seems?'

'Oh, my goodness, yes, Miss Grey; you shine whenever you're near him.'

'If that is so, it is because I believe in his principles,' I said firmly.

'But what *are* his principles, my dear? Can you be sure of them? If you don't mind my saying so, Mr Price's work strikes me as contradictory.'

'In what way?'

'Well, the fact is . . .' Mrs Smith looked down. She was choosing her words carefully. 'As I understand, there was a time when he was on record, publicly, for believing in such things. His name was once a shining light at the Society for Psychical Research. Then he broke away and set up on his own, changed his mind. Became a sceptic. But what if he witnessed a display of super-normal happenings that was irrefutable, completely undeniable, would he admit his scepticism was misplaced? Could he admit he was wrong and that some mediums have merit, I wonder?'

If it suited him, I thought.

'Yes, of course,' I answered, running a hand through my hair. 'I'm certain he would give his full support to any medium he tested who was capable of convincing him.'

'And what about you? Could you admit you were wrong to doubt the beliefs of Spiritualists?'

I thought it would take a very special sort of proof to convince me.

'I ask the question because I sense there is a part of you, somewhere deep down, that wishes it could all be true.' She took my hand in her own. 'Answer me honestly, dear: if there was the slightest chance that your father was looking down on you now and was able to communicate with you then you'd want to know about it, wouldn't you?'

'Yes,' I whispered, shivering slightly. 'Yes, of course. But—'

Before I could form my answer there came an interruption that brought Mrs Smith and me to our feet in alarm: the sound of smashing glass and the screams of two frightened men.

'Quickly, come with me!' I instructed and, taking Mrs Smith's hand, I launched out into the kitchen corridor, half running, half stumbling, until we reached the main hall and the entrance to the library, which opened via French windows into the glass-roofed verandah spanning the entire back of the house. Price and Wall were standing at the far end of the room, next to the windows. The floor around them was covered with broken glass. 'Harry! What on earth—'

'Stay exactly where you are, Sarah!'

I saw a large red brick lying on the floor, just at the verandah. Price picked it up carefully and examined it. 'This smashed straight through the roof above us.'

'Good heavens, what has happened here?' The disturbance had drawn the rector from the sanctuary of his study; he stood at the open door, one arm wrapped protectively around his wife, the other holding aloft an old storm lamp.

'Perhaps it fell from one of the chimneystacks?' said Mrs Smith, though even she sounded unconvinced by the idea.

'Perhaps,' Price answered somewhat distantly. He was still turning the brick over slowly in his hands. 'This brick is warm.'

'Warm?' I remembered what I had learnt back at the Laboratory in my early years of study. I threw Price a questioning glance. 'Harry, the first recorded incidents of poltergeist activity record that any object thrown or moved by the phenomenon is left warm to the touch immediately afterwards.'

Price nodded at my recital. 'Yes, that's right, Sarah. Something very odd is going on here.'

'You're telling me!' said Wall, and I realised then how unusually quiet he had been in the last few moments. He was glaring at Price, his cheeks flushed. 'Well, do you want to tell them or shall I?'

Silently Price turned his head away.

'Very well.' Wall faced the rest of us, took a deep breath and announced, 'I saw her. I saw the nun!'

WEIRD NIGHT IN 'HAUNTED' HOUSE

Shape That Moved on Lawn of Borley Rectory

Strange Rappings

Articles Flying Through the Air Seen by Watchers

From our Special Correspondent

Long Melford, Thursday

There can no longer be any doubt that Borley Rectory, near here, is the scene of some remarkable incidents.

Last night, Mr Harry Price, director of the National Laboratory for Psychical Research, his secretary Sarah Grey, the Revd G.E. Smith, Rector of Borley, Mrs Smith and myself were witness to a series of remarkable happenings.

All these things occurred without the assistance of any medium or any kind of apparatus, and Mr Price, who is a research expert only and not a spiritualist, expressed himself puzzled and astonished at the results.

To give the phenomenon a thorough test, however, he is arranging for a séance to be held at the Rectory with the aid of a prominent London medium.

The first remarkable happening was the dark figure I saw in the garden.

We were standing in the summer-house at dusk watching the lawn, when I saw the 'apparition' which so many claim to have seen, but owing to the deep shadows it was impossible for one to discern any definite shape or attire.

FALLING GLASS

But something certainly moved along

the path on the other side of the lawn and, although I immediately ran across to investigate, it had vanished when I reached the spot.

Then, as we strolled towards the Rectory discussing the figure, there came a terrific crash, and a pane of glass from the roof of a porch hurtled to the ground.

We ran inside and upstairs to inspect the rooms immediately over the porch, but found nobody.[1]

Note

1 *Daily Mirror*, 14 June 1929.

– 16 –
WALL'S CHALLENGE

Vernon Wall related his sombre encounter with such excitement, that it was a struggle for me to record every small detail with my usual care. But in the short time I had to consider the matter, I formed the intuitive belief that Price's version of the events in the garden – when we heard it – would probably differ in many respects from Wall's. And I was right, for when the rector asked Price whether he was able to substantiate the journalist's story, his question provoked a simple shaking of the head and an insistence that he had not seen anything unusual himself, and certainly nothing quite as startling as the appearance of a nun.

'We were stationed in the summerhouse,' he said, 'smoking. I had my gaze trained on the window of the Blue Room when Mr Wall here gripped my arm with a great flurry of excitement, pointing across the lawn. Before I could get a good look he had dashed off' – Price looked disapprovingly at the journalist – 'heading towards the Nun's Walk.'

'What did you do?' I asked.

'What *could* I do? I was quite taken by surprise as my attention had been solidly focused on the window of the Blue Room; and of course it was dark, so I waited a matter of seconds, directing my gaze at the area indicated by Wall.'

'And . . . ?'

Price hesitated. 'Certainly I saw something . . . *moving* against the darker background of the trees surrounding the garden. I suppose it seemed to glide, almost, down towards the little stream.'

'There you have it!' Wall exclaimed. 'A gliding apparition!'

'But I was not certain!' Price countered loudly.

And yet there remained the question of where the brick that had smashed through the roof of the verandah had come from and, more importantly, who had thrown it. Price, I could see, was bothered by the problem. But his bafflement did not prevent him from groping for any explanation he could find that would throw further doubt on Wall's experience.

'Our minds are such wonderful, powerful things,' he announced. He sighed and gave Wall a somewhat patronising look. 'Under the right conditions we can imagine all sorts of things. The light outside in the garden was not good, and our imaginations were on high alert. What you so readily believe was the nun, Mr Wall, could just as easily have been a shadow or a phantom of the mind.'

He was right, of course, but Wall had spoken with such conviction. Soon after, I took a seat in the deserted drawing room to gather my thoughts, and Wall joined me there, sitting beside me on a chaise longue.

I had to ask him. 'Did you really see her? You're certain?'

'I saw *something*, Miss Grey. I would swear it under oath.'

I said nothing for a moment or two, until I remembered that Mary had slipped away just after supper. 'Perhaps it was the maid playing a trick on us. She knew we were coming here and she knew why. Scaring us, tricking us, would have made a great tale for her to tell her friends in town.'

He shook his head. 'I don't think so – it was the most unnatural sight, a figure like a drifting shadow, half present and half not. And there was something else – a droning sound like a swarm of flies.' He shrugged. 'I didn't see any.'

This hesitant description only heightened my creeping sense of unease – call it a suspicion if you will – that all was not quite as it appeared at Borley Rectory. It was not that I suspected Wall of lying, but the animated manner in which he had described the event made me doubt him. The experience should have invoked at least some semblance of fear, some sign of alarm, but there was no evidence of either reaction – only his forthright, eager manner.

He could read me well. 'I say, *you* believe me, don't you?'

'Yes, yes, of course, but . . .'

I was about to ask him why he didn't seem more troubled by the experience when another question occurred to me. 'Mr Wall, when is your next newspaper article expected?'

He caught the cynical suggestion in my question. 'Tomorrow, actually.'

'I see.'

'Please, Miss Grey, surely you can't imagine that I would invent such a story just to please my editor?'

I said nothing, rubbed my forehead. He seemed to be telling the truth.

'Sarah, please.' He sighed, frustrated. 'This is Mr Price's doing, isn't it? He's turned you against me.'

'No – it's not that. Listen. It's in my nature to be sceptical. I've seen what lies can do.'

Wall looked unconvinced. 'I know Mr Price disapproves of

my being here, I can tell. But you don't have to protect him, or me for that matter.'

'Vernon—'

I had wanted to ask him what they had talked about in the garden. But before I could finish my sentence we both started, disturbed by a noise which sounded like a stone falling to the floor. It seemed to come from the opposite side of the room.

'What was that?' The urgency in my voice surprised even me.

We listened attentively, perched on the edge of the ugly chaise longue, but the only other sounds – apart from the ticking clock in the hall – were of Price and Mr and Mrs Smith, the three of whom were conversing in the next room as they busily swept up the shattered glass. 'Perhaps we should go and help them,' I suggested.

And then Wall slipped a comforting arm around me. My natural reaction was to go rigid, but I quickly relaxed, allowing my shoulders to loosen.

'Please, sit a moment with me,' said Wall.

There was a tense moment as, for a few seconds, we sat perfectly still, neither of us saying anything, looking everywhere except at each other.

'I hate this place,' I said after a while. 'It just feels wrong to me somehow. When we arrived I thought the silence was oddly soothing, but it's not soothing, is it? It's just unnatural. It doesn't make any *sense*.'

I saw him nod. 'I feel as though we're being watched even now.'

A gust of air passed me. Wall must have felt my nervous shiver, for he promptly squeezed closer to me; but the warmth of his embrace was useless against the creeping chill which seemed to be talking hold of the room. I reminded myself of

the date – June 1929 – as if to confirm that I wasn't imagining
the drop in temperature, to reassure myself that the capacity
for coherent thought had not abandoned me. Two and a half
years. Was it really so long since I had embarked on this journey
with Price? I tried to remember all that had happened in that
time, but the very notion that memories or coherent thought
were possible in this house or had any meaning here, where
the rest of the world seemed so very far away, felt misplaced;
indeed, if I had known then of the events still to come that
night, I would willingly have left the Rectory at that instant.
But I didn't know, and the growing strength of my conflicting
emotions towards Wall and Price was serving only to anchor
me here.

I glanced furtively at the door leading into the hall, afraid
we would be discovered in such an intimate embrace, and
was about to rise when Wall said, 'Sarah – in another time,
another place, more normal than this, when we're not frighten-
ing ourselves out of our foolish wits, it would give me the
greatest pleasure to see you.'

'See me? Oh, Mr Wall, I'm flattered; but really, I hardly have
any time to call my own. Harry keeps me so frightfully busy at
the Laboratory, what with setting up his experiments, interviewing mediums, answering letters, filing reports on our field
investigations . . .'

Wall was looking at me doubtfully.

And as I listened to the words falling from my mouth, I wondered where they were coming from. Why, indeed, was I so
reluctant to take a chance on someone so genuinely good? I
took a deep breath and said firmly, trying not to let my sudden
excitement show, 'Well . . . all right!'

Wall smiled cheerfully. 'Yes? For supper, perhaps? Or maybe

a walk on Rotten Row to take in the morning air? Or, if you're feeling a little more adventurous, a trip to Italy – to Como and the Pearl of the Lake? My father has a house there, in Bellagio. I could show you. It's a modest little place, but . . .' He cast his eyes grimly around the room, '. . . it's miles away from this world of darkness.'

I shut my eyes with delight and said, 'Yes, I would like that very much.' And immediately the sounds, sights and smells of the Italian countryside came rushing into my head – the fine wines, the fragrant summer breezes, the wonderful sunshine. Weather to warm the heart. They weren't vague imaginings either, but memories of the short time that Price and I had spent together in Italy the year before, when attending an auction of rare magical books. On the journey home we had stopped for a time in Italy – Milan – before taking the train onwards, across the border into France.

'I do so love Europe,' I said to Wall. 'It was in Italy that I spent what was probably the most memorable train journey of my life.'

Why memorable? Not because of the scenery, nor because of the delectable food we had enjoyed together for the duration, but because, an hour before reaching the French border, Price had panicked, suddenly seized with the fear that the vast quantity of books he had procured on our travels would be confiscated by the border police. 'I have an idea, Sarah,' he had announced with triumph. 'I'm going to walk the length of this train and hand the books out to the other passengers and ask them to pretend they are theirs. That will see us across the border, and then I will walk the length of the train again and collect them all back up!' He had actually done it, too.

Alerted by my account of the train journey, Wall's face became serious. 'You're obsessed with him, aren't you? Totally obsessed.'

He removed his arm from around me. 'What exactly does he do for you, Sarah?'

'Most things, actually.' The voice belonged to Price. I jolted at seeing him there in the doorway behind us, half hidden in the shadows. 'Not that Miss Grey's career is any business of yours, Mr Wall.'

How long Price had been eavesdropping on our conversation I couldn't say, but now Mr and Mrs Smith were behind him, their forms half swallowed by the darkness of the main hallway. The couple were the picture of concern, the rector with his arm wrapped protectively around his wife, and she standing nervously, twisting her rings on arthritic fingers.

I rose sharply. 'What's the matter?'

'The cold,' whispered Mrs Smith, stepping forward. It had become her habit to look over her shoulder as she entered every room and she did so now, as if a great beast might leap forward from behind and pin her to the ground. She rubbed her arms. 'Don't you feel it?'

'Well, of course we feel it,' said Wall, standing suddenly. 'We *all* feel it. All of us, that is, except – perhaps – Mr Price here.'

'I will need to check my instruments,' said Price grudgingly, turning away. 'I left a thermometer at the bottom of the main stairs.'

'*I* think,' Wall broke in, his voice rising steadily, 'that it's high time you actually *did* something.'

All of us stood in silence for a moment.

Price turned, his eyes narrowing. 'Such as?'

The reporter stepped forward. 'If there *is* a presence in this house – and I for one believe that indeed there is such a presence – then the thing clearly isn't shy. It wants to be noticed.'

'Let's assume, for argument's sake, that you are right.' Price's words had the tone of quiet menace. 'What would you suggest we do?'

'Speak to it,' said Wall. 'Ask it what it wants.'

Horrified, Reverend Smith said, 'No, we must not enter into any dialogue with it.'

'But why not?' Wall insisted. 'If there is the slightest chance that we might learn just something more about what is happening here then I see no reason not to question it. Mr Price, I demand that you lead us in a seance!'

'*You* demand?' Price was indignant.

'I do.'

'Oh yes, that would make an excellent story for your newspaper, wouldn't it? No, Vernon, I will do no such thing.'

'I agree with Mr Price,' said Reverend Smith. 'My boy, you must understand that there is such a thing as pure evil. Are you so confident in your standing in this world that you can be sure to recognise it when you see it?'

'And I agree most wholeheartedly with Mr Smith,' said Price. 'Under the present circumstances it would be irresponsible for us to take this any further.'

Wall looked intensely dissatisfied. 'What do you think, Mrs Smith?' he asked.

'I think we should do this.'

We all looked at the woman.

'*What?*' spluttered the rector. 'Mabel, you can't be serious.'

She took her husband's arm. 'Guy, if a seance will help us understand more about the occurrences in this house, help us to learn more about whatever it is that is causing so much trouble, then perhaps we can do something to help. And these things, whatever they are, might leave us in peace. Isn't it worth a try?'

Mrs Smith looked pleadingly at her husband. The rector sighed, patted her hand and said, 'Very well, my dear, if that is your wish.'

'It is. But we need guidance.' Mrs Smith turned to Price. 'Harry, won't you help us? You said yourself that ghouls are for the gullible. Well then, let us be gullible.' She looked down at the curious collection of objects that had come rolling down the stairs some moments before. 'Now you have seen for yourself what we endure in this house. You came here to help us. Please help us.'

Price considered the plea with obvious reluctance. I understood his dilemma. To agree to Mrs Smith's request would be halfway to admitting the fallibility of his science and, worse, the possibility that his staunchest critics had been right all along. But even I, in my constrained scepticism, had to acknowledge that the phenomena we had witnessed this night – ringing bells, falling bricks and fleeting shadows – had no easy explanation. Reliving these events in my head, I could well imagine Mother telling me how wrong I had been to doubt the possibility of an afterlife on earth, and for the briefest moment I questioned why I had.

I thought of my father and imagined the impossible.

'Do it,' I said, turning towards Price.

He gave me a quizzical look. 'Sarah?'

'We have nothing to lose now,' I said firmly.

Beside me, Wall seconded his support, catching my eye and throwing me a charming smile that touched me with excitement and a little guilt.

'Very well,' Price said. 'But I want to make myself very clear. During the proceedings, I will be watching everybody extremely carefully.' He turned to Mrs Smith. 'All right, madam?'

'So be it, Mr Price. Where shall we carry out the seance?'

'Most of the unusual events you have described focus in or

around the Blue Room upstairs. Shall we conduct it in there?'

Mrs Smith nodded her agreement, but she didn't look at all happy about the idea.

'Come on then. And please bring as many candles and lamps as you have available.'

Guided by the flickering flame of the rector's storm lantern, we followed him across the gloomy hallway and up the great staircase. Darkness and the smell of damp were on all sides of us. There was no need for us to turn the handle to the bedroom door, for it was already wide open, daring us to enter.

'In here,' said the rector, leading the way.

'But as the others filed into the dusty bedroom, I noticed Price hanging back. His attention was centred upon me. 'Sarah, a moment, please?'

I went to his side and looked into his serious face. 'What is it?'

'In here,' he murmured, before stepping into a shadowy doorway which led to the disused schoolroom.

I hesitated. Wall was waiting for me at the entrance to the Blue Room, his face mulish and etched with disapproval. I smiled awkwardly, embarrassed, then stepped aside, following Price.

The schoolroom was pitch dark. I could only just discern Price's shape silhouette. I shivered from the cold and flinched as he took my hand.

'Are you quite all right, Sarah?'

Although the words were caring, the tone was stern. 'Yes – of course,' I blurted out. Perhaps it was because I could barely see him, but his scent seemed more noticeable in the dark – stronger, thicker, more masculine.

He squeezed my hand firmly before leaning his head towards mine. 'If there was something wrong, you would tell me, I hope?'

'Whatever do you mean?'

'It's this house, isn't it? I sense that it is getting the better of you.'

'The house,' I acknowledged, my voice catching in my throat, 'the people in the house. And the . . . things. Harry, what are they?'

Price sounded thoughtful. 'Ancient echoes of the past.'

It took me a moment to realise that he was hypothesising rather than expressing a firm opinion.

'Or, more likely,' he continued, 'the work of a clever deceiver concealed somewhere in these walls.' A slight pause. 'Tell me, what is your opinion of our intrepid journalist friend?'

'Vernon?' I said, with noticeable surprise. 'Harry, no, you can't possibly suspect him in all this.'

'He claims he saw something outside that I did not see. Now, I'm not implicating him directly, but it is possible that he is intimately involved in the hoax. He has every motive.'

I pulled my hand away. 'Why are you so determined not to believe?' I demanded.

'Why are you so ready *to* believe?'

A wide silence opened between us. I wondered what notions about my suitability for this job were swimming in his head, what regrets, if any, he harboured about employing me; and I felt a stab of alarm to think that I had dissatisfied him. But facts are facts, and, reasonable or not, I could not allow myself to ignore them. I recalled, then, our conversation back at the Laboratory – so long ago now, it seemed – about one's entitlement to believe in genuinely paranormal phenomena, violations of natural laws. 'Do you remember, Harry, telling me that natural laws could never be broken?'

'Yes, I remember very well.'

'But surely,' I challenged him, 'we can't claim to have discovered every law of nature, every possibility? If that were so, it would never be possible for science to progress, to make new discoveries.'

'What are you trying to say, Sarah?'

'What I mean is, perhaps these events, these happenings – perhaps they are simply *ungoverned* by physical laws. And if that were so then there wouldn't need to be any violation of any laws. No contradiction!'

'Yes . . . Yes. Now that is an interesting idea.'

I was surprised to hear him admit that the possibility had not occurred to him previously. It warmed me to think that I had impressed him; but before I could settle into complacency he was speaking again in a sharper tone.

'Of course there is a long, inbuilt resistance to such ideas. And what we have here, in this house, though it merits attention, must be properly investigated. By us.'

'Are you suggesting that task is beyond me?' I asked coolly.

'I am suggesting that you are allowing your emotions, your personal biases, to cloud your judgement.'

'What? Harry, no—'

'Listen to me!' His face was inches from mine, his breath hot on my face. 'As we speak, Mrs Smith and her husband and that mischievous journalist friend of yours are busy preparing the bedroom for a midnight seance, the sort of thing you and I have witnessed many times with unimpressive results. And you, Sarah – you encouraged it! I will not jeopardise the integrity of this investigation just to indulge a personal bias. As soon as we return to London we will be asked what happened here tonight, and what we say will matter. Our critics, my attackers – every psychical researcher in London worth his salt will pore over every detail of what we are about to do. They will send arrows of doubt to darken our skies. I want you to know that. They will be acute in their scrutiny. And you – both of us – will have to stand the test of their judgement.'

'What are you saying?' I asked.

'If this is too much for you, too personal, then now is the time to step away.'

'Step away? No!' I was adamant. 'We're too close now, and if you think you're sending me packing back to London, you have another thing coming! Do you hear?'

Price hesitated. 'You would miss this job.'

'Yes, I'd miss it!'

'Like you miss your father?'

That stung. The question hung in the air and in the darkness I nodded, holding back my tears, thankful beyond words that Price wasn't able to see my reaction. I hadn't been able to express what bothered me most: the memory that came back to me in flashes of my father in Mother's bedroom, kneeling next to the wardrobe before an open trunk. He was sobbing quietly to himself. Why? I would have gone to his side, hugged him, consoled him, asked him what was wrong, but for some reason, I was too afraid. Like a spy, I watched him holding something. The light from the gas lamps in the street outside fell on three small white envelopes bearing a handwritten scrawl.

Unmistakably letters.

'You're not to go in there. Not under any circumstances.'

But why not? The noises that came at night signalling disturbances within Mother's room: the wardrobe door creaking open, the trunk inside snapping open.

Sarah . . . do you know what she is looking for?

Then a terrible thought: she wasn't looking for something, she had already found it.

Letters . . .

Was there a connection? There had to be, surely? I should just confront Mother and ask her for the truth. Why hadn't I?

Because you don't know how she will, react, do you, Sarah? You have no idea what she's hiding from you, or what confronting it will do to her. Or to you.

'Sarah?' Price's voice pulled me out of private reflection.

'Don't push me, Harry,' I said eventually. 'You can trust me. You can rely on my support.'

'If you're sure,' he said in a low voice. 'Then we will carry on.'

I followed him out onto the dim landing. The door to the Blue Room was ajar and I could see the flicker of candlelight. A voice from within made me start. 'Mr Price, Miss Grey, are you joining us?'

I glanced up at Price, whose eyes were fixed on the bedroom, his face a mask of tense anticipation. 'Harry?'

He jerked his head towards me, staring straight at me out of wide, wild eyes. 'Yes?'

'Do you have even the slightest idea what's about to happen?'

'None whatsoever,' he said, then reached for my hand. 'Well – are you coming?'

I must be crazy, I thought. 'Yes,' I said, placing my hand in his. 'I'm coming.'

And together we stepped out of the darkness to face whatever was to come.

– 17 –

A MIDNIGHT SEANCE

'Now, I must insist that we make this quick and work with the very best light,' said Price, 'so that we can all see one another and ensure that there is no interference by anyone.' He placed his lamp on a large dressing table on top of which stood a wooden-backed swing mirror while Mrs Smith lit a candle. There was only one armchair, into which Wall dropped, seemingly putting his notes in order. Price, the rector, his wife and I all sat down on the side of the bed facing the table, wedged in between the two pieces of furniture.

Shouldn't we sing some sort of hymn?' I suggested, recalling the traditional seances that Mother had described to me over the years. It was strange, but I had never even thought to suggest such a thing in the presence of mediums back at the Laboratory.

'Very well,' said Price, looking dubious. 'If you think it is necessary.'

'I for one certainly think that would be appropriate,' said Mrs Smith. 'In times of uncertainty like this, we need divine guidance.' Her husband nodded in agreement.

And so that is what we did, the rector's wife beginning, the rest of us joining in hesitantly:

Abide with me; fast falls the eventide;
The darkness deepens; Lord with me abide.
When other helpers fail and comforts flee,
Help of the helpless, O abide with me.

Swift to its close ebbs out life's little day;
Earth's joys grow dim; its glories pass away;
Change and decay in all around I see;
O Thou who changest not, abide with me.[1]

'Very good,' said Price quietly. 'Now join hands, please, fingertips touching.'

We did so. *Mother would be proud of me*, I thought, fully aware of the irony of this situation. To be honest I was a little embarrassed, but I was also curious and – after the incident outside and the falling brick and drop in temperature about the house – afraid. Was I foolish to have agreed to this? To have pushed Price into proceeding when it was obvious he would have preferred to spend more time questioning witnesses and searching the house for intruders.

'Miss Grey, are you all right?'

Wall's concerned voice cut across my thoughts.

'I address whatever intelligence may be present,' Price interjected, frowning at him. 'If any presence is here with us tonight and wishes to do so then please come forward and make yourself known to us.'

No sound followed, only the gentle spitting of the rain against the window.

'I ask again. If there is anyone present in this house, unseen to us but who wishes to communicate with us, please come forward now and make yourself known.'

And so we waited, the minutes passing like hours.

By the time the clock downstairs in the hall chimed half past eleven I had concluded we were wasting our time and would be better to retire to bed. However, before I could suggest as much there came, quite suddenly, a decisive tapping from the window. It was faint at first but as the seconds passed it grew louder.

'Do you hear that?' Mrs Smith whispered, her eyes wide. 'Tell me you do!'

'I should say so,' said Wall, standing. He went over to the window and pressed his ear against it.

'Come here and sit back down,' scolded Price. 'We should all be joined if we're to do this properly.'

Wall did as he was told, throwing Price a resentful look as he sat down on the bed next to me.

'Now then, I will repeat the question. One. More. Time.'

After he had spoken we waited, hushed and tense. This time within seconds of Price's question I noticed a shift in the atmosphere. The door was shut firmly and there were no windows open to account for the draught that sprang up, and from the far corner of the room shadows were encroaching on us, pooling around the bed and the table until I was convinced they would surely envelop us. Among the shadows was a sprinkling of tiny blue lights.

'Do you see that?' I whispered.

'I do,' said Wall, amazed.

I gasped at a sudden gust of cold air. The light from our storm lantern flickered; the candle that Mrs Smith had brought into the room spluttered and died. And with our hands resting flat on the table in front of us, each touching our neighbours', we waited for our world to meet the next.

The sound came again, just seconds later. 'It's coming from the back of the mirror,' Mrs Smith whispered. We all leaned away from the dressing table.

'All right then,' said Price slowly, his eyes ablaze with interest. 'Now we will proceed according to the following code. As you answer my questions, one rap means no, two raps means you are not certain, three means yes. Do you understand?'

Three decisive raps rang out. How can I describe them? Deliberate but quick, low and steady, as if someone behind the mirror were rapping their knuckles on its wooden backing.

'Very well then,' Price said somewhat hesitantly, 'are you the one who is responsible for the events in this house this evening, throwing stones, ringing bells and suchlike?'

We waited another minute. Then another.

Rap!

'Thank you. That's a no, then. Are you the nun that has been seen in the grounds of this house?'

No.

'Have you ever lived in this house?'

Rap . . . rap . . . rap!

'A yes. Are we in communication with the late rector, Mr Harry Bull?'

Yes!

At this, Mrs Smith pulled her hands away from the table and covered her mouth. 'This . . . this is all quite unbelievable,' she said, turning to her husband and myself. Her face was taut with alarm. 'This is all . . . *new*. We've never experienced anything quite like this here before. Mr Price, you seem to attract these phenomena.'

'Quiet, please,' said Price gently. The rector, who himself looked dumbstruck, took his wife's arm and squeezed it reassuringly.

Price continued. 'Hello, Mr Bull. We are grateful that you are able to join us. Quite a night we are having in your old house! In order that we may confirm your identify, would you please remind us how many members of your family lived here in the Rectory when you were alive?'

We counted nineteen raps, and Mrs Smith, who had researched the Bull family history thoroughly for her novel, nodded and said, 'Yes, I think that's correct, nineteen. Go on – quickly, ask him more.'

'And did your old friend, David Chipp, ever visit?'

Yes.

'Mr Bull, we have heard now, from many sources, about the apparition of a nun, which, it is said, patrols the grounds of this house; that during your lifetime, the phantom would peer in at you and your family as you took supper in the dining room. Are these stories true?'

Yes.

'Then tell us this, please. Does the nun pose any danger to us or to the people living in this house?'

Yes.

'Are you able to tell us the identity of this nun, or explain to us why she haunts this place?'

At this point Wall was scribbling frantically in his notepad and I could see from the confusion on his determined face that he was eager to discover how the discarnate entity was to convey the meaning of words to our party through raps alone. We did so in the laborious manner normally used by Spiritualists, and not usually encouraged by psychical researchers, by saying aloud each letter of the alphabet and making a note of those which coincided with a rap.

Letters were spelt out: *D-E-C-E.*

'What is that word? A date? December? The date of your death perhaps?'

Mrs Smith shook her head as Price dimmed our paraffin lamp before lighting it again. He did so a few times throughout the proceedings, claiming it was necessary in order to provoke the entity into responding.

Then more letters, a name this time: C-A-R-L-O-S.

'It's the same name I heard whispered in one of the bedroom passages,' said Reverend Smith. 'Perhaps it was a pet name for the rector when he was alive.'

Although Mrs Smith was nodding, I thought this explanation was rather clutching at straws and suspected Price did too, but we recorded the information nonetheless.

'I am sorry, Mr Bull, but we don't understand. Is there something that you wish to tell us?'

Yes.

'Does the matter concern this house?'

Yes.

'Are we in any danger from being here?'

Yes.

Then came five more letters. The word they spelt was unmistakable: C-U-R-S-E.

'Are you trying to tell us that there is a . . . a curse connected with the story of the Dark Woman?'

Yes.

And now more letters were coming through: D-E-C-E.

'I apologise, Mr Bull,' said Price, 'but we cannot understand that last word.'

'Then ask him something else,' said Wall impatiently, flipping over his notepad to begin writing on a fresh side of paper. 'Ask him about his death!'

'No,' said Reverend Smith firmly.

Wall interjected again. 'Mr Bull, you are obviously troubled. Please tell us, is there anything that you wish to communicate about the circumstances of your own passing?'

Yes.

'His wife, Ivy, was with him when he died,' Mrs Smith added, her voice low. Her face lifted as if a thought had come to her. 'She married into the family and was never much liked by the rest of them. Mr Bull, does the matter of your unrest pertain to your will by any chance?'

Yes.

Reverend Smith shifted uncomfortably. 'Mr Price, I think it would be best to draw this affair to a close.'

'I agree.'

'No, no,' said Wall, 'we must continue now. Mr Bull, was there money trouble?'

'Mr Wall, please!' interrupted Reverend Smith.

But the answer that came back was a definite 'yes'.

Wall's eyes were gleaming. His prize was in sight. 'Mr Bull, tell us, please – were you murdered?'

Yes.

'Are you able to tell us who killed you?'

Yes.

'Stop this now!' cried the rector, horrified.

'Then do so now. Tell us, Mr Bull, please tell us – who killed you? Was it a friend?'

No.

'A family member then? Ivy, your wife? Mr Bull, was it Ivy who ended your life with the sugar of lead found in the cellar?'

'Mr Wall!' Reverend Smith was appalled.

There was a long pause. Then finally they came: three definite raps.

'I knew it!' Mrs Smith cried.

Price and I leapt to our feet. Was it the answer that had startled us? No. It was the cake of soap that had jumped off the washstand on the opposite side of the room seconds afterwards, hurling itself against the wall.

'I've never seen anything like it,' said Price with wonderment, shaking his head. 'Such propulsion. Look! The cake is deeply dented where it struck the edge of the water ewer in its fall. Quite the most perfect poltergeist phenomenon I have ever seen.'

As if to challenge the assertion there came, rising from somewhere deep below us in the house, the shrill tinkle of a bell.

Wall stood up so suddenly I almost jumped. 'Here we go,' he said quietly, his face incredulous. 'What's this? More trouble?'

More bells joined the chorus – many bells.

'Great heavens above!' exclaimed Mrs Smith.

The rector regarded Wall with the gravest of expressions. 'I do believe you may get your newspaper story, my boy.'

Now it sounded as though every dusty room of that house was occupied with impatient guests tugging urgently on the bell pull. We knew that was impossible, because but for the five of us the house was empty, and all the bell wires had been severed.

Wasting no time, Price quickly took charge, hurtling past Wall and me, out of the bedroom and down the great stairs. 'This time we'll catch them, by Jove!' he bellowed above the clamour. 'Follow me!'

By now only a very small part of me believed there could be a logical explanation for this phenomenon. Indeed, upon reaching the kitchen passage we saw to our amazement and mounting unease that every one of the bells above our heads was ringing furiously of its own volition.

Mrs Smith, her husband at her side, had her hands pressed

to her ears. 'It's never been this loud before!' Reverend Smith shouted to Price. 'Your arrival in this house has only made things worse!'

Price meanwhile was frozen, his eyes darting this way and that as the world of science and order that he so cherished crumbled around him. Finally, he sprang into life. 'Come with me!' he ordered, taking my hand and leading us all back into the main hall. Then he was off, bounding back upstairs, checking the Blue Room for the intruders he was convinced must be doing this while I waited nervously at the foot of the great staircase. He had not been gone a few moments before Wall dashed after him, and it was a good two or three minutes before both men reappeared on the landing. I had never seen my employer look so thoroughly bemused. His face was white. This time even he was out of his depth.

The bells rang harder and louder.

'Mr Price, please do something!' Reverend Smith implored.

'I warned you!' Price shouted.

Both men were hurrying down the staircase when an object – I did not see what it was immediately – hurtled past them, missing Price by an inch or so. The missile flew past Wall towards me. I jumped aside, dodging it just in time. It landed with a crash near me and shattered into pieces.

Mrs Smith recognised it instantly. 'A candlestick, one of the pair on the mantelpiece in the Blue Room!' she squeaked as she backed into a far corner of the hall. Mr Smith followed suit, taking a protective place beside her.

I looked up fearfully, my hands over my ears to keep out the terrible noise of the bells, and saw Price standing halfway down the staircase. 'Right!' he cried, dashing down towards us. He landed in the hall with a graceful twirl and sped to the Rectory's front door. I thought he might throw it open to usher us all out of the house, but instead he stood firm and addressed the very air around us. 'I speak to address whatever intelligence or force is producing this noise!' he boomed.

At the instant the keys in the doors of the drawing room and library flew out of their keyholes onto the floor.

'That's impossible!' Price cried, looking around him.

But the racket of bells continued – almost, I thought, with greater ferocity.

Price was undeterred. 'Hear me now, spirits! Whatever your reasons for remaining in this Rectory, whatever the cause of your unrest, I must remind you that this is a house of *God*,' he snarled, 'and the lady and gentleman who are the present occupants of this home are good, loving, religious people, whose peace and patience and health are now under intolerable strain. Whoever you are – *whatever* you are – I command silence!'

A series of objects came tumbling down the staircase – first a mothball, then a hairbrush and some pebbles.

'Reverend Smith, give me your crucifix,' Price demanded.

'Whatever for, sir?'

'You know what for! Now don't argue – just let me have it.'

I sensed from Mr Smith's troubled face that he was unconvinced by this idea, but that didn't prevent him from slipping the small crucifix he wore round his neck over his head and handing it to my employer. Price stepped forward, then holding the symbol aloft, cried out: 'Saint Michael the Archangel, defend us in our battle against the world of darkness, against the spirits of wickedness. The sacred sign of the cross commands silence. *I will have it!*'

All at once the house was still again. Only the sound of rain hissing at the window remained.

'Remarkable,' Price muttered under his breath. 'I didn't actually expect that to work.'

The rector and his wife stood against the wall, wrapped in each other's arms. Only Wall moved, in the direction of the main door.

'Where are you going?' I asked.

'I have to get down to the nearest town and write all this up for tomorrow's edition.'

'At this hour?' I checked my wristwatch. 'But it's after midnight.'

'Absolutely! Someone has to report what has happened here.' He looked at me with concern. 'Please, won't you come with me, Miss Grey?'

'I . . .'

'Sarah will stay here tonight,' said Price sharply.

Wall's tone was challenging. 'I am sure the lady is capable of answering for herself.'

I should have been. But I was torn. When I look back, I realise that so much of what was to come began at that moment. I looked at Price, registered those wonderful eyes of his, remembered the opportunity he had given me, the financial help he had offered to the family of a dying girl he had never met, and realised I could not leave him – not now, when so much seemed within our reach. The rector and his wife looked away, embarrassed as the two men waited for my answer. 'My decision is to stay and help,' I said eventually, 'as we promised Reverend and Mrs Smith we would.'

'Very well,' said Wall, his face hardening. With a pang, I realised that I had offended him deeply. I'm sure now he thought I was foolish, and I probably was. 'I must be off.'

'Wait a moment,' Price ordered, his heavy eyebrows pulled

tightly together. 'I don't know what you're intending to write but I must insist your article does not refer in any part to the details of tonight's proceedings.'

'You can't be serious!'

'I am perfectly serious,' said Price. 'What we have just witnessed – although, I admit, fascinating – demands much closer examination before we can even think of making these details public.'

Wall took a deliberate step towards Price.

Undaunted, Price continued: 'The accusation relayed to us during the seance upstairs is a very serious charge, very serious indeed, and one that cannot be verified, least of all by us. You cannot make that information public, not under any circumstances.'

'Why not?'

'Because at best the evidence is unreliable, and at worst it is slanderous. Is that what you want, Mr Wall? A legal case against your' – he smiled, wryly – 'good name?'

I dropped my gaze but still felt Wall's incredulous eyes on me. 'Sarah, you don't agree with this ludicrous censorship, do you?'

'I . . .'

'My God! I brought you this case. You wouldn't be in this house if it wasn't for me.'

Price let out a sarcastic laugh. 'You and your lazy hyperbole. Yes, lazy! Like so many other young men these days.'

Wall's face flushed with anger. He moved towards Price slowly and with purpose, until they were only inches apart. 'Yes, there are plenty of men out of work. Plenty of healthy, competent men, who want to work and can't. They're neither dishonest nor idle, just unlucky. Because they were brave. If the General Strike taught us anything, it's that men want to do a hard day's work. I'm lucky, but I need to work. And I need this story.'

'Yes,' Price said softly. 'I'm quite sure that you do.'

'This is how it works then, is it? You can't generate any fantastic stories of your own, so you have to steal from other people. Mr Price, without this story I'll be back on a local rag somewhere, covering funerals.'

Price's gaze was frosty. 'That is not my concern, Mr Wall. But your concern, your *only* concern, is to report the basics of this case and nothing else. Do I make myself clear?'

'Perfectly. It's all very convenient for you, Mr Price. You get what you need, and I get nothing.'

'Need? What does he mean, Mr Price?' the rector asked. 'What is it that you need?'

'Ah now . . . Didn't you know, Mr Smith?' said Wall acidly. 'Our intrepid ghost hunter here is in something of a pickle; unless he returns to London with some exciting news to feed their hopes, every one of the Spiritualists who help fund his work will be shutting their doors against him. It's all rather convenient, don't you agree, Mr Price? That you should suddenly find what you've been looking for?'

Wall stood silently a moment longer, challenging Price with the fiercest of stares. I got the distinct impression that he knew something he hadn't yet mentioned and was struggling now to contain. Then he said, slowly and deliberately, 'This rascal thrives on bringing order to chaos and where there isn't enough chaos, he feels compelled to create it.'

Eventually my employer said, 'I take my work extremely seriously and I resent any insinuation against its veracity. I am asking – no, *insisting* – that you report what has happened here tonight with sensitivity and discretion. By all means report the basic facts of the matter, but for the sake of the Bull family – if no one else – leave it at that, or the damage you inflict could be irreparable. Do you understand?'

Ignoring Price, Wall turned to me and said, 'Do you think you'll ever stop, Sarah?'

'Stop what?'

'Following him.'

The words wounded me and I reached for him as he marched towards the front door and through it into the howling night. 'You can't possibly go out there!' I called after him. But the front door was now wide open, drawing in upon us the blast of wind and rain. 'Vernon!' I cried.

He looked back at me across the hall, his expression a mixture of anger, confusion and hurt, the same conflicting emotions that at that moment were washing through me.

'How could you do this?' he shouted. 'Side with him, when he is so clearly wrong! For God's sake, woman, I brought you here . . . I needed this!'

I moved towards him. 'Vernon, I—'

He raised his hand to stop me. Behind him, visible through the open door, lightning flashed. 'This house has its secrets, like everyone in it! You, me, even him. Can't you see what he's doing? I saw—'

'You saw what?' I cried. 'The nun? Something else?'

Wall hesitated, glanced at Price and said, 'You're a monster.' Then, fixing me with one last stare of disappointment, the young reporter turned on his heel and strode out into the night.

I stood perfectly still, helpless, as the front door slammed shut on any friendship I might have enjoyed with him.

As soon as he had gone my head dropped to my chest. It was bizarre that suddenly, without him, I should want him all the more. I contemplated following him, but what could I say to excuse my actions? And what about Price? This man was my employer, and the closest thing to a father figure I had known. I couldn't just walk out on him, especially as I had promised him that he could trust me. The last thing I wanted was to see him slip back into one of his depressions. If the bizarre events we had just witnessed – I cringed at even entertaining the notion of genuine ghosts – had impressed me, I knew they would have impressed Price too and that he would want to convey the fact to the widest possible audience. And the moment he did that, an army of critics would rush to attack him, driven by envy. He would need me to help him stave off such attacks, to protect his work and that of the Laboratory. Everyone would have to know what had happened here and the importance of Price's role in the matter. I needed to believe that his involvement had made a difference and would continue to do so because I was all too aware that this was Wall's story.

Looking back, it was inevitable that I would compare Wall with Price. Clearly, I didn't know much about how to handle difficult, ambitious men.

I thought of Wall's cautious warnings, his touching affection for me, his desire to ensure my well-being and the peculiar way he had made me feel.

Price's voice, stern and commanding, jolted me back into the hallway. 'Listen.'

'I don't hear anything,' I said.

He nodded. 'Precisely. The house is calmer now. I suggest we all get some sleep.'

I was relieved to hear that. The rector shot me a troubled look and offered to bless our rooms one more time. Politely, I agreed.

We went back to the Blue Room, where Price was to sleep, but he noticed immediately that there was something amiss. We all followed his gaze to the pillow on the bed, the same pillow on which his head was shortly to rest. Something like a large coin lay there, glinting in the fitful light thrown off by the storm lantern. I was sure it hadn't been there before.

Price picked it up, holding it up to the dancing light of his lamp. 'It appears to be some sort of medallion,' he said slowly, studying it. 'French, I should say and very, very old. Minted in brass, I think.'

'But where did it come from?' asked Reverend Smith, frowning.

Price's eyes met mine. 'It's an apport, Sarah,' he said. 'It must be.' And a smile spread across his face.

Reverend Smith looked lost. 'Apport?'

An apport, I explained to the rector, is an object produced by apparently supernatural means.[2] Such things were usually the focus of the controlled seances we conducted back at the Laboratory, when flowers, jewellery and sometimes even live animals would 'materialise' in the presence of a medium. Never had we encountered a genuine manifestation of the phenomenon; every alleged manifestation we had witnessed had been debunked as the product of fraud.

'May I see?' I asked. Upon inspection, I observed that the medallion was octagonal, bearing on one side the head of a monkish-looking figure and the inscription '*Vade retro me, satana*' On the other side of the medallion was the word *ROMA*, meaning Rome, which appeared beneath a design incorporating two impressive-looking human figures joined by a child. With the rector's help we quickly deduced that the medal was probably Roman Catholic in origin. It was chilling to the touch. And I hated it immediately.

The rector was bewildered. 'Whatever do you suppose it means, Mr Price?'

'Perhaps it's a clue, Mr Smith, to this whole peculiar business.'

With unmistakable relish, Price closed his hand around the medallion, a faint smile playing on his lips.

*

Although the summer storm soon passed, I slept fitfully that night, my bedroom serving both as a sanctuary from the rest of the house and as a prison.

The medallion we had found was lying next to my bed. Price had given it to me for safe keeping, but just knowing it was there in the room with me had destroyed any hopes of rest. We had heard the legends that connected the ghostly nun with a vague, monk-like figure and claims that the Rectory stood on the site of a thirteenth-century monastery, so this much made sense, but I failed to see how this English historical background connected with the French Catholic theme suggested by the medallion's other engravings. I decided I would have it examined the instant we returned to London.

The sun had not yet risen when a sound from outside my door stirred me from my slumber. As I rubbed the sleep from my eyes, I became increasingly aware of padding feet approaching my bedroom. Alert, I pulled the musty bedclothes up to my face and sheltered behind them. There came a gentle rap on my door.

Sitting up, I waited, hoping to God the sound wouldn't come again. But it did, louder this time. What was it Professor David Chipp had said about his stay in the house? That something in his room had pinned his shirt to the back of the door. *This room . . . ?* I speculated. *Was it this room?*

My heart was pounding. Alone, with the knowledge of what

had happened earlier that night weighing upon me, the image of Harry Bull from the painting in the Blue Room loomed up in my mind.

And then, to my horror, I saw the door handle turning. It clicked, and the door swung slowly open. A swaying light entered the room; behind it, only just visible in the gloom, was a pale face with huge black eyes.

The sight of it made me cry out in alarm.

'Shhh. Sarah, quiet now. It's me.'

'Harry?'

He shut the door.

'I can't sleep,' he said wearily, 'and my head feels ghastly.'

Price was prone to vicious migraines and it seemed that one was upon him now. In the flickering candlelight I saw that black patches had formed under his eyes, his cheeks were sallow and his high brow glistened with sweat.

'I want to get out of here, Sarah,' he groaned. 'I don't feel at all well. Let's go, now!'

'What?' I exclaimed. 'At this hour?'

He nodded and asked whether I would be willing to drive him back into Sudbury to catch an early train to Liverpool Street. Then he glanced back over his shoulder in the direction of the Blue Room. 'And I certainly don't want to go back in there.'

'Harry, you silly goose! We can't just leave. Poor Mrs Smith will wonder what has become of us.'

'We'll leave a note,' he said briskly.

'What time is it now?'

He sat down on the end of my bed, rubbing his eyes. 'A little after two.'

'A fiendish hour.' I thought of the labyrinth-like network of lanes we would need to traverse to find our way back. 'Harry, no, please just wait another hour. If you're still desperate to leave then, I'll come with you. But it's far too early to leave now; there won't be any trains at this hour anyway, not even the milk trains.'

I saw from his reaction that he did not approve of my suggestion, but he knew me well enough to realise that I was not going to be bullied into this.

'Very well,' he said bleakly, 'I'll go back to my room.' He stood up and turned to leave.

'Harry, wait a moment.'

'What is it?'

He looked down at me, his face still half-obscured in the shadows, and I searched his eyes for any hint that the same thought that was running through my own mind might be in his. I think he must have known that I did not want to be left alone in that room, but if he did, then he showed no sign of it. 'Nothing,' I replied quietly. 'You should get back to your room now.'

I'm uncertain that the words convinced me, let alone him. I lay there, cold and miserable, as he crept back out onto the landing. Before closing my door, he turned and looked back at me.

'Sarah?' he whispered.

'Yes?'

'Thank you.'

'What for?'

'For being the wonderful friend that you are.'

'Oh,' I said, closing my eyes, 'think nothing of it. Now be off with you!'

'Come and wake me in an hour or two, all right?'

'I will do. If I'm awake!'

He nodded and said softly, 'Goodnight, Sarah.'

'Goodnight.'

Long after those lonely words were spoken, my thoughts dwelt on the mercurial Harry Price. Then I remembered Vernon Wall, wondering whether he had made it back to the Bull Inn on his own, and confusion enveloped me.

If you have ever found yourself torn between two impossible options, one complicated but exciting, the other easy, so easy, and yet puzzlingly dull, then you'll have some idea of how I felt at that moment.

How sad it is, I thought as I willed myself back to sleep, that we love what is hard and run from what is easy, and only look back when it is finally too late.

SÉANCE HELD IN HAUNTED HOUSE

Mysterious Rappings in the Rectory of Borley

'FORMER RECTOR'
HOW QUESTIONS WERE ASKED AND ANSWERED
From Our Special Correspondent, Long Melford, Friday

An informal séance at the 'haunted' Borley Rectory, as a preliminary to an orthodox one with a medium, produced astonishing results.

This took place in the presence of the rector and his wife, Mr Harry Price, Director of the National Laboratory of Psychical Research, his secretary, and myself.

Mysterious replies to our questions were given by means of one, two and three raps on the back of a mirror in the room.

Light in the room made no difference.

The replies came clearly and distinctly. At times we lit the lamp and sat around the mirror with everyone in the room in full sight, but there was no hesitation about the answers.

EMPHATIC 'YES'

The only unsatisfactory feature was our inability to get a complete message by spelling out words; the 'spirit' was either a bad speller or speaking in Hindu.

Our first attempts were naturally to ascertain the identity of the rapper. We asked if it were the nun in the old legend or one of the grooms, and a single rap denoting 'no' was the reply.

Then I suggested to Mr Price that he should ask if it were the Reverend H. Bull, the late rector. I had hardly finished the name when three hurried raps came on the mirror, which meant an emphatic 'yes'.

The following dialogue then took place, sometimes with the lamp lit, sometimes in darkness: 'Is it your footsteps once heard in this house?'

'Yes.'

'Do you wish to worry or annoy anybody here?'

'No.'

'Do you object to anybody now living in the house?'

'No.'

SMOKING DURING SEANCE

'Do you merely wish to attract attention?'

'Yes.'

'Are you worrying about something you should have done when you were alive?'

'No.'

'If we had a medium here, do you think you could tell us what is the matter?'

'Yes.'

There followed a series of questions dealing with the late Mr Bull's private affairs, to which no answer at all was received.

The whole proceeding was entirely informal, and we even smoked and chatted as if we were in the Rectory drawing room instead of the room that is supposed to be haunted.

The worst part about these 'manifestations', from the rector's point of view, is that Borley is fast becoming a show place for the whole of Suffolk and Essex.

Crowds of visitors arrive on foot and by motor car to see the alleged haunted house.[3]

Notes

1   Henry F. Lyte, 1847.

2   Apport phenomena were first observed by Dr G. P. Billot. In *Recherches psychologiques ou correspondence sur le magnetisme vital entre un solitaire et M. Delcuzo* (Paris, 1839), he describes a session on 5 March 1819 with three somnambules and a blind woman. He writes: 'Towards the middle of the seance, one of the seeresses exclaimed: "There is the Dove, it is white as snow, it is flying about the room with something in its beak, it is a piece of paper. Let us pray." A few moments later she added: "See, it has let the paper drop at the feet of Madame J." Billot saw a paper packet at the spot indicated. He found in it three small pieces of bone glued on to small strips of paper, with the words 'St Maxime, St Sabine and Many Martyrs' written beneath the fragments.'

3   *Daily Mirror*, 15 June 1929.

– 18 –

THE BREEDING OF SECRETS

'You slept well, I hope?' From across the breakfast table, Mrs Smith's gaze swept from Price to me, then back to Price, as I buttered a slice of blackened toast.

'As well as can be expected,' I muttered.

'Well, I hope it was warm enough for you, Mr Price.'

'I slept with my clothes *on*, Mrs Smith. Absolutely nothing could have induced me to get undressed in *that* bedroom.'

I allowed myself the tiniest of smiles.

Since sunrise, Price had complained about a pain in his arm. He was keen to return to London, but I persuaded him that we should at least call upon Miss Ethel Bull and hear for ourselves her account of the ghostly nun. We might have done just that too, were it not for the unruly disturbance which suddenly broke the morning peace: men's voices, loud and accusatory, outside the house.

'Infernal racket!' Mr Smith cried, standing up. 'Whatever next?'

We followed the Smiths briskly through the hall and out on to the gravel driveway, whereupon Harry cried, 'Sarah, look out!'

An empty wine bottle hurtled past and shattered next to the front door.

'What the hell do you think you're doing?' raged Price, coming to my side.

His question was directed at a mob of youths and labourers, all rather odd-looking people, who had gathered at the main gates to the property. 'Leave us in peace!' one of them shouted. Another was brandishing a pickaxe.

'There we are,' said Price to Reverend Smith. 'Vernon Wall's gift to you, sir. They've come. And they'll keep coming until they get what they want.'

'Well, what *do* they want?'

'The truth. Or at least their version of the truth.'

With alarm rattling his words, the rector turned to me. 'My dear, do you think you could drive to the police station and summon some protection for us?'

'But of course,' said Price. 'It's the very least we can do.' Though somewhere between bidding farewell to the Smiths and unlatching the gate and driving down into Long Melford he changed his mind and asked me to stop the vehicle. 'You go, Sarah. I'll get the train.'

'But what about our visit to Miss Bull?'

'It's only two stops away. I'll call on her on my way.'

'Harry, this is ridiculous! What's wrong?'

The passenger door slammed behind him.

'So I'll see you back in London, Harry?'

He nodded once, but did not look back.

*

Feeling genuinely concerned for the Smiths, who I imagined were still stranded on the rectory lawn beating away the milling intruders, I drove at speed to the nearest police station, where the local constable reassured me a colleague was already en route for Borley.

Even so, the least I could do was find Vernon Wall at the Bull Inn and ask him to respect the Smiths' privacy in his future writings. I also wanted to see him for personal reasons.

'Sorry, Miss, 'fraid you missed 'im,' said the stocky woman on reception at the ancient Bull Inn. Her gaze lingered uncomfortably around my neckline. 'He not long left for the early train for London.'

God, I thought, *please not the same train as Price!* That wouldn't be pretty.

'You all right, Miss? You look a bit funny. Cup of tea, maybe?'

Trying to ignore her greasy hair and a lingering scent of musk, I told the receptionist I would like that very much and took a seat in the front bar beneath crooked timbered ceilings next to the widest stone fireplace I had ever seen. As I gazed out through the window at Price's cherished saloon, memories of the preceding night's affair swirled down upon me.

I had gone to his bedroom, as he had requested, at a frightfully early hour and found him – as I knew I would – fast asleep. This is embarrassing to admit, but instead of returning to my room I sat for a time watching him sleep in milky darkness; watching the rhythmic rise and fall of his wide chest beneath the sheets, difficult to see but oddly gratifying.

He must have heard me because soon afterwards his eyes flew open, his face grimacing with alarm. Then his vision adjusted, he recognised me, and his face melted into a mask of warm appreciation.

'I'm Ruth, by the way.'

The husky voice pulled me back to the Bull Inn with its leaded windows and suits of armour. From the corridor which presumably led down to the kitchen I caught a scent of bacon and eggs. Apart from the burnt toast I hadn't eaten anything that morning, and now pangs of hunger were pulling at me. I considered ordering something, but the broad-faced woman from reception who had returned with a wide tea tray was clearly more interested in the saloon just beyond the window than in serving me. 'That fancy motor car belong to you, does it?'

'My friend, actually. I'm looking after it for him.'

She nodded, laying the tea tray in front of me. 'Don't get many cars like that round 'ere, that's for sure. Only the big families like the Bulls 'ave 'em.'

My ears pricked up. 'You knew the Bull family?'

'Aye! Most round 'ere did. Best thing they ever did, leavin' that damned old house.'

'Borley Rectory?'

She nodded. 'Few people round here talkin' 'bout anything else, not since 'em reports of ghosts in the papers. Mike Oldman in town's thinkin' of startin' one of 'em tour buses, you know? Reckons he can make a few bob. Wouldn't catch me goin' up there, I can tell you.'

'You believe the stories, then?'

'Believe would be puttin' it a bit strong,' she said, catching herself, 'but you do hear some tales, horrid stories of somethin' that walks in the grounds of that place . . . Some years back there was a man who came into town, said he knew the Bulls, was at university with one of the family. He stayed here, in fact, in the room over the hall – said he was the headmaster of some posh school somewhere.'

I wondered if it was David Chipp, the academic who had written to us a few years before. 'Do you remember his name?'

She hesitated, casting her mind back. 'No. But I do remember him saying he wanted to spend a night up there, parked in the lane next to the Rectory, outside the church.' She shook her head. 'What a mistake that was.'

'He saw something?'

'Not saw exactly . . .' My informant clenched her jaw. 'When he came here, he had some dogs with him – two Labradors. Beautiful beasts they were. He took them to Borely. Had them sat in the back of his car as he slept through the night.'

I tried to guess what happened next. 'They started barking and woke him up?'

'No, Miss.' And now her face lost any trace of ease and her tone became grave. 'Because by mornin' there weren't any dogs left to bark. They were gone, completely gone – vanished they did, from right out of the car.'

I wanted to tell her that the story sounded impossible, that nothing just disappears. But the events of the preceding evening were beginning to alter my own conceptions of possibility.

'I heard rumours that *this* hotel is haunted too.'

'Here? haunted?' she cried. 'Why, it's alive, dear! You just try talkin' to the chambermaids, they've seen all manner of happ'nings – taps turnin' on, doors slammin, you name it.'

'What's that?' I asked, nodding to a large carving of a wild man with a beard on the opposite wall.

'The Woodwose,' said Ruth. 'Wards off evil spirits.' She startled me with a laugh. 'Or meant to – doesn't work very well, does it!'

At that instant there came a terrific bang from outside, so loud I dropped my tea. Heart skipping a beat, I raised my head and looked out through the window. 'Good God! Who the devil are they?' I hardly dared take my eyes off the two coarse-featured men who were crossing the road towards the saloon. One of them was short and loud and swearing profanities from under a twitching moustache.

The other was carrying a shotgun.

'Quickly!' I said, darting to the door.

'No, Miss – it's not safe!'

But I was already striding out into the hallway and unlatching the front door.

'This yours, is it?' The man with the moustache addressed me. He was standing next to the saloon, face purple with rage.

'If either of you so much as *scratch* that motor car, then you'll have me to answer to!'

He blinked. Hesitated. Then: 'Our quarrel's not with you. It's 'im we want – that scoundrel Harry Price!'

'Then I'm sorry, but your quarrel is indeed with me.' I took another step forward. 'I demand that you put down that silly weapon immediately.'

'You've no right speaking to us like that,' said the man, prodding the air with his shotgun. 'You've no place here, prying into our business. None of you. If there are demons in these parts then it'll be us who deals with 'em! Understood?'

'There's only one thing I understand and that, sir, is the insufferable arrogance of men!' I shouted. 'Now, you gentlemen can either stand there like idiots brandishing your weapon at me, or you can make yourselves useful and help me find what I need.'

'Oh yeah?' the man with the moustache grunted. 'And what's that, missy?'

I hesitated, realising the absurdity of the answer I was about to give.

'An antique shop!'

The shape of the ancient brass medallion we had found at the

Rectory hung uneasily in my mind. An unwanted souvenir. Just touching the thing made my hands tingle.

'Well, it is a fine piece indeed,' said the old gentleman I had consulted in his shop in Long Melford. His name, as I recall, was Daniel Weir. He was a quiet, sensitive sort of chap, with grey hair, thick glasses and a heavy brown cardigan. With bony fingers he turned the artefact over, examining it closely through a magnifying glass and paying particular attention – at my request – to the monk-like figure engraved upon its surface. 'Can you identify him for me?' I asked.

Weir nodded. 'Yes, I think so, young lady; this is Saint Ignatius, the founder of the Jesuits or the Society of Jesus. It is said that he was zealous in his attempts to bring people to God and spirituality.'

'But was he a kind man?' I asked, keen to see if this mysterious object possessed any symbolic meaning.

'That depends on which version of history you choose to believe. Ignatius was a loving, godly man, but he was also a soldier – an iron-willed, practical and stern man.

'Saints' medallions, medals and pendants are proclamations of personal faith as well as talismans meant to repel evil. You see this inscription in Latin, "*Vade retro me, satana*"?'

'What does it mean?' I asked.

'It's a phrase derived from Jesus's words to Peter in the Gospel of Saint Mark,' said Weir.

'Yes, but what does it *mean?*'

Weir's voice dropped almost to a whisper. 'The translation is "Get thee behind me, Satan." These words form a medieval Catholic formula for exorcism.'

He paused, turning the medallion over with his fingers, then frowned. 'Miss Grey, this item is at least three or four hundred years old; wherever did you find it?'

'A little place not far from here.'

His eyebrows shot up. 'Medals such as this are not commonly found in England. I was expecting you to name somewhere in Europe – Rome perhaps, or France more likely.'

'Why France?'

'Following the Reformation, medals like this were very popular as gifts between wealthy Catholics, as a symbol of dedication and loyalty to their faith. It was common for the medals to be worn suspended around the neck, as a sacramental object which inspires prayer. That fact alone establishes a theoretical link to bring about spiritual protection, much like the rosary.'

The rosary . . .

'Tell me,' I continued. 'Were these medallions predominantly worn by women?'

Weir fixed my gaze and nodded. 'Yes indeed, Miss Grey – principally they were worn by nuns.'

*

'Harry?' I marched stiffly into his study and, finding it empty, checked for him in the seance room and the workshop. 'Harry?'

No sign of him, but I didn't mind. I felt rejuvenated, more confident. Though I still couldn't fathom why he had left Borley so hurriedly, I knew the case was significant. We had witnessed objects fly about that house, projected by unseen hands. They had been aimed at us, thrown with intent. Yes, it was possible – unlikely but possible – that a telekinetic force from a human mind could produce such an effect, but if the intelligence of man could operate outside the body, at a distance from it, then surely it wasn't a huge leap to deduce that such intelligence could continue to operate once the human body had perished? I intended to suggest as much to Price when I saw him next.

But he didn't come to work that day, or the next day, or the day after that.

A week or two later, always late in the afternoon, the telephone calls started. I assumed at first that they were harmless practical jokes, but by then I hadn't seen Price for days so it was easy to let my anxieties run away with themselves.

'Ask him about his props,' my mystery caller instructed. 'Ask him!'

What props?

'Who is this, please?' I could hear the impatience in my voice. Someone was having a game with me. The caller never gave his name and I spent hours wondering which of Price's many enemies was responsible. Surely not Conan Doyle, I reasoned; he was far too much a gentleman.

'Ask him where he goes.'

'Ask him what he does when he's gone.'

'Ask him about Radley.'

Then nothing but a shallow intake of breath and a click before the line went dead.

Radley? My predecessor. I had asked Price what had happened to him on the morning of my very first day at the Laboratory. What was it Price had said in reply? 'Hard worker, intelligent, but I had to let him go.' Why?

As the months wore on, Price's appearances at the Laboratory became increasingly irregular. My mother had cautioned me that men were very adept at covering their tracks. He might be involved with other ventures I didn't know about – a business, perhaps. I entertained the idea briefly, but it seemed implausible that I would not have known about such activities, and I quickly discounted the notion. But that didn't stop me pressing the matter, especially the phone calls.

'Who do you think it is?' I asked him.

He appeared uninterested, irritated even. 'Probably just someone who misdialled.'

I felt my jaw clench. We both knew it was unlikely that someone would misdial so many times. Why was he being so devious? What was he hiding from me?

'No, actually the caller mentioned you by name a number of times.'

But the more I questioned him, the more he retreated from the world. It became his habit to barricade himself in his study with only his books, his pipe and a strong brandy for company.

It was easy to recognise the signs of depression. I had vivid memories from childhood of my father sitting on the stool at his piano, misty-eyed, staring vacantly at the keys. And when I came to Price one morning in early October, I found him in a very similar state. That morning, unusually, he refused the strong coffee that was usually delivered to his desk at nine o'clock exactly. Similarly, for the rest of the day he could not be distracted by any of his favourite journals or slow assessment of current astrological charts. Lunch, which he always ate in chilly silence, was left untouched. And when I tried to ask him what was wrong he glowered at me.

'Something is wrong, Sarah?' I hadn't heard him use that tone since our hostile exchange during the Velma Crawshaw experiment.

'Wrong?' My response came out like the squeak of a mouse. I found myself longing to reassure him – or was it myself I wanted to reassure? To convince myself that this strange new sensitivity which was creeping over my skin was nothing to do with the almost savage expression on his face.

'No. Nothing is wrong, Harry. I just thought that you—'

'But you are not paid to think.' His words sliced through mine ruthlessly, and I felt the heat of his pain as much as my own.

When Mother asked me – as she frequently did during those months – what it was like at the Laboratory, I'd feel myself burning to tell her just how peculiarly awful Price could be before guilt and my own dignity tempered the urge. *'You know what you'd say to your friends, Sarah, if they were in this situation. You'd tell them to run, wouldn't you? Run away from him; run just as fast as you can!'* During those lonely weeks I became very good at smiling; it was a convincing smile that covered a multitude of sins, some of them my own. Knowing as much pulled on my heart.

The letters and phone calls about Borley Rectory kept coming, yet Price became frosty and changed the subject whenever I mentioned them and on more than one occasion I passed his study and overheard him thundering at someone over the telephone about 'that house'. 'Libel!' he shouted. 'Libel!'

'What is all this about?' I asked him one day, barging into his office. 'What aren't you telling me? You can't just skip over everything that happened in that house, Harry. That's not how it works.'

I think we both knew I was talking about more than the haunting.

All of this ate away at me. When the telephone rang one chilly morning in September, I thoroughly lost my temper. 'Look! Whoever you are, just leave us alone!' I snapped into the receiver.

There was a brief silence and then a well-spoken woman's voice said coldly, 'I do hope that is not your usual telephone manner, Miss Grey?'

I caught my breath.

'I take it I *am* speaking to Miss Sarah Grey?'

'This is she,' I replied. 'Who is this?'

'My name is Constance Price. Harry's wife.'

'Oh.' I sat down, my nerves shredded. 'How nice to speak to you at last. I . . . I don't believe we've ever met, have we?'

'No. We haven't.' Her tone conveyed that she wished to keep it that way. 'This isn't a personal call, Miss Grey. I'm afraid I have some rather bad news. It concerns Harry.'

I felt the grip of fear in my gut. 'What is it? Is he all right? Do you know where he is?'

She took a deep breath. 'I'm sorry to have to tell you this, Miss Grey, but Harry has suffered a heart attack.'

– 19 –

MEMENTO MORI

'Please understand,' I wrote to him in hospital, 'that I never meant to put you under undue pressure. I am wishing you well and a speedy recovery. In the meantime, I am cancelling activities at the Laboratory until your return.'

The message spilled from my pen as my heart was breaking. There was so much I wanted to tell him, to show him, to ask him.

The year of Price's heart attack, the year of his absence, doesn't exist for me in any complete sense. I cannot measure it. The weeks caught me, folded around me. Lonely nights and empty months blew by, with days spent wandering the Yorkshire moors, worrying for those I had left behind – Mother and my best friend Amy, whose life since her wedding was an enviable antithesis of my own. Christmas, which I was dreading, brought no pleasure, and even the simplest comforts were dead to me – the sweet scent of roasted chestnuts or the open fire in the little cottage I had made my temporary home.

Yet all of this was necessary – for Price and for me.

When I returned to London shortly after Easter, I walled myself up within a prison of my own construction, rarely socialising. Until finally, more than a year later, Mother presented me with a letter scrawled in Price's familiar handwriting, beginning with the words 'Dearest Sarah'. Its message was simple: 'Prepare the Laboratory!'

Thank God, he was coming back at last!

I immediately checked all the equipment we would need, ensuring that the seance room was as secure as it could possibly be – absolutely no hidden props! When Price finally returned to work three weeks later, he was clearly impressed with my efforts and the adverts and news releases I had prepared for the newspapers announcing his return. My heart leapt with joy when he appeared at the entrance to my office, his decrepit hat in one hand, a cigarette in the other.

I rushed over and threw my arms around him. 'Harry!'

'My, you have been busy, haven't you?'

'More than you know,' I replied. 'Now, let me look at you!'

Although he was thinner, he did look better; the darkness that had shadowed his features had lifted and he looked brighter, though still businesslike. There was so much I hadn't told him, so much I wanted to tell him.

So much I should have told him.

'How are things at home, Sarah? You look different somehow.' He hesitated. 'Is everything well?'

The question came tentatively, as if he were afraid of my answer.

'Things could be worse.' I hesitated, catching myself. 'They're better now.'

'Good.' He smiled with relief, yet I sensed he was only half convinced. 'And your Mother? She's well too, I trust?'

'As a matter of fact, she's much improved.' And, to my relief, so was our house. There was a fine radio in the kitchen and in the drawing room a new, comfortable armchair. 'I had worried how she would cope after the stock market crash, but when I was away she started doing household chores for one of our neighbours in Gloucester Street.'

'Did she indeed?' The trace of a smile appeared on his lips. He edged nearer, laid his rough hand over mine. 'I know how difficult things must have been for you . . . what with . . . me not being here . . .'

I had been grieving for weeks, months. But once I had returned, so too did my enthusiasm. Later that day, I told him everything I had learned about the medallion we had found at Borley. 'All right, yes,' he said nonchalantly. 'We'll get round to that.'

'Aren't you intrigued, Harry?'

Although pleased to see him back at work, I was concerned to notice him grow quiet, his face grey and unsettled as he gazed absently into the middle distance. He had spoken briefly of his old friend, the medium Velma Crawshaw. He said she wasn't well, that her prospects weren't good, and if that were true I wondered how he would ever forgive himself for betraying her over the locked box affair.

'You seem distracted. Do you think perhaps you should go home, Harry? Get some rest?'

'Rest? Certainly not!' He waved a handful of papers at me. 'In just four months we're to be visited by Rudi Schneider at long last! The opportunity to test one of the most talked about mediums in Europe. There's no time to rest!'

'Schneider? But Harry, there are bags of letters about the Rectory. Surely we ought to capitalise on that interest?'

'No, no,' he said with a flick of his hand. 'I'll write up the case for the *Psychic Review*. That ought to keep people interested.'

Baffled, I sensed he wanted to drop the matter. And then I saw the note in his hand. 'What's that?'

His eyes flickered with watchful uncertainty. 'A letter from Sir Arthur Conan Doyle, accusing me of an intolerable indulgence of 'false and clumsy ridicule' against the president of the Spiritualist Alliance.'

'Harry, in the name of the Almighty!' I scolded. 'What were you thinking? They're the very people funding our work. We need them on own side!'

Price gave me a wounded look. 'And whose side are you on, Sarah?'

'Yours, of course! But you have to—'

'I'll write back!' he said, suddenly angry. 'I'll tell him he's thin-skinned; that most of his followers regard his doings and sayings as a joke.'

'You can't possibly do that!'

But he did, of course, and within a week the Spiritualist Alliance retaliated, threatening us with an eviction order.

'I told you,' I said, watching Price's brooding expression. 'You've really started something now, Harry. This public hostility towards the Spiritualists must stop, do you hear?'

'But don't you see?' he said. 'This is precisely why we must focus our efforts on Herr Schneider. When the Spiritualists hear that he is coming here to perform for us, they're bound to be satisfied.'

Perform? What an odd choice of word. 'Harry, he's not some sort of monkey.'

'Sarah, honestly . . . These experiments – if successful – will catapult us to new heights.' He gave me his warmest smile. 'And when this dreadful depression is over and the economy recovers we'll go on a little trip, just you and me. To Germany perhaps, or France.'

That made me smile. He had no idea how much I needed that smile – or perhaps he did.

I took hold of his arm. 'You need to slow down, Harry. And you need to open your eyes. Sometimes . . . the things that are best for you, the things that can help you the most, are a great deal nearer than you think.'

His finger flew to my lips. 'Now then,' he said softly, 'let us press on with what we have to do. Because it all depends on you now, Sarah.'

'What does?'

'Our future, together. The Laboratory, this quest we're both on.'

He seemed to be right, because shortly after that Conan Doyle resumed writing with letters beginning 'Dear Price' as opposed to the frosty 'Dear Sir' we had come to expect. 'I do hope,' he concluded in one letter, 'that behind the scenes of Spiritualism you have found some noble and beautiful things – consolation for sad hearts and hope for those who are hopeless.'

Harmony was restored. Temporarily. Because Price never did see Conan Doyle again. A few weeks later, on a bright afternoon in July 1930, the noted Spiritualist and author died peacefully at his home in Windlesham, Sussex, surrounded by his wife, two sons and daughter. To his last breath he remained an ardent champion of the spiritualist cause.[1]

'No one will ever take Conan Doyle's place,' Price wrote afterwards. 'There is not a Spiritualist living with the same dynamic personality, driving force, dogged grit, tenacity of purpose, fighting qualities, large-heartedness and world-wide prestige that the great High Priest of Spiritualism possessed.' It was a touching – if slightly puzzling – recognition of his worthiest opponent and Price wrote it carefully by hand. I watched him do so from the open door of his office. When he had finished he put down his pen, rose slowly from his desk and poured himself a single malt whisky before crossing the room and stopping at the widest window to look out across Kensington. And as he raised his glass into the sunlight that streamed in through the window, I saw that he was crying.

*

'No word from your journalist friend then? What was his name?'

'You know very well what his name was, Harry.'

'Forgive me, but he was a rather forgettable man.'

Considering that Vernon Wall's articles had succeeded in bringing us so much attention, I thought it ungracious of Price to refer to Wall in this manner, and I promptly told him so. But the comment was ignored and I felt my cheeks flush with resentment. I was, of course, pleased that our investigation had resulted in verifiable 'thrills', and I was grateful that the Laboratory's reputation might benefit as a result. But I had definitely returned to London a little less sure of the nature of the world and of my own place within it, and a little less sure of my feelings towards my employer. Only once did he ask where I had been while he was in hospital.

'Yorkshire – a village in the valley of Farmdale. Do you know it?'

He shook his head. 'You were gone a long time.'

'I had some old family to see. My aunt was unwell.'

'Your aunt?' He looked away. So did I.

It was, perhaps, telling that he didn't ask any more about the matter.

As the months wore busily on I thought of the charming Mr Wall more and more. Every day I checked the *Daily Mirror* for one of his articles. And yet when Price offered me the opportunity to visit the offices of the newspaper for a meeting with its editor, I didn't take it. I realised, to my disappointment, that for all my confidence I was anxious, nervous that if we met again he would ask me why I had chosen Price over him. And what answer could I possibly give to that?

I had asked Reverend Smith and his wife to keep us informed of activities at the house and they had done so through regular reports. From these I knew that the Smiths had left Borley Rectory in July. But even though it was unoccupied, strange events continued unabated. That month, the Smiths had found the small table in the Blue Room on its side, unaccountably 'hurled over from in front of the fireplace to the washstand in the corner'. On another occasion the windows were found 'unlocked from within and one thrown up'.

There had been more newspaper reports too. A piece in the *Suffolk Free Press* reported that the 'Borley Ghost' was now a 'Matter for Psychic Investigations'. *'The district,'* it read, *'has been thrown into a state of considerable excitement by an announcement that a "ghost" has been seen at Borley Rectory and the peaceful little village has this week by the notoriety it has gained, become "the hub of the universe".*

'It is a fact that both inside and outside the Rectory there have been certain strange happenings, strange enough for those engaged in psychical research to cause investigations to be made. What the eventual findings will be it remains to be seen, but from our enquiries the matter is worthy of the closest possible scrutiny . . .

'The Rector believes that some of the folk in the village are frightened to pass the spot at night. . . . Other people who have had close association with the Rectory in past years agree that there have been periodically strange happenings there which however they do not consider it desirable to talk about.'[2] Why, I wondered, would Price distance himself from a case as rich and as splendid as this?

It would be years before I discovered the truth.

*

That night, after going to bed, I read one of Price's books for a while. This one was about poltergeists. I never minded when he asked me to type his manuscripts. He was a brilliant writer and I wasn't at all surprised that recent reviews had remarked on the latent influence of his work. 'Mr Price's books,' one read, 'will bend your beliefs.'

I reflected on this for a moment as I creased the corner of my page and turned out the light, asking myself what sort of person would wish to change people's beliefs.

Someone who seeks mastery over others, said a voice in my head. A controller.

Then sleep covered my thoughts.

∗

Maddening as Price's lack of interest in the Borley case was, I wanted – more than that, *needed* – to believe his position was valid, or at least well-intentioned.

'Sarah, it is important to me that you understand.' We were in the seance room. His pleading expression drew me closer. 'How can I say I believe when I have already said that I do not? If I am to win their respect, I need to be consistent, don't I?'

I straightened his necktie. 'Forget their respect. All that matters is the truth. You taught me that. Each case stands on its own merits, remember?'

Uncertainty flickered on his face and I saw that the dark patches that stained the skin under his eyes had returned. It occurred to me then that in losing Conan Doyle Price had lost something integral of himself. 'Let his death set you free,' I urged. Conan Doyle's position in life had helped define Price's opposition. 'I know you think you have always been right, Harry, but what if you're not? Have you considered that your original conversion to scepticism happened so quickly and was so complete that you forgot what it was that opened your mind to the fantastic in the first place?'

He smiled, the gesture tempering his introspection, but only momentarily. He seemed distracted, his eyes registering private thoughts, and that distraction troubled me, bringing on other nagging questions about his honour and his elusiveness. What exactly had been bothering him before his heart attack? Who had caused him so much stress? Perhaps the same person I had overheard him arguing with about the Borley affair. The person who had been telephoning me, taunting me.

Late one evening, when I was sure I would not be disturbed by anyone, I took the key to his private study and went in search of a clue that might help me better understand. I soon found myself drowning in paperwork and battling with locked drawers to which I had no keys. I did, however, make one interesting discovery: beneath a mound of papers was a letter from Price to a university in Germany asking whether they would be interested in housing his Laboratory. Other letters, half-drafted, revealed that he was intending to make similar requests of other universities here in England.

Did I really mean so little to him that he should have started to look for a way out without even mentioning it? I struggled to rein in my anger, reminding myself that he had been unwell, but I couldn't help myself. It was too much. The following morning I marched straight into his study, prepared to confront him with everything that was bothering me.

'Harry, we need to talk. Now!'

His eyes were red as he lifted his gaze to meet mine.

'Harry . . . what is it? What's wrong?'

'It's Velma,' he said, looking down at his newspaper. I heard his voice crack and knew I had picked the worst possible moment.

'Breast cancer,' he explained, dropping his gaze, 'Horrendously aggressive.'

I went to his side, swallowing my anger. 'Harry, can I get you anything?' But there was nothing I could possibly say, nothing I could do, that would bring back the friend he had so callously betrayed at the public opening of the locked box.

'I need to be alone,' he said at last. His gaze was focused on the newspaper article with the terrible news, as if just by staring at the print long enough he might command the letters and words on the page to rearrange themselves and make Velma alive again. 'We will continue our . . . conversation . . . another time. All right?'

For me, sleep was slow coming that evening. I lay awake, staring through my window into the pale face of the solitary moon.

Solitary.

That was how Price said London made him feel. A strange reaction to a city that had won my love for its frivolities, fashions and friendships. But where were his friends? He had so many associates – too many, probably – but friends? Genuine objects of his affection and respect and love? I had seen little sign of these, except for Velma Crawshaw – and look how he had treated her. She had been so outgoing, so confident, yet oddly willing to subject herself to exploitation and humiliation. And all for what? I wondered: was it his indifference to the living that caused him to seek the company of the dead?

Then a terrible thought: was I becoming like him?

I rolled on to my side, inwardly rebelling against the idea, but how could I deny to myself that I, too, was terribly lonely? That shame and embarrassment and fear were keeping me – at just twenty-five – from enjoying everything that had ever made me happy: dinner and dancing with my friends, with young men. A memory of Amy at her wedding, imploring me to stay in touch with her, caught up with me suddenly, making my self-reflection uglier.

Anxiety scratched the surface of my thoughts. Something else was bothering me, something Velma had said. *I see nothing of my own future. Nothing at all.*

Strange, given what had happened to her.

You have to be careful, Sarah. There is a mark upon you.

I couldn't help but wonder what it was.

Notes

1   Just a few months before his death he led a Spiritualists' delegation to the Home Secretary, J. R. Clynes, protesting against police harassment of mediums under antiquated witchcraft and vagrancy laws.
2   'Extraordinary Incidents . . . Borley "Ghost."' *Suffolk Free Press*, 18 July 1929.

– 20 –

NEW MYSTERIES, OLD GHOSTS

29 September 1931. The visitor to our office had not been expected and by all accounts she should not have been welcome. After five years in Price's employment, I knew very well that he usually declined meetings with impromptu callers. However, on this occasion I showed the agitated middle-aged woman straight up to Price's study. I knew he wouldn't approve, but I was beyond caring. This was one meeting he absolutely needed to take, if not for his sake then certainly for mine.

He recognised the stocky woman immediately: it was Miss Ethel Bull, sister of the late Harry Bull of Borley and one of the original witnesses to the spectre of the nun. I could hardly believe that more than two years had passed since he had first met Ethel on his journey back to London from Borley, the morning after the Blue Room seance.[1] And now here she was, claiming to possess some new and important information about the case.

Ethel Bull was a woman who matched her name: she was both restless and forthright. She was insistent that whatever we were doing, however busy we were, she needed to be heard.

Price gave his best attempt at a polite smile, but I could see the impatience in his eyes. 'Please, won't you sit down, Miss Bull?'

She coughed, covering her mouth with a white handkerchief, then took the chair indicated, nearest the grate where a good fire was burning. I imagined she was glad of its warmth; indeed I was, for the morning was depressingly damp and bitter.

'Now then,' Price continued, 'what appears to be the trouble, Miss Bull?'

Our guest worked the strap of her handbag nervously. '*She* has been seen again, Mr Price.'

My employer arched his eyebrows.

'*Her*. The Dark Woman, the Borley nun.'

Price sank into his high-backed leather chair. 'I see,' he said slowly.

'Well, you needn't look so despondent, Mr Price.'

'I can't help my face, Miss Bull. When I was a child, bus conductors used to ask me if I was all right.' He regarded her ponderously, allowing the difficult moment to pass. 'Tell me: who, this time, has witnessed the spectre?'

'My cousin Lionel, who is the new rector, and his wife Marianne. Oh, Mr Price, they're having the worst time of it now, poor things. In the past year the Rectory has been turned over with all manner of happenings.'

'Is that so?' Price sounded surprised. 'I thought the house was empty.'

'Empty?' She coughed again, colour rising in her cheeks. 'Lionel and Marianne have been living at the Rectory for more than a year now. You wrote an article about the case. Why haven't you been out to see the Rectory since Reverend Smith left?'

Price stiffened, his expression full of angst. Here it was, the heart of the matter. I felt a surge of relief, for since our first visit to that house I had brooded on his lack of interest in Borley. I found the place deeply fascinating and there were plenty of aspects about the case that I was anxious to have explained to me. Was there really a Dark Woman haunting that little hamlet and the Rectory? What was the origin and meaning of the octagonal brass medallion that had appeared in the Blue Room? Who – or what – had communicated with us during the seance? Was it really the spirit of the late rector reaching out to us to settle the mystery of his death, or something else? And what was the mysterious message we received that began with the letters D-E-C-E?

These and other similar questions were mostly avoided in the explanation Price proceeded to give, but he did at least try to explain why the Borley affair hadn't commanded his full attention of late. 'We have been extremely busy, Miss Bull. It has been a trying time for us here in London.' He did not elaborate, but I knew he was referring both to his declining health and to the increasingly uncertain future of the Laboratory. Despite his efforts, he had yet to succeed in attracting interest from foreign and British universities to enable him to continue his work.

But Miss Bull pressed on. 'What could have kept you so busy that you stayed away from England's most haunted house? You, of all people, Mr Price, should—'

Again she gave a violent cough. I rose to fetch her a glass of water.

'The pressures upon us have meant that we have needed to prioritise,' Price said curtly. 'For the past year we have been managing a series of seances with Mr Rudi Schneider, a spiritualist medium of some surprising talent. You have surely read of him in the newspapers?'

Miss Bull nodded.

'The attention he has attracted has been well merited. We have conducted no fewer than twenty-two seances with Rudi Schneider and in every one he has impressed us under meticulously controlled conditions.'

'Mr Price isn't exaggerating,' I said, handing Miss Ethel her water. She looked relieved as she took it from me. I explained that I had been present at all of the Schneider sittings as note-taker. Price would divide the seance room into two portions by means of a fine mosquito net, which we would sit behind while observing the medium and the sitters on the other side. Imprisoned in this large net cage, each person was connected to a red lamp. If anyone moved either a hand or a foot, these lamps would blink, alerting us. In such conditions the young Austrian had time and again demonstrated the most brilliant and varied phenomena: tables that tilted of their own volition, ghostly fogs and vapours, raps that sounded from nowhere and ectoplasm produced from his mouth.

Practically everyone who attended the sittings was impressed.

'And where is Mr Schneider now?' Miss Bull asked pointedly.

'He has recently returned to Braunau,' said Price, 'but has promised to visit us again soon.' He smiled. 'The publicity has been extensive.'

Miss Bull seemed surprised to hear all this. 'Then, Mr Price, am I correct in thinking you now consider yourself a believer in Spiritualist powers?'

He nodded with an air of seriousness. After the dozens of fake mediums he had exposed, he had found someone he could stand behind while facing down his biggest critics. It was a position he had moved closer to ever since Conan Doyle's passing the year before. I have often wondered if the two events were connected somehow, for when Conan Doyle died I think perhaps something of the old, ruthlessly sceptical Price died too. 'And so this is why

I have not been back to Borley, Miss Bull. I simply haven't had the time. And when the last rector vacated the place, I did not have the means either.'

Miss Bull scowled as she opened her handbag. 'Then I wonder if you will make time for what I have brought to show you. Given that your mind is now so open, I would hope so,' she said curtly. 'As I said, the situation at the Rectory is rapidly deteriorating. Lionel looks upon the matter with the greatest seriousness and has spent countless hours compiling a detailed summary of the many peculiar incidents that are making life unbearable for himself and Marianne.'

'And who is Marianne, please?'

'I have told you already; do keep up! Marianne is his wife,' said Miss Bull, 'though I'm sorry to admit it. She's a beastly woman and mad as a hatter. But that doesn't change the facts of the matter.' From her handbag she produced a sheaf of papers covered with scrawled black handwriting. 'I believe he has more than one hundred and eighty typed sheets of notes now, perhaps more. Here are a few of them.'[2]

Price reached out his hand for the papers and placed them on the desk. 'Appalling handwriting, practically as illegible as my own.'

'My cousin suffers with chronic arthritis. His hands are so swollen now he's practically crippled.' She produced a small black-and-white photograph of the frail rector, then reached across the desk and took back the papers she had shown us. 'Here, I shall read you some.'

Price nodded and leaned back in his chair, never once taking his eyes off Miss Bull and the papers she held in her hands.

These are the passages she read to us:

'Since I have been asked by members of our family to tell what I know of the so-called Borley ghost, and since I think it is desirable that a record of our experiences should be preserved, I am writing this before the details have gone out of my mind. I should like to say, first of all, that had I been told by anyone what I am about to relate, I should not have believed it, unless I had the very highest regard for their general strict adherence to the truth. In fact I have, during these last few weeks or so, wondered more than once whether I should presently wake up and find it all a dream; I regret to say that I have not done so yet. As far as imagination goes, one can imagine one has seen things, or felt things, but one cannot imagine stones, bricks, books and pictures lying on the floor, things flying about the room and a broken window, when these things are still in evidence the next day and the next week.

'To begin then. We had, before we came here, heard about my predecessor's experience, and were rather inclined to attribute it to his imagination or to practical jokes played on him. When we came to Borley first of all we looked at the Rectory and another possible house, and decided to live in the former, neither of us feeling that there was an atmosphere about it.

'We came into residence on 16 October 1930. Our first experience of anything at all out of the ordinary occurred one evening a few weeks later. I was lying down upstairs when Marianne, who was sitting in a room downstairs, came to ask what was the matter as she had distinctly heard me call "Marianne dear" more than once. I had not called at all.

'A few days after this I went up to bed one night, and while I was upstairs I heard someone, whom of course I took for Marianne, walking about the hall. When I came down I found she had not left the room she was sitting in. I thereupon took a light and went around the drawing room, study and dining room, but could see no sign of anyone.

'Now I come to definite dates and the most extraordinary part of our experience. On Wednesday 25 February I mentioned to Marianne that I had missed the milk jug belonging to our breakfast set and some other jugs recently. She said she had looked for them, and a teapot, everywhere and could not find them, and added, "I wish they would bring them back."

'That afternoon I was away and she was alone in the house, except for our young daughter, so she locked the back door and sat in the drawing room, from where she could hear anyone coming in by other doors. Presently she went into the kitchen and found, on the table there, the jugs all together on a little plate that had also disappeared, on a table. She said, "I wish you would bring me back my teapot." That evening that also appeared.

'Thursday 26 started with our finding that two books had been placed under our bed during the night. Then the bells started ringing. First the front doorbell rang with no one there, and then two or three other bells. During the afternoon a whole lot of books were deposited on the rack for warming plates over the kitchen range; these included a number of Durham Mission hymn books that we use at the Lent weekday services (of which we were rather short, so they were a welcome addition) and two other large books.

'So far, it was just amusing; but what followed was not. That night, just as we were going to bed, I was in the bathroom and Marianne was on the landing outside our room with a candle in her hand when suddenly she was hit by a terrific blow to the eye. When she got to me in the bathroom her brow was bleeding, and she had a black eye for some days to follow.

'The following night we had just gone to bed when things started flying round the room. First something hit the wall and fell on the bed (it turned out to be a large cotton reel from the mantelpiece), and then something whizzed past fairly close to Marianne's head and fell to the ground with a great clatter. I lit a lamp and discovered the head of a hammer with the broken handle lying on the floor.'

There was a brief interruption as Miss Bull paused to ensure we were giving her our fullest attention. When she saw that we were, she nodded, turned a page and said with some excitement, 'Now then, we come to the apparitions.'

'I cannot remember the exact date, but we had not been in the house very long before Marianne began seeing Harry Bull. Twice she was with me when she saw him, but I saw nothing. . . . The last time she saw him was some time before Christmas. He seemed to be carrying something, so possibly he wanted to communicate about his will, about which he might well be uneasy since it is said that he talked about making another and possibly did so, and if so, it has been mislaid. Anyhow, I must not wander into conjecture.'[3]

When Miss Bull had finished reading aloud this curious narrative she closed the diary and stared across at Price. He raised his eyebrows expectantly before saying quietly, 'One question, Miss Bull. What sort of man is Lionel Foyster?'

'Why, he is a good man, an honest man. Intelligent and wise. Cambridge educated.'

'Would you say he is impressionable?'

'I know what you're implying, and I will have none of it, Mr Price. Lionel knows his own mind as well as the next man.'

'But does he know *your* mind?'

Her mouth fell open. 'I beg your pardon?'

'I will speak candidly,' said Price. 'The account you have just read to us, while undeniably sensational and striking in its content, sounds very much to me as though it has been coloured by your own biased opinions.'

'What opinions?' she asked, but the acerbic tone of her question suggested she had no desire to hear the answer.

'The extract you have read us implies that Mr Foyster might share your personal conviction, Miss Ethel, that this whole matter is in come way connected to the suppression of a will in your favour made by your late brother, Harry Bull.'

'Indeed, Lionel does think exactly that.'

'Except that Sarah and I have heard this tale already, from the Reverend Smith and his wife. I did not believe the tale then, and I do not believe it now.'

'Why ever not?'

'Because it is nonsense. Mabel Smith was even adopting it as her own literary project. It is the product of an overactive female imagination.'

'Harry!' I interjected.

Miss Bull looked very much affronted. 'How on earth can you know such a thing?'

'Because I have checked, Miss Bull, and double-checked.'

This was news to me. 'Harry, what do you mean?'

As Miss Ethel began another violent spate of coughing Price stood up and crossed the room to gaze out of the window. 'I did not want to bring this matter up in conversation as I consider it unseemly. But given that you have pressed the matter, I can see nothing else for it. You see, Miss Bull, after our first investigation at Borley, and at Mrs Smith's insistence that you believed some wrongdoing to have befallen your late brother, I took the liberty of checking the status of his death certificate with the local coroner and the status of his will. There was nothing suspicious about either of these documents. Harry Bull was not murdered. Nor was his marriage to Ivy Brackenbury bigamous, as you implied to Mrs Smith when she first occupied the house and discovered the sugar of lead in the cellars. The only people who truly benefited from your brother's demise were you and your sisters. That's right, isn't it?'

For a moment no one said anything. Miss Bull became still, and stared into the blazing fire.

'You're awfully quiet, Miss Bull,' commented Price.

Her eyes flicked up. 'Yes,' she said quietly, then her gaze settled once again on the dancing flames.

Price continued: 'The story you have willingly put about is slanderous, some would say cruel. That is why I prevented Wall from writing it in the *Daily Mirror*. He would have caused a scandal for your sister-in-law. However objectionable you may find Miss Ivy Brackenbury, she does not deserve that.'

Price sat down again behind his desk and eyed the papers still held tightly in Miss Bull's grasp.

'Now then, to return to the rest of your cousin's account, I think—'

'Just a moment, Mr Price.' Miss Bull was glaring at him. 'You said earlier that you received a communication concerning my brother's death during a seance.'

'That is correct. An article chronicling the event was written up in the *Mirror* by Mr Wall.'

'But that article was inaccurate,' our visitor said slowly, understanding gradually dawning on her face.

'Yes, out of necessity, as I have explained.'

'Then what else was communicated?'

'That information is private.'

'But I insist that you tell me. I grew up in that house. I was one of the first to see the figure of the nun. I have a right to know!'

He considered for a moment and then said, 'Snippets of information were relayed by an intelligence purporting to be the spirit of your dead brother. When we attempted to confirm his identity he told us, rightly, that nineteen people occupied the Rectory during his lifetime, and—'

'Nineteen?' Miss Bull was shaking her head and already counting on her fingers. 'No, that's not right for a start.'

Price caught my eye. It was a detail I should have checked.

'There were seventeen people in our household. Nineteen would have certainly been too many. What else was communicated during this seance?'

'Your brother's pet name when he was alive. Carlos.'

'Absolutely not.' She shook her head. 'I have never heard that name before.'

Price hesitated. 'There was as I recall some mention of a curse, and some letters were spelled out to us: D-E-C-E. Does any of that mean anything to you?'

Again she shook her head adamantly. 'I have to say, Mr Price, this all sounds rather vague and meaningless. My brother was many things – an eccentric who shot at rabbits from bedrooms upstairs and lounged for whole afternoons in the summerhouse, watching for spirits. But he was not the sort of man you are describing. Pet names indeed!' she grunted. 'You have been tricked, sir – misled.'

A thought struck Price and me simultaneously and our eyes met. What if the Reverend Smith had been right after all? What if we had not communicated, as we believed we had, with the spirit of the late rector but with someone – or something –altogether different, which had tricked us into believing we were communicating with old Bull? I felt very much alarmed by the idea, but it seemed to be stirring renewed curiosity within Price.

'This diary,' he said, 'you say there is more of it?'

'Oh yes, a great deal more. If you write to my cousin and ask to see the entire diary then I am sure he would share it with you. Only . . .'

'What is it?'

Her reply was carefully worded. 'Only you will need to convince him that your intentions are honourable.'

'Whatever is that supposed to mean?'

'I advised Lionel it would be sensible to call upon your expertise, but I have to say he was reluctant.'

'And why should that be?'

'You are, I assume, familiar with a Mr W. H. Salter?'

Price nodded. 'Why, certainly. He is the new honorary secretary of the Society for Psychical Research. What of him?'

She hesitated. 'Mr Salter visited the Rectory recently, and advised Lionel against your involvement in the affair.'[4]

The news made Price scowl and slam his fist on the desk. 'How dare he say such a thing!'

'My own views are rather different. I believe you could be useful. The occurrences at the house are worsening.' Giving another hacking cough, she placed the rector's handwritten notes back on Price's desk and pushed them towards him. 'There is still a story waiting for you in Borley, Mr Price, if you are willing to come.'

Whether Price was willing or not, our visitor's increased passion made me adamant that this matter would be resolved, and soon. I gave her my assurance that we would stay at the house for as long as was necessary to resolve its mysteries, and I felt entirely confident in making the promise. After all I had been through with Price, after all I had lost and had not yet divulged to him, I *needed* to know.

'Sarah?' Price looked shocked.

I could argue with you, I thought. I could challenge you, embarrass you, exactly as you did with me in front of Vernon Wall at Borley Rectory.

'Please excuse us for a moment, Miss Ethel.' I stood up and crossed to the door, nodding at Price to follow me. When we were alone in the corridor and the door was closed, I told him I thought we should deal with the matter. 'If you abandon something like this, trust me, it's never going to disappear. It's like a debt, Harry. It's going to come back.'

'A debt?' His eyebrows arched.

'We have to return to Borley,' I insisted. 'We're obliged to. The place haunts me still. And anyway, we're a good deal quieter now that Mr Schneider has gone home.'

He looked away from me for a long moment and I wasn't sure if he still trusted me – or if I still trusted him. 'You didn't have to send him away when you did – the experiments were showing promise. And yet once he'd given you your headlines, you sent him away as though you had something more important to do.'

He faltered, couldn't look at me. And suddenly I was filled with questions about who this man really was – where he disappeared to, sometimes for days on end; and why he wasn't consistent in his search for truth. When he looked at me again he seemed to see the doubt that was spreading through me, for he blinked and dropped his eyes.

'Would you like to know what I think, Harry?'

'From your tone? Not really.'

'I think Conan Doyle was right. Perhaps you *don't* want to find any ghosts.'

His flicked his head back to me and his eyes widened.

'And why would you think that? After all the progress we've made.'

'Because if you did prove that spirits are real you'd need to explain them, categorise them, break them down into little quantifiable pieces. Even you couldn't do that. You'd be lost, floundering for explanations. So you keep yourself at a safe distance.' I felt the heat of my frustration. 'We both know how much you cherish being in control.'

'That's enough, Sarah.'

'I'm not finished yet.'

'I don't like your tone.'

'I don't like yours!'

He stood back, assessing me shrewdly, and by the way the corners of his mouth twitched I could tell I had rattled him.

'All right,' he said at last. 'What would you have me do?'

'I know how badly, how bitterly, disappointed you were all those years ago, when you exposed William Hope as a fraud.' I took one of his hands and said quietly but firmly, 'But you must finish this case. Challenge yourself. Challenge us both.'

His gaze pierced me. To my relief, he nodded and smiled suddenly. 'There she is,' he breathed. 'My delicate, daring Sarah.'

I pushed down the warm sensation that was threatening to rise in my chest and stepped away.

'It's settled,' I said, leading Price back into the study. Miss Ethel turned in her chair to look at me. 'We will write to your cousin at once, telling him to expect us in a week or so.'

Our visitor nodded her relief and stood to leave. But as she did so, I caught the quick, secretive movement of her hand as she

tucked her handkerchief into her handbag. Her face tightened
with embarrassment. 'Just one thing, Miss Grey . . .'

'Yes?'

'Take good care in that house, particularly around Marianne.
She is a . . . spirited woman. And the misery in that Rectory . . .
it stays with you.'

We watched her go, and the dreadful sound of her hacking
cough carried up the stairs.

'Did you see it?' asked Price.

I nodded, hearing the alarm in his voice and feeling it too. But
neither of us mentioned what we had seen: the finely embroidered cotton in Miss Ethel's hand spotted with blood.

*

3 October 1931

Dear Mr Price,

Thank you for your letter of the 2nd. I am enclosing my account of
occurrences. I would explain that these were written chiefly to send
to members of my family and therefore no explanation is given to
matters that might be unclear to strangers . . .

My last account takes the story up to 24 June. Since then we have
been quieter on the whole, but we have had some outbreaks similar
to those recorded. One evening in August I was in the church when
my wife came rushing over and said that there was a tremendous
noise emanating from my study. We hurried back and when we went
into the room we found that the furniture had been thrown about.
Then, one night last week, I was woken up at around 3.30 a.m. when

I was hit on the head by something which proved to be a large water jug from another bedroom. We put it on the floor (it was not broken), and presently it was thrown at my wife.

Our chief trouble lately has been things disappearing, often from right under our noses; they are sometimes returned later. Doors have also been locked. Once there was no one in the house and my wife was locked in from outside; another time we were locked out of our room one night and had to sleep elsewhere; and one day our little girl was locked in her room, for which we had no key. These doors opened the next day after a 'relic' had been applied to them.[5] I should be very much obliged if you would kindly not mention at Long Melford what your business down here is, since we do not want reports to get around the parish. We have one indoor servant at present, but I think, with care, we can keep her from hearing anything. She is quite young – not fifteen yet – and has only been here ten days and as yet has not come up against any 'demonstration'. She has of course heard the gossip of the neighbourhood, but does not, I think, believe it. We should like to keep her as long as possible as she is a help to my wife, who is not well.

Yours faithfully,

L. A. Foyster [6]

9th October 1931

Dear Mr Price,

Thank you for your letter of the 6th in which you say we are to expect you next Tuesday evening. I trust you will not mind my asking that

all those who are taking part in any investigation sign an undertaking that they will neither themselves publish nor give cause to
be published in any newspaper or periodical, in this or any other
country, nor in any other way make public the facts connected with
the case. The condition I have made is in self-defence or we might
find our position here impossible.

I intended to say in a previous letter that I should like to have my
diary of the occurrences back when you have finished with it.

Yours faithfully,

L. A. Foyster'

Notes

1   Ethel Bull gave many interviews about the experience and many paranormal
investigators since Price have expressed their satisfaction with her testimony.
In June 1947 she offered the following statement to the BBC: 'I was walking
round the garden with two of my sisters, and they'd been to a garden party and
were telling me an amusing story that had happened. And then they wondered
I didn't take any notice and they looked down at me, and I said, "Look there's
a nun walking there." And I was terrified and so were they when they saw her
– and it sent cold shivers down our backs and we simply flew up to the house.
And then we saw my eldest sister who was staying with us and she said, "Oh
I'm not going to be frightened," so she came down, and when she saw the nun
she made to go across the potato bed to meet the nun, and the nun turned and
came as it were to meet her, and she was seized with panic and simply flew up
to the house' (recorded 17 June 1947).

2   There is documented evidence that Lionel compiled the diary partly at the
insistence of the Bull sisters themselves. He mentions it in *Fifteen Months in a
Haunted House*: '[Marianne], I am going to write a memorandum of our experiences before I forget them. Don't you think it would be a good idea? Then I
can send it round to members of my family; they seem to be anxious to know
what is happening' (p. 66).

3 *Summary of experiences at Borley Rectory*.

4 'Salter told Lionel that he shouldn't have anything to do with Price . . . and Lionel said, "Well, I am committed to it," and Mr Salter said, "You'll regret it," which we certainly did' (Marianne Foyster, quoted in *The Most Haunted Woman in England* by Vince O'Neil).

5 Lionel Foyster is referring here to an unidentified relic of St John Vianney, otherwise known as the Curé d'Ars. Vianney (8 May 1786–4 August 1859) was a French parish priest who is venerated in the Catholic Church as the patron saint of all priests. Interestingly, Vianney himself was the victim of poltergeist phenomena for a period of some thirty-five years.

6 Letter from Revd Lionel Algernon Foyster.

7 As above.

− 21 −

THE WATCHER

Price was late.

I had been waiting at least two hours for him on the platform at Liverpool Street station, inventing excuse after excuse that might account for his delay, such as the rain or some problem back at the Laboratory, but now I was worried. Was it his health? I wondered with dread. What else could account for such lateness?

I looked around me, scanning the movement of people along the platform for any sign of my employer. As I stood among the clamour of dragging cases, slamming doors, marching feet and whistles blowing, anxiety gnawed at me. It was intolerable, really it was; Price knew how important it was to me that we return to Borley and clear up its mysteries. What was I to do? Catch the train anyway and go without him, or return to the Laboratory?

I checked my watch. Five o'clock. I wished then that I had agreed to Price's original suggestion to drive, but there was no time to dally. A whistle blew, jolting me into resolution. I would go anyway, alone if necessary.

I pushed my way quickly across the platform and boarded

the train. To my relief, the carriage I had entered was empty. I quickly settled into a corner seat and laid my coat across my lap for comfort. Squeezing my eyes shut, I waited for my annoyance to pass. How pathetic I must have appeared: a sad young woman sitting alone, fighting back tears she was embarrassed to shed.

Where was he? With his wife? Or a mistress? When I considered the innumerable lunches and dinners he attended and the many afternoons that he stayed away from the office, it seemed inconceivable that he didn't have another woman in his life. I remembered the dismissive manner with which his wife had addressed me, both when we first spoke on the telephone and on numerous occasions since then. She called in the afternoon, struggling to maintain her dignified veneer as she enquired when Price could be expected home, but I was rarely able to answer the question truthfully because unless work was involved he told me very little about his whereabouts, and so I had either to invent a reason for his absence or simply tell her that I did not know.

The hardest part was to listen to her response, the sigh of disappointment. I heard her pain, and I understood. At the back of my mind there dwelt unwelcome memories of my mother standing anxiously at the telephone, calling around the local restaurants in Pimlico to enquire as to the whereabouts of my father. Children always know when something is wrong, and I knew that wherever my father had disappeared to those evenings in his melancholy, whatever his excuse, it could never be good enough. His rightful place was at home with us.

My father's absence had worried Mother deeply, and when I saw the pain in her eyes that lingered still after his death I pitied her and resolved never to allow myself to be treated in the same way. Women like that – like Mother, like Price's wife – were victims of circumstance, of their own false hopes of men. And now, sitting on the train, dwelling on Price's whereabouts, I was treading their path. You could change it all I thought, simply by walking away.

We rumbled on, the countryside rushing by, and I relaxed a little, relieved to have left London behind. Gazing out from my empty compartment I saw dark clouds gathering over fields of hanging mists and I decided I would not continue to the Rectory tonight but find a bed at the Bull Inn upon our arrival at Long Melford. Perhaps by the morning Price would join me.

I disembarked at Marks Tey to change for the train that would take me the remaining distance to Long Melford. It was a depressingly bleak evening with a blustery wind that dampened my spirits and made me yearn for the warmth of indoors. I stood alone on the platform, my suitcase at my feet, thoughts blowing through my head as the minutes passed. The connection was late and I was beginning to wish I had never come.

Then I saw, standing at the opposite end of the platform, the solitary figure of a man. His features were obscured by the darkness, but I could see well enough to discern that he possessed a broad, well-built form. I was struck then by an alarming thought: I was completely alone.

As apprehension fluttered in my stomach, I stepped back, praying he wouldn't see me. But my movement must have attracted his attention, for he lifted his head and held me in his sight for a few uncertain moments, then advanced.

'Sarah?'

It was not the stranger approaching me who spoke. I spun

round and saw Price, his battered hat pulled down low, his long black coat flapping in the wind behind him.

'Harry! What on earth are you doing here?'

Before he could answer, the train pulled into the station, dislodging the thick carpet of fog at our feet. Glancing quickly to my left I saw that the stranger was standing motionless, looking directly at us.

Taking my hand, Price said, 'Where the devil have you been, my dear?'

Of all the nerve! I shook myself free of his grip and exclaimed, 'Where have I been? Where have *you* been? I waited for you for two hours!'

The train whistle screamed. Price jerked alert. 'Come on, we must make our connection.'

'No, Harry. This time you're going to answer me. Where have you been?'

'There was a telephone call at the Laboratory, Sarah. It was important. I had to take it. I missed our train by minutes so took the next one to Bures, about five miles away, then a taxi here to make the connection. And just in time, it seems!'

'But how did you know I'd be here?'

'I didn't. But you *are* here, and that's all that matters.' He started towards the train. 'Come along.'

'Harry, wait! Who telephoned you?'

The compartment on the train was far less comfortable than the last – all wooden slats and rickety seats – but I was relieved to be no longer alone and to have shelter from the cold, damp evening. Price sat opposite me, looking thoughtful, unsettled.

'I apologise, Sarah. I came as fast as I could. I was sure you would come anyway, even without me.' He smiled. 'And here you are.'

'And here I am.'

I glanced to the corner at the far end of the carriage where the stranger from the platform was huddled. Although smartly dressed, his thick beard was badly kept. His head was turned away, but every now and again he would turn in our direction and his steely, suspicious eyes would catch mine.

I leaned forward and spoke in a low voice to Price. 'Who was it then? Who telephoned?'

Price was solemn. 'Rudi Schneider. Sarah, he wishes to take part in a further series of seances with us at the Laboratory.'

'That's good news, isn't it?'

He nodded slowly and spoke cautiously. 'It is, yes, but a few weeks ago Mr Schneider signalled his intention to make contact with someone very specific on the other side, someone he feels is close to this process we have embarked upon with him.'

I saw no problem with this, and told him so.

'You may feel differently when I tell you the identity of the person concerned.'

'Who is it?'

Taking my hand, Price quietly said, 'Your father.'

My stomach lurched. 'Sarah, Schneider is firmly convinced that he can communicate with the spirit of your father; he has spoken of him very specifically to me, and in exact terms. He wants to make him the focus of our next seance.'

I stared at him. 'I don't know what to say.'

Price nodded his understanding. 'I will understand completely if you think it is inappropriate or too painful for you. But you have seen now what Mr Schneider is capable of, the extent of his abilities. You and your mother can provide us with personal information Schneider couldn't possibly guess, and we can test him with that information. Imagine if he succeeds! The experiment could change everything.'

'I see.' I felt anger suddenly rising in my face. 'Harry, you really are the limit! Didn't you think to ask me this before now?'

'Well, yes,' he conceded, 'but I thought you'd say no.'

'I certainly am saying no!' I snapped. 'The idea of using my own father's memories as a control for an experiment ... it's too much, really it is!'

'There is something else,' he added quickly.

'Is there indeed! What is it?'

'Schneider tells me that your father has a personal message for you, something he wishes you to know.'

My stomach lurched sickeningly. I had wanted to keep his memory away from my work. Now that would be impossible. 'What is it, Harry?'

Price shrugged. 'I don't know. But there seems to be only one way of finding out, does there not?' His eyes searched mine. 'Will you agree to it?'

'This matters very much to you, doesn't it?'

He smiled. 'It matters to you as well.'

'But this is *your* passion, Harry; it always was. This journey we're on together now is *because* of you.' I let go of his hand. 'You've never said why. After everything we have been through together, you've never explained what started it all, this study of the spooks.'

'All right, all right.' His gaze faltered as he looked beyond me into the mists of his past. 'There is a boy I see every so often,' he said slowly, 'no more than eleven or twelve years of age. He's a quiet child, Sarah, insular, frightened, afraid of being alone and with an intense interest in the arcane. Loneliness can do the strangest things to a child, can it not?'

I nodded at him to elaborate.

'When I was nine, my father gave me a book for Christmas. The title was *The Tiny Mite, Describing the Adventures of a Little Girl in Dreamland, Fairyland, and Wonderland and Elsewhere*. Oh, what a curious thing that book was,' he recalled wistfully, 'full of tales of hobgoblins, witches, giants and magicians. It still fascinates me. I can see it when I close my eyes, that wonderful book. I think of it often. When I had finished reading it I read all I could on the subject of the occult.'

'You have never mentioned your father before.'

Raising his eyebrows, he pointed out that I rarely mentioned my own father. This I could not deny.

'I grew up in Shropshire, in the small village of Rotherington. Do you know it?'

'It is a lovely part of the world,' I acknowledged.

He nodded. 'My father, you understand, was an immensely successful man. In twenty years he had opened five separate businesses, each one outperforming the last. And so, by all accounts, I should have been a happy child.'

'Weren't you happy?'

'Happy? I was miserable. Never a word of encouragement from my parents. I learned to be lonely, I wallowed in solitude. I discovered I could do something other people would take an interest in and admire me for. I could write, Sarah. And soon I was doing precisely that for the school magazine, on subjects as varied as coin collecting, archaeology and the occult. The liberation it brought, the wondrous sense of superiority – I was addicted. Do you know what it is like to be addicted to something, Sarah?'

'I do,' I said quietly, averting my gaze.

'Then came the bullying, the most horrendous taunts. They

laughed at me because I was small, you see. I developed a nervous stammer. They laughed at that as well.' He looked across at me sadly. 'How cruel children can be. But in my subject, I found a way to escape.

'Then my father took me to a travelling fair and I witnessed the marvellous feats of the Great Sequah, an entertainer known far and wide as the best of his kind. Charles Frederick Rowley, born 1867, West Bromwich: a circus proprietor, a travelling showman, an entrepreneur, an entertainer. A scientist! Sarah, he could extract teeth, entirely painlessly, from volunteers selected completely at random. These subjects were strapped into a chair, and the Great Sequah would produce a sequence of objects from an empty hat – a pair of doves, flags, toys, sweets, you name it – and toss them into the audience. It all happened so fast, Sarah! Such sleight of hand – it was brilliant. Before one could blink, the offending molar had been removed painlessly and thrown out into the crowd.'

'You found it amazing?'

'Yes, but it was the novelty that captured my attention. I needed to know how the illusions were achieved. I needed to understand.' He smiled. 'That same month I had come across some of the wonderful reviews for A Study in Scarlet[1] and I though what a marvellous thing it would be to live such adventures, to become not only a brilliant detective but a psychic detective. Of course, I have good old Conan Doyle to thank for that.'

I understood now the source of Price's puzzling affection for his enemy.

'You two had more in common than either of you ever wanted to admit.'

Price nodded, briskly. 'Well, the Great Sequah did leave an indelible impression upon me. Afterwards, I rushed home and asked my father to buy me *Professor Hoffman's Modern Magic*. I devoured it from cover to cover in one sitting.'

'But why?'

'To discover the method by which the trick was done.' He nodded. 'It was the trombone and drum, of course.'

'The what?'

'The trombone and drum – the props he used. He would have his men play the instruments as he operated on his volunteers.'

'So . . . ?'

'They played *loudly*.' Price smiled. 'The sound drowned out the painful cries of his subjects. Clever man. I observed and I learnt the magicians' tricks. My mind was consumed even then with scepticism and critical faculty. I imagined myself addressing halls packed to the rafters with people eager to hear what I had to say. More than just a vulgar travelling show. My imagined audiences listened. They *listened* to me, Sarah, hanging on my every word. I was important. I *would* be important. Pathetic really, but at night I slept with copies of *Burke's Peerage* and *Who's Who* under my pillow.'

'Then it was a deceiver who started it all, this great obsession? The Great Sequah. And your father.'

The idea seemed to startle him. 'I suppose it was him unintentionally, yes. He had always held the highest expectations for me, always wanting me to rise as far as I possibly could.'

'That's a hope most parents share.'

'Yes, but in him, Sarah, it burned with the brightest ferocity. He tutored me every evening and every weekend as a schoolboy so that no examination would defeat me. Everything in my life was to be certain, no room for any doubt. He had to know that I would succeed. So I had to know it too.'

'And so you set yourself the greatest challenge of all,' I

observed, smiling, grateful at last for his honesty. I felt closer to him, as though knowing the man inside were possible. And, as I noticed the tears glistening on his lashes, I wanted to tell him everything I had been through, the sum of all I had endured and hidden from him.

'Was your father a believer in Spiritualism?'

Price nodded. 'Oh yes, very much so. He taught me that the dead were all around us.'

'And what happened to him?' I asked as our train rattled deeper into the countryside.

'Heart attack,' he said softly. 'It was a scalding hot Saturday in July 1906. I came home and there he was, sitting upright in his favourite chair. Just . . . sitting. Staring right at me. He was seventy-seven years old. A good life, Sarah.'

'And afterwards . . . ?'

'Yes.' Price nodded slowly, the word catching in his throat. He knew what I was asking. 'I saw him, or rather, I *thought* I saw him. Just one week after his funeral I woke in the early hours to see him sitting there at the end of my bed, daring me, challenging me, to test the mystery of his vision. These experiences were stepping stones for me, towards a conclusion I have yet to form. I thought William Hope was the real thing. I felt so close to the truth when I examined his photographs.' He hesitated, cleared his throat, and resumed a businesslike tone. 'But Mr Schneider is better by far. He has presented us with an opportunity to know, truly *know*, what all of this means, to discover what happens next. He gives me hope where I thought there was none. Just think what it could mean for you and for me, Sarah.' He hesitated. 'It was you who gave me the strength to open my mind again after Sir Arthur passed. It was you who urged me to dismantle my barricade of scepticism. Will you please consent to Mr Schneider's terms?'

'It's just so deeply personal, Harry,' I said tentatively. I didn't want to commit myself. 'What if Schneider fails? I can't begin to imagine how that would make me feel, or even how I would feel if he succeeded. And how would Mother feel?' It was such a logical reservation. But I knew, in spite of it, that I would consent. I cared for Price too deeply not to agree. When do we ever make good, rational decisions when we care for someone so strongly? Moreover, if there was the slightest chance that Schneider was genuine and Father had a message for me, and that this medium could succeed where others had failed and pierce the veil separating this world from the next, then I really had no choice. Curiosity, I knew, would compel me.

'If I do this you must do something for me in return, Harry.'

His eyes narrowed shrewdly. 'What is it?'

I asked him to make the Borley investigation the full focus of his attention so that we could finish what we had started together. He hesitated, and for a moment I thought he might decline, but eventually he nodded thoughtfully and said, 'Very well. It can do no harm.'

I smiled, blissfully unaware of how wrong he was. 'Then I agree to Mr Schneider's proposal.' I sat back, relieved and anxious, and asked him to show me Reverend Foyster's full diary, which had recently been sent to us. I wanted to read the document before getting to the house.

Price duly produced from inside his coat pocket a slim, leather-bound book. I thought he looked tired, older and worried, as though the weight of a problem was beginning to work upon him.

'And you're sure you're up to this?' I asked.

He flinched and replied abruptly, 'Yes, of course. Why wouldn't I be?'

'I'm only thinking of your health,' I said; then, seeing his dismissive reaction, wondered why I bothered. I took the diary from him.

'Take care of that, Sarah.' He lowered his hat over his eyes. 'It could be valuable one day.'

As Price slept, our train rumbled through the late afternoon and the rain onward to our destination. My feelings were scattered and confused, for I was both placated and troubled by our conversation. Although I had learned a little more about his motivations I couldn't shake the sense that he was keeping something from me, and not for the first time.

I sat back, opening the Reverend Foyster's *Diary of Occurrences*. And from the far corner of our compartment, the stranger from the railway station watched.

Note

1   Sherlock Holmes had made his debut the previous month in *Beeton's Christmas Annual*.

– 22 –
THE WRITING ON THE WALL

By the time our taxi from Long Melford had traversed the winding lanes up to Borley I had reached the conclusion that Reverend Foyster's diary provided a clear indication that something very odd was still happening at the Rectory. But my mind snagged on the peculiarity of the ominous stranger's behaviour. For the duration of our journey a smile of amusement had played across his features as he watched me reading the diary. Did he, perhaps, know something I did not?

We disembarked and stood in the lane. Borley Rectory was as bleak as I recalled. As I gazed at the dreary building, I noticed a tall cowled figure near the porch. It did not seem to be a shadow, and I called Price's attention to the form. But when we looked, it had vanished.

'It's your mind, Sarah – nothing more than that,' said Price dismissively. 'Remember that houses like this can play tricks with your mind, yes?'

I nodded.

Yet there was something disturbing about that figure, something – what was it? Something about its form, as though it were not quite solid.

'Now then,' said Price, 'what time is it?' Before I could check my wristwatch the clock in the church tower, buried in trees on the opposite side of the road, struck eight. 'All right,' said my companion. 'Let's get to it!'

He strode towards the great front door, his feet crunching on the gravel driveway as he whispered to me to stay close. We stood in the stone-pillared porch, rang the bell and waited. I felt fired up with enthusiasm and wondered briefly, given the lateness of the hour, whether we might be forced to spend the night here for a second time.

Eventually a tall man appeared in the doorway, partly conce-aled in shadow. He was holding an oil lamp and in its flickering light I recognised the frail, poorly shaven man from Miss Bull's photograph; this was Lionel Foyster. But his face was more gaunt than I remembered, strained, and the gaze he turned to us was full of suspicion.

'Yes?'

We hastily made our introductions and apologised for our lateness. When Price offered his hand for a moment I thought the rector would refuse it.

'I was beginning to think that perhaps you weren't coming,' he said, 'or that you would delay until tomorrow.'

'No, no,' Price said cheerfully, apparently oblivious to any offence he had caused. 'Time is of the essence, sir.'

The rector looked concerned. 'I say, did anyone meet you on your way here?'

'No, sir,' was my prompt reply, but I thought the question odd.

He seemed satisfied. 'Well then, I suppose you had better come in.'

We followed him through the gloomy hallway and into the large drawing room where the lamps were lit and a good fire crackled and spluttered in the great stone fireplace. The rector crossed the room and prepared a brandy for us. He moved slowly, as if carrying a great weight.

I told the poor gentleman how sorry I was for his predicament and he seemed to appreciate the sentiment. 'Thank you, Miss Grey,' he sighed. 'We are luckier than we might otherwise be. Marianne and I have some help around the house from time to time. There's the maid, of course, and a handyman – a good Catholic who lives in the cottage next door. But I will readily admit that we are quickly coming to our wits' end in this house. Please, won't you sit down?'

We took our places in the low chairs nearest the fire. I should have felt warmed, but already the sense of loathing and suffocation that my memory now associated with this house crept upon me, bringing goose pimples to my flesh. How reasonable it seems to me now, in retrospect, to dismiss such feelings as simple imaginings; except that I knew – *I knew* – my feelings had to have more substance than that. Something, somewhere, at the fringes of my own life or in the fabric of this house, was rotten.

'I trust that by now you have both familiarised yourselves with my *Diary of Occurrences*?'

'Indeed we have,' I said earnestly, though Price remained silent, his expression unwavering.

'You know, I never believed in ghosts until I came here,' said the rector, settling into a deep armchair. 'And Mr Price, I can see that even you are sceptical. Well, believe me, I used to laugh at the stories people told about the Rectory. I'm sorry to say we have discovered it is anything but a subject for laughter. Just listen to this. One evening a few weeks ago I found that all the pictures, except for one, that hang above the central staircase in the hall had been removed and laid face down on the hall floor. The only exception was a particularly large picture, and that was hanging crookedly as though it had been pushed aside. Another time, I had just finished writing a letter concerning the haunting to a family relative, when I discovered two pins with their points sticking upwards, one on the seat of the armchair, the other on the chair I had been sitting on. Whenever I have attempted to address the spirits – if indeed that is what they are – I have been pelted with stones.'

I made a mental note of these details and the rector observed my obvious surprise. 'Oh, that is not all. One night Marianne found pebbles behind her pillow; another time, just outside the Blue Room, she was struck in the face by some unseen force only to be turned out of bed, weeks later, three times in one night!'

'How was she afterwards?'

'How do you think? She was distraught! Day after day we found the bedding in our rooms dishevelled and scattered all over the floor and the beds themselves overturned!

'Afterwards we found a small fire had broken out by the skirting board in one of the empty bedrooms. And all the time, on the landing during the night, we heard the strangest noises: bangs, tapping on doors, and incessant bell ringing. In the corner of the library I keep a selection of walking sticks; those too have moved all on their own. I hear them sometimes on the floors of the rooms above. Thud. Thud. Thud. As though someone is up there, pacing the boards! And even my Sunday sermons go missing, only to turn up again later.'

We listened attentively as the rector told us of the male figure (Harry Bull, so he claimed) that he and his wife had seen in the Rectory corridors; of noises and lights in empty rooms; of books and other objects being thrown about; of unearthly whisperings; and, most intriguingly, of writing that had appeared on scraps of paper found about the house and on the walls of various passages.

'You understand,' said Price seriously, 'that if genuine, such writing would be one of the greatest catalogued occurrences in the history of psychical research.'

'I don't care what it means to you,' the rector snapped. 'I care what it means for us.'

'What does the writing say?' I queried.

'A great many things,' his tone was grave, 'although we haven't been able decipher all of it. I would welcome your assistance with that. The first writing appeared over a few days . . . random letters, swirling letters, scratched out. Then my wife's name appeared on the walls in the bedrooms and in the kitchen passage. The rest is just a terrible mess. The writing . . . I am convinced it is supernormal. That's the only word to describe it. Supernormal.'

'There are children living in this village,' said Price quickly, 'and many people who know the stories that go with this house. Is it not more likely that someone is playing a very mischievous and cruel trick on you both?'

'You think so, Mr Price? Well, consider this. One afternoon I was working in my study when I saw a pencil rise from my desk into the air. It just hung there. Floating.'

'Before your eyes?' I said with wonderment.

The rector nodded and spoke so quietly it was as if he were mouthing the words. 'Before. My. Eyes. No hand was visible. The pencil stayed that way, suspended motionless in the air, for some five or six seconds; and then it struck the wall, scrawling words and phrases right in front of me. Tell me, does that sound normal to you?'

We exchanged hurried glances, 'And what of the infamous nun?' Price asked. 'The Dark Woman, as I believe she is known.'

The rector's narrow face darkened. 'What of her? We feel her presence in the garden and about the house. She watches us. Judges us. As she has done with every family that has occupied Borley Rectory. And we live with that; it's all we can do.'

'Then you have seen the apparition?'

'My wife has seen her.' He made a sign of the cross. 'I sense her, all the time, around us, observing us. It's like living with a permanent shadow.'

Hearing these words I too felt the strangest sensation of being watched. I quickly shook my head and tried to focus. Notes! I had forgotten to take notes, so enthralled was I with his tale. I reached down to my bag, which I had left on the floor next to me, and retrieved my notepad and pen.

'What are those for?' Foyster asked. His tone was suspicious.

'Records for our investigation,' said Price. 'If we are to get anywhere near the heart of the matter then it is vital we document everything we see and hear tonight in this house. I trust you have no objection to that?'

With particular delicacy, Foyster rose to his feet. 'Oh, but I *do* object. Please, Mr Price, don't think me rude, but my wife and I have been warned about your – well, your methods.' As he spoke he went slowly across the room to his desk.

'My methods?'

'Yes, your fondness for the sensational.'

'My what?'

I quickly motioned for Price to be silent and shot him a reproachful glance.

The rector continued speaking as he delved in the top drawer of his desk. 'As I explained in my letter, I think it desirable that none of our personal details end up in the newspapers. Our predecessors had quite a bit of bother with the locals when details of your previous antics in this house were made public.' Though I conceded that the old man had a right to privacy, I couldn't help wondering whether there was more to his reluctance.

Moments later Foyster had rejoined us by the fireside brandishing a document we were politely but firmly requested to sign – an affidavit swearing us to complete confidentiality. 'I'm sure you both quite understand,' said Foyster, thrusting a pen into Price's hand. 'Just imagine what the people in the community would think if they knew what was happening in this house within a comparatively short distance of their own homes.'

To my great surprise Price signed the document without any hesitation or complaint and when he had done so said, 'Where shall we begin our inspection? Sarah, I propose you and I take a look around, familiarise ourselves once more with the old place, and then Mr Foyster can show us the curious wall writings.'

Reverend Foyster looked astonished. 'You're not proposing to undertake a comprehensive investigation at this hour?'

'But of course! Why else would we have come here?'

'I was under the impression that this would merely be an informal interview. My wife is asleep upstairs and—'

'Nonsense – we're here now; it would be a shame to waste the journey.'

There was a brief pause and then, reluctantly, 'Very well. But I'd be grateful if you tried not to disturb Marianne or upset her. It doesn't take much these days.'

'Whatever do you mean?'

'She is prone to outbursts, periods of excitement that come upon her, so I would prefer that she wasn't unsettled.'

'But of course,' repeated Price in a strained tone. 'We wouldn't wish that.'

Reverend Foyster scowled. 'Good. I am glad you say that, Mr Price. You see, I have been rather worried about your coming here. Mr Salter from the Society for Psychical Research warned us that—'

'Mr Salter?' Price was taken aback by the mention of the man. 'If I hear that name one more time—'

'I thought you knew that Mr Salter had visited the house.'

'Indeed,' answered Price sharply, 'but I wasn't aware that his opinion was considered relevant any longer. I suppose he was checking up on me, was he? Hmm? Now, let me make one thing absolutely clear, Reverend Foyster. Sarah and I have come at the request of a member of *your* family. We have *not* come out of the kindness of our hearts. I have a job to do, as does Miss Grey, and we fully intend to do it. I must insist that the Society you mention, and Mr Salter in particular, maintain an indefinite disassociation from the entire matter. This is my investigation now, not his; in fact, *no one* else's.' He paused, softening his approach. 'This is the way it has to be if we are to help you. Do you find these terms agreeable?'

'Yes, yes, all right, Mr Price. I . . . I can see that you wish to be in charge.'

'Yes, that's it, Mr Foyster. *I* wish to be in charge,' Price agreed with an unpleasant note of satisfaction.

The frail rector nodded uncertainly. 'Then my wife and I shall place our fate in your hands.'

The Rectory was pervaded by the same odour of dank decay that I recalled from my first visit. Little about the place had changed. The stillness in the air was so delicate it seemed that at any moment it might splinter, and it was that perfect quiet that conferred the mournful atmosphere I found so dispiriting.

Except now I was at one with the Rectory's sadness, a part of its history. The house was familiar with our sins. And wherever I walked, my secret walked too.

Finding our way by the light of paraffin lamps, we followed the rector upstairs, stepping carefully over fallen plaster and odd bits of rubble that made me question the cleanliness of the Foysters. And as we reacquainted ourselves with the grim house and its thick, thick darkness, I felt more unsure of myself than ever. An almost unbearable distraction began pressing down upon my senses; slight movements, barely discernible, flickered at the edge of my vision, and every couple of minutes my hearing became muffled as though I were underwater. In these giddy moments the world itself seemed off balance, and I managed to catch only snatches of the conversation passing between Price and Foyster, and one phrase in particular. The name of the house, whispered at me in short, puncturing bursts: *Borley Rectory. Borley Rectory. Borley Rectory!*

I raised my hands to cover my ears.

'Sarah?'

I watched Price's lips moving but could hear no voice. Either the house – its memories, and whatever presences dwelt within its rooms – was taunting me, or it was as Price implied: my own imagination was playing havoc with my senses. Whatever the truth, I had to pause for a moment and steady myself on the great stairs.

Now Foyster was speaking, his concern for me evident in his expression.

I waved them both away and squeezed my eyes shut, trying my utmost to fortify myself against the malign evil I could feel enfolding me. And now the very notion that there was another world, a real world, outside the Rectory, far away from it, felt no more than that: a notion, a vague idea entwined with physical and emotional confusion.

My eyes flipped open.

'All right?' asked Price. 'Ready to continue?'

Both men were staring at me. I motioned them forward. 'Yes, please – I apologise. I don't know what came over me.'

As we reached the top of the stairs I turned and saw, through an open door, a fine stained-glass window in the room over the porch – the old schoolroom, where Price and I had exchanged our private thoughts in darkness on our last visit. The stained glass was new and I remarked upon it, for it seemed oddly out of place.

'We had that room converted into a chapel,' said Foyster, and when I asked him the reason he looked at me darkly and said, 'Young lady, when you see what I am about to show you, I think you'll understand.'

To our right was the room in which I had slept on our last visit, the same room in which Price had visited me two years ago when he had woken me and asked me to drive him back to London. I could not help but look in as we passed, the memory of that time reaching back, taunting me. Stripped of furniture, the room appeared bare now, but it smelt and felt just the same. I looked up suddenly, aware of Price near me, and smiled uncertainly. I was hoping he had seen the room, hoping that he might remember also. But his eyes only flickered in half recognition, then he looked away. I hated him for that.

We came to a halt a little further down the dark corridor. 'Here we are,' said Foyster quietly as he pointed to the wall. The light from his lamp was playing on his face. 'Now Mr Price, Miss Grey, tell me: in all your investigations, have you ever seen anything quite like this?'

'It's extraordinary,' I whispered, casting my eyes over a mess of indecipherable pencil marks covering part of the peeling wall: scribbles, lines and, most intriguingly, four unmistakable words: *MARIANNE MASS LIGHT PRAYERS.*

'What do you suppose it means?' asked Reverend Foyster.

My companion leaned in, running his nimble fingers over the markings. 'Have you considered the possibility that little Adelaide did this, Mr Foyster, or her friend?'

'Indeed, it was our first suspicion, but the children do not yet know how to write; and in any event, they couldn't possibly reach as high as this. It's most odd. See, here, how the pencil mark slopes off, as if the writer has been interrupted, pulled away suddenly?'

Retrieving a length of steel measuring tape from the depths of his coat pocket, Price set it against the writing. 'And you say this appeared from nowhere?' he asked.

'Indeed, overnight, within several hours at the most.'

'Light mass,' said Price, deep in thought. 'Means nothing to me. Sarah?'

'Perhaps we're misinterpreting,' I suggested. 'Here the words are clearly spaced out. Perhaps that's intentional; perhaps each noun is intended to stand *separately*: mass, light and prayers.'

'It's possible,' said Price. 'Either way, there is a distinct Roman Catholic flavour to these messages. Reverend Fosyter, is there any more of this writing you can show us?'

'Indeed there is. Down here, please.'

We followed him round into another passage, which led to more empty and neglected bedrooms. Here, scribbled on the wall next to the entrance of one of these rooms, was yet more pathetic handwriting. I shone my torch a little further along the passage and saw, scrawled in the same unruly handwriting, the four words that have become immortalised in the history of the

Borley affair: *MARIANNE PLEASE HELP GET.* Another message read: *MARIANNE AT GET HELP ENTANT BOTTOM ME.*

'What is this?' asked Price, holding his lamp close to the wall to illuminate words immediately underneath: *I CANNOT UNDER-STAND, TELL ME MORE . . .*

'My wife wrote that,' said the rector. 'We wanted to see whether we could communicate with the entity.'

I looked up and noticed that Price's gaze had narrowed, latching onto the words. Then, abruptly, he said, 'The samples are rather similar. Aren't they?'

'What about this word?' I asked quickly, pointing to some other letters underneath: *TROMPEE.*

'I think it's French,' Price murmured.

'Well, of course it's French!' said a patronising voice from the dark at our backs. 'Silly man. *Trompée.* It means "deceived".'

Price and I spun round.

Reverend Foyster smiled. 'Mr Price, Miss Grey, allow me to introduce my wife, Marianne.'

*

Marianne's face was full of contempt. My first thought was that this woman couldn't possibly be the rector's wife, for she was closer to my age than to his and might easily have passed for his daughter. She was his opposite in almost every respect: healthy, confident and attractive, with a mass of dark hair and curves evident through her silk nightgown.

The rector took a step towards her. 'Dear, you should be in bed.'

'Oh, Lionel, do stop fussing!'

'Mrs Foyster, I do hope we haven't called at a bad time,' I said.

'Oh, not at all. After all, misery does love company.' She gave

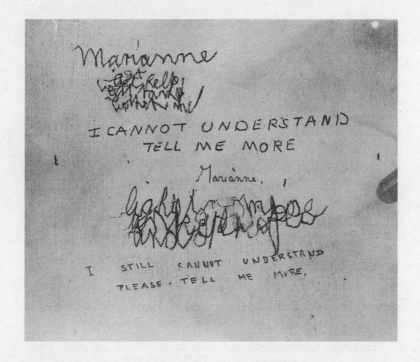

a pinched smile, glancing knowingly at her husband. 'Isn't that how the old saying goes, dear?'

'Mrs Foyster,' Price began, 'I'm—'

'Harry Price,' she said slowly, fixing her eyes on him. 'Yes, I know who you are. Although I must say, I hope your detective abilities exceed the quality of your French or else we might all be in trouble.'

He chuckled warmly at that. And although Mrs Foyster was smiling too, the same friendliness was absent from her eyes.

At the rector's suggestion we retired to the drawing room, where I was glad to sit by the warmth of the fire and in better light as we discussed the wall writings.

'Have you ever seen anything like it?' Foyster asked as he

settled back into his deep armchair cradling a brandy. Mrs Foyster hovered close by.

'Never,' I replied.

But from the far corner of the room where he was studying the contents of a bookcase, Price said firmly, 'I have.'

Mrs Foyster turned sharply towards him and gave a slightly nervous giggle. 'Oh? Tell us then.'

'Paranormal wall writing is extremely rare,' began Price, 'but there is a precedent. In fact, Reverend Foyster, you might have heard of the case. It occurred in 1878.'

The rector shook his head. 'I don't believe so; why would I have heard of it?'

'Because,' Price continued, still staring at the row of books in front of him, 'the affair to which I am referring occurred in a small town in Canada. A place called Amherst, near Nova Scotia. Perhaps you know of it.'

Although I failed to see the relevance of this remark it had an instant effect upon Mrs Foyster who turned and glared accusingly at her husband before crossing the room to the French windows. Her husband turned his head and stared into the fire.

'Ah yes,' Price said confidently, 'I thought you would. You lived quite near there, didn't you? You both did.'

This was news to me.

'Well, yes, but—'

'I do hope you don't mind, but I took the liberty of looking into your situation before we came here this evening. I made some very enlightening preliminary enquiries, in fact. Your cousin, Miss Ethel Bull, helpfully pointed me in the right direction on most of the relevant matters.'

The rector put down his glass cautiously. 'And what matters were those, exactly?'

His curiosity was matched by my own, for it was generally the rule that if a case under our investigation required background checking or additional research, it would fall to me to discharge such duties. But this time Price had not asked me. In fact he had never mentioned the question of any prior investigation. And this alarmed me because it confirmed what I had feared all evening: Price knew something about the case that I did not.

He continued: 'For one thing, an examination of *Crockford's Clerical Directory* of 1931, in which your previous incumbencies are recorded, showed that you were rector of Sackville, Nova Scotia, from 1928 to 1930. That's two years before you both returned to England and took up the living at Borley, is it not?'

'Correct.'

Mrs Foyster said with some heat, 'I don't see what relevance this has to the—'

'Don't you?' Price was watching her carefully. 'Sackville in Nova Scotia is a mere five miles from Amherst. Five miles. And there are certainly more than a few similarities between your problems here at Borley and those experienced in Amherst. I could list them, but I'm sure you're more than familiar with the matter.'

'We have never heard of this case you mention,' retorted Reverend Foyster angrily, 'and even if we had, I don't see what relevance it would have to our own predicament.'

'Allow me to jog your memory,' said Price, turning to look once more at the bookshelf. 'Because, quite conveniently, I see you have a book about the very case in question.' He slipped a thick volume from the shelf and held it out for me to see. 'Wonderful book this, Sarah: Walter Hubbell's *The Haunted House – The Great Amherst Mystery*.'[1] His eyes moved slowly over the pages as he leafed through the book. 'Oh, it's all very dramatic to be sure; it was a bad business, caused quite a bit of upset. Dr Nandor Fodor described this as one of the most famous poltergeist cases in the world. The young girl involved, Esther Cox, was a medium, or so she claimed. And she became the target of an alleged poltergeist infestation that was quite violent indeed. After a terrible time of stone-throwing and other disturbances, writing appeared on the walls of her bedroom.' He was turning the pages with increased eagerness now. 'Listen to this! One of them read simply, "Esther Cox, you are mine to kill."' At this he threw the book down on the floor and snarled at Mrs Foyster, 'Now, dear lady, is any of this beginning to sound familiar to you?'

I could not believe that he had known all of this and kept it from me.

Mrs Foyster stood motionless before the French windows, lost in her reflection in the black glass.

'Tell me, what took you to Canada in the first place?' said Price.

'Missionary work,' the rector answered quietly.

'And were you happy there?'

'Most happy.' He smiled sadly at Mrs Foyster, who had turned towards us. She did not return the gesture.

'Then tell me, why did you leave so suddenly to come here to Borley, this little out-of-the-way place?'

'There are many answers to that question, Mr Price. The first should be evident. Look at me. I'm bound to a wheelchair most days, my arthritis is so bad. I rely on Marianne to help me get around.'

As he spoke, Mrs Foyster drifted towards the drinks cabinet where she hastily filled her glass.

'We lost a great deal of our wealth during the Wall Street Crash. I was fortunate that my family were able to offer me residency here at Borley. But even now our situation could best be described as difficult.'

'You have moved about a fair amount in your time? Some might call it running.'

The rector was turning his head away now.

'Harry,' I said, 'that's enough.'

'But I wonder: what on earth could you be running *from*, sir?'

'Harry!' I raised my voice. This was an unforgivable style of questioning.

Price redirected his attention. 'Mrs Foyster, I can't help thinking this must be a very difficult house for you to live in, especially at this time of year. So many duplex lamps to be filled with paraffin each day, so many passages to sweep, and having to pump all that water by turning the wheel outside. However do you manage it all?'

Reverend Foyster answered for his wife. 'We manage. As I said earlier, we have a man who helps us.'

'Yes, I can see that you do,' said Price softly, 'but I can well understand that the loneliness and discomfort of this house would be hard for anyone to tolerate. And so many bad feelings in the building, stored up over so long, gathering about you. It's a wonder you haven't left the place already.'

'Like the Smiths?' said Mrs Foyster bitterly. 'The ghosts got them in the end, as we all said they would.'

'What do you mean by that?'

'Only that they had it coming. They weren't liked about the village. People in these parts don't take kindly to folk like them.'

'You knew about the house and its reputation before you came here, and yet you *still* came. Tell me why.'

Marianne turned and said bitterly, 'Because we had no choice. Do you know how much they pay my poor husband? I'll tell you

how much: the grand sum of six pounds a week. I know of chauf-
feurs who earn more than that.'

'Forgive me, but that's not quite the same reason that I have
been given.'

No one said a word. Price delighted in the moment. Once
again everyone's attention was on him. Finally he opened his
mouth to speak.

But before Price could utter a word a sudden noise from the
hall caused the rector to start up from his chair. 'I say! What the
devil was that?'

Armed with one of our lamps, Price hurried over to the door,
opened it and peered out into the gloom. As he did so, I fancied
I heard footsteps on the floorboards above us and the dull *thud*
. . . *thud* . . . *thud* . . . of a walking stick.

'Well?'

'Broken crockery,' Price answered. 'It's all over the floor.'

The rector joined him. 'All of this comes from the kitchen
dresser,' he sighed. 'You can see how unlikely it would be for
someone to fetch all of this, fling it down here and get out
of sight so quickly. I think we are going to have a bad night.
Marianne dear, I had better go and check that young Adelaide
is in bed.'

'No,' said Marianne quickly, 'no, I'll go.' And swept out of
the room.

The rector appeared peculiarly disappointed not to have gone
but quickly said, 'What a dear, kind help she is to me. How on
earth I would manage without her I don't know.' He eased himself back into his chair. 'Mr Price, I am genuinely puzzled by
your abrasive attitude towards our predicament. You seem to
blow hot and cold on the affair. One moment you believe it, the
next you do not.'

The same could have been said of Price's approach to the whole subject that was his passion, and the thought caused me to smile. When I looked at him, I saw that he was deep in thought again, watching as the Foysters' maid arrived in the hall with a pan and brush and set to work sweeping up the fragments of crockery. He walked over to speak to her.

'This happens a lot to you, does it?'

'Yes, sir, when there are guests about the house mostly.'[2]

'A ghost with an objection to house guests. Tell me more about that.'

The young girl looked at the rector, whose brow was furrowed. 'Well, sir, the Lord and Lady Whitehouse from Sudbury were here just a few weeks ago and had a terrible time of it. Poor Mrs Foyster became locked in her bedroom. The master had to say a prayer to let her out.'

'I see. And has that happened previously?'

'Oh yes, all the time, sir.'

Just then Mrs Foyster hurried back into the room. 'You needn't look so doubtful, Mr Price. My husband didn't believe it either, but he has faith; and if faith can move mountains it can most certainly change minds.'

'Perhaps. Is young Adelaide all right?'

He spoke politely, but there was no escaping the fact that the air of civility was strained.

'Yes, for now.' She sat down near the fire. 'Now then, I would think you ought to be getting off soon if you are taking a taxi back into Long Melford. And I wouldn't dally in those lanes either.'

'No, not yet, thank you,' Price replied. 'You see, I was in the middle of explaining to your good husband what I think is the matter in this house. As I see it, there are two possibilities. The first will appeal to those who are more open-minded. I have a theory that psychic abilities do, under certain conditions, produce phantasms or ghosts. Projections, if you like. My work with Herr Schneider has led me to this view. Whether we can apply this theory to the causation of poltergeist phenomena in this case is another matter.'

'Go on,' said Reverend Foyster.

Marianne was rolling her eyes as if to convey her boredom. 'Can someone remind me why I am here?' She shot her husband a scowl. 'Really, Lionel, bringing these strangers to our home . . . whatever next?'

There was an awkward silence as Price hesitated. 'Well, umm, your wife is a young woman with very firm opinions; perhaps there is some psychic connection between her and this phantom nun.'

The rector nodded his agreement. 'The wall writings and that pathetic appeal for help would seem to suggest so.'

'Indeed,' Price said. 'And except for a very brief period, there have always been many young girls – maids, the Bull sisters – living at the Rectory. Perhaps traces of their memories, their thoughts and experiences here, are still clinging to their old home. A sort of psychic residue, if you like.'

'What's the second possibility?'

'Now then, that's altogether trickier,' said Price. He sat down beside the rector, fixing him with his cool eyes, and I braced myself for what was coming.

But before he could say a word, there came from Mrs Foyster a startling cry. Then she leapt forward like a tiger before falling to her knees, her hands clasped in a gesture of prayer.

It was pitiful, like watching a child perform for attention.

'Marianne,' Foyster cried, getting slowly to his feet. 'Look now, you see what you've done – you've set her off!'

'Set her off?'

'My wife, sir, is prone to bouts of hysteria. Is it any wonder with all of this to contend with—'

I was about to go to the woman's aid when an appalling series of crashes sounded from the hall. 'What on earth?'

With unwise impetuousness, we all hurried to the door. Glass bottles flew past our faces. One hurled down from above, another came flying down the stairs and crashed at our feet, the glass shattering this way and that.

'Where are they coming from?' I gasped. 'Who's throwing them?'

'You see now!' cried Mrs Foyster. 'You see it is true. God save us all.'

'Get back,' said Price over the turmoil, and we did so. Indeed, I ducked down behind him. Only Mrs Foyster departed the scene, breaking out of the drawing room and bolting across the hall and up the stairs to her bedroom.

'Marianne!' the old rector cried out. Then he looked down, crestfallen and muttered, mostly to himself, 'Now there will be trouble.'

My heart was pounding, my hands trembling. I called desperately to Price for help.

'Come here,' he said soothingly, gathering me up in his arms. I was safe.

And then, as abruptly as it had begun, the disturbance ceased, and all was still and calm as before. Except for a single pebble that appeared as if from nowhere, skipped across the floor and bounced off the skirting board at the bottom of the stairs before rolling to a halt.

Foyster stood, trembling, then said gravely as if to himself, 'Is this my punishment? Is this what I am doomed to endure?'

I started. Punishment for what?

'Forgive me,' he muttered, shaking his head. 'It's this dreadful house. It plays the most terrible tricks on you.'

'Houses don't play tricks, Reverend Foyster,' said Price, 'but people most certainly do!'

And then he was at the nearest window, peering out as if some movement had caught his eye. He looked back at me. 'Check on Mrs Foyster,' he instructed.

I did so, following the route she had taken up to the first floor, while Price and Foyster began a thorough search of the downstairs rooms, diligently checking every door and window. I went first along the passage, past the wall writing, to the nursery to check that the young girl was still asleep. I was amazed to see that she was, and the sight calmed me.

But not for long; for no sooner had I closed her bedroom door and released a small sigh of relief than I noticed, next to the door frame, a set of markings that had not been present on our first inspection: a pattern of lines which reminded me of a crest – a royal emblem perhaps. Adjacent to these markings was a word, and it was clear as before: *TROMPEE*.

Somewhere in the bowels of the house a servant bell rung.

I need to get out of here now, I told myself, looking ahead of me, down the long, dark passage that led to the landing and the stairs to the hall. But before I could move an inch a piercing scream issued forth from the far end of the corridor. From the Foysters' bedroom.

I bolted forward, shouting Marianne's name. When I reached the door I found it locked. I threw my weight at it again and

again until finally it burst open and I stumbled into the room.
'Mrs Foyster, I—'

The sight before me stopped me dead.

Mrs Foyster lay on the bed, her left eye swelling and red,
her lip bleeding. Towering over her was a stout, dark-haired,
thuggish looking man.

I recognised him immediately.

It was the man who had approached me earlier that night,
alone on the station platform; the man who had followed us
into our carriage and watched as I spoke to Price. The watcher.

Before I could think what to say the assailant bolted past me,
out onto the landing and down the stairs, slamming the front
door behind him.

'Quickly, close the door!' implored Mrs Foyster in a hoarse
voice.

I did so, quite horrified. She stared at me blankly, silently.

Eventually I asked, 'Who was that man?'

She cleared her throat. 'Why don't you pull up a chair, Miss
Grey? I think perhaps I should explain.'

Notes

1   For a detailed account of the 'Great Amherst Mystery' see *Poltergeist Over England*, pp. 28–30.
2   According to Harry Price, the guests who visited the Foysters included Sir George and Lady Whitehouse, Mrs Richards, Miss May Walker, Miss Gordon, Mrs Wildgoose (née Dytor), Edwin Whitehouse, Mr L'Estrange, Mr d'Arles and Captain Deane.

– 23 –

MARIANNE'S WARNING

'Who was that?' I asked again.

'Just a friend,' she said.

'Mrs Foyster, forgive me but none of *my* friends behave in such a manner. Look at you – you're bleeding!'

Rising uncertainly from the bed, she fetched a robe from the wardrobe and slipped it on. Then she sat awkwardly on the edge of the bed beside me. I thought she looked lost, and in spite of her thinly disguised coldness towards me, I couldn't help feeling sorry for this wounded woman.

'It is a depressingly subjugated position we occupy in life, is it not, Miss Grey?' she said quietly, looking down into her lap.

I didn't understand, and politely told her so.

'We – women, I mean: such lonely little lives we lead, don't you find?' She sighed deeply and lifted her gaze to meet mine. 'The man you just met is our lodger. His name is Frank Peerless.'

'Lodger? But I thought only you, Lionel, the child and your maid lived here.'

'We haven't lied to you, Miss Grey. Frank lives in the cottage next door.[1] He pays us rent, attends to our needs. You met him, I understand, earlier this evening on your way here, at the station.'

'I thought he was following me.'

'How silly! Frank makes the journey from London every day. He has a flower stall outside one of the London cemeteries.'

'What was he doing in here?' I asked, though I already knew the answer. 'Why did he strike you?'

Mrs Foyster drew a tissue from a box next to the bed and dabbed her bloody lip carefully. 'You needn't be concerned for *my* well-being, Miss Grey. I can assure you, Frank is perfectly harmless.' She paused. 'I must remind you that you have signed an agreement of confidentiality regarding anything you see or hear in this house.'

'That is correct,' I said, though in fact it was Price who had signed the agreement, not me. But she seemed satisfied, for she promptly tucked herself beneath her bedcovers and propped herself up with pillows like a child preparing for a bedtime story. I had the strongest impression that here was a woman who had not enjoyed the company of another female for a long while. She wanted to talk.

'Frank can get a little excitable at times; he loses control. But it's nothing more than that.' She touched her wound again and flinched. 'Things got slightly out of hand, that's all. That happens sometimes. I'm sure you understand, being a woman of the world.' She saw my confusion. 'Really, you shouldn't think badly of him. He is perfectly . . . *acceptable*. Or at least,' she added with a grin, 'I find him so.'

'But your husband—'

'Lionel knows all about it,' she said nonchalantly. 'He pretends he doesn't, but really, he knows. Men are awfully good at covering their feelings, don't you find? It gives them dignity and a sense of power, pretending they can't see when actually they can. Especially when it hurts them the most.'

There was something chillingly calculating in her tone. I sat back, amazed that she had been so candid with me.[2] Of course, I knew there were women like her. They were the talk of parlour rooms the length and breadth of London – scarlet women.

'Oh, don't look at me like that,' she said defensively. 'I told you, Lionel doesn't mind. In fact, I think in a way he rather enjoys it. Do you know how long we've been married?'

'Tell me.'

'Ten years.'

'A lifetime.'

Her face hardened at my sarcasm. 'I can see you don't approve, Miss Grey.'

'It isn't for me to judge.'

'And yet that is precisely what you are doing. I can see so much, Miss Grey, even the things you cannot . . .' Her unsettling gaze held me. It seemed to linger around my neckline before floating back up to meet my eyes. She reached for a cigarette and there followed the scrape and flare of a match. 'You must understand, every so often this terrible urge comes upon me, and it's overwhelming. I don't suppose I should say that I am incapable of resisting men, but in these cycles I become quite desperate. Hungry for it.' I saw her arm move suggestively beneath the bedclothes. 'Have you never felt that?'

I shook my head. Then, in a manner that was noticeably more cordial, she asked me how well acquainted I was with Price. I said that I knew him very well but that this was hardly surprising given that he was my employer and had been for five years.

'But you'd like to know him much better than that, wouldn't you?'

It was like talking to a coarse teenager, and when I refused to answer the question she closed her eyes wearily. 'I understand, Sarah. Really I do. As I said, I can see everything.' Her eyes snapped open and once again her gaze settled on my neckline.

What was she looking at?

'But you must appreciate,' she continued, 'sometimes I feel I am dying in this house. It suffocates me with its perpetual melancholy. I'm entitled to some excitement, aren't I? I yearn for the bright lights of London, Sarah, the rush of the place, and instead I get *this*. Look at me! I'm stuck out here in the wilderness.'

'And Frank gives you excitement?'

'Yes, in many ways,' she said with a smirk. 'Imagine how it is for me every day: getting up, clearing up after Lionel, ensuring he takes his medicine, tending to his needs. He knocks everything over and blames it on "them", "the things". It's utterly pathetic.'

A thought struck her. 'I say, you don't suppose Lionel is responsible for some of the odd going-ons, do you? I've noticed that when he's in his wheelchair things happen far less frequently. And some days he makes no sense at all, barricades himself away in that little chapel over the stairs, praying like an old fool. In his mind, everything is a sin!'

'What does he pray for?' I asked.

'Forgiveness, I imagine,' she said with resentment. 'What I'm trying to say is, this isn't my life, and it never was my life, never should have been.'

'Then why did you come here?'

'There was some trouble in Canada. Mr Price was right about

that at least. I suppose you could say that we *were* running away, when I think about it now.'

'Running from what exactly?'

'Ourselves mostly, our darker natures. I suppose it was my fault mainly. Not *all* my fault, you understand; he played his part! And then some. But after that whole business . . . well, we had to move on.'

'It concerned men?' I asked.

'Doesn't it always?' she said bitterly. 'We had to come back. We had no money; as Lionel told you, we lost everything in the Crash. And now there's nothing left. I'm all he has.'

'So what you are saying is that you don't love him.'

'I have always loved him, Miss Grey. As I have loved all my husbands. But now . . . well, it's more the sort of love that one feels for a brother or a friend. Can you understand that?'

All her husbands?

'He wants me near him all the time, like some sort of doll. He can't stand it if I'm away from the house, even if only for a few hours.'

She paused and looked at me with determination in her eyes. 'But I will *not* be poor, Sarah.'

'What will you do?'

'Frank has a plan,' she said. 'He wants me to go with him to London. To start a business. Imagine that! Me, a businesswoman! A chance to start again.'

'Mrs Foyster, a moment ago you used the expression "all my husbands". What did you mean by that?'

'I suppose you might say I have a chequered past,' she said carefully, 'but that applies to most of us, doesn't it, Miss Grey?'

I looked away. 'You had more than one husband?'

Silence.

'Did Lionel know you were once married to someone else?'

'Of course not.'

'Were you divorced?'

She shook her head. This I could not believe. 'How old were you when you met Lionel?'

Her mouth fixed in a horrible grin. 'I was seven.'

If she had intended to shock me then she had succeeded. She looked at me the way a child might study an insect, analysing my reaction, assessing her skills in manipulation. It sickened me.

'Oh please, there's no need to look so alarmed,' she said. 'Lionel baptised me when I was seven – that was when we first met. As I grew up, he stayed in touch, until eventually—'

'He proposed marriage.'

'Exactly.'

And now I understood why earlier that night Mrs Foyster had prevented her husband from going upstairs to check on little Adelaide unaccompanied. He had been drawn to Marianne as a child. I felt sick. But I wasn't leaving until I had learned more about the mystery that had brought me back here. 'Tell me about the nun,' I said. 'The Dark Woman.'

Marianne gave me a long look and said rather nonchalantly, 'What of her?'

'Is she real?'

'I have seen her outside, near the summerhouse, a dark figure with head bowed. Yes, she is real; she is spoken of often enough, isn't she?'

'Harry seems to think that you might share some sort of connection with her,' I suggested. 'Some psychic bond.'

'How observant of him. Heavens, my name is written all over the walls!'

'And you think those words are messages from the nun?'

'Either that or they are the deranged inventions of my husband.'

'Then if it *is* the nun, what do you suppose she wants?' I asked.

'Everything suggests that she is Catholic: the word "Mass" on the walls, and the fact that when Miss Ethel saw her she was telling her beads.'

All of this made sense. 'What else?'

'I feel such an impression of violence in this house. I can sense it. Violence from long ago.' She hesitated. 'The word *trompée* is important . . . I think it means that the nun who walks these grounds was deceived by someone during her lifetime, here perhaps, at a house that once stood on this site. I sense that she didn't come here of her own free will – she was brought here from France.'

'Sense?' I repeated the word back to her. 'You speak with such conviction.'

'Lionel and I have found a number of ancient French artefacts about the house that would confirm the idea, together with other items.'

'Such as?'

'A French dictionary, for one. We found it on the first floor landing, just outside the Blue Room. Also a small gold ring – a wedding ring, I imagine – and some brass medallions inscribed with French and Latin.'

Medallions. Like the one found on Price's pillow in the Blue Room? Even the reference to a French dictionary stirred a memory.

'*Trompée*,' she whispered.

'What?'

But when she spoke next it was not with words, but single

letters. 'D-E-C-E . . . Deceived!' she cried. 'She was deceived. Yes, I feel certain that she was brought to England by a man who wanted her – someone important who betrayed her, deceived her, abandoned her, tortured and murdered her. She was escaping France and her life. She was promised the chance to start again, to start a new nunnery on her own. But he wanted her for his mistress and forced himself upon her. Such . . . such shame! She tore her medal off in shame.' My hostess put her hands to her throat. 'She's here somewhere; her remains are buried here, in or around the Rectory. She's leaving clues for us, guiding us, *warning* us.'

'Mrs Foyster?' I took hold of her arm. 'Tell me where you are getting this information.'

As she looked up at me, I felt as though she were capable of reaching into the innermost recesses of my mind, leafing through my thoughts as easily as one might browse through the pages of a book. She smiled at me knowingly. My skin crawled.

'What are you *really* doing in this house, Miss Grey?'

'I don't understand.'

'Oh, I think you do. I think you understand very well indeed. You came back. You didn't have to and yet you did. Why?'

'For the sake of our research,' I said. 'This case has such . . . possibilities.'

Her face hardened. 'No, this house possesses some personal significance for you. I can sense it: you've lost something.'

And then the most peculiar thing happened. The light in the room seemed to undergo a transformation. Shades of purple and black seeped into my vision, giving our surroundings an ethereal air.

'I told you, I can see things, Sarah. I see things in my head, events long since passed and events yet to come. I've had the ability since I was a child.'

'And what can you see now?' I whispered, though I was afraid to hear her answer.

'*You*, Sarah. I see you. A long time ago. Walking. It's cold and black, and you're walking somewhere with your mother. But you should have turned back. You should have turned back when you had the chance.' Her hand flew to cover her mouth. 'Dear God, you poor thing.'

I stood up, backing away from her with mounting fear. This was beyond my comprehension.

'You think you've lost so much,' she continued, 'but the worst is yet to come.'

I shook my head and, between fitful breaths, cried out at her to stop.

'The woman with two paths and one regret. There is a mark upon you.'

I froze. The words. I had heard them before.

'This house sees all. The nun that haunts this place wants revenge upon the deceivers who walk these halls. Whoever they are, wherever they are. Mark my words, whoever explores this house, delves into its mysteries, pursues the Dark Woman, will turn mad and never again know what it means to live a restful life. They will be followed from this place, haunted. Cursed. They will suffer the worst death. A bad death.'

Suddenly Marianne was still. Perfectly still and staring at the black glass of the windowpane. Then she said, 'They make so much more sense to me now, my visions.'

'Visions? What visions?'

'Whenever I lie down and close my eyes, I see things . . .

things other people don't seem to see. It's been that way since we arrived in this house.'

'Tell me,' I demanded, gripping her forearm tightly. 'What is it that you see in your visions?'

Before she could answer an urgent rapping on the bedroom door startled us both.

'Marianne, who is that you're talking to?'

'I am speaking to Miss Grey.'

'Will you come out here, please? Mr Price wants to speak to us downstairs.' It was obvious from Reverend Foyster's voice that something was wrong. He sounded agitated.

'Not now, Lionel – we're talking.'

'Now, please, Marianne. I'll be waiting for you downstairs in the library.'

His shuffling footsteps died away down the passage.

Marianne took a skirt and cardigan from her wardrobe and proceeded to dress slowly as if relishing the idea that I might be watching. I averted my eyes and waited politely. But as she made for the door I was impelled to call out, 'Mrs Foyster, please, what do you see when you close your eyes?'

'You're living in a prison of your own construction.' She looked back at me darkly. 'If you weren't aware, Sarah Grey, then you really should know.'

'Know what?'

'There is something you can't see. And it's around your neck.'

Notes

1   '[Marianne], ever on the lookout, discovered an advert in *The Times* for a small boy who wanted a home, etc. Correspondence and an interview ensued and eventually a little chap a few months junior to our wee girl came to share our home

for a while. Her father, a widower, brought him down' (Lionel Foyster, from his unpublished manuscript *Fifteen Months in a Haunted House*).

2　'Guy L'Estrange said he thought Marianne was very highly strung. He was alone with her for some time and she opened her heart to him and told him things he would never repeat to anyone. Once, during his visit, Marianne seemed to have a fit of hysterics – laughing and crying together. She recovered after a while. Her husband took no notice so L'Estrange did nothing either' (Guy L'Estrange in an interview with Peter Underwood, *Borley Postscript*, p. 117).

– 24 –

THE DARK WOMAN
OF BORLEY

'Wait!' I cried. 'Please, come back. I need to know what you mean!'

But she had slipped out of the room. I stood, adrift in my own confusion, the bedrooms walls seeming to spin around me until panic forced me over to the mirror on the bedside table. I looked and confirmed it: there was nothing at all around my neck, thank God.

I see more than you know.

I sat on the edge of the bed, trying to appeal to the rational part of me to tell me that this was all nonsense. But I had heard and seen enough to reason that Marianne knew far more than she was telling; that there was a connection between the deceptive practices of those attached to this house and the dark forces within it. And I was only too aware that I had lied to myself, to Mother and to Price for the past two years, though neither of them yet knew it. This was my private sin. And Borley Rectory could see it.

'Sarah?'

The voice made me start.

Price swept into the room. 'What's keeping you?' he asked impatiently. 'We're waiting for you downstairs.'

'Harry – this house. Something is very, *very* wrong here.'

He looked at me doubtfully but I begged him to listen to me, looking pleadingly into his eyes. 'I think this house, somehow, is dangerous. There is a ghastly atmosphere here. Mrs Foyster – she knows. She has some sort of ability. The wall writing, the nun, the medallion – it's all connected to some sort of curse on people connected with this house who tell lies.'

It sounded crazy even to me.

'Listen to yourself, Sarah.'

But I went on. I told him what Mrs Foyster had said to me, of her violent affair with Frank Peerless and her self-confessed bigamy. 'But you mustn't say anything to anyone,' I insisted. 'I promised her.'

He was quiet for a long moment, staring across the bedroom, before saying calmly, 'And so this fog of ghouls and poltergeists dissolves, and we see clearly the truth of the matter. Sarah, sit down.'

'No, there's no time. Please, just—'

'Sit down!'

His stern tone forced me to obey.

'Now then, I want you to listen to me very carefully, all right?'

I nodded.

'Marianne is behind all of this.'

'What? Harry, no, I don't think so.'

He nodded. 'The woman is so bored I think she would do and say practically anything to draw attention to herself and to escape from the Rectory. Think about it. Almost every item thrown at her husband in the time they have been here has come from behind him, with Marianne out of sight.'

'But that makes no sense,' I insisted. 'What about the bottles we saw flying about in the hall? Everything that happened in this house before we even came? The bells that rang when the Smiths were here?'

'Ah yes, the bells,' said Price cynically. 'The Foysters have reported hearing them as well, haven't they? And what sort of haunted house would this be without ringing bells?' He reached into his creased jacket and produced a length of cord which he held out for me to see. 'Look, I found this whipcord string dangling out of the ivy in the wall in the courtyard. I followed it and found it led through an open window into the house. Sarah, it was attached to a cluster of exposed bell wires at the back of the kitchen passage. Just one little tug and the bells ring. I rang it myself not long ago.'

'No,' I said, shaking my head. The idea that the bells were rigged with string just seemed too far-fetched; surely we would have noticed them? 'There were certainly no strings attached when the Smiths lived here.'

'Well, there are now,' Price said firmly. 'Sarah, there are cords like this running up to most of the bedrooms. I've had my suspicions about the Foysters since I learned about their time together in Canada. There they were known as the odd couple.'

'Lionel as well?' I asked doubtfully. 'He doesn't strike me as so odd.'

'Lionel especially. A rather unsavoury business, to say the least. And there is more.' Price reached into his jacket and produced yet another item, a small bottle. 'I found this in his study – opium. I hardly need tell you that this is a highly illegal drug which can give rise to all manner of hallucinations. Pencils which rise and float in the air?' He smiled and shook his head. 'I think not.'

I found little confort in this revelation. Mrs Foyster's words had infected me with lingering paranoia and I was convinced that there was more substance to the strange happenings than Price was willing to acknowledge. I tried telling him so then, but he interrupted and told me to go downstairs with him. I followed reluctantly, an inner turmoil slowing my step.

The Foysters were waiting for us in the drawing room. The night's proceedings had taken their toll upon Foyster who, looking weary, had taken to his wheelchair. Mrs Foyster hovered silently by the fireplace, a glass in one hand and a cigarette in the other. I took a seat by the fire. Price stood by the bookcase and announced that his investigation of the downstairs rooms had been fruitful.

'Well,' said Foyster testily, 'don't keep us in suspense.' He pointed at his wife who sat opposite him, her head turned away. 'Have you see Marianne's eye? She's black and blue. I tell you, *they* are at it again.'

Mrs Foyster shot me a warning look.

Before the rector could say anything more on the subject of spirits, Price puffed up his chest and approached the old man. I held my breath. *He's going to tell him!*

'Harry—'

'Mr Foyster, are you really so blind to the truth that you cannot see it, even when it is sitting immediately in front of you?'

'Whatever do you mean?' The light from the fireplace glowed on Marianne's cheeks.

Price gazed at Mrs Foyster with contempt. Then he said to the rector, 'Your wife is behind it all, sir.'

'What?' cried Mrs Foyster, putting her glass down on the mantelpiece. 'You think it's *me* throwing bottles and stones, harming myself? You think I'm the one dressing up in dark clothes, marching myself and everyone else up the garden path?'

'Yes,' said Price, 'or rather, to be more precise, you and your accomplice.' He wheeled round to face the rector. 'Mr Foyster, it's your wife who has been deceiving you.'

'With whose authority do you say so, sir?'

'Mine,' said Price. 'Only mine.'

And as the sole investigator of the case, that was all he needed. Price marched into the hall, gesturing for us to follow. We all did so, Marianne less eagerly than the rest of us. I soon understood why. Price was standing at an open window in the gloomy passage leading down to the kitchen. He got down on his knees and pointed to a small hole in the skirting board, which had come away from the floor. 'The house is riddled with holes like this,' he said, poking his finger into the crevice. 'Every one of these holes is pitted with phosphorous powder which ignites when exposed to the air. This explains the sporadic outbursts of fire.'

The rector shook his head. 'But the objects thrown at me . . .'

'Have always come from behind you, have they not?'

'Well, yes, but—'

'And look here!' Price remarked. From the fine gap which separated the skirting board from the floor he seized a delicate cord like the one he had shown me upstairs and held it up for us to see. It ran from his fingers up to the servant bells above his head. 'This leads from the bells in the kitchen passage immediately out to the bushes in the garden,' he announced triumphantly. He gave the cord a short, sharp pull and one of the servant bells above us rang out.

Reverend Foyster, slumped in his wheelchair at the entrance to the hall, looked stunned. I was surprised that he hadn't noticed the cord himself. Hadn't noticed or hadn't wanted to notice it.

'I should point out,' Price continued, 'that the bells can also be rung from the bedroom passage upstairs, near the Blue Room's door. Very clever indeed, Mrs Foyster! It must have taken you a good time to rig it all up. Ah, but then I am sure you had some assistance. Perhaps it's your accomplice I should be congratulating.'

'How dare you!' she retaliated. 'How dare you march in here throwing these accusations about like chicken feed! This is our home, Mr Price, and you are our guest.'

'No,' cried Price. 'I am your inquisitor, madam. And I have found you out!'

Mrs Foyster stepped back into the shadows of the hall.

Reverend Foyster addressed Price. 'What you are telling us is untenable, untrue. How do you account for everything that happened *before* my wife and I came here? Tell us that!'

'I believe Mary Pearson, the former maid, had a lot to do with it,' said Price.

What? I thought. Where has this come from? 'Harry, you never mentioned the Smiths' maid before—'

'And between you both, I believe you have carried on these deceptive practices and made this haunt your own.'

'No. This Rectory is disordered, I tell you!'

'Indeed it is,' said Price. 'It is disordered in the worst sense imaginable. It's bursting at the seams with physical, psychological and moral chaos. But this disorder has nothing to do with ghosts.'

'Harry,' I said. 'Harry, you can stop now.'

But he was ignoring me, his words chilly and clipped. 'Sarah, Mr Foyster, Mrs Foyster – this case has taken on more facets than

I ever imagined. It is without doubt the most intriguing and invigorating that has ever come my way. To expose it now as a hoax would be a revelation, a crushing disappointment to many thousands of believers. But that won't stop me.' He turned to the rector, his eyes flashing. 'Mr Foyster, your wife is engaged in a love affair with your lodger, Frank Peerless. They're in on it together.'

'That's a contemptible lie, sir!' Foyster snarled. 'Peerless came to us from an advertisement we placed in the *Church Times* seeking a companion for little Adelaide. He has a young boy, so the arrangement was ideal.'

'Yes, it *was* ideal. For Mrs Foyster at least. Listen to me,' Price ordered. 'It's not the spirits beating up your wife, Mr Foyster, it's her lover. He's consumed with jealousy and he wants you gone. They both do.'

'Harry!' I cried. My God, was there anything he wouldn't say?

'No, no,' protested Reverend Foyster, his face crumpling in despair. 'These stories, they're nothing; they're malicious gossip, that's all, put about by mean-minded people who are jealous of Marianne, her charm and her kindness. They have no factual basis.'

I thought Price would surely stop then, that he would recognise from the old man's evident pain and uncertainty that he had gone too far. I thought he would have mercy. I willed him to have mercy.

'Kindness? My good man, where is the kindness in *lying* to you, throwing things at you from darkened corners, whispering in the dark, just so that she can deceive you? I see no kindness in this.'

Reverend Foyster gave his wife an expression of such anguish and devastated betrayal that I couldn't help but pity him.

Marianne didn't even notice. She was standing like a naughty child at the bottom of the stairs, twirling a curl of hair around her finger.

'But what really interests me, sir,' Price continued, 'is how you never even suspected what the two of them were up to, playing these tricks on you.'

'No, I – I . . .'

But Price was relentless, unforgiving, his expression slyer than ever. 'Or could it be that you *did* know and all the time you have been playing along with the whole deception? Perhaps, sir, you enjoy seeing your wife and her lover together? Is that it? Their casual relations thrill you? Or perhaps you have been compiling your diary with literary ambitions in mind. You wouldn't be the first who has lived in this house and entertained such an idea. Your predecessor's wife was a very keen author, as I recall.'

Watching all of this play out, my thoughts were occupied not by the Foysters and their convoluted relationship with their lodger, but by Price's unforgiving attitude towards our hosts. They were feeling the ferocity of the sceptic's rage. Was he really so insensitive as not to question, even for a moment, how his words, his attacks on them, would make me, his companion, feel? How would his attacks, which anyone in my situation would have found embarrassing, affect the way I viewed him? Had he thought of that? Did he even care? The fact that I didn't know – couldn't even tell – was most disheartening, disappointing even; for as much as I still cared for him, still *wanted* him, the radiance of his personality was beginning to fade in my eyes, dimmed by his outrageous behaviour. It reminded me of how he had shunned me back in 1929 when I had gone to Yorkshire.

'This persecution ends now!' the rector growled suddenly. He was glaring at Price. 'Get out of my house. Get OUT!'

Price nodded and turned to face me. 'Come along, Sarah. It seems we have outstayed our welcome.'

'You were never welcome in this house, Harry Price!' Foyster's voice was deadly serious, his face flushed with anger. 'Yes, I know all about it, your last visit ended in disaster. That seance you conducted upstairs. You let something in, something evil. You're dangerous!' He held out his trembling hand and said, 'You have something that belongs to me. I want it back.' Shakily, he held out his arthritic hand. 'My *Diary of Occurrences*, if you would be so kind.'

I had never seen Price look so cold. 'I don't have it,' he said flatly. 'At least, not with me. I must have left it in my office at the Laboratory.'

'He's lying,' Mrs Foyster said suddenly. Her eyes were wild and red. 'They had it with them on the train. Frank saw them together.' She pointed at me and said, '*She* has it.'

'Is this true?'

When I said nothing Reverend Foyster held out his hand, opening and closing his fingers. 'My diary, please, Miss Grey. I won't ask you again.'

I had an opportunity then to set right some of the wrongs that were to come. If only I had known it. I stared at him blankly, feeling Price's eyes upon me, torn by the choice I had no wish to make. Eventually, to my shame, I said, 'I'm afraid your wife is lying to you, Mr Foyster. I don't have it.'

At that moment something cold and invasive, some peculiar pulse of air, pressed past me. It came so suddenly and with such force that I staggered to one side.

'I want it *back!* Do you hear me?'

Price's voice rose to a crescendo. 'I know perfectly well what you *want*, sir, and you will have none of it.' He stalked angrily towards the rector, stooping to place his hands on both arms of Foyster's wheelchair so that the old man was trapped. 'Indeed, you will have nothing but the truth!'

'No, Harry!' For the briefest moment an image flashed through my mind, quick enough to shock me but vivid enough to be quite unmistakable. It was the nun, her withered arms stretching towards me, black robes billowing out behind her. I cried out, 'Harry, please stop! Listen to me – they're not making it all up!'

'I know,' Price continued, glowering into the rector's face, 'that before Marianne married you her was name Greenwood – a name she inherited from a previous marriage. I also know that there is no record of a divorce, and Mr Greenwood is still very much alive. And I know that in 1914, in Belfast, she gave birth to a child – a little boy who she is hiding from you.'

At this Marianne emitted a piercing shriek. In horror I wheeled round to see her clawing at her arms and striking at her own face before collapsing to the floor, sobbing and gasping breathlessly, 'No, no!'

'What nonsense is this?' spat Foyster. 'What are you saying? That my wife is . . . ?'

Price was emphatic. 'The church register records the bond as having been made on the sixteenth of October 1914. She's still married, aren't you, *Mrs Foyster*?'

The rector reached out to his wife. 'Marianne . . . is this true? Tell me it's not.'

But her cries drowned out his words.

'Mr Price, you are a liar!' she screamed. 'You believe more than you're letting on.'

'The woman's hysterical,' Price announced, stepping back

from Marianne's accusation. 'This house is too stressful for her – she's overwrought. She slips easily into states where she is unconscious and apparently remembers nothing. Then she writes all over the walls, puts pebbles under your pillow, turns herself out of bed, hides your books and papers, throws stones, drinks your coffee, disturbs your study. She creates illusions, sir, and she calls them facts!'[1]

'Why, Marianne? Why would you do such a thing?' the rector cried, moving towards her with the wariness of one approaching a rabid dog.

'Because she *hates* it here,' Price snarled. He looked across at me. 'Come, Sarah, we must be off.'

As we made for the doorway I thought of Mrs Foyster, with cunning intent and to indulge her need for excitement, cruelly deceiving her family and friends, destroying their property and risking their health with booby traps, broken glass, hammers and stones. And what of her husband, poor, pathetic Lionel Foyster, who said so little but concealed so much? What would become of him? His health would decline and he would increasingly come to rely on his troubled wife. What would she do to him? How far would she go? The thought made me shiver, and as I did so I looked up and saw that she was watching me from the shadows, grinning, her face streaming with tears.

Mad, I thought. She's completely mad!

'You can see it all, can't you, little Miss Goody Two-Shoes,' she mocked. 'You think you're so clever, so perfectly proper!'

'Marianne, be quiet!' cried her husband.

But Mrs Foyster was ignoring him, advancing slowly towards me. She was wild, fiery-eyed with a mass of tangled hair, and she spoke with the coldest conviction, her words landing on me like blows. 'Do you really believe *I* am the only liar in this room?'

she said menacingly. 'You have the gall to think that, after all you've kept hidden from *him*?' She pointed at Price, who saw the gesture but ignored it.

Please don't tell him, I begged silently.

'Why not? How dare you, Sarah!' I felt the force of her words in a second, mysterious pulse of air. 'How *dare* you!'

I knew then that she was reading my mind. I suppose I had known it from the moment she had described my first tentative visit to the Laboratory in Queensberry Place on the night when it all began. *You, Sarah. I see you. A long time ago. Walking. It's cold and black, and you're walking somewhere with your mother. You should have turned back* . . . But only now did I acknowledge that this woman was in command of a genuine psychic ability. Oh, she had deceived her husband, I did not doubt that. But I was equally certain that some latent power stirred within her. And I was deeply afraid that now, on this dismal night, she would disclose to Price the secret I had so carefully concealed from him all these years.

Marianne Foyster opened her mouth to speak and I held my breath.

'You asked me what I see when I close my eyes, Sarah – the visions that come to me across the darkness. I see Her. Always Her. And She is coming for you, Sarah, for both of you. After the losses you will suffer, after the fire, after the proof that will be found, *the Dark Woman will return*.'

Note

1   Suspicions that the old rector was fooled by his wife are reinforced by W. H. Salter. He recorded visiting Lionel Foyster: 'I reminded him that a mutual friend, who had seen the wall writings, had pronounced them, and all the other queer

happenings, as his wife's work. He said that was all nonsense. Asked to describe one of the recent occurrences, he said a dreadful thing had happened only the last weekend. His sermon, which he had left on the study table on Saturday night, had disappeared when he went to pick it up on Sunday morning. He spoke of this as if it were obviously the work of the powers of evil, a view I was unable to accept. He seemed to me to have little worldly wisdom and to be entirely dominated by his wife' (*The Haunted Rectory*).

– 25 –

'TOGETHER WE WILL UNCOVER THE TRUTH'

My relationship with Price was never really the same after that.

I could not have known that my employment at the Laboratory would soon be at an end, or that we were about to be parted for five long and difficult years. But there were signs of the change that was coming. And as I look back over this manuscript, turning the pages across the years, I can see them all – the lost moments and the choices that led us there.

We returned to London immediately, and although I was glad to re-enter the sanctuary of my home, I could not shake from my mind the memories of what had happened. I slept fitfully, dark dreams of the phantom nun swirling about me. Marianne Foyster's prophetic words, which Price had dismissed as melodramatic ramblings, had stirred emotions that I had tried to suppress: guilt and shame, but most of all anger at myself for giving so much to a man who had given so little back to me.

Mother was more remote than ever. She rose early to fetch the post, as though it were an urgent task. Occasionally she came down to the drawing room in the evening and sat, listening in silence to the gramophone, but mostly she stayed upstairs in her bedroom with the door shut.

It was naive of me not to question any of this at the time, but it wasn't as if I didn't have my own distractions. Even if I had wanted to investigate, my attemps would have been prevented by her locked bedroom door. I sensed that it wasn't just me she was shutting out, it was the life without answers to questions she wasn't prepared to share or explain to me. I had given up asking about my father, about the mysterious visitor who had come to the house and poured questions and faith and renewed mourning into mother's head. She would tell me in her own good time.

The weekend passed in a blur, and on Sunday night I lay awake in bed, turning over dark thoughts. The idea of returning to the Laboratory, knowing that Price's attitude towards the case was so different from mine, for reasons I could not explain to him, filled me with creeping nervousness. The thought compelled me to reach for my lamp and, by its light, to retrieve my Holy Bible. But when I opened the drawer next to my bed I froze.

In the centre of the drawer, next to my Bible, lay a brass medallion bearing the figure of St Ignatius. I recognised it immediately, my mind rushing back in time five years to the Blue Room at Borley Rectory. But how it had come to be here, in the drawer next to my bed? I had no recollection of it having been there before, though when I tried to recall where I had stored the medallion, the memory refused to come. I hesitated before removing it from the drawer. It felt cold in my hand, and I shuddered. I hated to look at the thing. It was just an old brass medallion, I told myself, trying to ignore the malice it seemed to whisper.

Without delay, I threw the relic of Borley back into the drawer and slammed it shut.

And, from the partition wall that divided Mother's bed-room from mine, new and peculiar sounds made themselves heard.

Tap-tap, scratch; tap-tap, scratch . . .

The noises were muffled, barely audible, but definitely real.

Probably mice, I thought.

Or rats.

*

In the months that followed I became increasingly worried about Price's behaviour. I knew he had still not returned Reverend Foyster's *Diary of Occurrences*, but was at a loss to explain why. If the haunting was – as Price now believed – nothing but a shambling forgery perpetrated by Marianne Foyster, then why did he insist on clinging to the rector's recollections of the events in the house? It made no sense to me, and whenever I queried him about it he would quickly change the subject. It was insulting to be dismissed so easily, and humiliating to think that I ever tolerated such behaviour. I had lied to the rector so Price could keep hold of the diary; surely I had a right to know why? But Price never ever acknowledged he was keeping the diary. Nor did he announce to the newspapers – as he would normally do – his triumph in exposing yet another hoax, which was odd given his usual relish for such tasks.

He did, however, reach out to every psychical investigator who had expressed an interest in the case, informing them that the matter was now finally resolved. I hated assisting him with that task, for his was not a view I could agree with. He wrote to Dr D.F. Frazer-Harris:

> *It is the most amazing case, but amazing only in so far that we were convinced that the many phenomena that we saw were frau-*

*dulent because we took steps to control various persons and ro-
oms, [and] the manifestations ceased. We think that the rector's
wife is responsible for the trouble, though it is possible that her
actions may be the result of hysteria. Of course we did not wire
you because although psychologically the case is of great value,
psychically speaking there is nothing in it.[1]*

'What *is* the matter?' he asked, seeing my dissatisfied reaction
to the letter. I shook my head, knowing any attempt to explain
my contrary opinion would prove fruitless, and instead I asked
what he was going to do next.

'You mean we,' he replied earnestly. 'What are *we* going to do
next?' He was fired up with energy, dashing from one room to
the next as he consulted this book and that, delving restlessly
into dusty cupboards and trunks for equipment.

'Yes,' I replied, taking a deep reassuring breath, 'I mean we.
So, what next?'

When he had found what he was looking for, he raised his
eyes and fixed them upon me. '*This!*' he cried triumphantly, brandishing a camera. 'Surely you haven't forgotten that we were to
be visited soon by the great Rudi Schneider?'

Later that day, Price reminded me that the medium would
require a personal item belonging to my dead father. 'Schneider
says that a personal object will help your father's spirit connect
with this world.'

His request seemed heartfelt. His tone was tender and gentle,
but made me wonder: if he was so good, why did I catch myself
thinking, every day, about giving up this peculiar life at his
side? It seemed so contradictory that I began to worry if there
was something wrong with me.

'If it isn't too difficult, Sarah, do you think you can locate such an item?'

I thought possibly that I could.

At home later that evening, I crept upstairs whilst Mother sat reading in the drawing room. Her bedroom door was unlocked and slightly ajar. From within, a peculiar, musty smell caught my curiosity. Inside, dirty clothes were strewn across the floor. I was surprised, Mother was normally so tidy.

Something else caught my eye: in the far corner, next to the bed, the source of the odour: a pile of damp towels. Next to them, a bucket, filled up with water; and a sponge.

What on earth was she doing in here? No wonder I suspected we had mice in the walls. This room didn't look as though it had been cleaned in weeks!

As the seconds ticked by, my thoughts returned to the task at hand. At the back of my mind I was already telling myself that soon I would need to tell Mother about Schneider's imminent arrival, and about Price's abrupt change in attitude towards the supernatural. She needed to hear my doubts.

I knew she kept my father's old handkerchief in a drawer next to her bed. But that was too easy somehow. My eye was drawn to the huge oak wardrobe that she would open in the dead of night and rummage in. I stepped towards it.

'Come away from there, Sarah.'

I spun round: it was Mother, standing behind me at the entrance to her bedroom, looking down upon the heavy brown trunk I had pulled out from the back of the wardrobe.

'I was looking for some bedding,' I said quickly.

'Well you won't find it in there.' She advanced, coming round beside me to see if I had opened the trunk. 'What's inside it?' I opened my mouth to ask, but an inward uncertainty, a fear of not wanting the answer, held my tongue. Instead, my thoughts turned to the bucket on the floor, beneath the window. 'Why is that in here?' I asked.

Mother's face was surprised and somehow muddled. 'There was damp coming in, under the window,' she replied, hesitantly, before a quick blink restored clarity in her expression. 'I wiped it down.'

I had to tell her. It was now or never. 'Come with me downstairs, to the drawing room,' I said softly. 'We need to talk.'

As we sat by the fire I explained my concerns about Price's inconsistent behaviour, and his gradual conversion to belief in Mr Schneider. I thought she would say "I told you so." Instead, a smile touched her lips. 'I see now that perhaps I was too harsh on Mr Price.'

'Too harsh?'

She nodded 'This job has been good for you. It's stable, reliable.' An idea struck her. 'You're not going to tell me you're giving it all up now, are you? After all your hard work?'

'You *want* me to stay?'

'You've travelled to new places, seen things I never will. For all his complexities, I think Mr Price – Harry – is a good man.' He has taken care of you; of both of us.'

She saw my questioning expression and said, 'When you went away to Yorkshire, Harry was good enough to stay in touch with me. He wrote me letters, to check I was all right.'

'Harry did that?'

'Yes dear,' she smiled. 'Oh, I know he has made mistakes, shamed and disgraced legions of mediums, some of them my friends. But I see, also, that he was trying to help. Perhaps he recognises a true gift in Mr Schneider, an opportunity to end the infuriating war between Spiritualists and scientists.'

I couldn't speak: I had still to reveal the full story. And my part in it.

Mother was studying me; and I recognised at that instant, beneath her faded elegance, all the reason and wisdom that had been so evident when I was younger that had distinguished her as sensible, that had inspired me to become like her: smart and confident.

'Tell me this,' she asked, watching me carefully. 'Do *you* trust him?'

I remembered the warnings from my anonymous telephone caller: *Ask him where he goes*.

'He's a loner, Mother. Sometimes I feel as if I am in the way. Sometimes I feel as if I am the centre of his world.'

'But has he ever let you down, Sarah?'

Still I remained silent, unable to tell her what I held in my heart. There was no telling what the truth would do to her.

'Sarah, if someone as sceptical as Mr Price believes in this man, truly believes in him, so that he is willing to stake his own good word on the matter . . . well now, that surely has to count for *something* does it not?'

'I suppose so.'

She gave my hand a gentle squeeze. 'What's the matter, sweetheart? You look pale.'

When I told her about the planned experiment with Schneider, Mother seemed to melt before me. She let out a sharp gasp as her hand shot to her mouth.

A long moment passed until finally, dropping her voice, Mother said 'Harry *made* you agree to this?'

'He didn't make me. I agreed to the idea.'

I reached over, wrapped my arms around her, feeling her shoulders tremble beneath her woollen cardigan. When at last her sobbing subsided I summoned the courage to look at her again in the eye.

'I want to be there,' she said, firmly. 'If you father is . . . if he has something to say to us, if he is ready to answer my questions, then I am coming. Do you understand? You mustn't try to stop me. I've waited too long.'

'Mother, no . . . it's too risky.' But the expression of hardened determination on her face and the hope that had burgeoned in her watery eyes signalled to me that there was no sense in arguing now. The matter was decided.

'There is something else,' she added after a prolonged pause. 'Something I must tell you before this experiment can go ahead.'

'What – what is it? Mother?'

Her right hand was turning the rings on her left with nervous agitation. 'You know that I loved your father, in spite of the difficulties . . .'

'Of course.'

She lowered her head. 'He suffered badly, very badly with his nerves. We had a dinner party at the house once. He made every guest wash their hands. Twice.' Her eye caught mine and I felt myself look away. She had set my heart fluttering with unrest. 'At the end of the meal he said he had an announcement – a surprise. Kept us all guessing' – she smiled – 'he was good at that. I thought he was probably joking. *Hoped* he was joking. But then he led us all to the front door and showed us it parked right outside: a brand new Rolls Royce.' She blinked away a glistening tear. 'Oh, I smiled and laughed and pretended I knew. But of course, I didn't have a clue. And that was the way it was, when his obsessions became very bad: he made decisions, frittered away the money, and I was always the last to know.' She nodded to herself, staring past me over the other tables. 'I *still* don't know.'

'Go on,' I prompted her. We had come to it at last: the edge of the thing, the source of her enduring sadness.

'Sarah, his obsessions, made him do things . . . worse things . . . I only learned the truth, how bad it was, years afterwards, on the night . . . .' As she hesitated, choking back her tears, I resolved to broach the subject that was bothering me the most, to see if there was a connection here.

'I hear you at night sometimes, late, sorting through your wardrobe . . .'

She didn't deny it, but she was leaning away from me, looking down.

'It started the night that man came to the front door. Who was he?'

'Professor McDougall.'

McDougall. I recognised the name. 'He's a member of Harry's Laboratory.'

She nodded sharply. 'He was there on the opening night, singing Mr Price's praises. He invited me. His guilty attempt at reconciliation, no doubt.'

I thought back to that night. Mother in her sleek fitted jacket and matching skirt. The way she had conjured up in my mind the impression of a lost child. McDougall. She had mentioned the name. 'You sounded upset, insisted we leave – why?'

'It was Professor McDougall who treated your father, Sarah, before he went to war. Your father's condition . . . I kept it from you for as long as I could, but sometimes it was so dreadful . . .

He rose like a corpse some mornings, sitting unresponsive at the end of his bed, just staring. He had ceased to see the world in colour. He had ceased to see us at all.'

Of course I remembered. Not well, but enough.

'The Army would have called him mad,' she said, 'if they had known – they would have called him mad and sent him home from the war.'

I nodded, remembering Price's similar state of melancholy. 'Perhaps they'll have a proper word for it one day,' I suggested. 'Something other than madness. They'll understand it better. But he was brave to the end – remember that. At least we know he died a hero, and he did that for us.'

Mother's eyes flickered. I had no wish to heighten her distress, but my urge to know why McDougall had come to the house so many years after my father died, was too powerful to prevent me from asking the question. 'What did he say that upset you, ignited in you such a fervent belief in Spiritualism, made you hide Father's photographs?'

She inhaled deeply, stiffening her back, and said, 'I can't tell you the whole of it, but I will tell you some. Your father had a mistress. The man at the doorstep . . .' she inhaled sharply . . . 'Professor McDougall was her husband.'

Suddenly I felt so cold, felt my fingers turning to icicles.

Now Mother was looking back at me with pleading, sorrowful eyes.

'That can't be right,' I said. 'It just can't be.'

But Mother was nodding, and I was remembering. I couldn't stop. It was as if a curtain in my mind was thrown back, ripped down, revealing the horrible thing behind: there I was in the doorway to Mother's room, staring down at my father as he crouched on the floor, sobbing, clutching letters beside an open trunk.

'When Professor McDougall explained how long the affair had gone on, I refused to believe him. Until that night, when he came to the house and told me there was proof.'

'How could there be proof?' I breathed, already suspecting that somewhere, deep inside, I knew the answer. My hands had clenched into fists at the alarming idea that my father hadn't been the man I always thought he was. 'What sort of proof?'

Mother continued slowly, crying now. 'He told me there was a trunk, upstairs in our bedroom. That it would tell me everything I needed to know. Proof.'

Letters.

'I thought the old thing was full of junk. It was locked. When I broke into it . . . .' She stumbled over her words. 'Oh, Sarah, so many letters. So many years. So many mistresses.'

None of this was easy to hear. I had always remembered my father as a loyal and generous man. But now I knew.

'Those letters were his trophies.' Mother shook her head, as if to deny it. 'McDougall's wife told him everything. Your father wasn't the man you thought he was.'

'Why on earth did he keep them?' I wanted to know.

She shrugged. 'Perhaps they gave his life some order as his mind deteriorated. And now you can understand why I put his photographs away. I love him, of course, even though he wasn't the man you like to remember. You can see now, I hope, why I have been looking for so long, visiting mediums. If there's the slightest chance that your father can see us in the world beyond, if he can come through and explain to me why he did what he did,' she covered her heart with one hand, 'then maybe I can move on. The love that we shared, your father and me, is worth forgiving for.'

Then quite suddenly her expression changed again, her

anguish and sorrow replaced with a sort of hope and renewed confidence I hadn't seen since before she turned to Spiritualism. 'Tell me: when does this great medium arrive in London? We must be ready.'

The only words I could manage in reply were 'Soon, very soon.'

Mother stroked my hair, nodding with a smile that was proud and protective. 'My beautiful little girl. You used to say you were going to be an adventurer, see the world, meet a man who would change your perceptions. How right you were . . . .'

I was silent. What sort of daughter was I to have allowed this to happen?

'You realise what this means?' Mother whispered, taking my hand. 'He's returning to us, Sarah, just as he promised he would.

'At last your father is coming home.'

Note

1   Letter from Harry Price to Dr D.F. Frazer-Harris, 1931.

– 26 –
THE PARTING OF THE WAYS

We waited, Price and I, side by side on the platform at Liverpool Street station on a bitterly cold morning in April. Few words passed between us. His face was flushed, his hands raw as he fumbled in the pockets of his overcoat for his pipe.

'You're awfully quiet, Sarah.'

I listened to the wind and the way it seemed to whisper to me, and thought of the Rectory at Borley standing in the lonely Essex fields – a place where things were so utterly, despairingly different. I thought of the grim warning Marianne had issued to me and of the figure of the nun, the spectre of darkness, that in recent weeks had been a recurring and dreadful feature of my dreams. Then the problems at home: Mother's increasing fragility, the tapping, scuffling, scratching in the walls that occasionally kept me awake at night.

'Yes,' I said. 'I believe I have reason to be.'

As the last chime of the platform clock struck eleven our guest's train pulled into the station.

Rudi Schneider was exactly as I remembered him: an enthusiastic and cheery young man whose gracious and polite manner would, in other circumstances, have made me feel instantly at ease. His dark, handsome features meant he presented well for the cameras and he clearly enjoyed the great attention lavished upon him.

The two men clasped hands in eager appreciation of each other. 'Mr Price, how good it is to see you again.'

Price was smiling broadly. 'The whole of London is glad you have come, Mr Schneider. You have quite a following. But now you must rest. We will take you to your hotel. Miss Grey has reserved for you one of the finest rooms at the Splendide on Piccadilly where, in a few nights' time, we shall hold a dinner in your honour.'

After a brief presentation to journalists on the following morning, we took Schneider up to Price's study where we discussed a series of rigorous sittings that the young man had run the previous year, in Paris, at the Institut Metapsychique. The two men settled in high-backed chairs facing each other over Price's desk. I had pulled up a stool to one side of the desk and sat, notepad and pen in hand.

'I want to begin with a brief discussion of experiments undertaken in Paris,' said Price. His manner had undergone a transformation since the day before, from warm to merely cordial. 'I have heard that there, under the watchful scrutiny of the psychical researcher Doctor Eugene Osty, you consented to allow your purported telekinetic abilities to be tested with the aid of sensitive, automatic camera *and* infrared technology.'

'Correct,' said Schneider. 'I had only to move an inch and the camera would fire, then my physical influence would be caught on film.'

History records that the results of these experiments were indeed remarkable; movement *was* detected and the cameras had indeed fired, but it wasn't Schneider's hand that had moved, nor any other part of his body that had caused the mechanical set-up to activate. Instead, the developed photographs showed a sticky white substance – which Schneider claimed was ecto-plasm – leaking out of his body and passing through any objects that were put in its way.

'What does it feel like?' Price asked suddenly. 'The act of expel-ling ectoplasm. I can't imagine it's a pleasant experience.'

Schneider sighed deeply, his eyes misting over. 'Most of the time I have no idea what it feels like. The Rudi Schneider you see before you now ceases to exist; some very substantial part of me is replaced by whatever – whoever – wishes to communicate. It takes over, takes control.'

'You're happy for me to repeat the French experiments, I assume?'

Rudi nodded and smiled. 'Yes, but of course; I have put myself entirely at your own and Miss Grey's disposal.'

'You do understand,' Price continued, 'that I will need to make some changes to the methodology of our own experiments?'

Schneider squinted, though his smile never wavered. 'Changes?'

'This time your body will be more effectively immobilised. There will be a greater number of cameras too.'

'All right, yes, that will be fine.'

Price rose. 'Very good, then it is settled. Miss Grey and I will begin preparing the seance room without delay.' He crossed to the door. 'There are some journalists too, who will need to receive personal, handwritten invitations from me. Sarah, fetch me the full list of our closest friends at the national newspapers.'

As I left the room I heard Schneider say, 'There is just one thing I ought to tell you, Mr Price . . .' I thought nothing more of the remark and set about my task. However, I had not been gone two minutes before a loud, frustrated cry drew me back into the study. I entered to see Price standing over the seated Schneider, his hands raised in disbelief.

'I am startled that you would agree to this,' Price remarked. 'Your contractual agreement is with *me*, not the Society for Psychical Research.'

'Harry, what's the matter?' I asked. He looked absolutely furious.

'I'll tell you what the matter is, Sarah! Mr Schneider here has consented to be tested by our rivals!' He turned to Schneider, his face flushing. 'You are selling yourself to the highest bidder, sir, is that it?'

'No, no,' Schneider replied, 'but—'

'No buts! If you're so anxious to make money from your mediumship – your purported mediumship – then I suggest you go to the music halls instead, for this is a place of science and I have gone to considerable expense to have you here.'

Price's eyes were burning with anger. 'The sheer audacity of the Society for Psychical Research! If it's war they want then war they shall have. And you, Mr Schneider – you will withdraw from your agreement or so help me you will regret your decision for the rest of your life!'

He stormed out of the room and the heavy door slammed shut, leaving me alone with Schneider.

'My, he has quite a temper, doesn't he?' said Schneider.

'It's Harry's world. The rest of us just live in it.'

'And how does that make you feel, Miss Grey?'

'I – I used to feel helpful. I *wanted* to be helpful. But now . . .' I shrugged. 'He has changed me.'

'You feel as though life is passing you by, is that it?'

For a second I saw Vernon Wall's cheery, lean face and felt a pang of regret.

'Will you pull out of your agreement with Mr Price's rivals?' I asked.

'Surely,' he pointed out, 'they are *your* rivals too?' There was a slight playfulness to his tone. Was he digging for personal information that he could use later, during the seance? The possibility seemed highly likely, so again I said nothing.

Acknowledging my reticence Schneider said, 'I will not renege on my commitment to the Society for Psychical Research. I am bound by it. Mr Price will have to learn that there are many worlds beyond this one – beyond his own.'

'Then we shall see, Mr Schneider, the limit of your powers.' I made for the door. 'I must get on, I'm afraid; there are a hundred little things which need doing before your sitting: equipment to set up, third-party witnesses to invite to verify the proceedings.'

'Miss Grey – a moment, please.'

I wanted to leave then, but his hypnotic voice held me. 'Yes, Mr Schneider?'

'I know you don't trust me,' he said quietly. 'I understand. But you're going to have to face what is coming. I feel that your father misses you and your mother terribly, that he is sorry for you both; but I can bring him back.' He nodded, sure of himself. 'I *will* bring him back. But first, there is something I require – an item of some personal significance which connects your father with this world. I did mention it to Mr Price in my letters. Do you have anything like that?'

I was suddenly reluctant to give anything personal to this man, let alone Father's handkerchief which Mother still kept next to her bed.

I had said nothing, but Schneider's eyes suddenly narrowed. 'Very good, Miss Grey; thank you. That will do nicely.'

I caught my breath. How had he known? Had he guessed or had he *known*?

As if reading this thought too, Schneider nodded and said firmly, 'Bring the handkerchief with you to the seance tomorrow evening.'

The date stands in my memory like a tombstone. It was the 27th of April 1932. The day of the seance.

I began that working day by taking tea with Price in his study. 'You must calm yourself, Sarah; you look terribly nervous,' he said. 'Don't be. I am extremely hopeful that Mr Schneider will not disappoint us tonight.'

I wanted him to be more than hopeful. I wanted him to be certain. 'Then you've forgiven Rudi for courting the opposition?'

A shadow crossed his brow. 'I didn't say that.'

Just then, Rudi Schneider appeared in the doorway. Price saw him and scowled. 'Good morning, Rudi. Your big day has arrived at last!'

But Schneider was looking past Price and across at me with an expression of some concern, his gaze lingering on my throat.

'What is it?' I asked, alarmed. I touched my neck.

'Oh . . . nothing. Forgive me.' But a trace of anxiety remained etched around his eyes.

Price was issuing instructions as to what remained to be done before that night's demonstration: 'I want the world to know that the National Laboratory for Psychical Research has succeeded when Rudi triumphs.' He turned to our guest. 'Mr Schneider, I suggest you go back to your hotel now and rest. We will expect you back here no later than ten o'clock tonight, all right?'

'Very well. Good day to you both.' He gave a slight bow and was gone.

I can hardly express how nervous I was by this point, fearful of what the experiment would show.

Price's eyes glittered with excitement. Rubbing his hands together, he said, 'I have a sense that this is going to be quite magnificent, Sarah. The Society for Psychical Research will be shocked indeed.'

Just an hour to go. I went straight to the top floor, to give the seance room one final check before for the proceedings began. Everything was just as I had left it earlier that day: above me a net fastened to the ceiling, which later, just before the experiment commenced, I would pull down to separate Schneider from the rest of the room. Before me was the great wooden seance chair into which Schneider would be fastened, and next to this a small table with a red lamp resting on it. Cameras were positioned on all sides, each carefully primed. And beyond these, three rows of chairs – fifteen in all – for our spectators. Their view would need to be a good one. It was vital that every aspect of Schneider's movements be observed in acute detail. His only stipulation was that the seance take place in the customary red-light conditions, which was the norm.

I reached into my pocket and drew out Father's handkerchief which I had taken from Mother's room, caught the scent of colourful memories, then kissed it gently, folded it and placed it on the table next to the lamp. Finally, when I had given the room a final check, I knelt among the shadows to pray.

'Miss Grey, here you are!'

And there *he* was, the man who had promised the impossible. I got to my feet, but did not approach him.

'Forgive me, I did not wish to startle you.'

'What are you doing?' I could hear the tension in my voice. 'I'm afraid Harry hasn't arrived yet.'

'That's good.'

'Good?'

'It wasn't Mr Price I wanted to see.'

And in that moment I found myself wishing that I had never agreed to the deal that Price had offered me, and I longed for the chance to be free of the Laboratory, its unending darkness and its conduits to the dead.

'What's the matter, Miss Grey?'

'Please, no nearer,' I said, raising my hand. 'In fact, I'd prefer it if you left. Harry will be here any moment; he and I have some work to do.'

'Mr Price won't arrive for another forty-five minutes,' said Schneider darkly. 'In fact, as we speak his train is just pulling out of the station near his home.' I looked at his wrist: no watch. No clock on any of the walls either.

'But how do you—?'

'It's what I do, isn't it? Isn't that why you asked me to come here – to show you what you cannot see?' He stepped forward and this time I made no attempt to stop him. 'If we are going to do this properly, Miss Grey, then it is vital that you trust me.'

He had reached my side and was looking down at me, into me, with his gleaming, magical eyes.

'I never asked,' I stammered, suddenly short of breath, 'I never—'

'Oh, but you *did*,' he said quickly, his tone silky and soft. 'Not with your mouth perhaps, but in here' – he raised his hands and pressed his fingertips against my temples – 'deep inside in here, you have been asking for such a long time now.'

He closed his eyes. And against my will I was powerless to resist my own eyes closing too. 'What – what are you doing?' My face was cold, my head light. The ground beneath me seemed to fall away, and I was floating. It was not unlike the sensation I had experienced at Borley Rectory, when Marianne Foyster had reached out to me with whatever dark powers she possessed and rifled through my thoughts. Except this felt different, almost soothing.

'Trust me, please,' he whispered.

'No!' I pulled away sharply.

He blinked. 'You think that I have come here to play a game with you. Is that it?'

'I haven't ruled it out!'

'Tell me, Miss Grey, what is it you fear most? That I might deceive you, or that I am right?' He was calm, serene – as if my answer didn't matter, or he didn't care. Or he already knew what I would say.

The honest answer was probably 'both', for in agreeing to allow this man – the greatest medium in Europe – to attempt to summon my father's spirit, I had broken my own rules. Instead of distancing myself from my emotions, the memory of my father, I had stepped forward willingly and embraced them. As much as I had struggled all these years not to think of him, I had come now to the final reckoning. Because the agony of not knowing was too much. I *had* to know. And I had to know, also, that I wasn't about to be taken for a fool.

'Mr Schneider,' I exclaimed. 'You might have convinced Harry of your talents, but you have yet to convince me.'

'I'm not here to convince you, Miss Grey. I'm here to show you the truth; at your father's command. And then, I assure you, you will believe.'

'How *dare* you presume upon something so personal! It's *my* opinion that matters the most. Not yours, not Harry's – mine! Be under no illusions, Mr Schneider, if I find that you're lying to us, attempting to trick either myself or my mother, then so help me I'll make sure that you regret it!'

'Are you threatening me?' he asked in a low voice.

'Consider it a warning,' I said firmly. 'And here's something even Harry doesn't know. Yesterday I had some representatives from a firm of building contractors inspect our seance room, just to triple-check there was no hidden apparatus inside that you could have planted to simulate your effects.'

'You really don't trust me, do you?' He turned his head aside. His gaze latched on to a Ouija board discarded in the corner of the room and remained fixed on the item for some time as he drifted in contemplation. Finally, softly, he said, 'Would you like to know something of what it's actually *like* on the other side, Miss Grey? Of the nightmare the souls are forced to endure in the next world?' To this I gave no answer, but he quickly filled the silence. 'Forget heaven. The afterlife is a cold and dark place. The darkest. Imagine, if you can, the haziest dream you've ever had – that sense of personal solitude mixed with an ephemeral, half-tangible idea of who you are.'

I tried to remember my most recent dream – or was it a nightmare? – and stopped immediately.

Schneider continued, 'In such a nebulous state, the fabric of life is before you, floating, falling, drifting, Miss Grey. In our dreams we are like lost souls. And on the other side, after this life, that is how it is.' He looked up at me and I was alarmed to see that tears had formed in his eyes. 'They are all so desperately sad, Miss Grey, so despairingly isolated – so many wandering souls only faintly aware of one another, joined by the faintest, most fragile connections of thought. Psychic energy, Miss Grey, and half-remembered states.' He blinked. 'That's what we become, all of us. In the end.'

'It sounds dreadful,' I murmured.

'Indeed.' He nodded gravely. 'It's not life after death. It's death after death.'

*

The clock struck ten, and as the last chime sounded I entered the seance room, where Price and the sitters were assembled. Mother was among them. She wore a new black dress with bunched sleeves, and her eyes were fixed in hope on the man who had promised to contact my father. I could only imagine how she must have felt: she had waited for this moment for more than thirteen years.

I couldn't help but feel that this was the stupidest, most reckless exercise I had ever embarked on. *It's going to be fine*, I told myself, hearing my breathing deepen. But from the moment I saw Schneider's form silhouetted in the doorway, I felt my pulse quicken. How had I allowed it to come to this?

As the young Austrian entered the room, clad all in black, a suppressed whisper rippled through the audience. He saw me and I fixed him with a gaze of the strongest intensity I could summon, daring him to wrong me.

'Come along, Mr Schneider,' said Price. He took the medium's right wrist in his iron grip and led him into the centre of the room.

'What is this?' asked Schneider. He had seen the transparent mesh net which I had that evening hung from the ceiling and pinned to the floor.

'Just a small addition from Miss Grey,' said Price. 'The net prevents anyone in the audience from assisting you.'

But Schneider seemed quite unperturbed by this addition. Indeed, as he passed me on his route to the seance chair, he caught my eye, smiled and whispered, 'You have your father's eyes, Miss Grey.' The words ignited momentary hope in my heart, but it was easier for me to ignore them than to acknowledge them, so afraid was I that the seance would end in disappointment. I took my place at the back of the room, my hands trembling slightly, as Rudi planted himself on the chair and said to the room, 'Fear not, ladies and gentlemen, I will try to show you some very good phenomena tonight.'

With my heart in my mouth I watched carefully, taking meticulous notes, as Price placed a chair in front of Schneider and sat down facing him. On top of a four-legged wooden table, positioned just a few feet away from the two men, was a red lamp, already switched on, and next to this Father's handkerchief, which I had brought with me. First the two men stared at one another silently and then Price said, 'Very well, let us make a start. Rudi, I'm going to secure you now.' He placed Schneider's hands upon his thighs and firmly gripping his wrists so he could take his pulse, he clasped Schneider's knees between his own.

There were three cameras in position, all of which were set to trigger simultaneously in the event of any untoward movements.

Price asked the room for total silence, and only after I checked that all the doors and windows were tightly shut did he ask me to turn the main lights down. I did so, head bowed and bursting with hope that Schneider, who was already putting himself into a trance-like state by chanting and rocking his body, would not fall short of our expectations. Everything counted on this.

I caught Mother's longing expression. She was studying every-thing to the last detail. I knew she was too weak to suffer any greater disappointment, and that knowledge made me deter-mined that failure tonight simply wasn't an option. 'Schneider will come through for us,' I told myself. 'He must.'

A swarming darkness enveloped us, leaving only the soft red glow of the lamp on the table.

'Let the record show,' Price announced to the room, 'that our subject is going into a trance-like state that will enable him to better connect, mentally, with whatever – or whoever – wishes to communicate with us tonight.'

Schneider's breathing became laboured and spasmodic.

'Is he all right?' someone asked.

'Silence, please!' Price instructed through gritted teeth. 'This is a crucial moment for the medium. No more disturbances.'

So we waited, but there was no movement, no activity at all in fact, just the laboured breathing.

When it came, the change was sudden.

Schneider, whose breathing had been audible to us, became suddenly quiet. Then, quite abruptly, his body jerked backwards and he issued a penetrating gasp – one so deep it was as if he had just emerged from a lengthy spell underwater.

'Rudi?'

The medium was oblivious to Price, however, for he was gul-ping the air now, quicker than before, desperately. The change was alarming and clearly had an effect on Price, who was shaking his head in confusion. 'I count perhaps between two hundred and three hundred respirations per minute,' he said aloud. He didn't need me to tell him that the ordinary breathing of anyone not engaged in active exercise is between fourteen and twenty-six to the minute.

Schneider's eyes flipped open. 'I am . . . receiving a message,' he spluttered.

'Tell us!' Mother cried, leaning forward in her chair. 'My dear, I'm here! What is it you have to tell us?'

'Aaghhh!' And now Rudi's body was writhing in the great wooden chair, as if a surge of energy was crackling through him. His head jerked back, his hand spasmed, and his back stiffened.

'I'm struggling to hold him,' Price shouted. 'Sarah, help me!'

'Quickly, grab his arm!'

It was difficult to restrain him. Just like Velma Crawshaw, the first medium we had tested all those years ago, he seemed to have lost bodily control.

From somewhere behind the net I heard Mother's desperate voice: 'Sarah, for God's sake – be careful!'

Schneider's face seemed to be slackening and a fixating transformation was coming into his expression. I swear that his eyes actually changed colour. Price saw it too. 'Good God!' I exclaimed, 'Harry – what is *this*?'

The medium opened his mouth to speak, but the voice we heard next did not belong to Rudi Schneider. Nor was it the voice of my father.

'Harry. Price.' The speech sounded forced and came in short bursts. 'You were wrong. On a most incomprehensible scale.'

I saw Price's face turn the colour of milk. 'Oh God,' he whispered. 'I know that voice.'

And I knew it too. 'Harry, it sounds like . . .'

He blinked and nodded once. 'Arthur Conan Doyle.'

Gasps from the audience. We stared at Schneider as a wave of amazement passed over us. After a pause, the voice continued, Doyle's gruff tone unmistakable.

'I . . . did . . . not . . . recognise the difficulty there would be in getting through this wall or the density which stands between us. I would like you to know my location: that I am ... in a nebulous belt lying outside the world's surface and having life and being because it is of the same structure and matter as the earth itself. I am in no doubt as to my geographical position.'

'I am delighted that my old antagonist has returned,' said Price carefully, though 'delighted' was not the word that I would have used to describe his reaction.

'No reason why you should be,' came the reply. 'It was your fault that we disagreed.'

'But we were working with the same object in view but in different ways. I am trying to arrive at the truth!'

'I was always wondering what you were working for, to be perfectly candid. I always had my eye on you, and you used to watch me like a cat following a bird in a cage. It was I who kept Spiritualism going by my money.'

'Well, Sir Arthur, I am as much out of pocket during the past five years as you were!'

'Then, my dear sir' – the voice was becoming faint now, fading away – 'we may shake hands.'[1]

And then Schneider was still once again.

All Price and I could do was stare at one another.

'Did that really just happen?' I exclaimed.

'Hold him,' Price instructed. 'It's starting again!'

Sure enough, Schneider's body was becoming rigid, his breath quickening once more.

'Mr Schneider, are you all right?' I could tell that Price was trying to speak calmly, but he didn't fool me for a moment.

'His arms, Harry, they're twitching!'

'Hold him!'

But that in itself was proving difficult, because now his body was shuddering, jerking, jolting.

'Mr Schneider!'

'Hold him, Sarah – don't let go!'

But I *wanted* to let go, because what was happening now was barely within my comprehension. 'Harry,' I cried, 'his mouth – look at his mouth! Dear God.'

A sort of foam, white and sticky, was bubbling out of the Austrian's mouth, from his nose, too, and running down his chest to pool in his lap. It smelt dreadful, toxic almost. And then, remarkably – impossibly – this foam seemed to form shape, writhing as if it were itself a living organism.

I had never seen real ectoplasm, only the regurgitated cheesecloth produced by a charlatan medium during the first day of my employment, and this was nothing like it.

'Ouch!' someone exclaimed. I turned to see that they were glaring at Mother. 'You pinched me!'

'I did not!'

'Wait! Where's my coat?' someone asked. 'It's gone!'

By now the black curtains covering the closed windows were billowing and a cool breeze could be felt blowing through the room.

My heart was hammering. I worried that I might lose control and run from the room. Before I could seriously contemplate any such notion, however, I heard it: the purest, most unearthly melody. It seemed to seep in and out of the air, breaking through into this world as if from another, audible one moment then silent the next. I recognised it immediately.

It was the sound of my father's piano and the melody was a nursery rhyme from my childhood.

I released my grip on Schneider. Stood up. Blinked my astonishment.

'Look!' Mother cried, pointing past me, behind me.

From behind Schneider a mass of fog was issuing forth, swirling around and in on itself like a storm cloud, and within I saw what looked like hands reaching out.

Somewhere in the room an automatic camera clicked and flashed.

'But those are hands!' I cried. '*Hands!* Belonging to . . . *what*?'

The hands – if I can call them that – seemed to float towards us, out of the mist. Behind them, covered by the whirling fog, I thought I could just discern the form of a torso, the shape of a man, but the sight was fleeting. Was it him? 'It's me! Father, please, it's me!' I cried instinctively.

Schneider's mouth fell open to speak while his body remained in the great seance chair. 'Sarah, please, get away. Please, for your own sake, get away.' It was a different voice from before – younger, more even. Was it possible? Then came the words that would haunt me for the rest of my days: 'Sarah, I love you. I'm sorry. I'm so sorry.'

'Wait, Harold!'

The cry belonged to my mother, who was standing now, frozen like a statue, one arm outstretched, her features filled with longing as her gaze locked with the apparition behind the seated medium.

Then an ethereal voice said firmly, but not loudly, 'I love you, Frances. I do.'

I couldn't believe it. Schneider's mouth hadn't moved.

'Wait!' was Mother's repeated cry.

But the apparition seemed fainter suddenly, almost invisible, so much so that I had to wonder whether it had ever been there at all. Only the ghostly hands of the spectre remained now, fingers outstretched then fluttering as if conveying a final goodbye, but within seconds they seemed to have drifted away from Schneider and Price. We looked on with amazed silence as the hands took up the handkerchief that had been left on the seance table.

'It's him!' my mother cried. She was staring incredulously at the handkerchief as it danced around the lamp like a moth around a candle 'Oh, Sarah, it's him!'

Flashes of light ripped through the room as the phantom hands began to fade, receding into the smoke.

'Wait,' I cried. 'Please, don't go!'

An icy wind pressed past me. Then was gone.

I rushed to Mother's side as Price sprang to his feet, switching on the main light. He flew across the room to one of his cameras, then to another. Finally, he stopped before the last with a look of astonishment on his face.

My eyes met his. 'Harry?'

'We have it, Sarah!' he cried triumphantly, holding up a photographic plate. 'At last, we have it. Direct and undeniable proof of a world beyond!'

*

How relieved I was that Schneider hadn't let us down. That night I slept peacefully for the first time in years. My thoughts were quiet and, to my relief, so was the darkness. No faint scuffling or tapping scratching sounds came from the wall in my bedroom. No disturbing dreams either. The visions of the Rectory at Borley and its spectral nun that had plagued me had vanished, and the anxiety I had suffered for all the years I had worked at the Laboratory dispersed. We had taken a gamble and we had come through.

As our success sank in, I felt some forgiveness towards Price. Our work did have purpose after all. And when he released the evidence from our seance to the world – as I knew he would – who could say where our work would lead us?

But I was eager to find out more about the phenomena Schneider had produced. There were so many questions I had to ask him, and I wanted to see more; for although I had heard music I associated with Father, I had not seen his face or touched his hand. With this thought in mind, I arrived the next morning at the Laboratory deterininded to ask Schneider to take part in one final seance, to be performed exclusively for Mother and me in the privacy of our home. I doubted Price would object to the idea, but thought it better to check with him anyway, just in case. And I would have done just that, but from the moment I entered his study and saw him hunched over his desk, his face grim and his brow heavy, I knew something was wrong.

'Harry, what is it?'

The saturnine figure who was my employer, friend, mentor and object of all my desires looked at me sadly from across the room. In his hand he held a magnifying glass, which he carefully laid down on the surface of his desk. 'Ah, Sarah . . .' he said awkwardly, 'there you are.'

I felt my heart tumble. 'What . . . what's wrong?'

'I'm afraid,' he said slowly, 'that I have some upsetting news.' He looked down at a series of photographs he had spread out over his desk. 'Come and sit here, beside me.'

I did so, hesitantly. His face was heavy with tiredness, his cologne too strong.

'This morning I developed the plates automatically exposed last night during the seance.'

'Yes . . .'

'And I received something of a shock. One of the cameras in

the electrical circuit failed to make instantaneous contact with one of its two Vaku-Blitz bulbs.'

'So?'

'This caused the bulbs to fire one after the other, in quick succession, thus taking two superimposed and consecutive photographs on the same plate.'

He held an image out for me to see: Schneider strapped into his chair, Price holding him down, the ghostly mist hanging in the air before them. 'Look here – the plate in the overhead stereoscopic camera was fogged by the light of the flash striking the lenses.'

'Yes . . .'

'But see here . . .' He produced a separate image, this one much clearer than the first. 'The stereoscopic camera at the side of the counterpoise table reveals something quite different.'

I stared as my mind went blank. It wasn't possible. How could it be possible?

Somehow Schneider had managed to free his right arm and put it behind his back.

'Clearly,' said Price, 'the flash ignited before he had time to get his arm back into place.'

I rejected the suggestion immediately. 'That doesn't mean he faked it, Harry. How could he have done that? How could you not have seen it? You were sitting right in front of him! We saw hands, my father's hands – I saw a torso in the smoke. My father!'

'Sarah, I am afraid what you saw was nothing but the talents of a very clever man.'

'No, I—'

'Come now, you know as well as I do the wiles of the wizards; you know that no seance these days is complete without a materialisation. The production of luminous hands or faces is part of their routine. I admit it was an extremely convincing performance, but you and I have witnessed these tricks many times; you know how it's done. Trapdoors, sliding panels with a waiting accomplice dressed in wigs, costumes and make-up, balloons painted with luminous faces. What you saw last night was no different. The only tangible difference is that you had an emotional investment in this experiment. I don't have the full answer, not yet, but I will. I'll work it out. But one thing I do know: these photographs can make us certain it was an illusion.'

For seconds, perhaps a whole minute, I was speechless. I tried as best I could to frame an explanation. 'Perhaps . . . perhaps the flash startled him and . . . and he jerked his arm away. Or perhaps, like Marianne Foyster, he connects with occult forces he can't always control, and his powers are . . . unreliable, and when they wane he resorts to the occasional attempt at trickery.'

I could hear how ridiculous I sounded. Price was staring at me sadly. 'I don't think so. Earlier this morning, before you came in, I confronted Schneider with these photographs and made him understand that I believed he had cheated.'

I attempted to steady myself. 'What did he say?'

'Nothing,' said Price. 'He met my accusation with complete silence. And silence, my dear, is the first refuge of a scoundrel.'

I cradled my head in my hands as the world around me fractured. 'Harry . . . this is too much.'

'You must believe it. There is no doubt. The entire performance was fraudulent.'

My eyes floated up to meet his as I shook my head in denial. 'You normally explain how, but this time . . .' Price stared at me. 'You don't know, do you? You have no idea.'

'I know he got his arm free. That is enough.'

He amazed me with his apparent lack of concern. He had believed in Schneider faithfully, had spent hundreds of pounds courting the man, testing him. 'But there was music, Harry – my father's music. I heard it! A nursery rhyme. Didn't you?'

'I heard nothing.'

My hands flew to the side of my face as my temper threatened to explode. 'How can you be so calm?' I demanded. 'There's something else, isn't there?' I could sense it from the way he was pursing his lips. 'Harry?'

He held my gaze. 'Sarah, all you need to know is that Schneider said something to me which convinced me he was lying.'

I rose shakily out of my chair, my heart racing. 'I will decide what I need to know. Tell me now. What did he say to you?'

'Very well.' Price sighed deeply. 'I asked Schneider this morning what effect the seance had on him, what it felt like, what he heard, sensed and saw.'

'And . . . ?'

'He told me a message was imparted to him from beyond, a message . . . from your father.'

My fists clenched as I braced myself. 'Well?'

'He said your father was a weak man.' Price hesitated. 'He called him a coward.'

I stepped back into an endless silence. Then, when at last I found the words: 'But my father died fighting for his king and his country! A coward? He was a hero!'

'I know,' Price said quietly. 'So you see now – complete and utter nonsense. We would be wrong to waste any more of our precious time on Schneider.'

I could barely contain my rage. I flew to the door, but before I could step out into the hallway a mumbled remark from Price made me stop dead.

I turned slowly, feeling something close to dread rising within me. 'What did you say?'

Price shook his head. 'What?'

'Repeat what you just said!' I demanded.

'I said, we will tell the world about this.' He pronounced these words as if nothing were more obvious or straightforward. 'I'll write a detailed report explaining why Schneider is a fraud.'

'No, you can't!'

'Sarah, you must know that I have to make this public. It is my duty.'[2]

There followed another prolonged silence as the gravity of his words pulled me down into a mood of bleak resentment. From the street below I could hear every sound of normality – the bell of a passing bike, the hum of an engine, a dog barking. They seemed a world away from this room.

'You knew all along that Schneider was a fraud. Just like Velma Crawshaw! You must have known; you were so keen to have him visit us.'

Price's silence incriminated him.

'You encouraged him,' I continued, my limbs trembling uncontrollably at the realisation, 'so that you could bring him down – and you used *me* to do it, Harry. My own father!'

'I needed to ensure Schneider gave us his best performance, Sarah.'

'Harold Robert Grey will not become a chapter in your next book,' I said, turning away from him in disgust. He reached for my arm.

'Don't you *dare* touch me!' I cried, spinning round. 'You've done enough damage to me as it is without this.'

'What . . . what do you mean?' I had never heard him so hesitant, so worried.

I longed to fire at him the secret I had kept, to hurt him as badly as I had been hurt. But the words refused to come.

'All this time you've been waiting for the perfect opportunity to show the whole world that you were right, just to grab a quick headline, just to show all your competitors at the Society for Psychical Research that you were in control.'

'I *am* in control,' he snapped. 'After this, it will be necessary for previous investigators to revise their findings.'

'You used me! My own father, Harry. How could you do that? What on earth will Mother say? This could ruin her – she thought this was real! *I* thought this was real!'

My tears broke through then as the hopelessness of my predicament and the full impact of my remorse washed over me. I stared helplessly across at the glass cabinet full of the items that Price had collected from the many fraudulent mediums we had worked with, scrutinised and exposed. And there, on the top shelf, in prime position, mocking me, was the handkerchief that Rudi had made dance around the lamp.

If Price had said something to me then I wouldn't have heard it, for the pain I felt filled my head, obliterating my blind love for the man. Something inside me withered and died.

'Sarah—'

'No. No more,' I said, trying my hardest to stem the flow of my tears. 'I gave you my trust . . . you deceived me.'

'Sarah, please—'

I knew what I had to do. I spoke in a resolute tone, taming the trembling within. 'Albert Einstein once said the definition of insanity was doing the same thing over and over again and expecting different results. I must be insane to have imagined this could ever be any different. To even hope you could change for me. I can't do this any more, Harry.'

Then I stood, turned my back and prised myself away from the man who had plucked me from an ordinary existence and dropped me, so carelessly, into his peculiar, uncharted waters.

'But why? Where will you go?' The tremor of concern in his voice made leaving him so much harder.

'I'll find somewhere,' I muttered, feeling lost and scared, knowing that I needed to collect my thoughts and focus on finding another job away from this peculiar subject, if only for a short while; then I would be able to stand alone. Independent. Free from all of this. But where to start?

Suddenly I was struck with a wonderful idea. Films. Yes! From my brief days in modelling for *Eve* magazine I knew something about how performers were cast. I had developed all the right skills while working with Price to be able to promote people and events, to whip up publicity where it was needed, not to mention a good knowledge of photography. I made my mind up then. I would apply to one of the new film companies operating out of Soho. I would act as though the Laboratory and Borley Rectory and everything in between had never happened.

Suddenly Price was beside me, his weighty hand on my shoulder, his voice soft and somehow distant. 'Please stay. I need you, Sarah.'

'You never asked how I coped, Harry. When you were away in hospital and I was here alone. You never asked where I went, what I did.'

He looked away guiltily, then met my gaze. 'But I can help . . . financially. You and your mother. Like before—'

'Before?'

And suddenly it all made uncomfortable, terrible sense to

me: the new kitchen wireless, the new armchair that appeared in the drawing room when I had left London two years earlier. 'You gave her money, didn't you? When I was away in Yorkshire. No wonder she agreed to the experiment with Schneider. You bought her trust! You put her – us – in your debt.'

'It wasn't a loan,' he rushed to assure me, his eyes red and wounded. 'You weren't working. I wanted you both to be all right. I was trying to help.'

I thought back to the night before we had gone to the Rectory in the summer of 1929. The night he had escorted me home. 'You'd kept Mother's bracelet all that time. You used it so that you could win her trust.'

He looked confused now, as if he had expected me to be grateful for his peculiar generosity. 'No, you've got it wrong. Do you really think I could be so devious? Sarah, look at me. We can forget all about this.'

'Do you realise what you're saying? What you're asking me to do? What sort of person do you think I am? Do you think I can just walk away from this and pretend that it doesn't matter?'

'But you can't leave. I rely on you now.'

'And who do I rely on?' The words caught in my throat. I swallowed. 'We don't want your money, we never did! How . . . how could you do this? Our greatest fear was that Schneider would trick us, and you cheated us into it. You manipulated us.'

'No, no.' He attempted a smile. 'Do you remember, this was where we met? Right here in this room. I asked you whether you could type. I asked you to be my assistant. Remember?'

How long will you follow him, Sarah? How long?

'Miss Grey,' he said hopefully, remembering, 'can you type? I believe there is a vacancy.' He smiled; he was trying to be sweet, but the words stung.

'I respectfully decline,' I said, wiping away a tear as I stepped backwards, away from him, towards the door. My head pounded as I fought against my trembling legs. *You must keep control now, Sarah,* I told myself. I took a deep breath and said, 'This isn't the end, Harry Price. I'm sure one day I'll see you again. But I need time. I need to begin again. Can you understand?'

He looked past me, staring dejectedly out of the sash window. 'I will miss you, Miss Grey.'

The finality and acceptance in those words brought a numbing pain to my head and heart.

'I will miss you too,' I said quietly, with the greatest effort.

And then I walked out of the door, out of the Laboratory and out of Harry Price's life.

Notes

1   'An Authentic Interview with Conan Doyle from Beyond'.

2   Price seems not to have made this decision immediately. A few weeks after developing the photograph he wrote a particularly intimidating letter to Rudi informing him of the 'suspicious-looking photograph': 'I am just commencing my report on the series of séances we held with you in the spring. I have not yet decided what to do with the photograph we took of you when trying the handkerchief experiment. It is so suspicious looking that there really is only one construction to be put on it' (27 May 1932).

Part III

The Bad Death of Harry Price

'It is fatal to have anything to do with Borley.'

– Sidney Glanville, Harry Price's 'Chief Investigator'

– 27 –

THE GATHERING STORM

Now began an uncertain but exciting period in my life – though at first it hardly seemed so. Weeks passed, months passed, and as the blank seasons flew by life seemed to me altogether less interesting. Gone was the nervous anticipation at the thought of what new discoveries the day might bring; gone were the thrilling night-time adventures to strange places; and gone was the rush of excitement that came each time Price took my hand, looked into my eyes or whispered to me to follow him. And though I tried to forget, my every attempt was met with failure that was fraught with frustration – at him and, increasingly, myself.

Of course, I didn't tell Mother that Price suspected Schneider was a fraud. What would be the point? I still hoped there was a chance he would keep his doubts private, and spare us both yet further sadness. Nor did I ever mention the money she had accepted from Price: her pride and dignity were too valuable to me.

I lived in habitual monotony, dragging myself out of bed each day, following routines robotically. A mechanical existence. I wanted to move on, to pursue the new career I had dreamed of, to see Amy again if I could only cover my embarrassment. But like a ghost I returned week after week to the places in my past that were familiar to me because I had visited them with Price: the restaurants, bars and cake shops on Piccadilly. Wherever my mood took me, the shadow of his memory went too. I saw him everywhere: in the reflections of shop windows, at street corners and in my dreams, his broad silhouette outlined against a vast isolated moor, the outline of the Rectory visible in the distance behind him.

I had only one item by which to remember him – the St Ignatius brass medallion. And this alone restored my confidence in the life change I had committed to, for a bad air seemed to hang about it like a disease. On the few occasions I dared to pick it up, I did so carefully and only for the briefest period. Then I would remember. And my world would turn dark.

I could at least keep the thing away from me, keep whatever evil I sensed radiating from it at bay. I left the medallion in the top drawer of the cabinet next to my bed, resting on the brown leather jacket of the Holy Book.

It was less easy to deal with the faint sounds that came occasionally from the partition wall that divided Mother's bedroom from mine.

On a blustery night in December 1932 I was lying in bed when I noticed it again: *tap-tap-scratch; tap-tap, scratch.*

I got out of bed, shivering in my nightdress, and went gingerly to the corner of the room nearest the window, pressing my ear to the wall. No squeaking, rustling or scurrying. And no mouse droppings in the house.

The faint, insistent sounds taunted me: *Tap-tap-scratch; tap-tap, scratch.*

I slapped my hand against the wall. Silence, quickly followed by the scrape of Mother's bedroom door on the carpet as she came out on to the landing.

I joined her in the gloom

'Did you hear something?' I asked.

'Only you,' she replied. Her face was pale and blank, and unquestionably innocent. 'Try to get some rest, Sarah, please.'

Oh, but how I longed for rest! How I wished for the cobwebs in my head to blow away. I sat, hour after hour, watching the rain run down my windowpane, contemplating with regret the countless opportunities I had forfeited because of him. All around me old attitudes were changing, class barriers being dismantled, women occupying all manner of professions beyond domestic employment – in factories, on the land and even on the buses. It had been that way for years but I hadn't really noticed. I had been left behind.

By January 1933, ten months after Price had detected the suspected fraud in the photograph of Rudi Schneider, I was simmering with resentment not only of him, but also of the other ladies my age who were embracing the new egalitarianism of the times, flocking to the dance halls and jazz clubs of London and exchanging weekly invitations to afternoon tea. I wondered how my old friends spoke of me now. How did Amy, who was married with a family of her own, remember the old Sarah, the ambitious, glamorous Sarah who had loved life? I imagined her mocking me with her new friends: 'the ghost hunter's assistant'.

And of course I couldn't help wondering what had become of Vernon Wall. I had heard nothing from him. No phone calls, not even a letter. Nor had I noticed any more of his newspaper articles, and believe me when I say that I scanned all of the newspapers every morning. According to Mother – who had heard as much from a friend – the young journalist had taken off, deserting London for a woman in Italy. Lake Como. Whether it was true, I had no idea. I hoped it wasn't.

The preponderance of my negative thoughts was so great that by February I began to feel unwell, waking each morning to a dull ache pulling at the bottom of my spine. I felt bloated and quickly lost my appetite. Something, I was sure, was wrong, yet I did not respond with the urgency I should have done, or would have done had I been in a healthier frame of mind. It was Mother I had to thank for eventually persuading me to see a doctor. I did so reluctantly, little imagining I would soon find myself admitted to the Chelsea Hospital for Women for an operation. A small growth – they called it a subserous fibroid – was growing from the outside wall of my uterus into my pelvis; it was removed and afterwards I spent fourteen days recovering. And as I lay in my bed at night, listening to the sounds of the hospital and the other sick women, for the first time in many months my spirits rose. I was lucky. Unlike some of the women around me, I was going to be all right.

When at last I was released from the hospital I decided that I would heed the doctors' advice and take myself away from London for a short time to somewhere relaxing, preferably near the sea, where I could properly recuperate and clear my head of its brooding melancholy. Solitude is rarely desirable, and I did not relish the idea of spending such a long time alone, in a part of the country I didn't know, but I needed to escape. So when Mother drew my attention to an advert in the classified column of the *Sunday Dispatch*, I decided that the 'remote, peaceful cottage' in West Wales sounded ideal.

'How long will you be gone?' she asked me. We were sitting in the drawing room at home. My cases were packed and waiting in the hall. 'Not as long as the last time, I hope?'

I suddenly realised that she might have regretted urging me to get away, and perhaps that she was afraid I wouldn't be coming back. I stood, went round to her chair and took her hand, squeezing into it some gentle reassurance. 'No, not nearly as long. You'll be all right without me?'

'Yes, of course. You need this.' The warmth and loyalty in her voice was touchingly sincere. Her face was lined and her hair grey, but she was still a striking woman. My eyes roamed from the faded curtains to the stained carpet and tarnished silver to settle again on Mother's face. 'You can tidy the house, perhaps? Brighten the place up a bit?'

'Yes.'

As I entered the hallway to collect my coat and suitcase a chill air pressed past me, and I wondered if I was making a mistake: if leaving Mother alone was ill advised. It wasn't just the occasional scratching in the walls that made me hesitate: the house itself was beginning to feel different to me; as if our home was sheltering something hidden just beyond the limits of normal sight.

'Sarah dear, are you all right?'

She was standing behind me. I turned, and for the briefest moment I fancied I glimpsed something alien in my mother's gaze, as though a dense cloud was drifting in, covering her thoughts.

I blinked, and saw nothing at all abnormal in her expression. Only the familiar loyalty and unquestioning love I had come to rely upon.

'Are you sure you don't mind me leaving you?' I asked again, and she quickly responded with a decisive nod. 'Don't worry about me. You must get away and enjoy yourself.'

That was comforting, if I overlooked the fact that I had felt something oddly recognisable – I might almost say something menacing – in the chill movement of air that had pressed past me and brought gooseflesh to my arms.

'No more ghostly nonsense either,' I instructed her, making her promise to leave seances and books about the paranormal alone.

Then a depressing thought hit me: *Your mother may socialise with Spiritualists, Sarah, but at least she has some friends.*

This is what ghosts do, I thought as I wrapped my mother in my arms. They bleed us of life and potential and hope and happiness. They make us shadows of ourselves.

That afternoon I left London determined to begin again.

✳

Overhurst Farm, the cottage that was to be my temporary residence, stood on a wide cliff above an expanse of deserted beach with an uninterrupted view of the sea. I discovered it at the end of a half-mile track that led down from the hamlet of Talbenny, just outside Broad Haven, and on first sight my heart leaped. All around me was the cool fresh air I had come for and I drank it in eagerly, quickly dispelling any misgivings entertained about this trip.

My hostess was an elderly spinster who introduced herself as Miss Golding. She was welcoming and kind and I warmed to her immediately. She was, I think, glad of my company and I was grateful for her support. We sat together each morning at breakfast, looking out over the beautiful bay, discussing our lives and the newspaper reports that interested us. Then, during the afternoons, I would take myself off alone for short walks along the isolated stretch of beach, watching the birds wheel in the brilliant blue sky above me, before sitting for a while and resting in the long grass at the foot of the hill which rose from the beach to the spot where the cottage stood. Even at night, when the sense of isolation was at its highest and thick mists rolled in off the sea and gathered about the house, I never felt vulnerable; I had spent too long in the company of shadows to find anything in this natural splendour that could upset me.

Nothing had ever felt so perfectly right. Which made what happened on the Sunday of my third week at the cottage especially disappointing.

I arrived at the breakfast table just as the clock over the mantelpiece chimed eight, poured myself a cup of tea and reached for the morning newspaper. The news at that time was full of stories about the escalating troubles in Europe, and with some family on my mother's side residing in Germany I was keen to learn more about what was happening there since the Reichstag fire the week before. But where was the newspaper? I looked about but couldn't find it. Then I noticed that Miss Golding was watching me worriedly. When I asked her about it she became evasive, muttering something unconvincing about a late delivery due to the worsening weather. I held her gaze until she flinched and looked away. 'What's the matter?' I asked. It was only then that she sat me down and reluctantly told me the name she had seen in the paper.

Harry Price.

I felt sick. But when at last she handed me the morning edition of the *Sunday Dispatch*, I realised the situation was even worse than I had imagined.

The headline screamed at me: '*Price Detects Fraud – Sensational Exposure of Spiritualist Medium Rudi Schneider*'. And below this was the damning photograph I had first laid eyes on some fifteen months earlier, which showed that Schneider had freed his hand while the phenomena occurred.

'Let us face facts,' Price was quoted. 'Life after death has not been proved. The report has upset a great number of people, including some of our own Council who suggest that Rudi's free arm had only been a trance movement. That is only a theory and I prefer to believe that the boy deliberately took advantage of the fact that I was ill that night and evaded my control.'[1]

Why had Price kept the fact of Rudi's fraud a secret for so long? To shelter me from the humiliation of the truth? That hardly seem likely. Only when I cast my mind back to the night of the experiment did I remember the crucial information I had overheard in conversation between Price and Schneider, and the truth became apparent: 'If it's war they want then war they shall have.'

My old employer had played a long game, set a trap, spited his enemies, thrown Schneider and me to the wolves. I realised now that he must have suspected from the beginning that Schneider was performing separate seances for his rival researchers, the Society for Psychical Research, whom he loathed and resented; and to an ego the size of his, the idea was intolerable. So he had waited, insidiously courting the Society for Psychical Research in the process, all the time cultivating the necessary information to cause them maximum damage. When he had learned they were convinced of Schneider's veracity he had waited until they had announced as much to the world's media. And then, when he was certain he could refute their conclusions and embarrass them beyond measure, he had exacted his revenge.

By the spring of 1933, this was my assessment of his behaviour. And time has shown I was mostly correct. But what I could not have known then was that a deeper, more insidious kind of wickedness was also at work.

Note

1 *Sunday Dispatch*, 5 March 1933.

– 28 –

THE LONDON
TERROR

I resume my account at a point six years after the last. If you were to ask me why I chose to skip such a period, I would reply that these were the years of my greatest contentment and the longest time that elapsed without my having any direct association with Harry Price.

I had returned from Wales determined to find new and fulfilling employment among other people of my age, and I soon did so when the Jupiter Film Locos Publishing Company, at 186 Wardour Street, London W1, accepted my application for the permanent position of secretary. I was delighted, and a wonderfully active social life soon followed. Though I knew little about the industry, it was an exciting one in which to work – the public was going wild for the 'talkies' and the new modern colour stereoscopic flicks were simply marvellous! By 1934 I had become a sort of general manager with a secretary of my own. The fact that I had not married did not concern me because married women were at that time prevented from enjoying the privilege of work.

My new job brought freedom to enjoy myself. Though I was still living at home, I could now afford to treat Mother to some luxury, whether it was our visit to the seaside that summer or our many shopping trips in the following year to Dickins and Jones. Although for most of the time she seemed content, there were enough signs in her behaviour to make me suspicious. Like the afternoon in October 1935 when, over tea at Lyons Corner House, I glimpsed a glassiness in her eyes, as though she was listening not to me but to a different voice coming from somewhere else.

I preferred to spend as much time as possible away from our home. Although we had improved the decor, bought new furniture, even bought ourselves a pet – a small black cat we named Charlie – something about our house, particularly the landing outside Mother's room, no longer felt 'right' to me, and all the idiosyncrasies about the place – the faint and intermittent tap, tap, scratching in the walls, the unexplained cold spots and chilly wisps of air – began taunting me. I didn't want to believe there was anything wrong; I valued my new life too highly to permit the intrusion of such thoughts. Instead I sought comfort in alternative explanations. Perhaps Price was correct when he had hypothesised that houses like Borley Rectory somehow 'kept' human memories. Perhaps that was happening to us.

I see now what I was doing: using elaborate hypotheses to keep the past at bay. But for how long? Every so often someone would ask me about the time I had spent with Price all those years ago, and when that happened I would laugh off the question, giving him an excellent character and carefully omitting the juicy bits.

In this way I became very good at ignoring the lingering sense that there was unfinished business from my past. I learnt to resist the dreams of Borley Rectory and its dark nun. For a time the distance I had imposed between the past and myself enabled me to blow them quite easily away.

Until one night in 1937, when I arrived home from a late work supper in Soho to find Mother crouching in darkness at the top of the stairs.

'What are you doing?' I asked, feeling at once intrigued and alarmed. But she didn't answer me. She didn't flinch. Even as I reached the stop of the stairs and knelt beside her, raising my hand to take the wet sponge from her grasp. The wallpaper was damp and smudged.

I asked again, 'What *are* you doing? It's approaching midnight.'

My voice was strained, and I could see now that Mother's eyes were wide and empty and shining like glass.

Then she did flinch. Blinked once. 'Sarah, dear . . . there you are.'

I could hear the uncertainty and confusion in her voice, could see it in her eyes as they dropped from my face to the wet sponge in my hand. The mystery took hold of me as I helped her to her feet and led her downstairs, remembering that years ago she had done this before.

'The wall needed to be washed,' she said quietly from her chair next to the fire. 'The damp is getting in again. It's rising.'

Somewhere in my heart I felt a knot loosen as Charlie advanced into the room and paced restlessly around the coffee table. 'There is no damp,' I said patiently.

Mother's gaze faltered. Charlie leapt into her lap and hissed at me.

'Tell me how I can help you,' I said, feeling my stomach tighten. Mother was my best friend. No thought was more distressing, more alarming to me, than the possibility that she might be losing her faculties.

'My dear, you've already helped. I hope you know I'm grateful for everything you've done for us,' she said, directing a wistful glance at my father's old piano. 'I don't want to be a burden on you, not on anyone.'

Any irritation I had harboured down the years at knowing she had once secretly accepted money from Price dissolved. She could never be a burden on me, and the idea that she thought of herself in this way was too horrific, too sad.

'You and I,' I said softly, 'we're a team. And I have a good job now, one that will keep us secure.'

'I do *want* to work,' she said with a trace of sadness, and I nodded my encouragement. She was one of the bravest, proudest women I had ever known. 'But Sarah . . .' She paused, struggling to release the words. 'I worry that there is something the matter with me. Sometimes I feel . . . different, not myself. Like tonight. I wake and find myself downstairs, collecting the mail, moving things.'

'Sleep-walking?' I smiled, wanting to feel relieved. 'That's common enough. And you've always been the first to collect the mail.'

'No.' Her voice was stern, her eyes wide and uncertain. 'Not always. It's worse now. I find myself . . . doing things, dreaming things. Things I can't remember. Do you understand? I washed the wall on the landing, and another in my bedroom, without any memory. I don't even know how long I was sitting there doing it! I did it in my sleep.' She held up one hand. 'I know how this sounds, but sometimes I feel as though something is taking me over, taking control.'

As I registered the shakiness in her voice, my worst fear took hold: her mind was deteriorating. All of her wisdom and intelligence and companionship, everything that made her mine, was suddenly in jeopardy. I wanted to reassure her with an explanation, but an explanation resolutely refused to come. So instead

I said in an unsteady voice, 'Perhaps you need some rest.'

'Rest? How can I rest with those terrible noises in the house?'

'Noises?'

'A very faint tapping, scratching sound,' Mother explained. 'Coming from the walls. Every month or so. It's driving me mad!'

And now my heart was pounding. Our cat's eyes tracked me as I stood up abruptly and approached Mother's chair. 'Then you've heard it too?' I ventured.

'I thought it was in my head. Sarah, why did you never say?'

'I did, remember?' Her blank expression told me she didn't. I took her hand and knelt beside her. 'After that I didn't mention it again. I didn't want to scare you. I thought it might be mice, or—'

She stared at me silently until eventually, in a cracked voice, she whispered, 'There's something wrong with this house, isn't there?'

I deflected the question with another of my own. 'How long have you been feeling not yourself?'

'A long time – years. But never as odd as I feel now.'

I gazed hard into her fearful eyes. 'Please try to remember. It might be important.'

After a long moment's consideration she nodded and said, 'Since you went to that place with Harry Price. That house on the Suffolk border . . . What was it called?'

I froze, and watched her lips with mounting horror, as Mother mouthed the two words I had hoped never to hear again.

*

Harry Price was the last person I wanted to ask for help.

What little I saw of him in the newspapers made me glad to be separated from him. The only time I felt any real envy was when I heard that he had become the first Chair of the British Film Institute. His 'experiments' were becoming increasingly outlandish, with newspaper articles recounting his bizarre escapades in Europe, where he had investigated the case of a talking mongoose that could apparently read people's thoughts and sing hymns. Next came his inquiries into fire-walking and the Indian rope trick and his examination of the bite marks of a 'devil girl' from Romania.[1]

Knowing his beginnings, it made me sad to see that my old employer had been reduced to such cheap popularisation. But, as I was to discover shortly, any sympathy I had was grossly misplaced. For just when it seemed he could stoop no lower, Price was preparing news that would awe a generation and secure his name in history forever. At a terrible cost to us both.

Perhaps it was denial that made me close my eyes to the problems at home – a reluctance to reassociate myself with phenomena that defined a life I had left behind. I told myself we didn't yet need outside help, that Mother and I were all right on our own. And there were many distractions at work which helped me convince myself of this lie. The months flicked by in a blur of late nights at the office, film premieres and parties. At the Silver Slipper in Regent Street, with its polished glass dance floor and walls painted with lush Italian scenes, I danced away troubles I hoped would never catch up with me.

Until one evening in late November.

It was close to 8.30 when I locked the office and stepped out into the cobbled alleyway that cut through to Old Compton Street. Soho was dead. This in itself wasn't unusual for a Thursday evening, but I was keen to reach the bright lights of Leicester Square as quickly as possible. After an absence that had lasted far, far too long, I had arranged to meet Amy for a trip to the cinema to see *Modern Times*, the new Charlie Chaplin film, and I didn't want to be late. We had a lot to catch up on. Afterwards, if there was time, we would go for cocktails together in one of the bars opposite the new Windmill Theatre, and laugh together at the married men who were enticed there by the nude shows. They were hilarious to observe, like guilty schoolboys.

Walking on, I spotted up ahead a broad-shouldered uniformed police officer who was standing watch by the side of a gated townhouse. Stamping his feet and looking about him, the poor man looked rigid with cold. And something about his general demeanour hinted to me that all was not well. My curiosity led me right to him.

'I hope there's not been any trouble?' I asked.

'Trouble?' His breath frosted on the air. 'That's putting it mildly.'

I tried to catch his eye, but he was glancing furtively to either side of me, then behind me, almost as though he was afraid that at any moment someone might leap out at us from the dark.

As it transpired, that was exactly what he was afraid of.

'You'd best be moving on now,' he added. 'It's not safe out.'

'Not safe?'

'Not for women like you – perhaps not for any of us.' He looked up. 'You must have read about the attacks?'

I hadn't. I explained to the officer that I had been so busy at work that week I hadn't had time to read the newspapers. The way he was shaking his head now, looking away from me and pursing his chapped lips, led me to the conclusion that something was very wrong. I didn't care at all for the look on his face. I had seen that look before, in the pale faces of the Foysters at Borley Rectory.

'Are you guarding this house?' I asked.

He shook his head. 'Not guarding, miss. Waiting.'

He cast a quick glance behind him.

'It's all right,' I said with quiet diplomacy. 'There's no one around.'

His sharp eyes locked on me. 'Sure about that, are you, miss? I've seen him,' he said suddenly. 'Once this week already – Monday. Came charging out of the dark, he did.'

'Who did?'

'Whatever he – it – is. Dark and fast – such a terrible size. I didn't see its face. It was no human, I know that. There was a sighting late last night, on this street. A young lady living at this house answered the door to a figure – said he was covered in a dark cloak. A man like a giant bat. Stood right where I am now, just staring at her with blazing red eyes and shooting blue and white sparks from his mouth.'

'Was she all right?' I asked. 'No one hurt, I hope?'

'Before the poor lady could cry for help, the attacker had clutched for her dress with steel claws. Then he ran off.'

Steel claws? I checked my watch. Amy would be wondering where I was. I returned my gaze to the sociable policeman and was about to bid him goodbye when something – it sounded like a dustbin lid – somewhere behind us clattered to the ground. Nothing remarkable about that, I told myself. It was a cat, probably, or an urban fox. But the policeman's pupils had become wide circles. 'Tell me more,' I said. 'Tell me everything.'

His name was Officer Westron, and as he recounted his own peculiar encounter, I found myself wanting to produce a notepad and pen and take down every last detail. I felt as if I was back at Price's side, questioning anxious witnesses like Reverend Smith and the Foysters whose lives had brushed with the unknown. And though a piece of me wanted to walk away – to find Amy at Leicester Square and enjoy an evening on the town – I couldn't resist asking yet more questions.

'It was a tall figure, and thin. Moved too fast for me to see – leapt out at me from the alleyway. Jumped right over that wall.'

I took a sharp intake of breath as I remembered something Price had said, years ago, about a ghost that could leap over fifteen-foot walls – a man with steel claws who shot fire from his eyes. *The Terror of London. One hundred years ago, sightings of the ghost were common.*

'Spring-Heeled Jack,' I said under my breath.

By the expression on his face, Officer Westron must have thought I was speaking another language.

'Reports of The Terror appear across history,' I explained. Sometimes he is said to be gigantic in size. In London he came to prominence in the winter of 1890 when *The Times* ran a series of articles about unexplained assaults on women by a demonic figure, much like the one you say happened here last night. And now . . . it's happening again. Maybe.'

'But how do you know about this?' His tone wasn't suspicious, more fascinated.

I hesitated, unsure how to answer.

'You might be able to help us,' he continued.

'No.' My answer came out without thinking. 'No, I have to go. I'm meeting a friend.'

'Wait, please.' Westron reached out an arm. 'Come down to the station with me.'

Help the police? On a matter of psychical investigation? The idea shimmered, beckoning. This predicament was both crazy and comfortingly familiar. During my Laboratory days Price and I were frequently called upon to give evidence against fraudulent mediums prosecuted under the Witchcraft Act. But that was my other life, behind me now. So why did I suddenly feel so confident, so curious?

'It won't take long,' Officer Westron insisted.

Against my better wisdom – perhaps out of a sense of duty – I nodded and stepped forward.

'How do you intend to take control of this situation?'

Detective Mayfield was silent. Since my arrival at Charing Cross Police Station, I had heard very few answers. Only questions, which Officer Westron and his superior evidently thought I might help answer.

I tried again.

'Any physical evidence?'

'We found a gentleman's cane in the alley. That was all.'

'Do you have any suspects?'

'Who could possibly match the profile? I mean –' Mayfield threw up his fat hands in exasperation – 'how can any man appear out of nowhere, outrun six officers, leap fifteen feet into the air, and just . . . disappear?'

'A man can't,' I said directly, 'but the human mind is very capable of imagining that he can. Tell me, did your officers actually *see* this figure leap into the air?' I rose from my chair and turned to face the mild-mannered officer Westron, who was installed behind a much smaller desk, scribbling on a notepad. The vulnerability in the young man's expression was so pronounced, so incongruous with his otherwise sturdy, robust appearance, that I couldn't help wondering if he was in the wrong profession. 'Officer, were your eyes on him when he leapt?'

He blinked.

'I didn't think so.'

The detective looked puzzled. 'But they chased him into an alleyway and found he was gone.' He shook his head. 'The only way out was over the wall.'

'The only way out *as far as you know*,' I corrected him. 'How many reports have there been now?'

'Seven. And many more in the newspapers.'

'Then witnesses may be unreliable, prone to seeing what they have heard from others,' I said, and before the words were out of my mouth I was remembering the hysterical crowds that had surrounded Borley Rectory when Wall had published his article on the haunting. They'd become drunk on their imaginings. The same thing could be happening in this case. The power of suggestion could make people believe anything.

Another question occurred to me.

'Do any of the eyewitness testimonies match?'

Detective Mayfield, whose tie was loosened and whose shirt was more grey than white, heaved his broad frame out of his chair, chewing his lip as he pondered the question. He was around fifty, pale-skinned with a midnight shadow looming on his jowly face. 'The details are scant. No one got a good look at the assailant's face. The attacks happened at night, so . . .'

'So it is easy for the witnesses to exaggerate their reports,' I said vigorously. 'What they don't remember, their mind fills in for them.'

'You think they're lying, Miss Grey?'

I met the detective's gaze and saw that it was laced with envy. Whatever did he think of this fiery young woman who was telling him how to do his job? In truth, I didn't care. They were the ones asking for my help. And my qualifications were, well, unique.

'Not lying. But possibly mistaken.'

Catching an unpleasant scent of sweat and beer, I went to the detective's cluttered desk and leaned over the map on which he had marked the locations of the attacks.

'The way I see it, you have two possible scenarios. Either there *is* a ghost, or you're dealing with someone who is impersonating the legend of Spring-Heeled Jack – someone who wants to fool people there is a ghost at large. Mass hysteria and fear of the unknown do the rest.'

The detective glanced at the younger officer who had brought me in. 'You're right, Officer Westron. She seems to know her stuff.'

'And *she* is still here,' I said forcefully.

'You're a sceptic, Miss Grey?'

I blinked. Memories flashed across my mind: Mother at home, scrubbing damp from the walls; the wretched outline of a dark figure, encroaching ever nearer.

'I've met ghosts. They don't behave like this. They certainly don't drop their cloaks or pull women's dresses with steel claws.'

I turned and went over to Westron, who was already feeding a sheet of paper into his typewriter, presumably to write up his handwritten notes. 'Here's what I recommend you do: put an article in the newspapers, laying out the evidence. Shoot down the myths that have built up around this character, Spring-Heeled Jack. Because I can guarantee you, it's not a ghost stalking London, it's fear. When people are scared, they'll believe anything.'

I turned to face the detective. 'Take the fear away. Expose

the facts, shine light upon the problem, and watch it dissolve.'

'You think that will work?' Mayfield asked. The frown etched into his weighty face suggested he didn't.

'I guarantee it.'

As if a switch had been flicked, the detective nodded and instructed Officer Westron to telephone 'that expert in South Kensington. What's his name?'

'Harry Price?' Westron ventured.

'No!' I heard myself say, and both men snapped their heads round in my direction, clearly surprised.

I took a deep breath and lowered my voice. 'Let me do it. I'll write the article.'

'So it seems this city is blessed with two psychic experts, Miss Grey.'

Three months had passed. In his office on Fleet Street Bernard Jenkins, the editor of *The Times*, was smiling as he leaned back in his chair, admiring the pages of that day's edition. 'We had an excellent response to your piece on Spring-Heeled Jack. The letters pages have been humming with speculation ever since.'

'Splendid. I'm glad.'

In truth I was annoyed with myself for letting down my friend. I had telephoned Amy and apologised but every time I had asked to see her she had said she was busy. Half of me felt guilty but I was satisfied too. Reports of 'The Terror' had fallen since I had forgone an evening with her to help the police. And my boss at Jupiter Film Locos was impressed with my article's reception. Indeed, when he learned that I had worked for a ghost hunter, he even joked that I might assist with the scripts on future horror films.

'Perhaps you'd consider writing more for us?'

'No, thank you. When it comes to psychical research, I suppose you might say I've retired.'

Yet even as I said this, I wasn't sure I believed it.

Looking back, it seems ridiculous that I should have seriously considered agreeing to the editor's request after the lengths to which I had travelled to distance myself from the subject. Yet the idea was oddly appealing, and not just because it was flattering to be asked or because I sensed I was making myself useful. No, the temptation to agree was far more visceral than that.

'Won't you reconsider, Miss Grey? You'll be handsomely paid. Surely there are some unusual affairs you might investigate, and write about for us?'

I remembered, then, the way Price had reacted when Wall's articles had threatened his own popular status, the way his jealousy had erupted. If I did this, I knew it would anger him intently. And of course I was still bitter.

'I'm sure I can find some. *If* I do this,' I replied.

'Wonderful,' said Jenkins. He was smiling, I think because he sensed my latent desire to say yes. 'Mr Price . . . he's not the easiest man to deal with.'

'Why do you say that?'

'Someone warned me about him a while back,' he said, choosing his words carefully. 'An old colleague. Said he's had his fingers burnt with Price, that he can't be trusted.'

Naturally I asked him who had said this.

'Vernon Wall. He's a journalist. Do you know him?'

'I used to know him.' Then I thought, I wish I still did.

Did it strike me as unusual that the journalist who had expressed such interest in me at Borley had never tried to contact me since – no telephone call, not even a letter? I can honestly say that it didn't. Since our time together at the Rectory, I'd had leisure to reflect. I saw now what had probably been true all along: that I had treated Wall poorly by siding with Price. It was Wall's story first, even if he had been responsible for drawing crowds of visitors who upset the Smiths' lives.

Jenkins shrugged. 'Trust or not, Harry Price pays his bills.'

'Bills?'

He nodded. 'Just this week he placed an advert with us calling for assistants to help with an investigation of a haunted house somewhere in Essex.'

'An advert . . . What investigation?' I leaned forward. 'What house?'

'I won't pretend your letter didn't surprise me, Miss Grey.'

The old man I had tracked down at his college rooms in Oxford spoke with such a rasping voice I assumed he must be a keen smoker. He wasn't. Indeed, something far worse was at work upon him.

'How many years is it now since we corresponded?' he asked me on the staircase at the entrance to his set of rooms.

'Ten,' I said, with a note of apology in my voice.

'And not a word from you since then.' He gave a reflective sigh and then, perhaps seeing a wider problem not yet evident to me, he nodded and his expression grew serious. 'I assume you are here because of Borley?'

I told him I was.

'Then you'd better follow me.'

He led me along an oak-panelled corridor into his rooms which, for such a wealthy college, were colder and less welcoming than I would have expected. The threadbare carpet and the lingering odour of damp were impssible to ignore. Impossible, also, not to see the troubling thoughts brewing behind my host's eyes as he invited me to sit with him at a large oval table.

'Dr Chipp, I know you went back to the Rectory all those years ago, after you were at university with Harry Bull. I know you had an . . . experience. The story of how your dogs vanished from your car while you slept is the talk of Sudbury town even now. The villagers are still frightened.'

His mouth had tightened. 'That was a long time ago. Why have you come to see me?'

'Because I need to speak to somebody who understands about that place,' I answered.

I told him then some – but not all – of what had happened since he had written to Price at the end of the last decade with details of the Borley problem. Wanting his help and at the same time fearful of what he might tell me, I felt as if I was about to receive the results of a dreaded medical test. 'I realise I might be overreacting . . . but I feel there is danger around me. As though something is drawing me to the Rectory even now.'

I reached down to my handbag, which I had left at my feet, opened it and took out the cutting given to me by the editor of *The Times*:

HAUNTED HOUSE

Responsible persons of leisure and intelligence, intrepid, critical, and unbiased, are invited to join rota of observers in year's night-and-day investigation of alleged haunted house in Home Counties. Printed instructions supplied. Scientific training or ability to operate simple instruments an advantage. House situated in lonely hamlet, so own car is essential. Write to Box H.989, *The Times*, EC4.

Dr Chipp was silent, his expression hovering somewhere between sadness and fear. Finally he said, 'You think it's the same house?'

'I know it's the same house.' The editor at *The Times* had given me the details. What I didn't know was why Price was suddenly involved with the case again, after he had so readily dismissed it.

'Your companion is making a grave mistake,' said Dr Chipp. His statement was devoid of doubt.

'He's not my companion,' I said. 'Not any more.'

But this detail seemed irrelevant to Dr Chipp. As he sat in silence, I had the impression that this was a man who had lived for too long with a burden – something, perhaps, that he wanted to share with others, but didn't feel able to express. 'That place is thoroughly evil,' he said eventually. 'The Rectory stains you, pollutes lives.'

I hesitated, feeling the apprehension his words evoked.

'You've been there, I assume?'

I nodded. 'Oh yes, a couple of times.'

'Then you will already have experienced troubled thoughts, no doubt. Strange phenomena, nightmares?'

If Dr Chipp harboured any doubts, they didn't show. His voice was adamant.

The terrifying thing, of course, was that he was right. My dreams had worsened and were always the same: the figure of a woman in robes advancing on me. And now, suddenly, whenever I looked in a mirror I glimpsed something below my neckline. I had begun avoiding mirrors for fear of what I might see.

Of course it didn't help that Mother's mental lapses were worsening. She still rose early to collect and open the post, but began to forget she had done so, forgetting also to lock the front door. Her mental condition wasn't the sole cause of the distance that was opening between us. That was due to a bigger mystery: the partition wall that divided our bedrooms and, from within, the faint but insistent tapping, scratching sounds. Like everything else we didn't understand, we had learned not to speak of those sounds, to do our best to ignore them even if they refused to ignore us.

'I've come because I believe something is wrong, something is happening to me. And because something needs to be done.'

'Then you *have* felt it too?'

He wanted me to level with him, I realised. *Folie à deux*: a madness shared by two.

The old man leaned forward. His face in the low light was sallow.

'Some years after visiting the Rectory I came here to the college, but within weeks I heard a restless rapping coming from the walls. I never located the source. Soon I started seeing things – quick movements out of the corner of my eye. Oh, I tried to ignore them, but when my scout informed me, in a state of some distress, of what she had seen one morning while cleaning my office – well, I knew then that something had followed me from Borley.'

'What did she see?' I asked.

'A woman, dressed from head to toe in black robes.' He pinched the bridge of his nose. 'After that, the troubles became progressively worse. As you can see, my health is not good. And there have been too many . . . accidents over the years.'

'Accidents?'

'Fires, family deaths. Everyone close to me has gone.'

'How do you explain it?' I asked quickly.

'I'm not sure I can.' He hesitated in a way that made me anxious. 'It was said that Henry Bull, who built the Rectory, was taken in with stories of haunting, that he would study the occult, try to summon up evil. If that's true, who knows? Perhaps he let something through from the other side which drained the life from him.'

'You mean a curse?'

He frowned. 'Possibly. I disapprove of that term. It diminishes the gravity of the thing.'

'Then what would you call it?'

His lips curved downwards as he contemplated my question. 'I would call it an execration: an attempt to inflict harm upon the living through supernatural influence. Hexes are associated with places, people, or, more commonly, objects.'

'All right, well, if there is a curse – an execration – at work, then how do we stop it?'

'I was hoping you might tell me.'

Marianne Foyster's warning came back to me then.

'I think that whatever is haunting us feeds on the lies of the living,' I said. 'Deception. I think a woman – a nun – was murdered in that house centuries ago by someone who deceived her, and that some fragment of the suffering he caused her remains.'

Dr Chipp was frowning. 'You're saying her soul is punishing the living for her murderer's sin?'

'I know how it sounds . . .'

But did I? Or had I become a woman who could no longer differentiate between what was real and what was not?

I had to know, so I asked him the only question that seemed reasonable – the question that was the reason for my visit.

'Dr Chipp, are *you* guilty of some deception?'

He did not say what his sin was. He didn't need to.

'We all tell lies, Miss Grey. That's what humans do. Even you, I imagine.'

He knew. And if I was in danger, it was because I had hidden too much – from Price, from everyone. The greatest and guiltiest secret. I pictured the ancient brass medallion we had found in the Rectory – octagonal, embossed with the likeness of St Ignatius – the wall writings and the fury burning in Marianne Foyster's eyes; and beneath these memories, playing like a terrible record, the curious scraping sounds from behind the wall at home.

'You must clear up this mystery,' Dr Chipp said, 'or our sins will engulf us both.' There was a slight pause, then, 'You know, the dogs that disappeared from my car were never found. You understand, Miss Grey? Those animals are gone. Forever.'

He stared at me and said nothing more.

Note

1 'Fire-walking': The act of walking barefoot over a bed of hot embers or stones. In an attempt to elucidate the mystery, Price placed an advertisement in the personal column of *The Times* on 23 October 1934, inviting 'amateur and professional fire-resisters to come forward and perform the feat' (*Confessions of a Ghost Hunter*, p. 363).

The Indian rope trick has been described as the world's greatest illusion in which a magician hurls a rope into the air which then stands erect, allowing the magician's son or assistant to climb up it before disappearing after reaching the top. 'Has the Rope Trick ever been witnessed in its traditional form? I do not think it has. I have carefully analysed all the accounts of the Trick which have come under my notice, and in each case there was a flaw, such as a faulty memory, incorrect sequence of events, mal-observation, ignorance of deceptive methods – or sheer lying. There was always *something* that would not stand up against cold analysis' (Harry Price, *Confessions of a Ghost Hunter*, p. 345).

– 29 –
THE LOCKED
BOOK

The Dark Woman did not relent but encroached ever further; whenever I closed my eyes she was there, her arms outstretched in a gesture of condemnation. Real or imagined – and I doubted the latter – she would not leave me. I knew that now. I carried her with me, the penalty for my deception that I had yet to confess.

And someone else had my scent.

On a cold evening in February 1939, I was working late when a noise in the corridor that led to my office caused me to start.

I looked up, focusing my gaze on the glass partition wall that ran the length of my room, but I saw no one. Soon the sound came again, and when I looked up for a second time I was alarmed to see the silhouette of a man standing at my open door.

I leapt up but his words prevented me from crying out. 'Miss Grey, I presume?' He held out his hands. 'Please, don't be alarmed. I didn't mean to startle you.'

My visitor had an air of authority about him and in his right hand he carried a black briefcase. In the dim evening light he seemed to resemble Price himself. In fact, for a moment I thought it might actually be Price.

'My name is Glanville – Sidney Glanville,' he said quietly. 'I've come with a message for you, Miss Grey, and to make a request. Excuse my interruption, but may I come in?'

I motioned him forward, saying nothing, and sat down at my desk again.

'Thank you,' he said, taking the chair opposite me. 'I am relieved to have found you here at this hour. I would have called in the morning, but I was passing and saw the door downstairs was open, and—'

'Will this take long?' I interrupted, my voice firm. 'Because I'm a busy woman, Mr Glanville. If you're here on business then come back during business hours.'

'I was worried you would react in this way.' He smiled awkwardly, apologetically. 'I am a close friend of Mr Harry Price – his closest friend. And I've come at his request.'

My stomach knotted. 'I'm sorry,' I said briskly. 'If you would excuse me . . .' and I rose from my chair to make for the door.

But as I rounded the desk he also stood and reached out to me. 'Miss Grey, please, just five minutes of your time, and then I will go.'

My visitor's face was fresh and tinged with pink from the evening chill, his hair silver and neatly combed in a side parting, and he wore a pair of spectacles which gave him the gravitas of a schoolmaster. He seemed reasonable enough, but what did I owe him, this stranger? And yet, I reasoned, he must have good reason to be here in my office at such a late hour. The thought tempered my impulse to ask him to leave and I returned to my seat. 'Five minutes, that's all.'

Nodding, Glanville reached for his briefcase, opened it and removed a black book that was bound with leather and fitted with a Bramah-lock. 'Harry wanted you to see this.'

'Who are you?' I asked sharply.

'I am your replacement, Miss Grey. Harry's principal investigator.' He laid the leather book carefully on the desk in front of me. 'This private and confidential report chronicles every aspect of my investigation of the events at Borley Rectory.'

'*Your* investigation!'

'Please, don't be offended. I know you take an interest. I had a meeting recently with Dr Chipp. He told me you had visited him. Since you left Harry's employment there have been many exciting developments, Miss Grey. With Harry's support, I've spent almost two years at the Rectory, re-examining the old evidence and exploring that which has only recently come to light.'

'What new evidence?' I asked. These comments made little sense to me for I knew that Price did not believe in the Borley manifestations and never had.

'As I said, Miss Grey, the situation has changed dramatically. Harry is writing a book on the Borley affair, chronicling his involvement with the case all the way back to 1929, when the two of you first visited the house.'

That surprised me.

'It's to be published next summer. I've read an early draft, and I have to say a most convincing case has been put forward. I believe it will be found totally absorbing. It's all in there: Lionel Foyster's diary, the wall writings, the prophecy – everything.'

I heard his words but still didn't understand. I *knew* that Price had debunked the Borley phenomena, albeit in a very understated fashion. What had happened to change his mind? And what was this prophecy Glanville had mentioned?

'I will explain everything; it's all here in this report.' He patted the item lightly. 'All that I ask is that you listen with an open mind, and only *after* you have heard the evidence we have gathered do you make your decision.'

'What decision?' I asked.

He smiled as he produced a small key from his pocket and unlocked the book. 'Whether to return to the Laboratory. Harry would like your assistance to help him complete the investigation. He knows how important it is to you. And he sees, I think, that he made a profound mistake in allowing you to leave.'

'He didn't *allow* me,' I cried, rising abruptly. 'I decided to leave, and for my own sake, not for his!'

And why should I return? I asked myself. I had a life now; all this was in my past.

It was as if my visitor heard my unspoken question. 'Miss Grey, I firmly believe that when Harry's manuscript is published it will send shock waves far and wide. It could very well shake the foundations of the scientific materialist world view. And when you see what I have come to show you, I think you'll understand why.'

He handed me the book. I drew the lamp closer and examined it intently. The room and the noises of Soho beyond receded as I silently leafed through the pages. I was amazed at the quantity of work before me. There was masses of correspondence between Glanville and Price, Glanville and the Smiths, Glanville and the Foysters; pages and pages of photographs depicting Borley Rectory from every angle imaginable; detailed observation reports; tracings of the wall writings and what appeared to be transcriptions of table-tipping and planchette seances.[1]

'Well,' I said, 'you have been busy.'

'*We*,' he said evenly. 'We have all been busy.'

'All?'

'Myself and the other observers.'

I was about to ask, 'What other observers?' when my eyes settled on a copy of the advertisement which had appeared in the classified column of *The Times*, inviting men of leisure to join a year-long vigil in a haunted house.

'I think you already know that it was Harry who placed the advert,' said Glanville. 'I knew the moment I saw it that I had to reply. You see, Miss Grey, I'm an engineer by trade but retired now, with far too few activities to occupy my day. But this' – he gestured towards the book – 'this was thrilling. Perfect, in fact.'

'Mr Glanville, there is nothing even remotely "perfect" about that house.'

'It is indeed a most unsettling place, unlike anywhere else on earth. Every time I visited the Rectory I came away in lower spirits.'

His words brought gooseflesh to my arms, yet I was intrigued. 'Tell me what precipitated the recent investigations.'

'Four years ago, when the Foysters vacated the Rectory, the place was locked up and it remained empty for a year. Even then people who passed the house at night swore they saw figures at its windows, shadowy silhouettes staring out, and because of these rumours the ecclesiastical authority decided that the Rectory was to be closed permanently. The place was just too much work, too run-down. So the parish of Liston was combined with Borley, and in due course the Reverend Alfred Henning was made responsible for both.'

'Why didn't they just sell the place on?' I asked.

'Oh, they tried, many times. But who wants to live in a house with a reputation like that? Harry himself was offered the building for a song.'

'He didn't *buy* it?' I asked. The idea startled me.

'No. The Rectory is some one hundred and fifty miles away from his home. It would have been quite impractical for him to take care of the building.' Glanville hesitated. 'He's not in the best of health now, Miss Grey; he suffers regularly with angina. I'm forever telling him to slow down.'

'Good luck with that! Harry Price doesn't do anything slowly.'

My visitor smiled at me with thoughtful deliberation. 'I think I understand. His world does sometimes feel like a whirlwind of chaos.'

'So if he didn't buy the Rectory, what did he do?'

'Ah, well now, that was the clever part. He rented it. For twelve months. His tenancy began in May 1937. Such wonderful foresight on his part.'

I couldn't believe this. He had rented a property he had already debunked as being subject to fraud! Why?

'Don't you see?' Glanville continued. 'It was quite the perfect experiment! He wanted to examine the place methodically over a sustained period, discover whether the manifestations were still ongoing, and then—'

'Attempt to discover the cause,' I said flatly, understanding. 'As he has always done – to explain it all away. Am I right?'

Glanville nodded. 'Precisely.'

'Some things never change.'

'But therein lay the most surprising part of it.'

'You're going to tell me he has discovered some ingeniously clever explanation for all the queer events at that house, aren't you? That it was some local children all the time, playing tricks on people? Or some other explanation' – I listed them on my fingers – 'malobservation, exaggeration or natural causes? Really, Mr Glanville, it's all so predictable. What's the real reason he has sent you? Come on, out with it! He's jealous, isn't he? Of that piece I wrote for *The Times*. He's afraid I'm setting myself up against him.'

'Harry has enough enemies. He doesn't want to make one of you too.' My visitor sat back slowly, his eyes narrowing as he inhaled. 'But you have quite misunderstood. Let me put this as clearly as I can. Harry has reached a profound conclusion. He believes that the evidence for paranormality if you want to call it that – evidence for the events at the Rectory – is as conclusive as human testimony can ever be. He is convinced. He is willing at last to state, on the record, that the events in question *are* entirely supernormal.'

'But why?' I cried. 'I told Harry long ago that the case had substance. I explained to him I believed there was something sinister about the house that couldn't simply be waved away as trickery, and he rejected the idea out of hand. He told me I was wrong!'

I neglected to mention the dreams that had plagued me. Nor did I mention Marianne Foyster's prophetic warning to me about the Dark Woman of Borley and her alleged curse upon those who deceive. It was not a statement I had any hope of substantiating; I had only a vague sense that the legendary apparition of a nun witnessed at the Rectory had been a woman deceived by someone during her life and then cruelly murdered. But how and by whom?

These were questions I had long since abandoned hope of answering. Until now.

'Perhaps Harry's mind was on other matters, the Schneider seances, for example, or maybe he suspected you were drawn to the house for other, more personal reasons,' Glanville suggested.

'Is that what he said?' I asked sharply. Price had never been strong enough to acknowledge the truth about our relationship even to me; the idea that he had discussed his feelings with another person was outrageous.

'No,' said Glanville. 'He has not said as much. But whenever I mention your name, or question him on the circumstances of your parting, I observe on his face an expression of the deepest melancholy. And from that, well' – he shrugged – 'I draw my own conclusions.'

'You would be unwise to draw too many assumptions about the internal machinations of Harry's mind,' I said.

'Perhaps. But to understand how we have come to the situation we are now in, the change in Harry's beliefs, you must hear what has happened recently at the Rectory and during his tenancy.'

As he spoke I found my curiosity piqued by his words. 'Go on then.'

'The advertisement in *The Times* produced a wealth of applications, some from mediums and Spiritualists. These were discounted. You see, Harry wanted impartial observers – educated and honest men, with no prior interest in matters of the occult or psychical research. There were forty-eight observers in all, myself included. We were strangers to one another, united by our common curiosity. Between us, in separate teams and at different intervals, we spent many nights and days around the Rectory, watching and waiting for specific phenomena. If we saw anything unusual, we were to report it.'

'So he didn't visit the house himself?'

'Only very occasionally. Mostly he conducted and managed the affair from his Laboratory.'

'But how did you know what to do? Where to look, what precautions to take?' Ghost hunting, I remembered well, was a rigorous exercise.

'We were furnished with a helpful document – Harry called it a Blue Book – containing detailed instructions as well as a history of the Rectory and advice as to what sort of phenomena we could expect to see, and where. Actually, I have a copy with me. Would you care to see it?'

Against my inner will I found myself nodding yes to his question, and seconds later I was handed a slim document which Glanville produced from inside his coat. Flicking through it, one passage – on the subject of apparitions – stood out. It advised:

> If seen, do not move and on no account approach the figure. Note exact method of appearance. Observe figure carefully, watch all movements, rate and manner of progression etc. Note duration of appearance, colour, form, size, how dressed and whether solid or transparent ... If figure speaks, do not approach ... Enquire whether it is a spirit. Ask figure to return, suggesting exact time and place ... Note exact method of vanishing. If through an open door, quietly follow ... Make the very fullest notes of the incident. The nun is alleged to walk regularly along the Nun's Walk in grounds.[2]

I was amazed. The Harry I knew would never have created such a document, a tool capable of furnishing investigators other than himself with so much information, and I quickly said so to Glanville.

'Nevertheless, Miss Grey, Harry advised us to examine all the passages and walls for pencil markings or writing, and to ring any we found with chalk; and we were encouraged to work in pairs so that one could rest while the other kept watch. Groups of three were discouraged.'

'Now, that doesn't surprise me,' I said, remembering my first visit to the Rectory and Vernon Wall's presence on that occasion. 'What else?'

Anything we did see we duly recorded and sent on to Price at his London office.'

He told me then of the phenomena witnessed, and as he spoke I felt a chill creep across the flesh of my bare arms.

'The house was full of sounds, especially during the night – thuds, scrapings, tapping and knocks. They came sometimes from far away, sometimes within a few feet of us. We were able to account for some: vermin, dripping taps, and so on.'

'Some?'

'But by no means all. On one occasion my son was alone in the library when he distinctly heard light tripping footsteps descending the stairs. And then they stopped. On another occasion one of our most active observers, a gentleman named Mark Kerr-Pearse, was showing some interested visitors – three women – around the Rectory. At first nothing happened. But then, as they were crossing the landing and making to descend the main staircase, immediately outside the Blue Room one of the ladies came to a complete standstill. She was trembling all over, couldn't move, as if paralysed. She said that her hands were freezing with pins and needles all over them.'

I knew instantly the place on the landing of which he spoke. Glanville was watching my reaction carefully. 'Now, I see I have your attention. But there were other things I must tell you about.

'We knew, of course, that objects were said to move from one room to the other, especially during the residence of the Foysters, so we placed items at various points throughout the house – mantelpieces, shelves and so on – and ringed them with chalk so that we could see whether they moved. Well, I can tell

you, that they did move, and frequently. And we found objects
as well – objects that appeared *out of nowhere*.'

The words jolted me as the shadowy figure from my dreams
flashed into my mind. I heard Marianne's voice speaking to me
across the years: *The Dark Woman will return.*

'What did you say?' I whispered.

'Sarah, what's the matter? You're as white as a sheet.'

She is coming for you, Sarah.

'Tell me again what you said,' I repeated urgently.

'Objects,' he repeated slowly, his eyes never leaving mine. 'We
found objects, occasionally, around the house. No one could
account for them. Harry had a name for them. He called them—'

'Apports,' I said quickly.

'Yes, that's right, apports. You're familiar with the term, I see.'

'Very familiar,' I replied, remembering the St Ignatius medallion we had discovered in the Blue Room. 'You must tell me what
you found.'

'Many things: pebbles, mothballs, a dictionary,' he said. 'A
French dictionary, to be exact. And a small gold ring. We gave it
to a psychic to examine – Lieutenant Aitchison, who has shown
some promise in experiments conducted at Price's Laboratory.
The moment he held it in his hands he dropped it and shouted,
"Murder." He refused to hold it again.' Glanville paused, observing my reaction. 'Miss Grey, are you all right?'

'Tell me quickly,' I said, my head reeling, 'where exactly in the
Rectory did you find this ring? And the dictionary?'

'Miss Grey, what is the matter?'

'*Where?*'

'On the landing upstairs, just outside the Blue Room.'

It was the same place.

I drew in a breath and said, 'Mr Glanville, that is the same position where, ten years ago, the Reverend Smith reported hearing voices and whisperings. It's the same place where Marianne Foyster later reported being struck in the face, where she found a French dictionary and a wedding ring. The scribbling on the wall – "mass, light, prayers" – appeared right at that spot. And it's the same area where scores of witnesses have reported the sensation of coldness. You just said so yourself!'

'Yes, I know, but—'

'Dr Chipp!' I explained. 'He said in his original letter, all those years ago, that when he was at the Rectory, he lost a French dictionary.' I was struggling to get the words out. 'I must go and see him and ask him about this.'

It seemed like a sensible suggestion. So why was Glanville now shaking his head?

'Dr Chipp is dead, Miss Grey.'

I shivered. The old man's warning rushed back to confront me: *Our sins will engulf us both.*

I felt suddenly so small, so intimidated, I might have been sitting at St Mary's School for Girls, cowering under Sister Regis's punishing gaze.

'Shortly before he died, Dr Chipp wrote to Harry explaining that you had been to see him,' said Glanville, and with something close to horror I realised it wasn't just concern I saw in his face, but pity. 'My dear, Dr Chipp said that you were frightened. Tell me why.'

I knew the only way to help Glanville understand was to tell him my own secrets, and that was unthinkable. But what was the alternative? To allow suffering to creep steadily in? To end up like Dr Chipp, Ethel Bull and the others?

I shook my head, recovering my concentration with a question that seemed obvious. 'Is there a floor plan of the Rectory?'

'Yes, I drew one myself.' Glanville took the book, flicking through its pages. 'Here it is.'

The diagram he presented clearly showed the layout of the cellar, the ground floor, the first floor and the attic. I studied it for a moment and then carefully tore the page in two down the middle.

'Wait!' Glanville cried. 'What are you doing?' But it was too late. All he could do was watch as I carefully overlaid the two parts of the diagram.

The pieces of the complex jigsaw puzzle slotted together.

'Miss Grey, what is it?'

'I'm beginning to understand,' I said slowly. 'I think I know what all this means, what we have to do.'

And then I was on my feet, flying towards the door.

'Wait! Where are you going?'

'To Borley,' I said without looking back. 'To end all of this.'

Notes

1   The word 'planchette' is derived from the French for 'little plank', and is a small piece of flat wood – usually heart-shaped – which moves about on a board to spell out messages or answer questions, allegedly under the influence of paranormal voices. Table-tipping is, similarly, another type of seance in which participants sit around a table, place their hands on it and wait for the table to move, or tip, in response to questions. Answers are spelled out according to letters of the alphabet called out over the table.

2   'Instruction Booklets for Observers at Borley Rectory'.

– 30 –

A PROPHECY
FULFILLED

'Sit down, Sarah!'

The voice pulled me back into the past. I stood rooted to the spot on the threshold of my office, one foot in the corridor outside, facing into the thick darkness. I could smell the familiar scent of fresh pipe tobacco air, could feel my hands and legs beginning to go numb.

'I know it's you,' I whispered.

And Harry Price was before me once again, stepping out of the darkness.

I uttered a sharp gasp, tottered unsteadily back into the room and collapsed into my chair.

He looked down at me uncertainly, like a child coming to apologise. 'Hello again, Sarah.'

Sidney Glanville became concerned. 'I'm sorry, Miss Grey; I was going to tell you he was here. I wanted to explain first—'

But I had turned my head away from both of them and was staring at my reflection in the window. My heart was hammering as I wondered what I would say to Price and how I would say it without losing my composure. But it was Price who spoke next, not to me but to Glanville, whom he asked to leave the room.

When he had gone I turned my head warily towards Price. He looked so much older, with heavy circles under his eyes. His teeth were even yellower than I remembered, his skin white as paper. Even his eyes, once so brilliantly blue, seemed to have lost their radiance. He saw me looking at him and said, 'The years haven't been good to me, have they?'

'They have been harder to me, Harry. Since we last met I've measured the full distance between happiness and despair.' Just seeing him again reminded why I had needed to leave him. 'What made you think you could drag me along for all that time as an addendum to your life?' His eyes grew wide with sorrow. Real sorrow this time. 'That you could make changes at the Laboratory, plan for its future, without involving me? Allow someone – a stranger – to hurt Mother and me, to indulge his deceptions just to punish your enemies? How did that make you feel, Harry? Well,' I nodded at him, raising my voice, 'it wasn't just *them* you punished, was it?'

He coughed hoarsely. 'Sarah,' he said softly, 'I am truly sorry for what I did to you and your mother. I never intended to harm either of you.'

A quick memory of Mother's pained expression after the Schneider seance. As my nightmares had worsened, she had become a shadow of her former self. I hardly saw her any more. She was always in her bedroom and never allowed me inside. 'The pain you caused us both, the false hope you allowed us to entertain – you can't take that back.'

He kept his eyes lowered and said only, 'You know how I can be.'

'No, that's not good enough,' I said, raising my voice against him. But I was furious with myself too, for the fact that I was still there talking to him. Walking away wouldn't have been easy. His magnetism held me, threatened to draw from within me questions about his life: whether he was happy and fulfilled, whether he had missed me as I had missed him. My heart and head did battle. How could I ask him any of these questions? My dignity was too dearly bought to be suddenly handed back to him on a plate.

'Don't you ever stop to ask yourself whether it's worth it – the quest you're on? Whether it's worth the pain and suffering?'

'Yes, every day. It's exhausting.'

'I don't mean your suffering!' I cried, exasperated. 'I mean the people you leave behind, the ones whose lives you blow through like a hurricane.'

'You're no different from me, Sarah. We are the same.'

'We're not the same.'

He nodded, detecting the tremor in my voice. 'Perhaps not always, but now – yes, we are the same. You want the truth just as badly as me, for your own reasons.' He left a weighty pause. Then, 'I wonder if you're willing to tell me what they are.'

His eyes cut into me. I faltered, looked away.

'No. I didn't think so.' He stepped forward and I flinched as he touched my arm. 'Sarah, come back with me, please. I need you.'

As he spoke, Velma Crawshaw's haunted face floated into my consciousness. I remembered what he had done to her and a voice in my head said, '*Nothing good will come of this. Walk away, now.*'

I followed that voice as far as the door to my office. Until something – perhaps my determination to correct whatever was happening – made me shut it out.

I turned. 'Why are you here, Harry?'

He looked thoughtfully at the book that lay open on my desk. 'If you had asked me what I thought about the Borley case ten years ago, I would have said it was one hundred per cent bunkum. But now I think it is only ninety-seven per cent bunkum.'

'Tell me why,' I insisted.

'There have been developments, huge advancements, since you have been away, Sarah; notably the appearance of apports, written messages obtained through seances and a most alarming prophecy.'

'What sort of prophecy?' I asked with some apprehension, for the word made me think of Marianne Foyster's warning to me years before.

'After a few visits to the Rectory, Glanville remembered an old planchette and rescued it from a lumber room at home where it was stored. He took it to the Rectory and used it first late one night in the library with the help of his daughter. No sooner did their fingers come into contact with it than it started to write in large and well-formed letters. It ultimately produced words, dates, phrases, even drawings. Some of it was gibberish, some plainly untrue, some unverifiable; but Sarah, a certain amount was true *and has been* confirmed.

I held my breath.

'On March 27th, 1938 we received the most remarkable message of all – a prophecy which tells of the one thing that is unimaginable to anyone wishing to study the mystery of the Rectory any further,' said Price. 'It foretells its destruction.' He picked up the book and flicked through its pages and then handed it back to me. 'Here, see for yourself.'

This is what I read:

Does anyone want to speak with us? *Yes.*

Who are you? *Sunex Amures and one of the men mean to burn down the Rectory tonight at nine o'clock end of the haunting go to the Rectory and you will be able to see us enter into our own and under the ruins you will find bones of murdered . . . under the ruins means you to have proof of haunting of the Rectory at Borley the understanding of which game tells the story of the murder which happened there.*

In which room will the fire start? *Over the hall. Yes, yes you must go if you want proof.[1]*

We were sitting beside one another now, at my desk, surrounded by piles of unsolicited film scripts – the sort that are poorly bound and arrive in scruffy envelopes. The book before us was more interesting than any of these. I stared, puzzled by the text. 'This appears to foretell that the Rectory will burn . . .' I trailed off. The rest suggested that under the ruins would be found the bones of a murdered person – the nun perhaps? The idea would certainly corroborate Marianne Foyster's suspicion that the nun's remains were buried somewhere in the Rectory grounds. But still, the message made little sense. 'It's almost a year old.'

Observing my confusion, Price nodded and said quickly, 'Precisely!' Then he raised his eyebrows in question. 'So?'

'So . . . what?' I demanded.

'So, surely *now* you agree I am duty bound to reconsider the matter? In light of what has happened?'

'What do you mean?' I asked. 'What *has* happened?'

His mouth fell open with an expression of incredulity. 'You mean you haven't heard? You don't know?'

'Know *what*, Harry?'

'Sarah . . .' He turned a further few pages of the book until he came to a black-and-white image of the Rectory. 'This photograph was taken just last week.'

I felt the shudder of my own alarm.

'You understand now?' he whispered. 'The prophecy has already been fulfilled. Borley Rectory burned down two weeks ago. The fire started over the hall, at exactly the place this entity, "Sunex Amures", had foretold and at the time prophesied.'

The Dark Woman will return.

Through short breaths I asked Price whether anyone was harmed.

'Thankfully, no,' he replied. 'The Rectory was empty when it happened. And yet . . .' His eyes misted over and I imagined him standing on the lawn of the Rectory looking up at the flames that licked its turrets and leapt from its windows.

'And yet?'

'The locals who watched it burn swore they saw rushing figures amid the smoke and flames.'

Note

1   'The Haunting of Borley Rectory. Private and Confidential Report'.

31

REVELATIONS

'Now then,' said Price as he laid his hand on my arm, 'you said just a moment ago, before Sidney left us, that you had something important to tell me, something about the case. What was it?'

The muscles in my shoulders tensed as an image of Marianne Foyster's troubled face watching me from the recesses of the main hall at Borley Rectory came into my mind and I thought of her sinister warning: *After the losses you will suffer, after the fire, after the proof that will be found − the Dark Woman will return.*

'Her,' I said at last. 'It's all about her, Harry. The Dark Woman. The nun. Who *she* is, what happened to her.'

It was clear to me now that Marianne Foyster was right: beneath the veneer of fantastical events at that place lurked a quiet human agony crying out for release. The force of it was bitter and malevolent; and if Marianne was right, if the spirit of the nun brought a curse, an execration, upon those who deceived others, then I would need my sharpest faculties about me.

'What more do we know of her?' I asked.

'The legend of the nun is the most compelling aspect of the case,' said Price, 'and you'll be relieved to hear that I am quickly coming to the opinion that it is more than a legend. We have now uncovered many more witnesses to her haunting. By our estimation, she has been seen by no fewer than twenty people in the last fifty years. Twenty, Sarah! Most of those people are either gravely unhappy, unwell or now dead. The weight of the evidence convinced Glanville to look into the matter. His family arranged an experiment, an attempt to communicate with her spirit.'

'Go on,' I said slowly.

'Using the old planchette he retrieved from the attic of his home, Sidney and his family conducted a seance in the library of the Rectory. On this occasion, as you can see here' – he pointed to the book – 'words, dates, drawings and phrases spelt out meant nothing to any of the individuals at the time. But among all of this there was, I am amazed to say, a message.' He turned another page. 'A message that purportedly came from the spirit of the dead nun herself.'

'Well, what did it say?' I asked, my heartbeat racing now.

'Here,' said Price, turning the book towards me. 'See for yourself.'

This is the script he showed me:

Séance of 31 October 1937

The circumstances under which the following scripts were produced are as follows: Upon our return from the Rectory I showed my daughter Helen the scripts that had been produced there (25 October). She had not previously used a planchette, and we had given her no detailed account regarding our own writing. In our absence, and unbeknownst to us, she used the planchette with the results that follow. During the course of the writing there were many ordinary domestic interruptions, such as telephone calls, callers, etc., when the board was temporarily left.

Who is there? What is your name? Marie Lairre.

How old were you when you passed over? 19.

Were you a novice? Yes.

Why did you pass over? (No reply.)

Where did you hear Mass? (Indistinct.)

Will you please spell each letter? B-o-r-l-e-y.

Have you a message? Chant Light Mass.

Do you want it yourself? Yes.

Why? I am unha . . . (Three letters indistinct.)

Were you murdered? Yes.

When? 1667.

How? Stran . . . (Last letters indistinct.)

Were you strangled? Yes.

Will our Mass be sufficient? No.

What Mass do you want? Requiem.

Where did you come from? Havre.

Are you French? Yes.

What was the name of your nunnery or convent? Bure.

Do you want a burial as well as Mass? Yes.

Do you wish to leave Borley? Yes.

Are your own past actions the cause of your being unable to leave? Yes.

What was that action? Death.

What shall we do to help? Light Mass Prayers. Get a priest.

Can Reverend Henning help you? Yes.

Did you write the messages on the wall at Borley? Yes.

Do you want the Mass on any special day? Yes.

Which month? June.

Which day? 13.

Can you tell us why you want the Mass on that day? (Indistinct.)
Please repeat carefully. My murder.[1]

'So you see,' said Price, studying my face as this information
sank in, 'a name was revealed.'

'Marie Lairre,' I breathed. Then I turned to look at my old
employer. His heavy brow was creased into a frown in a way
that made me wish him younger. 'Harry, this is remarkable.
Such detail.'

'Yes. On the whole, I don't know quite what to make of it.'

But I did know; because ever since Glanville had told me
about the French dictionary that had appeared next to the cold
spot on the landing outside the Blue Room, my mind had been
drawing together the clues. I showed Price the floor plans I had
torn from the book. 'Look,' I said. 'When laid on top of each other
the cold spot on the landing of the first floor correlates with the
area in the cellar beneath and the place where you first found
the older bricks, the remains of some earlier building, in the
earth. Do you remember?'

'Yes.'

'And at the same time, before we went upstairs, Vernon Wall's
foot crashed through a well cover nearby.'

'I remember. I was slow to help get him out,' said Price with
a grin. His eyes drifted, studying every detail of my office: the
film posters on the wall, the piles of letters on my desk, invitations to film premieres and fashion shows. Here were clues to
my new life, about which he knew so little. I wondered then
if I had become as much a mystery to him as he had been to
me.

'So you see,' I continued, 'that well must sit underneath the cold spot on the landing, two floors above it. You remarked upon it yourself.'

His eyes widened with the memory. 'Yes, I did, didn't I? You're theorising that the cold spot and the well are connected.'

'No, not theorising; I know! Harry, these planchette writings confirm exactly what Marianne Foyster told me she could sense: that the nun was French, was brought to Borley and was murdered. According to these writings, that's exactly what happened: she was brought by someone important, someone who loved her, from a convent at Le Havre in France to a house that once stood on the Rectory site in Borley. And there she was betrayed, deceived, murdered. Look,' I pointed at the page, 'the word is explicit – "strangled" – as is the date: 13th of June 1667. This is it.' I looked up at him. 'This is what we've been looking for!'

'What is?' he asked. The look on his face hovered somewhere between envy and admiration.

'A clue – she wants us to find her remains and lay her to rest with a requiem Mass, Harry. "Mass, light, prayers." Everything we need to know was written on those walls. Don't you see? It's all in this book,' I said earnestly.

He drew nearer and rested his hand gently on my arm as I leafed through the book, stopping at the relevant pages. 'It all fits – the wall writings, the plauchette messages, the cold spot over the landinh, the prophecy – all of it.'

Price raised his eyebrows. 'You're saying the clues were there for us from the first time we ever set foot in that house?'

'Yes,' I said urgently, 'and the bricks you noticed protruding from the earth? They could be the remains of Borley Manor, Harry – the manor the Smiths told us about, the manor mentioned here in the planchette writings. The manor that was the residence of—'

'The Waldegrave family,' finished Price, wide-eyed. 'Good God, Sarah, you realise what this could mean?'

I nodded. 'That a member of the Waldegrave family murdered the nun, Marie Lairre. Harry, that's it!'

I thought I could see admiration in his eyes as they skimmed over my face. 'My goodness, look how far you have come,' he said with gentle appreciation. 'I taught you well.'

'I taught myself in the end, didn't I? I had to.'

He nodded and looked down. 'Though I think perhaps we're getting ahead of ourselves. 'Those wall writings were written by Marianne Foyster herself, or her husband.'

'It's possible they wrote some of them,' I said, 'but I don't believe they wrote them all. I saw one, right next to me, which had not been there before.' A thought struck me. 'Perhaps Marianne was channelling the messages psychically without knowing it. That's possible, isn't it? Marianne told me years ago she felt certain the nun's bones were buried somewhere on the Rectory site.'

'So?'

'So,' I said earnestly, 'this could be our opportunity to find them. Perhaps we're *supposed* to find them! Perhaps—'

He didn't allow me to finish my sentence. 'And show the world that we have faith in the reliability of planchette data? You know I have my reservations about the evidential merits of automatic writing, Sarah. It would hardly reflect well on my reputation to be seen suddenly championing its application.'

I glared at him. 'Forget about your precious reputation for a moment, Harry! Until now you have ignored me every step of the way on this investigation. You haven't seen me in years! After all this time, I think I have earned the right to be trusted.'

He nodded but said nothing and I felt anger colouring my face.

'Harry Price, you really are unbelievable. It was *you* who came here today asking for my help.'

'All right,' he said, holding his hands up in protest, 'all right.'

'*No!*' I cried, 'It's *not* all right! You have no idea, no idea at all, what I went through for you, how much I sacrificed, the other people I had to give up.' I gasped for air. 'If I'm doing this, I'm doing it for me! Understood?'

'Very well,' he said softly. 'What are you proposing?'

'That we dig,' I said simply. 'Gather a team of men and excavate the ruins.'

'But that could take months! The cellars will be full of debris. It won't be the easiest of tasks to clear it, especially if war comes. Essex would be right in the middle of any enemy flight path. The site is huge. Where would we begin?'

'Where we've been told to begin. Look,' I said, pointing to a photograph of a segment of wall writing in the book. 'We interpreted this message as reading: MARIANNE AT GET HELP ENTANT BOTTOM ME. There is no doubt that the first word is Marianne. But compare the clarity of these letters to the scribbles underneath. They're barely legible. And first interpretation makes no sense whatsoever. You can see here, on the left, the words "GET HELP". That's fine. But over here, on the left, further down, there is the letter "W". With me so far?'

Price leaned in, nodded and said, 'Go on.'

'From here the pencil seems to have curved upwards and then down. Do you see, Harry? It doesn't leave the wall.'

'Yes.'

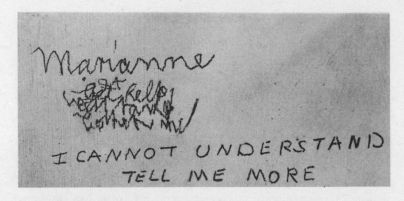

'It begins a new word again, immediately beneath. Here, you can quite clearly discern the letter "E". You interpreted the two letters that followed as "T". I don't think that's right, They look more like the double letter "I". Which would spell 'WELL".

He nodded and blinked.

'You thought the last letter was "T". But look at the odd way the base of the letter is drawn.' I stared at him. 'It's not a "T", Harry, it's a "K".'

I reached for a pencil and paper and frantically scribbled the words out:

WELL TANK BOTTOM ME.

Price stared down in awe at the newly deciphered message, and then looked at me in wonder, shaking his head and clasping his hands together. 'We are playing different chords now, Sarah, but we are still making music. That's brilliant! Simply brilliant!'

I smiled with pride. Now we knew where to dig. 'The bones of the murdered nun are beneath the Rectory, in the well in the cellar. The prophecy said "you must go if you want proof". Well, let's go!'

Price was looking at me uncertainly. 'You're suggesting we ask permission from the Queen Anne's Bounty[2] to dig the place up on the basis of some wall writings and automatic writing gleaned from seances.'

'That's exactly what I'm suggesting. The sooner we do so, the better.'

I could see he was uncertain about the idea.

'Harry,' I said, lowering my voice, 'you owe me this.'

'I had forgotten how stubborn you are, Sarah.'

I had to admit that in this affair, I was. And I would not apologise for it; I was driven by a conviction to know the truth, to find reassurance that I could still escape the dark fate that Marianne Foyster had foretold. Whoever reads this will wonder, I am sure, about the secret I carried that connected me with that house. I wondered about it often too, and I knew I had to lay it to rest.

'I won't take no for an answer. Come on, Harry! Why knock on a door you're not prepared to enter?'

'Very well,' said Price, getting to his feet. 'Then the Rectory will yield its secrets after all. Come, Sarah, let's begin!'

I sprang up to follow him. As I passed the mirror on my office wall my eye was caught by a gleam of light reflected in its glass. But when I turned and looked, I saw only my reflection and my eyes, wide with alarm, staring back at me.

'What is it?' asked Price. 'What did you see?'

I had wanted to tell him oh so badly. That he might understand at last. I thought in that moment that perhaps I could explain and offer us both some release from perpetual confusion. This haunting. I wanted to take it all back, to relinquish the hurt, to return to that night when Mother and I had walked together to his Laboratory, back when I could have chosen another path: worked for a charity or become a teacher. I tried to remember what life had been like before Harry Price but couldn't.

'Sarah, what did you see?'

'Nothing,' I said. 'Really, it's nothing.'

Of course that was a lie, another secret I kept from him. For how could I have admitted what I thought I had seen in the mirror? A chain glinting in the lamplight hanging like a noose around my neck.

Notes

1   'The Haunting of Borley Rectory. Private and Confidential Report'.
2   The Queen Anne's Bounty was a fund established in 1704 to augment the incomes of the poorer clergy of the Church of England. The bounty was funded by the tax on the incomes of all English clergy, which was paid to the Pope until the Reformation, and thereafter to the Crown.

32

A PSYCHIC
FETE

Just six weeks before the Second World War engulfed Europe a party was held in the gardens of the ruined Rectory to raise funds for the restoration of Borley Church. Reverend Alfred Henning had suggested, rather cleverly I thought, to theme the event as a 'psychic fete' with attractions including a guided tour of the ruined building by its new owner, one Captain Gregson, who had purchased the building when Price's tenancy had ended. Captain Gregson was the last owner of Borley Rectory and had moved into the house on 16 December 1938, just two months before the fire.[1]

On Wednesday 21 June 1939, I took a day's holiday and travelled with Price back to that strange and out-of-the-way place along with twenty-five members of the London Ghost Club. I was curious to see the present state of the dilapidated Rectory for myself of course, but more importantly I wanted to ascertain the viability of excavating the cellars before the whole area was cleared and the bricks taken away. Anyway, I reminded myself, the event might actually be fun.

However, I regretted attending from the instant I set foot in the Rectory grounds, for as I wandered around the tangled garden beneath the heat of that dusty afternoon, passing the games of skittles, the coconut shy and the white elephant stall, my mind soon returned to the many events I had witnessed there ten years before and I began to feel increasingly uncomfortable and detached, as though I was viewing the games of darts and the pig-pelting competition along the Nun's Walk through a pane of glass. I couldn't even stand still long enough to participate in the other ladies' insipid conversations. Their words were lost in the rustling summer breeze, drifting around my head as intangible as smoke. I smiled, but had no idea why, because none of this seemed quite real to me. It was deceptively perfect, for it all too thinly disguised the truth.

War was coming.

Everyone knew it, though few in this picturesque setting of English gentility wanted to know. Children played, women laughed, men talked lightly of their horses and of politics and of how war on the scale they had witnessed before 'could never happen again'. But their eyes showed their true fear, and the laughter was hollow. Here was an England clinging to the last vestiges of hope that would soon crumble, like the old Rectory looming over us.

After a while Mrs Butler, wife of the then Undersecretary of State for Foreign Affairs, took to the wooden stage to deliver her welcome speech. Behind her, Borley Rectory had been reduced to little more than an abandoned shell of blackened bricks. Its windows gaped where the glass had shattered and blown out from the heat; its high roof was gone, collapsed inwards upon the rubble below; no doors remained, only deep spaces leading nowhere.

My observations quickly gave way to reflection. Had I never come here in 1929, I might never have learned of this place's secrets or been touched by the malevolent, hateful presence that dwelt within these grounds – a spirit intent on observing and punishing deceit. I wished I could go back. I wished I could protect my mother from the hatred and bitterness and seething malice that I suspected was the cause of her long drawn-out suffering.

On her best days she answered questions perfectly coherently. Those were moments to savour, moments to remember during the other, darker times, when confusion reigned in her fluttering, darting eyes.

Standing in the Rectory grounds that summer afternoon, I rubbed my bare arms against an unnerving chill that shuddered through me. In my head I heard peculiar sounds from Mother's house, which ran now like a soundtrack through my life:

Tap-tap-scratch; tap-tap, scratch.

'Sarah, come and meet Captain Gregson.' Price's voice made me turn. Before me was a tall, robust man in his fifties. 'Shall we go over here?' Price suggested, and we walked away from the light-spirited garden function towards the old summerhouse at the far end of the grounds. I looked back at the Rectory and at a cloud of birds swooping slowly around one of its crumbling chimneys. Swooping *too* slowly, as if the sky was thickening. And then, impossibly, the summer's day was blowing away, dissolving. The years turning back as darkness gathered and folded around me. I spun round to face the garden, seeking the reassuring presence of the other guests; but there was nothing. Every soul had vanished.

I blinked.

Once.

Twice.

Opened my eyes.

Before me now, was the Rectory – but not my Rectory. This was the Rectory as it had once been – clean, intact windows, roof unbroken, red brickwork glowing softly, solidly, under the moon. And at the front of the house a window that hadn't been there before.

I scanned the gardens, the path skirting their perimeter, and through the darkness I thought I saw a gliding figure. *This is a dream*, I thought. *This can't be real.*

Suddenly the air was thick with heat and crackling sounds. A dreadful scent of smoking wood brought tears to my eyes.

Time tilted, balanced itself. I was back in the garden. In my time. How far into the past had I gone? To Price and the Reverend Henning, I had travelled no distance at all. Their conversation babbled in mid-flow, as it had when I had left them. I had been with them, I had gone, I had come back. And like the Rectory, I had been here all the time.

Looking towards the Nun's Walk, I asked Captain Gregson for his opinion on the matter of the haunting. He had been living in the cottage adjoining the Rectory, which had escaped the fire, for longer than a year. Did he believe the tales that went with the house?

'What I believe is neither here nor there,' he answered. 'It's what I know that matters. And I *am* obliged to trust the evidence of my own eyes and ears.'

He told us then how his two cocker spaniels refused to enter the Rectory courtyard, how each went mad with terror at something they sensed beyond the threshold.

'What is the explanation? Who knows. I don't. But I have a feeling you might . . .'

It seemed the right time to make our request. We wanted, I said, to excavate the ruined grounds as soon as possible but would need men and tools to assist us. Would the captain agree to help us?

He gave a short shrug. 'Well, it's an unusual request, Miss Grey, but I don't see the harm. Yes, why not? Might be difficult though, what with the prospect of another war.'

Price raised a doubtful eyebrow. 'Oh, I don't know. I'm not sure that things in Germany are as bad as they were. I know many people who have just returned from holidays in Germany and who report that everything appears normal and they were treated kindly.'

'You approve of the German culture, Mr Price?' The captain seemed surprised.

'Indeed I do,' Price replied, insensitively I thought, given that it was at the hands of a German soldier that my father had perished. 'I want, once more, to dine on the terrace of the Molkenkur restaurant. I have never taken you there, Sarah, but one day I will. From that marvellous elevation one can look out over the town of Heidelberg and its castle, like a collection of model houses hundreds of feet below. I want to observe the peasants making quaint cuckoo clocks on the doorsteps of their Black Forest homes.' He paused and then said, 'I am sure that Mr Hitler is a reasonable man. Let us hope, even at this eleventh hour, some means will be found to adjust the differences between our two countries.'

I had never seen him so passionate about a subject other than the supernormal. Had the comment any meaning? It certainly struck me as odd.

'I will do my best to help you,' said Captain Gregson, 'but it won't happen quickly.' He promised to clear the arrangements with Reverend Henning, whom he was sure would be compliant, and to let us know when would be convenient. Then he returned to his guests, Price following in his wake like an eager child as he prepared to take to the stage to regale the punters with stories of spirits and table-rapping.

I lingered a while longer by the summerhouse and closed my eyes, breathing in the sweet scent of honeysuckle. A warm breeze carried music from the fete upon its breath and somewhere, beyond the blackened ruins of the Rectory, the thin cry of a child.

Note

1   Gregson paid £500 for the property, which was initially valued by the Halstead estate agent Stanley Moger at £450. Mr Moger visited the house shortly after Price had left. The inventory he prepared for the Ecclesiastical Commission on 26 May 1938 describes the interior of the house as '. . . roaming and quite out-of date, requiring much expenditure in refitting and modernising. The decorative condition is decidedly old and of cold appearance.' Elsewhere in the document Mr Moger records the building's reputation thus: 'LOCAL RUMOUR. The Rectory is supposed to be HAUNTED, and a few years ago was the Hunting Ground of many hundreds of Spiritualists and Inquisitive persons, in fact, so many visited the site that the Police had to handle the matter. This, as you may imagine, is a considerable detriment to selling, as many view but turn away on this account.'

– 33 –
'THE MOST HAUNTED HOUSE IN ENGLAND'

The sun was burning a fierce orange high over the lonely Essex fields when the first pickaxe broke through the floor of the Rectory cellars. I hoped I would feel some relief once we started digging but the scene was tense and I felt unwell, and had increasingly for some months. The scar from my operation ached. I put it down to agitation that it had taken so long to be granted access to the Rectory site. Three years! The war, as predicted, had rather interrupted our plans.

Price strode around the site as if he owned it, jacket off, shirt sleeves rolled up to the elbows as he directed each of us to do this or that. My own task was simple: I was to take detailed notes on the proceedings so that Price could draw on these later as he compiled his second monograph of the case – a work he had already decided would be titled *The End of Borley Rectory*.

He called down earnestly to the man digging, 'Do you see anything?'

'No, sir, not yet.'

Price's strained heart prevented him from doing any of the digging himself, so Reverend Henning had enlisted the assistance of a local gentleman called Ted Jackson. He was a tall, bespectacled man whose thin frame did not reassure me that he would be equal to the task, but we were grateful for his willingness to help.

'She's been seen again, you know,' a voice behind me said quietly. It was Reverend Henning.

'You mean the nun?' I asked.

He nodded. 'Just recently, out there.' He looked past a belt of elm trees toward the lane which separated the Rectory grounds from the churchyard. 'By a doctor this time. Reckons he saw a figure all in black robes, bending down at the side of the road. Skin like leather, he said, with just black holes for eyes.'

Jackson's pickaxe struck hard into the cellar floor a second time. I felt my stomach lurch with anxiety. I knew that if Marianne Foyster was right and some awful curse had befallen me then I had but one hope: to find the remains of Marie Lairre – if that truly was her name – and lay her to rest. Then, perhaps, I would finally be free from her shadow.

What if we don't find anything? The idea was too terrible to contemplate. For too long I had suffered prolonged restlessness, at home and at the film company, where I had not progressed nearly as far as I would have liked. I was sleeping fitfully, sinking ever deeper into depression. I had even fallen into the habit of avoiding mirrors for fear of what I might see. I was beginning to fear for my sanity. How long before I became like Mother, scrubbing the walls in our house and forgetting?

Suddenly, frighteningly, anything seemed possible.

As I stared down into the blackened pit of rubble it occurred to me that everything had led me to this moment. All clues converged here. It had taken weeks to clear these cellars of all their debris, but now at last, the excavation had commenced.

I watched everyone and everything, afraid that some important detail might be overlooked. But I needn't have worried:

Price was diligent in applying his scrutinising eye to every inch of the scene. It was easy to see why, for he too had a lot riding on what we might find. His book, *The Most Haunted House in England*, had been a publishing sensation. Chronicling his involvement with Borley Rectory from our first visit in 1929, the finished article was a thorough deconstruction of all the mysterious events and legends associated with the house. Even the charming Vernon Wall was given a starring guest appearance in the opening chapters. I wondered what the journalist would make of it, wherever he was now, and what the Reverend Foyster would think, for the book even included – to my surprise – a full duplication of Foyster's *Diary of Occurrences*, which Price had never returned to the old man. I remembered that he had signed a confidentiality agreement and could only infer that he had used the diary with the certain conviction that the rector would not take legal proceedings against him, for any such action would inevitably have dragged the Foysters into an unwelcome public exhumation of their darker past. The result was a readable and convincing account and the story was believed. University scholars, scientists, the clergy and the nobility sanctioned Price's findings. Sir Ernest Jelf, senior master of His Majesty's Supreme Court, confessed in *The Law Times* that he was 'at a loss to understand what cross examination could possibly shake it'.[1]

It was a valedictory moment that could at last allow the great 'psychic detective' to challenge his detractors. Price had come full circle. Sceptic turned believer. He had proved his theory and sold his story to the world.

But the story was far from over.

A black dog, wandering aimlessly among the rubble, seemed to sense my unease. It came close and then padded off, before stopping and sitting on the other side of the pit formed by the opened cellars. Its eyes, black as coal, watched me.

The date was 16 August 1943, the time 11.30 a.m.

The question will undoubtedly be asked, why didn't we commence the excavation sooner? Dig up the cellar ourselves? If only it had been so simple! The truth of it was that the wartime conditions made this idea practically impossible. Manpower was scarce, and the beds that would be needed in the inns and hotels at Long Melford and Sudbury for every participant and onlooker were all given over to military personnel. Nevertheless, as the years wore on and my spirits dampened, we never stopped trying.

Progress at last came in the spring of 1943, when Price discovered, to his concern, that the rector was preparing to sell the remains of the Rectory. He told me that the new owners might never permit an exploration of the cellars. It was now or never. So I wrote to Reverend Henning myself, insisting that he help us find some men to assist us with the job.

Just a few weeks later Price telephoned me with the news that the reverend had finally found help for the task. Apparently not everyone approached with the idea was enthusiastic and it had taken some cajoling to persuade them to come. I was hardly surprised. Beneath me the cellar walls, like the rest of the ruins, were stained black from the fire, the floor littered with rubble, dead leaves and other debris that had accumulated here. Gone now were the piles of mouldy boxes, the old wine bottles, the wooden rocking horse with the melancholy eyes. All that remained to indicate that this was the same cellar we had explored all those years ago with Vernon Wall and Reverend Smith were a few bricks, the foundations of an earlier dwelling, protruding from the earth.

'Well?' cried Price after we had been standing for so long that my legs felt weak. 'Anything?'

'Afraid not, Mr Price. Nothing yet.'

Price's face registered his disappointment.

I checked my watch and recorded the time in my notebook: 12.45 p.m.

Those present at the scene were Reverend Henning and his wife; Dr Eric H. Bailey, senior assistant pathologist of the Ashford County Hospital; Mr Roland F. Bailey, his brother, who was a barrister; flying officer A. A. Creamer; Captain W. H. Gregson and his two nieces, Mrs Georgina Dawson and Mrs Alex English; Johnnie Palmer, a dubious looking observer from one of the local cottages; Price, of course, and me.

Only Sidney Glanville, who had helped lead us here by telling us of the planchette messages received by his daughter, was absent. I wondered why. He was, after all, Price's 'most loyal observer'.

Everyone was intrigued by what we might find in the earth. But more than anyone, I was keyed up with anxiety. I hadn't noticed until Price instructed me to stop grinding my teeth. 'You've been working that jaw all morning,' he said. 'Relax now.'

It struck me as curious that he could remain so calm in the face of such an important development in our investigation. But then, he wasn't living each day under the Dark Woman's gaze; he didn't feel the problem as I did. For him, this was merely an exercise to complete the remaining chapters of his second book. I, however, was contending with a proliferation of nightmares and unsettling noises which now came almost weekly from my bedroom wall:

Tap-tap-scratch. Tap-tap, scratch.

Those insistent sounds reminded me of something – but what? School perhaps . . . Yes, that was it. St Mary's and my teacher, Sister Regis . . . her chalk striking the blackboard.

Everything I was learning about the insidious long-term effects of the Rectory's haunting, made me certain now that somehow its legacy had affected Mother, as it was sure to affect me. If the two were connected – the house and our problems – I had to know how, to make us both safe and to end it.

It was shortly after a quarter to two when, having shovelled and sifted tons of earth, Jackson finally pulled some bricks from the ground and threw them aside. Then he tipped more earth and clay into his sieve. 'Well?' I asked hopefully.

He looked up at me and shook his head.

I was about to suggest that we take a break for lunch when a cry from behind caused me to look sharply back over my shoulder. 'Wait a moment, I think I might have something here.'

I rushed forward, Price close behind me. Somewhere nearby a dog began barking. 'What, what is it?' Price demanded.

Jackson retrieved something from his sieve. He studied it closely, his moustache twitching, his face grey, and then held it aloft for us all to see.

There was no mistaking the object in his grip.

'Dear God,' whispered Price.

'Is that what I think it is?' I felt my heart squeeze.

'Yes,' said Price quietly, 'I do believe it is.'

At the end of the afternoon I went with Price to the rectory at Liston, at Mrs Henning's invitation, and wrote up my notes. Over dinner that evening Reverend Henning told us of a local woman, one Mrs Collett, who had recently attempted to divine the floor of the Rectory with a hazel twig. When she had passed over the spot where we had dug that day, her twig had snapped. An innocuous occurrence? Perhaps. It would have been easy to think that. But I knew better.

Because next to the exact spot where Vernon Wall had first crashed his foot through the cellar floor and into the well tank, underneath the cold parts of the house where the planchette messages had instructed us to dig, we found a few curious items: a large antique brass preserving pan, a silver cream jug and, beneath, a fragment of a skull – a jawbone with five teeth in it. Dr Bailey examined it carefully and declared with certainty that it was a left mandible, definitely human, probably from a woman.

The next day, when we resumed excavations, we found two religious medals.

I shuddered as I recalled the tantalising prophecy revealed to Glanville's daughter six years earlier: '*Under the ruins you will find bones of murdered . . . Proof of haunting.*'

Note

1 *Law Times*, 9 August 1941.

– 34 –
THE LAST RITES

The jawbone and fragment of skull were all we ever found of the supposed phantom nun who referred to herself as Marie Lairree. I considered this odd. Where was the rest of the skeleton? Price pointed out that the remains might have been disturbed and scattered when the foundations of the Rectory were built, or parts buried elsewhere intentionally.

Whatever the explanation, the absence of a complete skeleton wasn't going to prevent me from insisting that the remains should be given a proper burial, as the planchette messages and wall writings had instructed. It had to be that way, otherwise I could never have hoped for the chance to gaze into a mirror without feeling apprehension. And thankfully Price had demanded as much, although, I think, for reasons very different from my own. Following the success of his first book, his publisher was keen to follow it with another: *The End of Borley Rectory*. The location and eventual burial of the phantom nun's remains provided him with the best ending he could have hoped for.

Curiously, the chosen location for Marie Lairre's final resting place was not Borley, as one would have expected, but the nearby Liston churchyard. I assumed that Liston was a more convenient location for Reverend Henning, who lived there, and that he had little wish to risk drawing any further unwelcome attention to Borley itself, which had been overrun with overeager ghost hunters since the day Price's book was published.

We waited a further two years before it could be done. They were the longest two years of my life. I remember them now as little more than a white, fearful haze. For as much as I tried convincing myself that I was overreacting, the continuing disturbances at home made me worry we were wasting valuable time.

But what more could we have done? Permission had to be sought for the burial and Reverend Henning thought it would be more appropriate and respectful to the other members of the parish if we waited until the worst of the war was over.

So we waited until finally, in the honeysuckle heat of a glorious May evening in 1945, our small group gathered for the simplest of ceremonies in Liston churchyard. Those present included the Rector of Borley cum Liston and Mrs Henning and their young son, Stephen; Mr Eric G. Calcraft, who took photos of the session; the sexton; Price, of course, and me.

Price had placed the fragments of skull and jawbone in a cedarwood casket measuring five inches by four that would, in his own words, 'be quite immune from insects and other corroders.' On its surface was a brass tablet which bore the date we had excavated the remains. Only when the lid was finally nailed shut did I allow myself the briefest of sighs.

The casket was lowered into the grave, then the rector said the Committal. A movement caught my eye. Behind a low stone wall at the far end of the churchyard stood a man, smartly attired in a brown suit and hat, the rim of which was tipped down just low enough to obscure his face. In one hand he held what I thought was a notepad, and slung around his neck was a camera. His stance seemed familiar. And though I wasn't able to discern his features I was certain he could see me, indeed that he was discreetly watching the proceedings.

'Who's that?' I said, turning to address the sexton who was standing a short distance behind me. But he had a face like stone, and instead of answering me he shook his head.

I would have probed further, such was the peculiarity of his reaction, but the rector was commencing drawing the service to a conclusion. I allowed myself a moment to cherish this, the end of the affair. As he recited the prayer, blessed relief washed over me.

At last it was over and I could begin again. I could live my life free of regret and misery, and guard the secret I had held all these long years. I breathed in deeply, closed my eyes and thanked God.

The time was approaching seven. The light was fading, the day draining away. Price posed for a photograph – that now famous image of him standing with Reverend Henning, looking solemnly down at the grave. I was about to suggest to him that we have a photograph of us together when I noticed a small crowd of people gathering at the perimeter of the churchyard, some of them children. A sense of unease began to creep over me, for on their faces were expressions of utmost disapproval bordering on disgust. I glanced at Price. He was consumed with the task of capturing himself on film from the best possible angles, but every now and then his eyes flicked furtively in the direction of the crowd, until at last he stopped and suggested we return to Reverend Henning's residence.

Unusually for him, Price seemed rattled by the spectators. One of them, a woman with blonde hair, paused a moment, shaking her head from side to side as she fixed her eyes on him.

'Are you coming, Sarah?' Price called as he saw me lingering by the grave, which the sexton was preparing to fill in. I told him to go on without me and that I would catch him up. I wanted to stay a moment and reflect. 'Very well,' he called, striding after the rector and his wife. 'Don't be long. We'll have tea waiting.'

When he was gone I stood for a short while in silence, watching the sexton work. He did not acknowledge my presence. Eventually I said, 'You seem ill at ease, sir, if you don't mind my saying so.'

'Aye,' he said curtly without looking up. He seemed quite put out by his task, as if it was a waste of his time. His manner was disrespectful for the setting and I told him so.

This time he did look up, turning his head slowly away from the ground until his eyes met mine. 'Disrespectful, you say? I see.'

'Whatever is the matter?' I asked, my patience waning.

He patted the turf over the grave back into place. 'Never seen anything like it in my life.'

'What do you mean?' I demanded.

'This!' he cried, pointing at the ground. 'A farce if ever there was one. And at a time like this, with so many innocents losing their lives – why, it's not right. He said so himself!'

'What? *Who* said so?'

'Him!' He pointed towards the wall behind which I had glimpsed the man in the long coat. 'Well, he was there a moment ago.'

'You spoke to him?'

'Aye.'

I drew in a breath. 'Well, what did he say?'

'Full of questions, mostly about the burial. Wanted to know who it was for, why we were doing it.'

'He called it a farce?'

'That's right. He told me straight: That the bones unearthed at the Rectory never belonged to no woman, and everyone knows it!'

'What?' I raked my fingers through my hair. 'That can't be right.'

He laughed. '*He* knew it very well. Been asking the locals all kinds of questions. Said he was going to tell others the truth too. That's why he was here. Some reporter come from London, I think.'

The clock tower struck seven and my heartbeat drummed in time.

'A reporter,' I repeated. 'Did he give you his name?'

'He did. Can't quite recall it now.'

'Please try.'

He thought for a moment. 'Wall, I think he said it was. Yes, that's it. Something Wall.'

And then I ran.

I had left the churchyard at Liston behind me, the evening shadows lengthening as I took the narrow country lane that led east towards Borley. I knew from the sexton, who had seen Wall steal away from the scene, that this was the route he had taken.

The journey to Borley was some two and a half miles and soon it would be dark, for dusk was gathering. Price and Reverend Henning would be wondering where I was. But as I strode along the narrow country lane I gave none of these facts the slightest consideration, my mind instead returning to the sexton's remarks.

It was nonsense, of course. Had to be. It was over. We had done as the nun had instructed.

But I had to know.

My mind was resolved: I would find Wall and demand he tell me what he knew. This affair would end, just as it had begun, with the tale of a journalist.

With some nervousness and a little excitement I wondered as I took chase what his life had been like; what he would think of me now and what I would say to him. I suppose that after all I had endured – after all the pain, regret, longing and loss – I considered him to have had a lucky escape. Why had he come back? Why now?

By the time I reached Hall Road my feet were tired and the gloom made it hard to see where I was going. But soon, through the tall, menacing trees on either side of me, the dark shape of a ruined building loomed into view.

I stood in the quiet lane immediately adjacent to the Rectory grounds, looking about me, when a small blue car parked on a dirt track leading into a nearby field caught my attention. I went quickly towards it, following a route that brought me to the rickety wooden fence that enclosed the Borley churchyard. Then, in one of the church windows, I saw the glow of a lamp.

I knew I had no choice in the matter. I might have stopped, returned to my life safe in the knowledge that we had put the whole matter of this mystery to rest. Closed the file and been done with it. But that was never an option, not really; for I had the profound sense that I was *meant* to be here at this moment, that by some unearthly law I was supposed to be reunited with Vernon Wall and that everything had been building towards this.

I scraped open the squeaking gate and took the narrow path that led me to the church's Tudor porch and ancient looking door. With rising apprehension I lifted the heavy latch and went inside.

35

THE REVELATIONS OF A JOURNALIST

I was standing at the back of the nave concealed in the gloom, looking down past the rows of pews to the side of the altar where, kneeling before a great monument – the vast Waldegrave family monument that the Smiths had first told us about – was a man with broad shoulders and a long brown coat. He heard my movement and turned, and by the light of the oil lamp he held aloft I saw that this was the person I had come to find: Vernon Wall. Seeing him again, the advice he had given me years before sprang to my mind: *For every moment in your life that passes, there is always another that might have been.*

'Hello?' he called, straining his eyes in the darkness. 'Who is it?'

I had heard from Reverend Henning rumours that Borley Church was haunted; that the ghosts from the Rectory had moved here since the fire, that sometimes the organ was heard playing itself. *Perhaps*, I wondered as I watched him from the shadows, *he thinks I am a ghost.*

The man rose slowly, collecting his brown trilby from the floor, and began walking towards me, his footsteps echoing in the draughty space. 'Hello there?'

I stepped into the tallow light. 'Hello again, Mr Wall.'

He stopped, blinked and raised his hand in acknowledgement. But he did not smile 'Well, well . . . Sarah Grey . . . isn't it? My God, what a long time it has been.'

'Almost sixteen years.' I paused, looking him over. He was the same handsome man I had last seen charging out of the Rectory that fateful night of his argument with Price, but something about him had changed. His face told the story of his years. He looked tired, worn down, and I told him so.

His mouth tightened. 'War does that – changes people.'

I moved towards him then, my footsteps echoing. He stood perfectly still watching me, his face troubled. And I too felt a curious mix of emotions: regret, mostly, for the wasted opportunities, as well as sadness and affection, for in spite of everything, he was still disarmingly attractive.

'They sent you away?' I asked miserably.

He nodded. 'Germany, for a short time, then France.'

'What was it like?'

'Horrendous. I was lucky, Sarah. That's all. Others . . . not so. They say it'll be over soon, any day now . . . Who would have thought it? That it could all have happened again?' He shook his head, snapping out of his reflection. 'What *are* you doing here, at this time?'

'I might ask you the same.'

'You realise they say this church is haunted now, that spirits speak in here, that the organ plays when the place is empty? I don't know,' he smiled cynically. 'What do you think?'

I saw the great Waldegrave family monument looming in the darkness behind him and shivered. 'To be honest, I have the strongest sense that we should not be in here.'

'Then why did you come?' he asked, his voice businesslike.

So I told him everything we had learned – deduced – about the murdered nun Marie Lairre. I told him of the planchette messages, the prophecy that the Rectory would burn down, and the many clues that had helped us eventually locate her partial remains beneath the ruins of the house, as the prophecy had foretold. But most of all, I told him of Price's transformation from sceptic to triumphant believer that had come about as a result of our renewed work on this extraordinary case with Sidney Glanville's assistance, and the fact that he was preparing a second book on the affair with a wealth of new evidence.

From the way Wall's mouth turned down, I could see he disapproved of what I had said. And the lack of interest or surprise in his eyes as I related events suggested he possessed prior knowledge.

'You already know this, don't you? The sexton at the churchyard in Liston told me as much. That's why you've been interviewing the locals: they know something about the bones. What is it? Why have you come back after so long?'

He was watching me coolly, the glow of his lamp playing across his chiselled features. Finally he said, with some heat, 'To be honest, Sarah, I am amazed that you are even able to look at me after what you did, and that you – or Price – can dare to show your face in this village.'

He began with the war. 'I've often thought that the most enduring casualties are the bereaved who get left behind. As a journalist, you can't help but feel sorry for them as they look longingly to their past, their loved ones, wishing them back. I've done it myself. So many dead, Sarah. Again. Good men. Gone.

'For these last years I have worked as a war correspondent with *The Times*. When you've seen what I've seen, it changes you, believe me. You learn to shift your conception of what's important, you see more and you understand more. You, Sarah, understand more than most – or at least you did when your father was taken. Isn't that what drove you to Price's Laboratory in the first place – the need to save the deceived, to shine a light on the tricksters? And then, perhaps, to find a way to cope with your own grief?'

'You know it is,' I replied.

His eyes widened in grim response. 'Well, haven't you noticed?' he said evenly. 'History is repeating itself. Now another war is ending, every Sunday in London there are at least forty Spiritualist meetings. The movement is enjoying a resurgence, just like before. Charlatans popping up everywhere, capital-ising on grief.'

He was right, of course, but there was nothing in itself unusual about this; Spiritualism had flourished in the wake of every major war and I told him so, pointing out that Price's investigations had at least been rewarded now with strong, con-vincing evidence for spiritual survival. 'Of course there have been disappointments along the way,' I said, remembering the Schneider seance that had so destroyed my hopes, 'painful ones too. So painful. But the Borley phenomena prove—'

Suddenly he was shaking his head, his expression one of angry consternation. 'You believe it all, don't you? *Everything.*' He looked back over his shoulder at the fine Waldegrave family monument. 'You think it all leads here, to *this*? That a Walde-grave man strangled this woman you can't even prove existed – Marie Lairre – and buried her bones somewhere at Borley? Sarah, have you any idea how ludicrous that sounds?'

'It's not ludicrous. I am certain of it,' I said, approaching the monument. I ran my hand along its smooth stone surface. It was in perfect condition, a flawless example of sixteenth-century craftsmanship. Sure enough, as Reverend Smith had told us all those years ago, on one side of the monument was a coat of arms resembling the Prince of Wales feathers. 'These match,' I said to Wall, 'almost exactly the wall markings I saw in the Rectory during the Foyster residency. I thought then that the markings resembled an emblem, some sort of crest . . . There's a connection. She was telling us who murdered her.'

'One of the Waldegrave family?'

I nodded. 'I believe the drawing was an attempt at a representation of the Waldegrave crest. And now we have located her remains, and we are safe.'

'Safe from what?' His abruptness suggested he wasn't interested in my answer.

And because I sensed that he thought I was talking nonsense I told him then, with some relief, of the curse of the Dark Woman. I told him that I had laboured under the anxiety of this belief for many years, since the very first night we had stayed at the house when Price had come to me. 'You saw the apparition yourself, Vernon, in the garden!'

He hesitated. 'I saw something. Why are you so afraid, Sarah? You seem so convinced that there is a curse at work upon you. Why?'

I knew he would ask me what I could possibly have to fear from such a curse, what information I had concealed that was so terrible it was tantamount to punishable deception. He did ask, but I refused to answer.

Wall frowned and was silent for a moment. He looked deep in thought, his face hardening as he reflected. Then, by the light of his lamp, he examined the markings on the side of the Walde-grave monument. 'Yours is an impressive undertaking, Sarah,' he said, 'and as a journalist I have to respect that. I admire your investigative skills greatly. But it seems to me you have asked yourself every relevant question except the one that is *most* relevant, the biggest question of all.'

'Which is?' I pressed him.

'Harry Price's own role in all of this – your blessed psychic detective.' He spat out the words as though they were bitter as lemon.

'I know Harry better than anyone.'

'But exactly how much do you know *about* him?' He watched me keenly as I stepped away from the Waldegrave monument and sat in the first pew. 'Let us see, shall we, who is the real psychic detective.'

What did he mean? Why was he looking at me now with such cold conviction? He moved to the altar and took from the briefcase he had left there a black folder, and then came to sit beside me on the pew. The title emblazoned across the dossier made me go numb: 'Harry Price – a Private Report.'

Wall followed my gaze and said, 'I've been watching him for years, watching both of you in fact. You did well to get away, even if you did end up running back to him.' He shook his head sadly, then opened the file to reveal a sheaf of papers interspersed with photographs.

'Where was his grandfather born? Do you know?'

'Shropshire, I think.'

'Actually, it was Worcestershire. Let's try an easier one. Where was *he* born? Where did he grow up?'

This I did know. I said, 'In the village of Rotherington.'

'Close, but no cigar, I'm afraid,' said Wall with mock sympathy. 'The correct answer is New Cross.'

New Cross. South London. 'But why would he lie?' I asked.

'Why indeed? He appreciates the finer aspects of life, prefers the company of the upper middle class.' Wall gave me a tight smile. 'Well, forgive me, but there is little that is middle class about New Cross.'

I thought this over for a moment and remembered the cadence of a South London accent I had thought I defected the first time I heard Price speak in public, the way his voice had drifted between registers. Was it possible that he had lied to me about such a personal piece of information? If so, what else had he lied about?

'Let's turn to his profession,' Wall continued. 'How much do you know about that?'

'More than anyone, I should think!'

'Tell me, then.'

'Why, you know very well: he is a psychical researcher.'

'At some times of the day, yes,' Wall acknowledged. 'When he isn't tending to his other business.'

'What is this?' I asked slowly, shifting over in the pew to put more distance between myself and Wall.

'When his father died, Harry inherited his paper bag business. Did you know that?'

My mind was alive now with memories of the strange ways he had behaved: the odd change in his work patterns, the secrets he couldn't confide. It could all be explained if he had another job.

'Did you know that he still runs the business, even to this day? Oh, and he never attended university, never gained the letters he so brazenly lists after his name. He is a canny but dishonest man who has used the mysterious to enhance his standing in life, and anyone who examines that life, as I have done, will find a minefield of fabrications and contradictions.'

My mouth opened to respond, but failed to form any words. The scale of Wall's accusations was making me dizzy.

'It began in the early twenties, when he exposed William Hope. That case made him famous. But it was the Society for Psychical Research who set him on to it – not that he gave them any credit! From that day he swung between scepticism and belief, straddling the domains of the Spiritualists and scientists. The inconsistency made him radical. Anything halfway true was sensationalised. Any medium that showed promise, he kept to himself. Any medium he could expose, he did, and to hell with the consequences!'

'No, he wanted the truth!' I said sharply.

'Fame and fortune, that's all he wanted. And there's more,' said Wall with relish. 'There are signals from Germany that Hitler is taking a special interest in the potential of psychical phenomena. According to my sources over there, the Third Reich has given permission for the founding of a Department of Psychical Research at Bonn University. Sarah, before the war Harry was engaged in discussions with them about donating his Laboratory and his work to their research.'

'No! He wouldn't.'

'He and Stuart Worsley, acting principal of the University of London, visited Bonn as official guests of the Third Reich on the thirteenth of April 1937. It seems he was willing to go to extraordinary lengths to obtain the academic recognition he has sought all these years. Sarah, I'm sorry to say it, but I believe – and I intend to make it known – that Harry Price is very likely a Nazi sympathiser.'

I stared at him in disbelief. Apparently realising my inability to speak, Wall pressed on.

'Over the years you were apart he made numerous visits to the Rhine and held many meetings there with the relevant authorities. In November 1938, while the synagogues were being raided,

Jewish shops destroyed and Jewish people murdered, he was off enjoying himself at concerts in Bad Godesberg, taking dinner in Bonn and tea in Cologne with the people he thought were going to help him. He even wrote to Hitler asking to attend – in comfort, I might add – the Nuremberg Rally in August.' He shrugged. 'It came to nothing when war began.'

I found myself able to speak again and asked Wall how he could possibly know all this. The answer was reasonable enough.

'Price told William Salter, the prominent psychical investigator, and Salter, in turn, told me.'

Salter. I remembered. He had been there at the beginning, all those years ago, at the grand opening of the Laboratory. Plotting to bring Price down.

'But why?' I asked, caught in bewilderment at how the past and present were meeting like this. 'What on earth is your interest in this – in him – after all this time?'

He pursed his lips, then, looking at the folder in his hand, said, 'I mean to bring him down. I mean to bring *both* of you down, unless you give me what I want.'

'Which is . . . ?'

'Closure,' he said quickly. 'Harry is collecting information for a second Borley book, isn't he?'

I nodded.

'I intend to stop him, and I want you to help me.'

'What? But why, why would you ask that of me?'

'You work in the film business, don't you? You can help me get this out.' He grinned. 'Come to think of it, the whole story would make a suitable film.'

'You can't be serious,' I managed to say.

'Sarah, it's *my* story!' His shout rebounded around the cold, musty church. 'It was always my story! Even at the beginning, before the two of you ever came to Borley. And he – you – cheated me out of it.'

'No, that isn't fair!' I cried. 'I had nothing to do with it!'

'You were complicit! You can't expect me to believe you never knew.'

'I went to him because I needed someone.'

'And look what he did to you,' he said numbly. 'You must help me. We must be rid of Harry Price.'

My mind was racing now as I scrambled for explanations. 'After we left Borley, Harry took little interest in the case. His mind was on other things – securing the Laboratory against the Spiritualists, testing Rudi Schneider. He wasn't involved with the Borley case for years.'

'But clearly he was involved,' said Wall, glaring at me. 'He's been collecting information on the case all the time, squirrelling it away for publication. He just never told you.'

'No,' I argued, 'that's not possible, I would have known, I–'

And then I remembered Price's odd behaviour after we had left Borley for the first time and returned to London. The long disappearances without explanation. The phone calls that came when I was left alone at the Laboratory, taunting me, just before he suffered his heart attack. *Ask him – ask him where he goes. Ask him about the props.*

I looked up and saw that Wall was looking at me, and in his expression I registered sadness mixed with anger, frustration and betrayal. 'You?' I could hear my own disbelief. 'You made those calls to me. You were the one I heard him shouting at down the phone in his office!'

He nodded slowly, sadly, and as he did so, the words he had spoken during our first visit to the Rectory drifted back: '*The telephone bell is a rather simple device, but it still rings with vital messages.'*

'Oh, but *why*? Vernon, the stress brought on his heart attack! Why did you do that? Why? What did you mean, "ask him about the props"?'

Wall took a deep breath. 'I'm sorry to be the one to tell you this, Sarah, but Harry . . .' He hesitated.

I stared at him, wishing he would just tell me and be done with it.

'Do you remember the first time we went to the Rectory? The candlestick that hurtled down the stairs, the pebbles rolling about in the hall? All that happened after the seance, even *during* the seance.'

I remembered all of this vividly and told him so.

'And in the saloon, on the journey we made from London, his coat pockets were filled to the brim with odds and ends?'

'Yes, yes.'

'Props,' he said quietly, 'that's all they were, like the curious items he keeps in that cabinet of his at the Laboratory – props for a clever magician's conjuring act. Harry brought them with him, and when our backs were turned he threw them all about that house, down the stairs, along the corridors, wherever phenomena were observed.'

'What? No, that's not true. He would never do that. He *couldn't* have done it, not all of it. How could he? He wasn't standing in the right place to have done those things without our noticing.'

'There is much he *could* have done. His pockets were stuffed full. You said so yourself. Remember he is a trained member of the Magic Circle. Even the Smiths agreed that when Price arrived in the Rectory the phenomena became worse.'

I couldn't accept this. 'Harry is a man of ability. His training with the Circle was impeccable. If all he could do to fool us was throw a few stones around, he wasn't a very good magician, was he?'

Wall shook his head, his expression somewhere between frustration and pity. 'Think back, Sarah! The blue lights which appeared during the seance? The Smiths said it themselves: such things had never happened before! Don't you find that an intriguing coincidence? Today, poor Mrs Smith thinks tricks were being played all around her, on all of us, and she was in no mental state at that time to be rational. Put yourself in her situation: in coming to Borley, succeeding the Bull family, hearing of Miss Ethel's family feud, she and her husband had walked straight into a psychological drama. At every turn the locals were telling her and her husband to beware and not to stay at the house. *Psychological*, Sarah, not supernatural.'

'We found a medallion. It appeared from nowhere. An apport.'

He shrugged. 'Harry Price is an avid coin collector. Did you know that? He probably has hundreds of the things at his home.'

'But what about the bells that rang, the cake of soap we saw hurled across the room, the brick that crashed through the verandah roof right above your head? Vernon, the haunted mirror? We all heard it tapping at us.'

'Nothing but hocus-pocus,' Wall insisted, gripping my arm, his voice urgent now. 'The heat and moisture from our lamp could have caused the wood in that mirror to expand, thus creating what Price led us all to think were spirit raps. He turned that lamp on and off repeatedly, remember? That alone would have induced a constant change in the air's humidity.'

'I'll hear no more of this!' I exclaimed.

'Listen to me,' he demanded scornfully. 'I *saw* him do it, as clear as I see you now. I *saw* him throwing pebbles when we ran upstairs together. His pockets were full of them. I am so sorry, I really am, but you must allow yourself to believe it. Harry Price had a mundane existence with a wife he kept hidden at home and a paper bag business of which he was ashamed. He wasn't scientist or an academic. He was a fantasist, Sarah! A fraud, a humbug, a psychological liar.'

I could not, would not accept it.

But Wall, clearly, already had. 'Take this,' he said, handing me the file of documents.

'What is it?'

'All the evidence we'll ever need to prove it, to bring him down.'

This was just ridiculous. The idea that Price, who had dedicated his life to the exposure of fraudulent mediums, had himself turned deceiver was alien to every understanding I had of the man. I said to Wall, 'Harry went to Borley at your request, not to prove it was genuine but to debunk it. And now you're saying . . .'

'That the man has been playing a long and cruel game with you, laying clues from day one so he could finally solve the case for publication and financial gain. His team of untrained observers gave him everything he needed. He prepared them for what might happen there: his briefings, his Blue Book of activities. His observers saw things, heard things, because they were told that they *would* see things. All he had to do was write them up in the appropriate way. Which is precisely what he has done.'

I was shaking my head, but Wall continued. 'It's understandable that you should resist it, after everything you've done for him, but you're holding the evidence right there in your hands. Take my word for it, his best-selling book is nothing but an impressive blend of legends, fantasy and lies twisted around some facts. A stone was thrown and the ripples have spread.'

His words were slaying me. But were they the truth? I had good reason to doubt it. Why hadn't he tried to warn me or get in touch? 'Not one letter, Vernon! And why didn't you say anything at the time? If you saw him hoaxing phenomena, if you knew, why didn't you warn me?'

'I wrote, many times. To the Laboratory and to your home address. I tried to warn you, Sarah! And I wanted to go public. I threatened Harry that I would – just before his heart attack – but my editor forbade it. Said you and Price would fight it in the courts, two to one against us. So he made me suppress what I knew.'

There had been no letters to the house from him. None that I had seen.

'*I wake and find myself downstairs . . . doing things I can't remember . . . collecting the mail . . .*'

Mother, always up before me . . .

The realisation hit me with a thud.

She collected the post.

'*I know how that sounds, but it's as though something is taking me over, taking control.*'

These thoughts slashed through my mind, cutting away any clinging doubts. I wanted to pause and reflect, make sense of all of this. But the moment was overtaken as a single newspaper clipping dropped out of Wall's file and landed at my feet. 'What's this?' I asked.

As Wall retrieved the cutting he told me it was a letter recently published in the *Daily Mail* written by Mabel Smith, whom we had met on our first visit to the Rectory.

I took the article from this hand and read:

A SPOOK IN THE WHEEL OF SUPERSTITION

On May 23rd the *Daily Mail* published a story 'Whiff of Evil at Borley Rectory' describing Borley Rectory as 'the most haunted house in England'.

As the wife of a previous rector of Borley, I would like to state that we lived in the rectory for over [*sic*] three years and did not think it was haunted (except by rats). It was an old house, and very creaky and broken-down. The 'wall of perfume' can well be explained as pigsties were adjacent.

It is because of local superstition that we called the Psychical Research Society in, hoping to show the people that there was nothing supernatural and, to our lasting regret, the place was made a centre for sightseers.

Surely now that fire has demolished the place, all this absurdity should be dropped and could it not be stressed that the supposed haunted house was not the rectory but an exchanged residence?[1]

Please help to clear the reputation of Borley, Essex, for it is a sweet little country place.

I have no reason at all to think Borley was haunted. Of course, our minds were turned towards the subject, owing to so much gossip; but in spite of this, nothing occurred which I consider could not be explained.[2]

'"Absurdity", "nothing supernatural" – how can she write that?' I exclaimed.

'She has written it because it is true,' said Wall. 'I interviewed her again recently to be sure. The footsteps her husband heard were attributable to rats. His hockey stick never whistled through the air, he simply used it to frighten away the vermin. She states emphatically that she saw enormous rats in the place, and is certain these were responsible for bell-ringing and many noises attributed to the supernatural. It makes sense, doesn't it? Rats would scratch the boards. The house had been empty for such a long time it's easy to see how vermin could have taken up their abode in kitchens and cupboards.'

'No,' I insisted, 'that isn't right. Reverend Smith told us rats were *not* the cause. What about the bell-ringing that night? You remember *that* happening, don't you?'

'Oh, yes,' said Wall, 'they most certainly *did* ring, but not because of ghosts. They rang because the rats made them ring, and perhaps with a little intervention from Price.'

The comment ignited a memory which made me start: Price, two years later, just after confronting Marianne Foyster, standing in the servants' passage holding a thread leading out through the window. Could it be? Was it possible? If so, then everything I had known – or thought I had known – about the man had been a lie; he had perpetrated the most cunning and elaborate deception imaginable; he had known all along about the others' deceptions – the Smiths', the Foysters', even Miss Ethel Bull's – and manipulated them towards his own ends, fabricating evidence when he saw the case's commercial appeal. And if he had interfered with the evidence, I couldn't help but wonder: what else had he tampered with? The idea was just too awful to contemplate.

Now Wall was removing from the file a letter which he passed to me. This one was dated 19 October 1935. The note was addressed to Sir Arnold Lunn. Referring to Marianne Foyster and the events at Borley, it read: *'I think she wanted to drive her husband away from the rectory, which is a very quiet and lonely spot. But I cannot print this explanation. I daren't even hint at it, so that part of the doings of the most haunted house must remain.'*

The signature underneath was clear: Harry Price. It was an extraordinary confession from a man who had previously announced to the world, in a blaze of publicity, that he was 'engaged in investigating one of the most extraordinary cases of poltergeist disturbance and alleged haunting . . . for years'.[3]

'Everything has a natural explanation, Sarah,' said Wall. And now he was producing from inside his jacket pocket another sheet of paper, which he handed to me.

No more, please, no more.

'I have here a statement from one of Price's official observers, Major Henry Douglas-Home.'

With the greatest apprehension, I unfolded the note. It read as follows:

> *After dark we toured each room, every hour, my friend leading, and Price bringing up the rear. The first few hours we found a number of extraordinary squiggles on the walls which we all swore had been unmarked on our previous hour's visit.*

'But this happened,' I insisted, remembering my own experience on the night of my confrontation with Marianne. 'I saw it myself, unexplained writing on the wall that appeared from nowhere—'

'Finish the letter,' Wall instructed.

> *We each carried a torch and I was so intent on examining each new mark that I failed, at first, to realise how they were being made. The last man (Price) had a pencil up his sleeve and as he swept his torch over the wall ahead, he made new squiggles in the darkness, which would be found on the next inspection.*[4]

'Of course you understand I will have to make this public,' said Wall.

'But you said yourself at the time that you believed it! You began it all, with those articles of yours. You singlehandedly put Borley on the map with your media circus. You stayed there. You were frightened; you saw the unexplained light shining in the window of the empty room. Mr Wall, you saw the nun!'

He stared at me.

'You're telling me that none of it was true?' My chin tilted up in defiance.

'None of it.' He paused and then smiled. 'Well, perhaps some of it.'

'Mr Wall!'

'I exaggerated! I'm sure that whatever I saw was probably just a moving shadow, a trick of the light, nothing more. Listen to me. I was young, just starting out, and it was a great story, Sarah. Tricks of the light don't sell newspapers but ghosts do. And I think Harry has come to understand that very well indeed.'

'But you're forgetting something,' I said. 'The Rectory *did* burn down. The prophecy was fulfilled.'

'There was nothing mysterious about that fire,' said Wall. 'Captain Gregson was stacking books in the hall. He left a few damp volumes near an oil lamp which toppled over and set them alight. Minutes later the place was ablaze. All very convenient for him too.'

'Whatever do you mean?' I asked tightly.

'Hasn't Harry told you? Captain Gregson filed an insurance claim, a total of £7,356, I believe. It was rejected on the suspicion that he torched the place deliberately.'

'He wouldn't do that,' I said, my voice heavy with revulsion. 'The captain seems to me a fine, upstanding citizen.'

'So you didn't know that he was until just recently an area organiser for the British Union of Fascists, Oswald Mosley's Blackshirts?'

'What? No, I—'

'Or that since the Rectory burned down he has been charging psychic investigators for access to the site? Or that just two months ago he accepted the sum of three guineas for the radio broadcast he and Price did together on the case?'

'No . . . but that doesn't mean—'

'Sarah, they're in on it together. The pair of them. And when Price's book is published, their combined profits will soar.' He handed me the dossier. 'It's all there, everything you need to know. I have provided a copy of this work to the Society for Psychical Research. Perhaps, being aware of Harry's fading health, they will wait until after he is gone before publishing what they know. But I should tell you now that they plan to re-examine the whole affair. There is so much to question.' He stood up. 'I'm quite sure their investigation will confirm what I already know: that Price is no better than the charlatans he's spent his career exposing – a trickster, an old humbug.'

I was aware now of the worst emotions pressing down on me, crushing my hopes. 'But if all you say is true then surely somebody must have known,' I protested. 'Someone would have worked it out.'

'I believe that someone *did* suspect what he was up to, yes, even in the early days, before the Borley case ever came our way.'

'Who?' I asked numbly.

'A gentleman by the name of Joseph Radley.'

'Radley – I remember him! I met him on the night of the Laboratory's opening, with my mother.' And I remembered, too, asking Price some months later about Radley's whereabouts and the evasive way in which he had responded. 'What happened to him?'

Wall's expression was dark. 'We don't know what happened to him, Sarah. That's just it. My enquiries with the Society for Psychical Research have led to nothing. As far as I can ascertain, he disappeared. No one saw him again after the night the Laboratory opened. He vanished.'

The church clock tower commenced striking nine, the clanging bell startling us both.

'I ought to be getting back,' Wall said. He cast his eyes with admiration over the magnificent Waldegrave monument. 'It's a wonderful specimen, no doubt,' he said, 'but I'm afraid it's the red herring in all of this. You're wasting your time. The real enigma is Harry. Always has been.'

I sat staring uncomprehendingly at the dossier of evidence he had given me. I needed to make sense of the anger I could feel burning within me. 'What am I supposed to do with this?'

'Do as you wish. But my advice is to confront the old crook, discover redemption in the truth. Tell him what you know and insist that he gives up on his second book and apologises to all those he has betrayed. Lionel Foyster should be top of his list; it was that poor man's *Diary of Occurrences* he bastardised for this book. He's left in poverty now, bedridden and lonely.'

'Wait!' I cried with the briefest hope. 'There's one thing you haven't told me. The sexton said you knew something about the remains we discovered at the Rectory; he said you claimed they weren't a woman's remains.'

I heard his firm, decisive reply. 'That's right. They most certainly were not. They weren't even human.'

'But the remains were examined by experts; they confirmed they included the jawbone of a young woman.'

'Don't you see, Miss Grey? Harry switched the bone fragments you found on the day of the excavation with human remains he brought with him from London. He used a conjurer's sleight of hand. One of the men who observed the dig *saw* him do it – Johnnie Palmer says he made the switch as he took the remains from Jackson and passed them to Mr Bailey. Very convenient, wasn't it, that he just happened to have a pathologist on the scene to identify the remains, *and* a barrister to act as a witness to the find?'

'Then what . . . did we find in the earth beneath the cellar?'

'The bones you discovered beneath the Rectory, your so-called proof, Sarah, were nothing more than the remains of a pig.'

I stared, contemplating the prospect with a pang of fear and relief, then dropped the file he had given me at my feet. 'He. Couldn't. Have.'

Wall walked down the church to the south nave, turned and looked back at me. 'How did we ever come to this?' he asked sadly. And then his lean face softened and I caught a semblance of the man who had caught me, sixteen years ago, on the rotten staircase descending into the basement of Borley Rectory – a man who might have rescued me from myself, saved me from the encroaching darkness, saved me from the enigmatic Midnight Inquirer. 'Find me, if you need to, Sarah. When this is over. Come back to me.'

I managed to give him a weak smile as he placed his brown trilby on his head and slipped out of the church. The urge to go after him was almost irresistible.

But something stopped me: the sharp sound of a pebble clipping the floor.

It had landed at my feet. Who had thrown it and from which

direction was impossible to tell, but its abrupt appearance set my pulse racing and quickened my resolve. Was it a sign?

Conflicting thoughts pulsed through my head: the hateful visions of evil and bitterness that came to me in nightmares, my mother's deteriorating mental health and the insidious disturbances in our house. If the Borley saga really was bogus, then how was I to interpret these events? As mere products of my imagination? Symptoms of insanity?

I had to know.

Now there was only one person I needed to find, and it wasn't Vernon Wall. Somewhere in the night, beyond Borley, in the safety of his compartmentalised private domain, Harry Price would be waiting.

And I had a job to do.

Notes

1 Mrs Smith appears to be alluding here to the sightseers who were then pestering the current incumbent, Revd Henning, at Liston Rectory.

2 *Daily Mail,* 26 May 1949.

3 *Journal of the American Society for Psychical Research,* pp. 435–436.

4 This quotation was due to be broadcast by the BBC on 4 September 1956, but the programme never aired due to fears that Marianne Foyster might sue the broadcaster.

36

GETHSEMANE

It must have been a little over two hours before I reached London. I recall very clearly that my hands were trembling as I climbed into the taxi that took me from Borley to the station, and I remember, upon arriving in Liverpool Street, that they were still trembling and my head was throbbing. But of the journey itself I recall very little. The shock of what I had learned from Vernon Wall had blurred my thoughts.

As a taxi took me the remaining distance to Queensberry Place, I was sure of one thing: Price was coming for me. By now, my absence at Liston would have been noticed. Reverend Henning would doubtless have asked the sexton where I had gone. He would have made enquiries with the nearest taxi company. He would have discovered my route. He would have passed that information to Price; and Price, knowing I had returned to London, knowing how uncharacteristic it was for me to just take off like that, would have become suspicious. He would have got into his Rolls-Royce at once and returned to the city.

I glanced at my watch, fretting at the wasted minutes, and wound down the window of the car. The evening's earlier warm breeze had whipped itself into a strong, blustery wind and the sky was black with leaden clouds. Nature itself seemed to have fallen sick. I felt a speck of rain on my cheek. Or was it a tear? The answer hardly seemed to matter, but the changing weather heightened my unease. As we pulled into Queensberry Place I felt physically sick with an anxiety which pulled at the pit of my stomach. 'Leave me here,' I said to the driver, getting out of the car.

I stood for a moment to collect myself. I thought of the first time I had walked down this road as Price's employee, of my alarming confrontation on that first morning with the medium who had appeared before me like a monster, regurgitating cheesecloth, and an awful thought occurred to me. If Wall's accusations were correct – if Price had fabricated evidence, switched animal remains for human remains[1] – then that made him far worse than any of the mediums he had exposed and vilified. Wall's accusations painted my former employer, the man I had loved, as an abominable creature.

I wondered whether Price even realised how far he had gone, the true extent of his deceptions. I doubted it, but I had to know.

The street ahead of me was deserted. I checked my watch and saw that the time was fast approaching midnight. I would need to be quick; I had little more than an hour, perhaps less. As I hurried down the street the sky cracked and rain pelted down around me. I ran as fast as I could until I reached the entrance to number 16, the Laboratory, his hall of mirrors.

No lights were on, no sound came from within, and from behind the windowpanes there was no sign of any movement. Stepping into the wide, pillared porch, glad of the shelter, I stared at the heavy black door behind which we had worked so hard and for so long. All that counted for nothing now.

I stepped forward and tried the main door, expecting it to be locked, but to my surprise it opened immediately. Inside, the gloomy hallway reached ahead towards the wide staircase. I took the route slowly, fumbling in the dark, tripping over objects invisible in the gloom, until I reached the top floor and the outer office. The door here was locked, but only until I threw my weight against it and the force of the attack granted me access. Stumbling into the outer office, the door swinging shut behind me, I turned on the spot and looked around.

There, on an old desk, was an electric torch. I reached for it, clicked it into life and illuminated the abandoned Laboratory.

Among the dust and shifting shadows I saw only the remains of what had been: files of paper strewn around the tables and the floors, boxes packed and placed in corners ready to be taken away. This was no longer a functioning establishment. Price was moving on, clearing up. He had been warned, perhaps, of the danger looming, the attacks that were destined to rain down on him.

There, at the corner desk, I had sat, sometimes for hours at a time, waiting for him to return to me from his endless appointments, worrying about the state of his health, wondering how on earth I could ever tell him what had happened to me during the period he was away unwell. Over there we had examined together the mysterious locked box that had allegedly belonged to Joanna Southcott; and there, at the threshold of the door that led into the main corridor, Price had stood and announced that we would discover the mysteries of the universe together.

As I entered the network of corridors and rooms I had first seen with Mother almost twenty years before, the memories came rushing back. I saw the jostling crowds, heard the clamour of journalists shouting Price's name, the flashbulbs on their cameras making his eyes wide with delight and suspicion. The contrast with my present surroundings was stark. The place seemed in every way to have lost its colour. Its shelves, once crowded with rare books, were empty now, layered thick with years of dust. Old furniture lay hidden beneath dirty sheets. The Laboratory corridor, once adorned with prints, was bare now, its pictures packed away, I imagined, in some of the many tea chests that stood around my feet.[2] Why was everything packed up? Where was he sending it all?

I waded deeper into the Laboratory, drawn by an intuitive certainty that somewhere among this debris of the past were the answers I sought.

Now coming up on my right was the seance room, where I had witnessed many an episode of unmasked fraud. It too had changed beyond recognition. The seance cabinets that had held our innumerable test subjects had been dismantled and lay discarded in the corners, and the room's windows were dark no longer, their shutters rolled back and admitting the deathly glow of the moon. But the worst feature remained. The seance chair dominated the room. I remembered Rudi Schneider sitting in it the night he had promised to reunite me with my father; I remembered the kindness of his tone as he whispered to me, 'You have your father's eyes.' I remembered the shock of realising that he, too, had lied to me.

The painful memory sent me across the corridor to Price's office. I found the door unlocked, and as I stepped into the room I was struck by the thick scent of pipe tobacco and then a new, more alarming thought: what if he's already here? In the building with me, now?

I went quickly to the filing cabinet where I remembered he kept his most extensive photographic collections and heaved the heavy drawer open. The sight of the files inside, crammed full of papers and photographs, took me back to an age long since passed, when working at the side of London's foremost psychic investigator was thrilling and exhilarating. How I wished I had recognised the danger sooner.

'Come on, come on,' I whispered. It had to be here: something that would substantiate Wall's accusations. I did not have to search long. At the back of the drawer, behind the many thick files packed with spirit photography, was a folder slimmer than the others, conspicuous by the fact that it carried no label. With mounting trepidation I opened it.

The first photographs – of buildings I recognised from Berlin and Cologne – were harmless enough. But clipped behind these were the damning images that confirmed what Wall had told me, images of Germany's symbolic power: the Kongresshalle in the Luitpoldhain in Nuremberg, the Köningsplatz and the Brown House, the National Socialist Party's headquarters building in Munich, a flag bearing the swastika.

I threw the file down in disgust. I wanted to tear myself away from these rooms, to never again to see the man who occupied them or to contemplate the fact that I had associated myself with the place. But I had yet more to discover, for I knew that if Wall was correct then proof of Price's deceptions in the Borley Rectory affair would be here somewhere.

I turned to leave, to explore the workshop, when the corner of an object protruding from beneath Price's desk caught my eye. I had never known him to keep anything under his desk, so it struck me as odd. Intrigued, I went over, crouched down and shone my torch on it. It was a wooden trunk. It was too heavy to pull out, but I managed to prise open the lid to make a gap sufficiently big to peek through. The light of my torch revealed the evidence I had dreaded, but somehow known I would find.

'*What* are you doing in here?'

I leapt to my feet, away from the trunk.

I could see a figure outlined against the doorway at the far end of the room, and then he switched the light on, revealing himself.

'Harry, I, I—'

'Don't speak, Sarah. Don't say anything.'

He came towards me.

Price stopped a few steps away, the desk between us, dividing us, protecting me from him, for I now believed he was capable of anything. Did he know? Had he seen me looking in the trunk? His gaze moved down to the floor. From where he was standing I doubted very much he could see it.

He stared back at me appraisingly. He seemed to be deciding what he should do.

Finally, after a long silence, I said, 'Harry, tell me it's not true.'

'Tell you what's not true?'

'That you were planning to relocate this Laboratory to Bonn in Germany; that you've been courting the Nazi Party; that you asked Hitler if you could attend Nuremburg; that you're not really a scientist at all; that you've no qualifications to speak of; that you lied to me, to everyone, about who you really are; that you lied about your family background, your secret paper bag business.'

Price said nothing but his eyes were frosty, glinting with the possibility of malice.

Suddenly I was no longer afraid. I reached down to the wooden trunk and opened it to reveal its horrifying contents. Bones. Human bones. Where they had come from, I had no idea. But now I was as certain as I could be that Wall was right: that Price had collected these, taken one of them to the dig and switched it with the animal remains he was confident we would find in the ground.[3]

I took out something that looked like a finger bone and brandished it at him, raising my voice, 'Tell me, *tell* me it's not true!'

He stepped back, his face uncertain.

'You lied to me about Borley from the very beginning. You invented phenomena at that house, fabricating evidence. You leased the building with the express intention of capitalising on its haunted reputation. Captain Gregson bought it for the same reason and torched it as an insurance fraud. It was you drawing on the walls. And you deliberately made us think that we had found human remains in the excavation. That's why we never found the rest of the skeleton. There was no skeleton!'

He seemed dazed by my accusations. 'Where on earth did you hear these things?'

'From Vernon Wall. It's over, Harry.'

I expected he might say something then to defend himself. But instead he moved slowly away from the desk and went over to the window, all the time keeping his back to me. He moved like an old man, unsure of himself, as if at any moment the floor might vanish beneath him. He coughed, a wrenching, painful sound. He stopped before the cabinet filled with the contraptions of fraud he had confiscated from so many mediums throughout his career. Then he said in a thin voice, 'Sarah, do you suppose there really is a world awaiting us after this one?'

'I used to think so,' I replied, 'if the phenomena at Borley were anything to go by.'

He turned and regarded me. 'Yes, well . . . in that case, perhaps we are all in trouble.'

'Harry?'

He crossed to the window and stared out into the howling night. 'It's all very clear to me now, Sarah. We've been wandering in the dark, going the wrong way, you and I, for so very long.' He faced me. 'Because it's the bunk they actually want, not the debunk.'

His statement made me go numb. I hesitated. Seeing the confusion in my face, Price filled the silence between us.

'Don't you understand? The hopes of these wretched people cry out for it – to hold the hand of their dead brother, to hear again the voice of their father. They remember because they must. And mediums rescue them from their pit of sorrow.'

'What are you saying?'

He gave a slight shrug. 'Supply and demand, that's all it is. They provide a service. And who was I to take away their business? If it's answers people demand then answers they will have!'

'So you fabricated evidence?' I demanded.

He nodded reluctantly. 'Do you remember the photograph of the flying brick?'

I cast my mind back. A few years earlier an article had appeared in *Life* magazine with a photograph of the Rectory ruins, half demolished. It appeared to show a single brick, suspended in mid-air. Price, who was present when the image was captured, later wrote: 'if this was a genuine paranormal phenomenon, then we have the first photograph of a poltergeist projectile in flight.'[4]

'It was thrown,' he confessed, 'by a workman just out of the frame.'

Even as he spoke, I had a sense that this was only the tip of the iceberg. How much more had he embroidered and embellished?

'Harry, I want to believe that you are better than this.'

'The phenomena at Borley met the public's insatiable demand for mystery,' he continued, warming to this wretched attempt to justify himself. 'Let's not fool ourselves now, Sarah; all who lived in that house, every one, twisted the truth to suit their own ends.

Reverend Smith and his wife, so sincere, so polite, so concerned that their house be inspected for spooks, but only because they thought there was profit to be had. Mrs Smith wanted to write a book on the whole thing. And as for the Foysters, where do I start? Each as deranged as the other.'

At hearing him say as much, my anger flared. 'That "deranged" old man is living in poverty now, Harry, because of what you did – stealing his manuscript, turning it into a book for your own selfish reward. How could you do that?'

'Because it was necessary.'

'Judas!' I spat the word out.

And I understood then why he had done it. It had not been for his amusement, or even for money. He had done it to be noticed. And when the world had stopped paying attention to that, he had taken the next available route to fame. Why show them fraudulent mediums when he could show them a genuine haunted house, fill it with 'official', 'credible' observers, only to solve the case and lay the offending spirits to rest? It was marvellous and appalling in equal measure. And I was one of the few who knew. *One of the few*. The thought made me nervous.

'If it's any consolation to you, I wasn't responsible for all of it. How could I have been? The first sightings of the nun were in 1900. I hadn't even heard of Borley then.' He began to move towards me slowly, intent in his cold eyes.

'Harry, wait—'

He kept coming.

'Harry!'

And then a thought hit me. 'Who was Joseph Radley?'

The question made him freeze. He paused, frowned. 'You know very well who he was. Radley was my assistant.'

'Tell me what happened to him!' I screamed.

There was a further pause, and then Price said, 'Joseph Radley was employed by the Society for Psychical Research, though I did not know it at the time. He was a spy, Sarah, a traitor. They sent him here to keep tabs on me, to check my work wasn't outpacing theirs. And when I discovered the fact, shortly after we first met – well, it made his position here untenable.'

'Untenable? He hasn't been seen since! Not by anyone! What did you do to him? My God! What *are* you?' But I hardly needed to ask. The answer was staring back at me with dangerous eyes that never wavered, not once.

And as he advanced towards me once more, I knew what I had to do. It was now or never.

So I told him. Finally I told him the one thing I had been incapable of telling anyone, the one secret I had carried with me all this time since that dusty summer of 1929 and that fateful night when we had visited the Rectory for the first time, the night of the seance when afterwards, under cover of darkness, he had come to me.

I told him the truth as plainly as I am telling it now.

That I had been a mother.

That, from the summer of 1929, I had carried his child.

He was staring at me with his mouth wide open. And because he seemed quite incapable of asking me anything, I gave him the answer to the question I knew he wanted to ask. 'It was a boy, Harry. His name was Robert.'

On hearing this, his face changed, its expression melting from bewilderment to wonder and finally to hope. His eyes darted left to right, as if he expected the child to appear in the far recesses of the room.

Had he known? Marianne Foyster certainly had; but Price? I doubted it. He would not have noticed at the time, for in the months I was carrying his child he was in hospital, recovering from his heart attack. Certainly, if he had known then he had long since buried the truth in the deepest part of his mind where he wouldn't have to feel the guilt that attended such a thing. I made him acknowledge it now, in the room where we had first encountered one another. He listened attentively, his face powder-white, as I reminded him how, on the night he had come to me pleading that I take him back to London, I had lain awake after he retreated to his room, thinking of him, and shortly before dawn I had gone quietly to his room and slipped into his bed.

I told him how, when the pregnancy was confirmed, I had gone from the doctor's office on Tachbrook Street and wandered for close to an hour around the streets of Pimlico, my head swarming with confusion at the impossible future that had been forced upon me. I remember I experienced the briefest excitement at the news, and then the crushing fall, hating myself, hating him, for at that time there really was no worse shame than for a woman to be in my predicament. There was absolutely no one I could have told – not my closest friends, not even my mother. And especially not him. He who basked in the public limelight, whose public image sustained him. Who was married.

Price was struggling to catch his breath as the barrage of revelations crashed over him. 'What happened to the child?' he managed to gasp at last.

My mouth tightened. I backed away from him.

'Sarah? Tell me, what happened to the child? My child. *Tell me. What happened to him?*'

And then he realised; I saw it in the tragic understanding that flowed into his eyes, in the trembling of his hand, the pursing of his lips. I could so easily have stopped then and said nothing at all. I wish I had stopped. But instead I said, 'I could never have kept the child, Harry. How could I? He's gone.'

His face crumpled and he emitted a terrible, tortured cry as thunder crossed his brow. His ferocious gaze turned upon me.Then he lunged, approaching with a speed that took me unawares. 'You took my boy!' he thundered, grabbing my arm. '*My* boy!'

But he couldn't hold me for long. Somehow, I slipped free and stumbled towards the door. At the threshold to the room I paused and looked back, bracing myself to run at any moment. But he had stopped following me. And as I watched him groping hopelessly for words, shaking his head wildly, I knew it was no longer necessary for Vernon Wall or anyone else from the Society for Psychical Research to bring Price down. I had done it for them.

'You know, I think I can hear them now, Sarah. At last. At last I can hear them.' He was nodding, his eyes glittering with tears. He went, shakily at first then with firmer footing, to his glass cabinet of wonders. When he reached it he rested his hand upon its surface, the glass forming the only barrier between him and signed confessions from fraudulent mediums. He stared at them intently with a look that seemed to say '*Where did I go wrong?*'

'Hear who?

'*Them*,' he hissed. 'The ghosts, Sarah. I can hear the ghosts.' He raised his head up to face me, reaching out with a shivering hand, pointing past me, beyond me, into oblivion. 'Do you see? There! *There* they are! I *hear* them, Sarah.'

His eyes were fixed intently on something, but I saw no one. 'It's only your conscience you can hear,' I said. 'And I hope you never stop hearing it.'

'You must believe me,' he pleaded, and he slid down to the floor, his back to the cabinet. 'It wasn't all me. It wasn't. I might have embellished a few things, thrown pebbles, planted evidence, yes, but the rapping mirror? The cake of soap which jumped off the washstand? The ringing bells, the candlestick which hurtled down the stairs? I couldn't have done those things – how could I? And the medallion. I assure you, Sarah, that had absolutely *nothing* to do with me. Or the nun. How could I have invented the story of that apparition, Sarah? How could I possibly have done that?'

All can be achieved by a clever man.

'You're nothing but a sham,' I told him. 'All you ever wanted was validation, to be famous. And you played everyone off against one another to get where you wanted to be. That's why you were inconsistent. It wasn't the truth you cared about, it was yourself.'

He raised his pleading eyes to meet mine. 'People have never meant much to me. You were the first that did. I could see something wasn't right for all those years, that you were keeping something back from me. I wanted to protect you,' he said quietly. 'Don't you see? I had to make you not like me. You think I haven't felt it too – the darkness approaching?'

I looked down at him, not knowing what to believe. The man who had brought a glittering luminescence to even the most mundane tales had been reduced to a cowering shadow. His hands were clasped together in a gesture of prayer, his head dropped back, eyes scanning the ceiling. If it was solace he was looking for, from the noise of his conscience or the glaring gaze of God, I doubted he would find it now.

I moved towards the door.

'Wait! Where are you going?'

I looked back at him, hardening myself against the pull of his eyes, my head swimming with visions of how different my life could have been without him. 'It's like you said, Harry. Pain and loss. The two inevitable consequences of life.'

I should like to say that he said something profound at that moment, *anything* to redeem himself. Instead he raised his eyes to me and asked, 'Do you suppose that those who hunt ghosts are hunted, in turn, by them?'

'Yes, Harry,' I said coldly. 'I have no doubt of that.'

Then I went quickly from that place, leaving him desperate and alone with nothing but ghosts for company.

Notes

1 Corroboration of Price's suspicious behaviour in connection with the excavations comes from Mr R. F. Aickman, one of the official observers, who contributed an essay, 'Postscript to Harry Price', to *Mystery. An Anthology of the Mysterious in Fact and Fiction*. He writes, 'Price's secretiveness could try the patience. Although I was in full communication with him when my friends and I made the visits to Borley recorded in *The End of Borley Rectory*, Price never informed me that he himself was visiting the place almost immediately before and after my visits, and in order to carry out the vital excavations in the cellars as well' (p. 272).

2 A thorough examination of the Harry Price Magical Library at Senate House confirms that there were eighty-seven tea chests in all.

3 Animal bones had been found in the grounds of the Rectory before, as the Smiths told Price and Sarah on their first visit to the house in June 1929.

4 *The End of Borley Rectory*, p. 285.

37

AFTER THE
AFFAIR

There is little left for me to tell. Only the worst of it.

When I was young, Mother warned me that my lies would find me out. I never paid much attention; I heard the adage so often it became something she said rather than a warning to be heeded. But when I look back across these pages, when I think of the awful thing that happened to Price and the distressing ordeal I am now suffering, I think perhaps she was right and I wish I had listened.

Some months after my final confrontation with Price I became unwell. The nightmares that had haunted me all these years, which I had expected to recede with the knowledge of his fraudulent behaviour, did not cease but instead grew into serrated dreams, each worse than the last – visions of a wild windswept moor, a dark rectory and a hooded figure robed in billowing black.

As I lay awake fighting the darkness that came each night, I became fatigued and prone to moments of melancholy, which quickly gave way to a deep depression. I drowned in it. I couldn't work, couldn't leave the house, couldn't even eat. Throughout this time my only companion was Mother, whose mind, over the years, was gradually being taken from me. And it was she who unwittingly, devastatingly, showed me the truth.

'I have seen this before,' she said sadly, sitting next to my bed. Her wrinkled old face was a mask of pain, but in all other respects she was having a good day. She was mentally present, lucid, which made a refreshing change from her usual behaviour. 'All a mother wishes for her family is for them to be happy and healthy. That's all I ever wanted for you and for your father.'

I looked into her caring eyes, which for the first time in weeks were possessed with nothing else but her own spirit – that same wonderful resilience that had served her so remarkably when she had given her time to the Voluntary Aid Detachment. I remember saying to her: 'I don't know what's wrong with me; my moods, they're almost uncontrollable.' And it was true. I drifted through the world like a shadow of myself, clutching at old familiar pleasures, but all too often I found the simplest tasks – running errands in town, meeting friends, getting out of bed – required the greatest summoning of will. Too often I felt that when I smiled I was inwardly crying.

'I know, dear, I know. It's an illness and no one knows its effects better than me.' She leaned closer and placed a gentle kiss on my forehead, then stroked my hair. 'Your father suffered so badly with it. I tell myself that daily – that he was ill. That's why he did what he did . . . You're like him, Sarah – my brave little girl.'

'Then I'll get better, like he did?'

She gave me a half smile. Then her mouth turned downward and her eyes became dark and drifted into the distance. She was remembering.

'Mother?'

'We tell each other everything, don't we, Sarah, you and I?'

'Yes, of course . . . Why?' Something in her tone made the hairs on the back of my neck stand up. She was twisting her wedding ring nervously.

'I'm old now, Sarah. Seventy-three?' She shook her head, looking wistful. 'In here' – she tapped her chest lightly – 'I'm still your age, full of hopes and dreams. And regret. It's been so very long. There is something I never told you. Something you have a right to know. Something you *need* to know.' She stared beyond me to a faded photograph of my father hanging on the wall. Her expression filled me with a creeping sense of dread.

'You don't want to make the same mistakes I did. Perhaps the truth will help you see how fruitless it is to wallow in misery.'

If she was intending to comfort me, it wasn't working. 'Mother, please, what—?'

Tears glistened on her dark lashes. 'Your father, Sarah, died in the trenches, killed by a single gunshot wound to the head.'

'I already know this!' I said, sitting up. 'I do know how Father died.' And somewhere in my head a voice said, '*How can you know it? You never read the telegram, did you, Sarah? You were never allowed to read it.*'

'Sarah, please – let me get this out. I may not have long, and when I'm gone you will want to know.'

I drew in a breath, alarmed that I might unwittingly have prompted this detour to the past.

'You remember, before the Schneider seance all those years ago at the Laboratory, we spoke, you and I?'

'You said there was something I needed to know before the experiment could proceed.'

'That's right. And during the seance a message came through for us.'

An image flashed through my mind: Schneider writhing and

convulsing in the seance chair. 'Yes, I remember. An apology. He said he was sorry. He said he loved us. But none of that was real. Harry showed he was a fraud.'

'Your father was one of life's casualties, Sarah. The gunshot which killed him was fired by his own hand. I'm sorry,' her voice cracked. 'I couldn't tell you. I'm so sorry. Your father took his own life.'

'Don't say that,' I pleaded. 'Please don't.'

Mother's hand stifled her broken sobs. 'Will you ever forgive me, Sarah? I should have told you, I know I should, but how could I?'

I flinched at this awful news, and even as my bottom lip began to tremble, Price's voice from that time, the day after the seance, the day I had walked out on him, the day he had betrayed me by announcing his intention to denounce Schneider as a fraud, was inside my head: *He said your father was a weak man . . . He called him a coward.*

A flash of understanding.

I thought back to that fateful night, to before the experiment – Price announcing his intention to photograph the seance with the greatest rigour he had ever applied; Schneider's uncompromising cooperation; Price's mounting hostility to our guest as it dawned on him that other researchers, rival investigators, were keen to test Schneider too, to bask in the reflected glory of his talent.

Then I remembered something else: the rapidity with which Price had rushed to judgement on Schneider's probity; the photographs he had shown me, clearly depicting Schneider's hand freeing itself from his grasp. I remembered the spasmodic way in which Schneider's body had moved, and the panic in Price's eyes when he had realised it was a power that he alone was unable to constrain. Had Schneider really cheated? Or had Price, in exposing the fake, been the one using trickery to create *the false impression* that Schneider was a fraud? Exposing Schneider helped put him on the map, validated his work. Could he have released Schneider's hand deliberately just to take the limelight? It was possible. As for the photographs, Price was skilled in the practice of photographic exposure; he could easily have tampered with them.

'Then Rudi Schneider might have been telling the truth?' I asked Mother, realising that the young medium's apology during the seance had come not from him but *through* him, channelled by my dear father in the world beyond.

Mother nodded, smiling. 'There,' she said, wiping a tear from my face. 'You see, Sarah, there is hope for us yet.'

I wanted so badly to believe that as I shut my eyes against further tears and Mother wrapped me in her arms, stroking my hair and whispering gentle words of reassurance.

But even though she had been honest, a part of me rebelled at the idea of accepting that all would be well. Because as I pondered her confession and everything that had happened since my first visit to the Rectory – her changing behaviour, her moments of hypnotic detachment, the recurrent *tap-tap scratching* in the walls – I knew the only reasonable conclusion was that something was very wrong with our lives; a canker that had grown beneath the skin of our family.

I opened my eyes and looked up into her kindly face. 'Vernon Wall tried to stay in touch with me. You opened his letters and kept them. Didn't you?'

She turned her head with embarrassment.

'It's all right,' I said soothingly. 'I'm not angry.'

'It's a dreadful thing, Sarah' she sighed, 'not to know your own mind. To let other people down because you don't know yourself any more. I didn't know what I was doing, my love. Sincerely. Some days, I still don't.' She shook her head as her voice cracked with fear. 'I don't want to go mad. You will you look after me, won't you?'

'We're a team, remember?' I cupped her face in my hand. 'I'll get better and I'll look after you, whatever happens. I promise.'

But even as I uttered the words, I didn't know if I could muster the strength to confront what was really wrong with her: she thought she was losing her mind, whereas I suspected, with mounting dread, that something else, some malign presence, was taking it from her, stealing her from me by degrees.

I had met possessed women. I had met Marianne Foyster, who had read my mind and cast fearful prophecies upon me. Something of the glitter in her eyes when we spoke that night in her bedroom at the Rectory – the glitter that had drugged me with possibilities both fantastic and fearful – I had recognised in Mother's eyes too on the night I came home and found her scrubbing the walls.

As if hearing these thoughts, Mother said suddenly, 'We will face it together, my darling. Whatever it is.'

And Marianne's words from years before drifted back to me: *She is coming . . . After the losses you will suffer . . . the Dark Woman will return.*

*

I remember the date vividly – 11 February 1948, my birthday – though I can only recall the morning of that day. The rest is a blur.

I rose early and stumbled downstairs half asleep. My mistake. If only I had been more awake I might have noticed the warning.

I might have seen the small pile of pebbles heaped on the floor at the foot of my bed.

We were in the kitchen when the thing happened. With a kindness that was typical of her, Mother presented me with a gift to lift my spirits. I remember smiling as she handed me the jewellery box and the brief thrill of anticipation as she told me it contained a necklace, one she had troubled to make herself.

I closed my eyes as she looped it around my neck. But the moment she did so, my eyes snapped open. I recoiled on feeling the cold chain against my skin, the heavy object suspended over my heart. *Sarah Grey, there is something you can't see. And it's around your neck.*

An acute terror rose within me, choking me. I snatched the awful thing from around my neck and threw it violently at the wall. It landed on the floor in plain sight, and I saw that I was right.

The last relic of Borley Rectory – the ancient Catholic medallion! Stumbling backwards, I tripped and fell. There was a sharp crack as my head connected with tiled floor but I did not lose consciousness. My only thought was to get this thing far away from me. I had not seen it in years. Mother had found it in the drawer where I had left it with the Bible, and now she had unwittingly given it to me as a gift without even knowing what bad feelings attended it, with no idea of its history. But I knew. Now it was clear to me: all these years it had been there, in the background of my life, polluting my existence with its wickedness.

That afternoon I sent the medallion to Price, with the briefest of notes explaining that I wanted nothing to do with it. 'This belongs to you,' I wrote.

His reply was instant, which did not surprise me; by then he was well under way with preparations for a third book about the Borley affair. I hadn't bothered to read his second, *The End of Borley Rectory*; I didn't need to.

But in the following weeks I began to doubt myself and wonder if elements of the tale had been true, for as soon as the medallion had left my possession I felt lighter in spirit, younger. A shadow seemed to have lifted from me. The change caused me to reflect and I recalled that the Borley victim had, according to some testimonies, worn a Roman Catholic medallion. So eventually I put pen to paper and wrote to Price for the last time: 'Tell me, Harry, have you noticed any difference in either your mental state or your physical health since having the Borley brass? Certainly since getting rid of it I have felt better in health and in a happier frame of mind. I would be glad to hear your view.'

I waited. The days crawled by, and with no reply from my old companion the weight of my anxieties grew heavier upon me. Price's original letter had stated his intention to have the medallion photographed. I knew it was his custom to delegate such tasks to the services of A. C. Cooper Ltd, a reputable art photographer based in Bond Street, Mayfair. Perhaps they could tell me something useful. It seemed unlikely but, in light of Price's silence, worth pursuing. The idea led me there late one afternoon, but I was alarmed to find that the shop was gone. All that remained was a blackened space where plush, respectable rooms had once been. There had been a fire.

A local shopkeeper directed me to Mr Cooper's temporary business premises a few streets away. There I explained to the photographer the reason for my interest and my past association with Price. When I mentioned the medallion he turned pale and said gravely, 'So it is true. Strange events *do* happen.'

Apparently, while setting up the medallion to be photographed, one of his men had dropped it on the floor. The moment it hit the ground, a very expensive oil painting fell off its easel, with no explanation, and crashed to the floor.

'A coincidence, surely?' I said.

'Call it that if you will, Miss,' he said gravely, 'but is it also a coincidence that a grandfather clock we have kept in that same studio, which has not worked for some fifteen years, sprang into life again at that precise instant? And days later we came into the office to find things had moved about. One of the men . . . It sounds so silly, but one of the men thought he heard a mirror tapping.'

I tried my best not to show my alarm, but he saw it anyway and gave me a knowing nod. 'Just a few days later the fire broke out in the dead of night.'

Another fire; there had been too many of them.[1] And Marianne Foyster's words from years ago were screaming prophetically in my head: *She is coming . . . After the losses you will suffer, after the fire, after the proof that will be found – the Dark Woman will return.*

All this time I had assumed Marianne had meant the great fire of Borley Rectory and the partial remains we unearthed beneath the house. I felt foolish. Had she not warned me of the Borley curse, that the fate of anyone connected with the Rectory who deceived others was to be haunted and suffer a horrible death? In my limited knowledge of Price's deceptions I had assumed – dangerously – that she was wrong; there was nothing to fear because he had made everything up, had planted the brass medallion in the house for us to find.

But what if he *hadn't* planted it? *Dear God!*

I had to find Price. I had to warn him, for both our sakes.

I battled through the crowded London streets, dread in my heart. For I was as guilty as all who had ever exploited the ghosts of Borley Rectory to their own ends. The night I left Price broken and alone in his Laboratory, I had done so knowing I had wounded him with a version of the truth. I had let him believe that his little boy was dead, that I had terminated my pregnancy. I hadn't.

Robert Michael Grey was born on 16 April 1930. He was the most beautiful child. The midwife and the other women – many of them in the same, unfortunate predicament as me – spoke endlessly of his blue eyes. I could never have harmed anything so precious; so many years watching mediums converse with the dead had granted me an appreciation of life. However, I had prepared to give the baby away, so far as it was possible to prepare for such a thing. It was horrific, watching him being carried away from me at the convent in Yorkshire. I mourned my son from the moment he left my arms, and I have mourned him still further since discovering the identity of the family to whom he was given.

Memories of the child I had given up to protect Price, to protect us both, assailed me as I hurried through the rain-washed streets. By the time I arrived at Queensberry Place evening was setting in; a glance at my watch told me it was seven o'clock. Would he be there at this hour? I hammered on the door with my fists, I cried out his name helplessly. No response. A passerby looked at me as if I was losing my mind. I think perhaps I was losing my mind, for at that instant a low humming filled my ears and I saw her at last.

The Dark Woman.

The dismal figure stood – floated – at the farthest end of the road, merging with the London fog which swirled around her. Her outline was hazy, blurred, perpetually shifting and flickering, like a picture on a badly tuned television. I could feel her rage and betrayal and vengeance burning me with human torment.

And suddenly the darkly clad form was nearer, the droning sound louder. I dared to look at the spirit's face. Saw deep black holes that might have been eyes. Saw her skin, like grey leather, stretched across her bony features. An immense cold overpowered me as her mouth cracked open and her jaw dropped. Shadows seemed to slide out of her, thrusting forward. And from the gaping cavity that was no longer a mouth but just an inky space, untold misery and malignant feelings poured out of her, flowing into me.

> *Trompée,*
> > *trompée,*
> > > *trompée.*

My arms shot up in a vain attempt to shield myself from the words flying at me, fired by the phantom's mind.

'Stop it!' I cried, pressing my hands to my ears as a tortured wail rose up.

The nun's scream – not mine.

'Please stop it, stop it, stop it!'

Her long wasted arms hung by her sides, her withered hands closed tightly. At the edge of the road, suddenly, as if from nowhere, a large black Labrador caught my eye, its teeth bared and its hackles up. I had looked away from the nun only for a second, but when I glanced back the diabolical form was just a few feet away, raising one arm, extending it towards me, opening what remained of her hand.

Lying in her smoky palm was the brass medallion.

In that moment I knew that whatever end awaits me in this life, I am powerless to resist it.

I blinked. The phantom suddenly dispersed into thousands of individual parts that broke away, humming and buzzing – a thick, swarming mass of flies.

I ran from the Laboratory, from Queensberry Place.

When I arrived home I noticed my watch had stopped at precisely seven o'clock that evening. That was significant, but I didn't yet know how significant. I didn't have time to think about it. I was far more concerned to know why Mother hadn't answered when I had called her name.

I looked about me manically, dashing from room, flicking on the electric lights. As I flew into the hall, stumbling, the main light overhead dimmed then exploded, showering me with glass. 'Mother!' I screamed. 'I'm coming, I'm coming!'

By the time I had reached the top of the stairs, I could hear it from behind her bedroom door: the all too familiar scraping, scratching sound: *tap-tap-scratch; tap-tap, scratch.*

It was louder now than ever.

The door handle rattled but refused to turn.

'Mother, please let me in!'

Panic gripped me. I threw my shoulder against the door once, twice.

The lock broke on my third attempt. I stumbled into the darkened bedroom, and froze.

The scratching sound in the wall hadn't been a mouse or a rat. Something far, far worse had entered our house.

Scrawled across the walls and the floor and every other surface in Mother's bedroom was one word scratched out in chalk, hundreds of times, over and over:

Trompée . . .

   Trompée . . .

      Trompée . . .

Mother stood facing me in the corner of the room, one hand raised. Gripped in her fingers was a stick of chalk.

My blood ran cold as I looked into her eyes, which were like black pearls, and saw that all humanity had burned away. I had seen the same thing in Marianne Foyster's gaze at Borley Rectory. I knew then: whatever vengeful spirit had turned the rector's wife out of her bed and made her write on the walls was here with me now, perhaps always had been, since the day I had brought the Ignatius medallion into the house. There was no doubt about it: Mother was possessed.

She dropped the chalk. It struck the floor and snapped. And as Mother slumped to the floor I dashed forward to catch her, too late. God forgive me – I was too late.

I knew she was dead. Even before I gathered her up in my arms.

Time slowed down for me as all the fear that had built up in me dissolved into uncontrollable sobbing: tears of guilt. For all these years, it was she, Frances Helen Grey, who had kept me safe.

I have no idea how long I remained sitting there on the floor, cradling her body like a broken doll and stroking her thinning white hair. My heart was heavier than a dead weight. Now the Nun's curse had found us for our deceptions.

Who else had it found?

As if on cue the tall black telephone jangled beside me. I flinched. Fingers trembling, I fumbled the receiver to my ear. 'Yes?' I managed to say, 'what now?'

'Miss Grey? This is Sidney Glanville.' Price's old assistant.

He sounded downbeat, apprehensive. But he didn't need to say anything else.

I already knew why he had called.

As I write these concluding words, I am sitting alone in the study in my house. Before me on the desk lies the St Ignatius medallion. I am afraid to gaze at it for too long, afraid of its potential; but as much as I would dearly love to be rid of it, I know I never will be. I have tried many times. I have taken it down to the ponds on Hampstead Heath and dropped it into the water. I have left it on tables in cafés in Piccadilly. I have buried it in the garden. Every time it comes back to me, appearing, as it had first appeared, on a pillow. Except this time on *my* pillow.

Your lies will find you out. The adage was as true for Price as for me.

Three days ago I read in the newspaper of the Society of Psychical Research's intent to reinvestigate Price's handling of the Borley affair. They will want to know what I know, they will want the truth. But they will not hear it from me. When I have completed this narrative I will go from here to Bloomsbury, to the eighth floor of the Senate House Library at the University of London where Price's fantastic library now rests, and I will hide these pages there, among the dusty stacks – the only appropriate place for a tale such as this.

As I sit here, listening to the rain drumming on the roof, longing for that safe time before the Rectory, before the darkness, I thumb through the pages I have written and I wonder whether there is any significance in this story.

I think of Father and of Rudi Schneider and how no satisfactory explanation for the miracles he produced at the National Laboratory for Psychical Research was ever found. I think of

Velma Crawshaw, the young medium who had told me there was a mark upon me and who, just months before her tragic death, had told us she saw nothing of her own future. I think of Reverend Smith, of the last thing he said to me when we left the Rectory the morning after the fateful seance: that Borley Rectory was evil from top to bottom and it should have been burned to the ground years ago. Well, now the house has burned, and all the rectors who once lived in it have passed away. I think of Vernon Wall and how different my life might have been if I had heeded his early warnings and walked away from the Laboratory. I think of Marianne Foyster, how later in her life she changed her name and claimed that her husband was also her father. I think of Lionel Foyster who, I heard, spent his remaining days locked in his bedroom, his bed soaked in urine, as he rambled about a haunted house and his lost *Diary of Occurrences*. I think of the reports in the papers of ghosts lurking still in Borley.

And I think of my beautiful son, Robert, given to the Caxtons, a doctor and his wife living in the valley of Farndale. Because for all those years, across all that time, it wasn't only the Dark Woman I had seen in my dreams but my beautiful baby boy's face, his cheeks the softest pink, his skin so new and smooth. I cried through the night until my child was taken from my arms. I cried until the weeks and months rolled by and carried me back to London. I never stopped crying.

Son, if you should ever read this, believe me: always and forever, I was crying for you.

What on earth will you make of me? I hope you will consider me a good woman who led a bad life; a woman who had much in common with the legendary Dark Woman of Borley, betrayed and abandoned. If you survived the war I hope that you are more content than your parents ever were, and I hope you have inherited our better qualities – my zest for life and your father's keen and probing mind. I like to think of you as a distinguished professional, a scientist perhaps or an academic. But mostly I hope that you do not probe the supernatural; for as Price realised that night in his office, those who hunt ghosts are hunted, in turn, by them. They find us eventually as the Dark Woman found your father and will – I am certain – find me.

But know this: Harry Price will always be part of my family. He is your father so I will always care for him, whether I want to or not.

I had waited and waited for him to answer my letter but of course he never did.

Harry Price's body was discovered the same afternoon I encountered the vision in the road at Queensberry Place, the time of death seven o'clock, the exact time at which my watch stopped. It was his wife who found him, slumped over his writing desk, working on his new book on the Borley affair. His face was frozen, she said, in an expression of absolute terror, the fingers of his left hand still gripping his pen; and in his right hand, securely attached to his gold watch chain, he held a curious item she had never seen before:

A brass St Ignatius medallion.

Sarah Grey

November 1955, London

Note

1   It is interesting to observe that bizarre and strange accidents were reported at the site of Borley Rectory also. The *Suffolk Free Press* carried an editorial passage on 24 May 1944 entitled 'Queer', which reads:

'I understand that the fire-ruined Borley Rectory ... is being demolished and the bricks carted away for rubble. I heard an interesting story
the other day which supports the idea that there is always something
queer about the place. A local firm was engaged in felling some trees,
and 'everything seemed to go wrong'. Three axes broke in the course of
the work; one man received a shoulder injury; and two trees which were
roped and cut so as to fall into the grounds, fell into the road instead,
the ropes breaking, and a tractor had to be fetched to haul the timber
off the road.'

EPILOGUE

by Doctor Robert Caxton

*Fear no more, says the heart, committing its burden to some sea,
which sighs collectively for all sorrows, and renews, begins, collects,
lets fall. And the body alone listens . . .*

                      – Virginia Woolf, *Mrs Dalloway*

The sun was creeping up as I slipped the weighty manuscript back into the leather pouch with the broken lock. I sat staring at it.

Was it possible?

You might think that a middle-aged psychologist would have little about himself to doubt. But when I had finished reading Miss Sarah Grey's memoir of hope, terror and betrayal, I sat in my study at home in Oxford, unravelling as the shape of the world and my own sense of belonging within it dissolved.

That manuscript dropped a conclusion on me, like a hammer on the mind.

As someone who has spent my career helping people cope with trauma, I admit only with grim reluctance that I have evaded the truth about my past since I was eleven. Since the day my parents decided to sit me down at the kitchen table in our farmhouse on the snarling North Yorkshire moors and tell me the truth: that I wasn't really their son.

The truth of my adoption rattled through me. All my life I had felt out of step with the rest of my family and now I knew why.

'Your real mother was from a respectable Catholic family in London,' my parents told me. 'She was just twenty-six when she came here to give birth to you.'

They explained to me how difficult it must have been for a woman of her age to have a child out of wedlock; that little else could bring more shame upon a family.

I felt no animosity towards the woman who had given me away, but lacking knowledge of her identity, my true father's identity and thus my own heritage cast me adrift on doubt, leaving me certain only of one thing: the fundamental essence of my identity did not descend from my adoptive mother. Or my father.

He was a doctor of medicine, but also held a degree in physics and could easily have pursued a career in that field. Quite brilliant, he read Einstein and Bohr in his recreational hours. He understood them.

I could not. Something in me recoiled from the notion that everything, including thought, was ultimately reducible to chemical reactions in my brain. I felt it with every shred of my being and found the evidence in every pungent smell, every vivid colour. There had to be something more. Not necessarily a soul, but something more than bits and pieces. Beyond the particles.

I became fascinated with finding it, looking for evidence of it. It became my secret hobby to read about people who claimed abilities in extrasensory perception and out-of-body experiences. I consumed everything I could access that was written about world religions and belief systems, folklore and ancient mythology.

My adoptive father did not encourage these pursuits. While I was young he tolerated my interests with pursed lips and heavy frowns, consoled that I was interested in reading even if the subject matter was not as orthodox or intellectual as the Greek scholars he had mastered as a young man. He was always a loving and decent father, but as I grew towards adulthood his tolerance evaporated. 'If you want to be taken seriously,' he insisted, 'then you must choose a serious path.'

I know he would have been pleased for me to choose medicine, though he never pressed it upon me. Perhaps he thought the subject beyond me. One thing I did know: his curiosity about my ancestry was growing. Where did my fascination with 'pseudoscience', as my father scornfully disparaged it, come from if not my mysterious birth parents?

We knew nothing else about my biological mother, but my parents were unstintingly generous in their offers to help me find her. I shook my head against the idea. I already had a mother, sweet and dedicated to my well-being above all else. She had more than earned her claim to the title of Mother, and no one would take it from her.

My parents – for that is what they were – had left London in their late thirties, and sold their house to begin a quieter life in the cottage that came with fifteen acres of pastureland. He took a more relaxed position than the prestigious but life-encompassing post of consultant neurologist; being the only General Practitioner within a fifteen-mile radius was still lucrative and respectable and allowed time for him to write monographs on various ailments of the brain.

She, inevitably, retired from her job as a primary school teacher to devote herself to keeping house and home for the family. They were good people, generous and, with only one significant exception, unfailingly supportive. What right did I have to risk dishonouring them by searching for my birth mother?

I wanted for nothing. Our village in the valley of Farndale was remote and peaceful, and notwithstanding the sombre, bleak atmosphere that characterised the late winter afternoons, my upbringing was stable. My life was happy. I had no desire to change it.

Thankfully, the tension with my father never degenerated into outright hostility, but even so there are few things more corrosive for a young man's spirits than a parent's thinly concealed disappointment. I learnt to conceal the more outré theories that caught my interest beneath the academically respectable cloak of psychology.

The most modern of the sciences, of all academic disciplines psychology offered the greatest possibility of delivering an explanation of the mind that did not rely purely on molecular actions in the brain.

My father agreed, through gritted teeth, to fund my study of Philosophy and Psychology at Cardinal College, Oxford.

Yet conflict raged within my heart. By the time I had left university the need to find my biological mother had returned, more urgent than before. The compulsion was almost irresistible but resist it I did. Whatever my birth mother's reasons for giving me up, I knew her suffering must have been unbearable. Was it fair of me to risk finding her when she might not want to be found, to risk embarrassing her with shame? I couldn't do that.

Nevertheless, the questions continued and eventually a visceral need to know opened a hollow space at my core. I filled that space by carving out my own route through the world: a career in psychology, first as a counsellor for children receiving the dubious benevolence of the social services and later in academia; a return to Oxford for my doctorate, then as a lecturer and eventually a Fellow of my old college.

Psychology may have been enjoying a wave of popularity, but I worried that if I publicly announced the full range of my scientific interests in areas such as extrasensory perception and telekinesis, my colleagues would laugh at me. That I would never publish again. At least, not in my own name.

That was the solution I deployed. I conducted my research into these esoteric fringes of psychology in secret, and published my findings under assumed names, in heretical journals. Journals that sold a great many subscriptions in plain, unmarked envelopes.

The work was my therapy, helping pacify my mind and banish, or so I thought, the residual doubts about my unconventional preoccupations and my unknown parents.

I helped children with traumas that eclipsed my own and in the process I helped myself. I learned to quiet my questioning mind; I brought my thoughts to order and subdued them. I learned to be at peace with the past.

And I was, for a time. Until John Wesley's letter. Until Senate House and its curious library on the eighth floor.

Until Sarah Grey.

Now, as dawn broke through the shuttered windows of my study, I was overcome with an all consuming anger. All my life I had wondered about my birth mother, hoping she had enjoyed a happy, fulfilling life, only to discover, so late, how mislaid those hopes were.

The truth about my real father's identity lunged at me from the manuscript. Harry Price had been a rogue and a fraud, had abused the trust of my mother and of the whole world. He had presided over a carnival of gaudy lies, and covered his deceptions with the charm of a showman. The idea that my abiding interests were the legacy of his blood was intolerable.

How could John Wesley, a stranger, have kept this from me? How could I have been the last to know?

I spent all morning gazing into my coffee, struggling to make sense of the information I had read. I began to redefine my own identity in the language of Harry Price's shortcomings. I recalled my arguments with my adoptive father, and realised with dismay that I wanted him back.

Maybe, just maybe, I was mistaken. Growing up in North Yorkshire, I was very well acquainted with dark tales of ghosts and superstitious legends. Perhaps this explained why, like Harry Price, I had held a lifelong interest in matters of the peculiar.

The argument raged back and forth in my head. The clues were compelling: same dates, same name, even the same village. I had to know the truth, if not for my sake for that of my dear wife Julia and my little ones.

Where to start? Who to ask? My adoptive parents had taken their offer to help me track down my parents with them to the grave. There was only one way to know for sure.

By lunchtime I had informed Julia that I was I stepping out, heading back to London, to Senate House and the Harry Price Magical Library.

I found the curator, John Wesley, as before, on the eighth floor, sitting at a large desk before a high leaded window. I strode towards him, past playbills from the 1930s and framed posters for performances by various mediums, magicians and entertainers. Something about the gloomy room was different; there were more boxes than I remembered and fewer books.

'How long have you known?' I demanded once I was standing over him.

The old man raised his head into the weak light. At the corners of his eyes, beneath yellowing skin, blue veins crawled away. 'Too long,' he said with grit in his voice. 'Long enough to have watched you from a distance to be certain that you were the one to help me.'

'*Help* you?' I slammed the leather pouch containing the manuscript down in a puff of dust. 'Help you with what?'

'Please sit down, Dr Caxton.'

I did so reluctantly, keeping my eyes on the curator's wary features.

'Dr Caxton, I've preserved this odd collection my entire life. But now I'm retiring' – his gaze dropped sadly on a box already packed full of rare books – 'the University wants to close it down, be rid of old Harry's legacy for good.' His chest rattled with another cough. 'Someone must ensure that never happens, that these great questions about the occult and the mysteries of the universe aren't left unopposed and unchecked.' He darted me an expectant look. 'You.'

I couldn't help scanning my surroundings even as I recoiled at his suggestion and feeling, in a peculiar way, joined to them now; I could hear the artefacts whispering to me. There was something unnervingly compelling about those voices. They spoke, rustling and seductive, directly to my soul, directing their enticements at my secret interests. Like my father before me, I could lie to the academic community, to this man before me, to the whole damn world – but not to myself.

If the infamous Harry Price really was my father, then who

else was better fitted to carry on his work? Work which would vindicate my own clandestine research and resolve the questions that had obsessed me all my life or take me to the brink of ridicule and professional ruin.

'It's out of the question,' I blurted, scrambling for reasons to refuse him. 'If Sarah Grey and Harry Price learned anything, it's surely that these things are evil, better left alone. Borley Rectory took the better part of them both.'

I turned my head away only to find myself staring directly at the stone bust of Harry Price.

'You can't run from yourself, Dr Caxton. It's in your blood – Harry Price's passion, his quest. You were conceived in that house by the original investigators of the case; you are the child of the Rectory. It is your duty now to continue what your parents, your father, started.'

He was a tactician of truth, this gnarled and wily man. His exhortations pierced my feeble protests and thudded like arrows into the bullseye of my secret heart.

'Sarah Grey,' I said firmly. 'Why are you so certain? Where is your proof?'

'We'll get to that,' he said with a conviction that obviated the task. The proof was in his pale transfixing gaze. In his cracked and antique voice.

'Then tell me where she is buried. I shall need to say goodbye, to pay my respects.' I held his gaze defiantly even as my lip trembled. At last the doubts burned off like morning mist and golden rays of certainty came blazing through.

'Your respects? Oh, my dear man.' Wesley raised his eyebrows and the faintest trace of amusement crinkled the corners of his mouth. 'Sarah Grey is alive.'

The words jolted me to my feet and for a dreadful moment I felt the truth of his remark. The room swayed with me. I gripped the ladder-back chair to brace myself, in a surreal echo of that day in Yorkshire, decades away, at the kitchen table.

Behind his half-moon spectacles, Wesley's eyes narrowed with shrewd watchfulness. 'You *will* help me,' he commanded with gentle menace, 'if you want to know the truth.'

Against my inner reluctance I could feel myself nodding. No sooner had I returned to my seat than he reached beneath his desk for a battered briefcase. Buckles snapped and the case flipped open, releasing bundles of old papers – among them, a faded photograph of Sarah in a slim black dress standing next to Price on the doorstep of the Laboratory in Queensberry Place.

'Was she mad?' I asked.

'She was in love . . .' shrugged Wesley. 'The same thing, perhaps.'

He slid something towards me across the desk: a small envelope, which I took and proceeded to open.

The note within, seven months old, was scrawled in black ink:

> Overhurst Farm
> Broad Haven,
> Wales
> 6 March 1977

Dear John,

I wanted to thank you for your prolonged efforts to keep interested investigators at a distance from us both. We appreciate your discretion more than you'll ever know.

It's odd. Sarah always said she believed that the curse of Borley Rectory fell upon those who deceived others; but after she wrote the manuscript she entrusted to your care, her spirits lifted. Her confession exonerated her, somehow, from whatever dark punishment she believed was waiting for her.

Although life has been very kind to us here in Wales, I do worry for my Sarah; that when I am gone she will be left behind, alone with her fears. When that day comes, and if it is within your power, please do your best for me and ensure she is not neglected.

You see, John, there are mysteries here, in Wales, too. Odd things. Something very strange happened at a local school just recently. The children witnessed something most bizarre, something predatory. It needs the attention of an expert . . . you will know the sort of expertise I mean.

Although I think Harry Price did psychical research a disservice with his occasional tricks, I do believe that, so long as mysteries endure, there should always be someone like him following in close pursuit. For all our sakes.

Yours in trust,

Vernon Wall

Wesley was at my side, laying a bony hand on my shoulder. 'Afterwards, she spent her life with Vernon in the one place she felt safe, the farmhouse she ran to in 1933.' He gave a pained sigh. 'And all these years I did as they wished . . . I kept Vernon and Sarah hidden – kept their location secret.'

I tracked his gaze down to the weighty leather pouch resting in the glow of the table lamp, then looked again into the old man's face. His eyes revealed a quiet expression of hope.

'It was you,' I ventured finally. 'You brought them together. Vernon and Sarah.'

He shrugged. 'What else could I have done? Some ghosts haunt buildings; some we carry around with us. When Sarah entrusted her manuscript to me, I saw the weight of the thing had taken its toll upon her – she was haunted . . .'

'By the Borley curse?'

He nodded and, pausing for thought, added, 'That and the rest: her own false hopes, her squandered desires. Well . . . I knew where to find Mr Wall . . .'

'So you ensured they found one another.'

'My good deed. Although I'm sorry to say it did not go unpunished . . .'

He reached into his cardigan pocket, then held out a trembling, clenched hand and opened it.

'Oh God . . .' I stepped back, feeling the hairs on the back of my neck prick up. In the palm of his hand lay a small brass medallion.

'The lies have their price,' said Wesley, before breaking into another frightful bout of coughing.

'You took it from her? Why? Why did you keep it?'

'I can't get rid of it,' was his next remark. 'It always comes back. And helping Sarah was my calling. I answered it, as you must answer yours now, Robert. Vernon Wall died seven months ago and Sarah is alone. She needn't be.' He gripped my shoulders, studying my face. 'The ghost hunter's son! His quest passes to you now.'

I glanced again to my right, to the stone bust of Harry Price, the man who was supposed to be my father, the collector and discoverer. And then, another thought struck me: 'There must be more . . . other stories Sarah never shared. The places she

and Harry went to together, their investigations into the supernatural, other adventures.'

Wesley's eyes glinted. 'Oh yes, Robert. And if you're willing to
listen – if you're able to find her – Sarah will tell you.'

I looked up ahead and through the rain-soaked windscreen saw
the gloomy lane open into a small clearing beyond which wide
fields sloped down towards the cliff edge. Directly ahead was
an old well, and immediately to the right, behind a low, crumbling stone wall, was the farmhouse. Once, perhaps, it had been
gleaming white, but now its walls were weathered yellow and
the paint around the windows had peeled.

No phone calls. A chain of letters, lengthening, culminating.
Eventually a meeting. Here in West Wales.

Her handwritten notes described me as a 'beautiful child'.
They told me how much I had weighed, that I had been a strong,
happy baby. The nurses had smiled when they saw me.

Her last note:

*After you were born, I went to a convent which stood on
the outskirts of Ilkley Moor. You slept in my arms all the
way from the hospital. When the time came to say goodbye,
I froze. The waiting nun had to prise you from my arms.
She walked away with a part of me, and from that day I
wondered – every year, every birthday, every day – what
had happened in your life, who you had become and what
you looked like.*

And at that point, I had known that John Wesley was right: I had
to find her, not just to learn about my father and myself but to
show her what I had done with my life. To explain that what-

ever torment she had endured by giving me up, I had been all right. Had done well. Become a respected academic. She needed to know that she could be proud of me.

My mouth was dry with the unconscious fear of rejection, and as my car rolled to a halt I caught the movement of a curtain at the closest window. I reached for the glove compartment and clicked it open. Inside were the photographs I had brought to show Sarah Grey: my beautiful girls and my wife, posing together in the earlier summer outside the Colosseum in Rome.

I waited, my chest tightening around a thundering heart, mentally rehearsing everything I would ask the woman who had brought me into the world. I was about to meet someone who had only ever been a name to me. What would she be like? I pictured a frail, elegant woman in a wool cardigan. Any time we had left would be painfully limited. There would be smiles. There would be tears. And I would embrace her in a hug that lasted fifty years.

My eyes roamed as I climbed out of the car. Beyond the farmhouse, out to sea, which was wild and black and forever, lightning shredded the sky. And somewhere, beyond the curtain of rain, in another place, I imagined Harry Price was watching.

THE END

Author's Note

The haunting of Borley Rectory and Harry Price's investigation are legendary. Rumours and stories abound and have fuelled many books on what might – or might not – be lurking in that bleak and isolated hamlet perched on the Essex–Suffolk border. But what is the truth?

During my first visit to Borley in 2010, I was unable to find anyone willing to admit to any unusual experiences on or near the site of the old Rectory. The few residents I did meet were keen to emphasise that any stories of ghosts were fictitious and that the legend of the Rectory was nothing but an elaborate hoax. I even wrote a letter to every resident in the village, requesting that they share any personal experiences of haunting. None did.

But then came a curious and unsettling development.

An old friend who accompanied me to Borley on a later date revealed in confidence that he had heard strange noises as we approached the churchyard. In his words, 'the sound of a coach and horses pounding the road'.

The odd thing was, we hadn't seen any coach or horses.

When I mentioned this to an elderly woman living close to

the site of the old Rectory, she became serious and said quietly, 'Yes, people do keep reporting that . . . But if strange things *do* still happen here, I'm hardly likely to tell you. Don't expect anyone else here to discuss it, either.'

Whatever the truth about that mysterious, out-of-the-way place, it is the legend of Borley rather than its historical detail that I have sought to re-imagine. This novel is certainly not a faithful retelling of Harry Price's association with the house, but a fictional representation of what might have happened. I owe a debt of gratitude to the source material in Harry Price's original books, *The Most Haunted House of England* and *The End of Borley Rectory*.

The following elements in the story are true:

★ The Harry Price Magical Library was looked after for forty-two years by the late Alan Wesencraft, who died on 3 December 2007. For many years, the collection was stored in a room on the eighth floor of University of London's Senate House Library, which is itself reputedly haunted. Yes, there really are rumours about the eighth floor, and the collection is one of the largest and most important of its kind anywhere in the world. More information is available at *www.neilspring.com*

★ The National Laboratory for Psychical Research was based on the top floor of 16 Queensberry Place, the headquarters of the London Spiritualist Alliance. Whereas the setting remains consistent for my story, in reality Price's lease with the LSA expired in 1930. The following year, the Laboratory was relocated to 13 Roland Gardens in South Kensington. It was dissolved in 1934.

★ In 1927, at Church Hall in Westminster, Harry Price staged a sensational public opening of Joanna Southcott's 'locked box'.

★ The Bull sisters observed the apparition of a nun in the Rectory garden on 28 July 1900. From that day, 28 July became known in Borley as 'the nun's day'.

★ The Borley case came to Harry Price's attention in 1929 via Alexander Campbell, the editor of the *Daily Mirror*, after Mrs Smith wrote a letter to the newspaper asking to be put in touch with the Society for Psychical Research. Vernon Wall did not lock horns with Harry Price. He resigned from the *Mirror* in 1932 and became a freelance reporter.

★ According to Harry Price, the title of his book – *The Most Haunted House in England* – came from a labourer whom he stopped and asked for directions on his way to Borley Rectory.

★ Price's arrival at the Rectory on 12 June 1929 coincided with a range of unusual happenings; stones and mothballs were thrown, bells rang, a candlestick came hurtling down the stairs and a brick crashed through the verandah roof. Vernon Wall also reported that he had seen a dark shape moving in the garden and caught his foot in a rotten well cover in the Rectory cellars. The order of these events has been altered significantly in my story.

★ The Blue Room seance on the night of 12–13 June 1929 lasted three hours and was attended by the Bull sisters, Mr and Mrs Smith, Vernon Wall, Harry Price and his real secretary at the time, Lucy Kay. During this seance, a cake of soap was indeed thrown at the wall and raps were heard on the back of a mirror, spelling out names and messages by an entity purporting to be the spirit of the late rector, Harry Bull, who claimed he had been murdered.

★ Many people working at the Bull Inn, near Borley, claim to have experienced paranormal phenomena. Interviews with some of these witnesses are available at *www.neilspring.com*

★ Harry Price sat with the Austrian medium Rudi Schneider many times, and in May 1932 obtained an incriminating photograph which he later claimed was his revenge for Rudi associating with the Society for Psychical Research. During another seance in his Laboratory, Harry communicated with a medium who appeared to be speaking with the voice of Sir Arthur Conan Doyle. These seances were entirely separate events, and on neither occasion did events transpire as the Rudi seance is presented in my story.

★ Although the scenes involving Harry Price and Sarah Grey with the Reverend Lionel Foyster and Marianne are imagined, it is true that Price returned to Borley Rectory in October 1931 with a group of interested colleagues. It is also true that he was persuaded to return to Borley by Ethel Bull; that Lionel Foyster sent Price a copy of his *Diary of Occurrences*, which Price did not return; and that Price signed an agreement of confidentiality with the rector. He left the house with the impression that the phenomena in the house were caused by Marianne, but paradoxically later wrote up the case as an apparently genuine incident of poltergeist phenomena.

★ Marianne Foyster was born in 1899 and died in 1992. It is true that she married a man by the name of Greenwood at just fifteen and that when she married Foyster in 1922 there was no evidence of any divorce. According to evidence from Trevor Hall and Robert Wood, author of *The Widow Of Borley*, the Foysters' lives were extremely dysfunctional, with Marianne pursuing a sexual relationship with Frank Peerless, the lodger at Borley Rectory.

★ During the fire which destroyed Borley Rectory on 27 February 1939, a police constable and locals watched what they thought were ghostly figures walking in the flames. Captain

W. H. Gregson's son, Alan William Gregson, later claimed that the fire started while his father was shelving books in the library when an oil lamp accidentally tipped over; but another son, Anthony, claimed that the house was torched for insurance purposes.

★ My character Sarah's interpretation of the wall writings 'well tank bottom me' is based on an elaborate theory devised by Canon W. J. Phythian-Adams, who wrote to Harry Price in January 1941 urging him to dig in order to substantiate the theory. Although the writings appear to have been written in Marianne's hand, some witnesses claimed that the wall writing appeared in front of their eyes.

★ In July 1943, human remains – the jawbone of a woman and the left side of a skull – were discovered at the site of the Rectory. The jawbone was analysed by a dental surgeon, Leslie J. Godden, who found it was severely infected and was likely to have caused great pain during life. Harry Price theorised that this was the reason the phantom nun of Borley was always seen looking pale and haggard and unhappy.

★ Harry Price died suddenly of a heart attack at his home in Pulborough on 29 March 1948. The St Ignatius Borley medallion was found on his body, after his former secretary, Lucy Kay, sent it to him at his request. Until recently, the location of the Borley medallion was unknown; but shortly before the completion of this novel, its whereabouts were privately disclosed to me.

★ In January 1956, Eric J. Dingwall, Kathleen M. Goldney and Trevor H. Hall published their 'Borley Report' in the *Proceedings of the Society for Psychical Research*. The results of their five-year investigation destroyed Price's reputation as a reliable psychical researcher, accusing him of fraud in practically all aspects of the Borley case. Professor Anthony Flew, who reviewed the report in the *Spectator* on 27 January 1956, referred to the Borley case as 'a house of cards which Harry Price built out of little more than a pack of lies'. By then Charles Suttton, a journalist, had gone public with the news that he had witnessed Price throwing stones at the Rectory.

★ In March 2004, the fourteenth-century tithe barn, which was positioned just next to where the Rectory had stood, was converted into a handsome private house. During the course of the work human skeletal remains were unearthed in its foundations: fragments of skull, ribs and leg bones. Analysis of the remains confirmed they were female.

★ Reports of unusual sounds and occurrences at the site of Borley Rectory continue to this day.

As for Harry, his character – brilliant and ambitious, impatient, selfish and unreliable, charming and riddled with contradictions – is based on the true Harry Price, who was born to a working-class family and certainly embellished his upbringing and his credentials. I have exaggerated and imagined aspects of his character. The real Harry Price was not, for example, a good public speaker and showed much greater initial enthusiasm for the Borley investigation than is implied in my story. He never employed an assistant named Radley and he never kept his paper bag business a secret. Nor is it necessarily true that he sympathised with the Nazi regime, although he did possess a great many photographs of German architecture, and in July 1939 he drafted a letter to Hitler, requesting 'facilities for attending – in comfort – the Nuremberg Rally in August'.[1]

Harry's foil, Sarah Grey, is my creation. I found some small inspiration for her character in Harry's former secretary, Lucy

Kay (born Violet Lucy Kaltenbach). Lucy,whose father was a commercial clerk named Maximilian, was a young actress of German descent who trained at RADA, and was first introduced to Harry at the opening of his Laboratory. Their meeting wasn't at all hostile or dramatic in the way Sarah's encounter is presented. Nor did she move to Wales and live out her days with Vernon Wall. In fact she died from cirrhosis of the liver in Hammersmith on 7 May 1955, and although she was only involved in the initial investigation of Borley Rectory – having left Price's employ in the early 1930s – unlike Sarah, she was a willing believer in the phenomena encountered there, as well as a staunch defender of Harry Price. 'It is my considered conviction that Harry Price never, at any time, faked phenomena,' she wrote. 'I am convinced he was a man of unimpeachable integrity.'[2]

There are indications that Lucy Kay led rather an unpredictable, irresponsible life. According to her son David, she frequently moved between addresses in the Paddington area of London, enjoyed betting on horses and was not sensible with financial affairs. In fact, she even borrowed money from Harry Price, whom she found 'hypnotic'. The pair formed a close friendship which lasted until Price's death, after which Lucy had replicas of the Borley medallion made, and sold them for profit.

Despite suspicions, there is no conclusive evidence that Harry and Lucy's closeness ever developed into a romance. In my novel, Sarah's Grey's child by Harry, Dr Caxton, is entirely fictional. His character brings us to the heart of the book through layered narrative – a well-worn technique in the ghost-story genre.

When people ask me what makes a good ghost story, I invariably tell them that the reader must be made to care about the ghost. We have to know something of their life on earth if we are to care about them in death. So it might seem odd that in this novel we learn very little about the phantom nun, but we do learn a great deal about Harry, Sarah and the residents of Borley Rectory. This is deliberate, because ultimately they are the true ghosts of the piece.

I like to think that Sarah and Harry are still out there somewhere, chasing ghosts and solving mysteries, a conception I hope will be realised one day through dramatic adaptations. Harry Price, ever the showman, might approve of this idea.

I hope so.

Neil Spring

London, 2013

Notes

1   Letter from Harry Price to Eric Dingwall, 28 July 1939.
2   Lucie Meeker, quoted in *Borley Postscript*, p. 143.

Bibliography

Adams, Paul, Eddie Brazil and Peter Underwood. *The Borley Rectory Companion*. Stroud, Gloucestershire: The History Press, 2009.

Banks, Ivan. *The Enigma of Borley Rectory*. London: Foulsham, 1996.

Clarke, A. "The Bones of Borley." *The Foxearth and District Local History Society*, 2005. <http://www.foxearth.org.uk/BorleyRectory>

Dingwall, Eric John, Kathleen M. Goldney and Trevor Henry Hall. *The Haunting of Borley Rectory*. London: Duckworth, 1956.

Aickman, R.F. "Postscript to Harry Price." *Mystery. An Anthology of the Mysterious in Fact and Fiction*. Ed. Negley Farson, et al. London: Hulton Press, 1952.

Foyster, Reverend Lionel Algernon. *Summary of Experiences at Borley Rectory*. University of London: Senate House Library [HPC/3G/2], 1938.

Foyster, Reverend Lionel Algernon. Untitled Letters. University of London: Senate House Library [HPC/4B/74], 1931.

Glanville, Sidney H. *The Haunting of Borley Rectory. Private and Confidential Report.* University of London: Senate House Library [HPC/3G/5]

Hall, Trevor Henry. *The Search for Harry Price.* London: Duckworth, 1978.

Henning, Reverend A.C. *Haunted Borley.* Colchester: Shenval Press, 1949.

Mayerling, Louis. *We Faked the Ghosts of Borley.* London: Pen Press, 2000.

Meeker, Lucie. *The Ghost that Kept Harry Price Awake.*

Morris, Richard. *Harry Price the Psychic Detective.* Stroud, Gloucestershire: Sutton Publishing, 2006.

Price, Harry. *Confessions of a Ghost Hunter.* London: Putnam, 1936.

Price, Harry. *Leaves from a Psychist's Casebook.* London: Gollancz, 1933.

Price, Harry. *Journal of the American Society for Psychical Research* (1929).

Price, Harry. *The Most Haunted House in England.* London: Longman, Greene & Co Ltd., 1940.

Price, Harry. *Poltergeist Over England.* London: Country Life, 1945.

Price, Harry. *Search for Truth: My Life for Psychical Research.* London: Collin, 1942.

Price, Harry. *The End of Borley Rectory.* London: George G. Harrap & Co. Ltd., 1946.

Tabori, Paul. *Harry Price: The Biography of a Ghost Hunter.* London: Athenaeum Press, 1950.

Underwood, Peter. *Borley Postscript.* Haslemere: White House Publications, 2001.

Wood, Robert. *The Widow of Borley.* London: Duckworth, 1992.

BIBLIOGRAPHY

Other

Dingwall, Eric John, Kathleen M. Goldney and Trevor Henry Hall. *The Haunted Rectory* [BBC script]. London: British Broadcasting Company, 1956. Republished at http://www.foxearth.org.uk.

'An Authentic Interview with Conan Doyle from Beyond.' New York: *Cosmopolitan*, January 1931.

"Instruction booklets for Observers at Borley Rectory." University of London: Senate House Library [HPC/7/6], 1937.

Websites

http://www.harrypricewebsite.co.uk

To learn more about Borley Rectory, other mysteries and future novels, visit:

www.neilspring.com

Acknowledgements

My sincerest thanks to Guy Chambers, dear friend to whom I owe a debt of gratitude for fishing the opening pages out of the sea (yes, it's true – that doesn't just happen in movies); the fabulous Sharon Kendrick, an early encourager; my excellent literary agent, Cathryn Summerhayes at William Morris Endeavour; everyone at Quercus – my copyeditor, Margaret Histed, the publicists and especially my fantastic editor, Jo Dickinson, who saw the potential and the heart of the story and made it so much better; Tom Winchester and Jo Wright at Bentley Productions, for acquiring television option rights; Portia Rosenberg for her atmospheric illustrations; Alex Harris and Andrew Hiles for a website that does the book proud; all the helpful librarians at the Senate House Library for their permission to reproduce extracts from the Harry Price Library; the employees at the Bull Inn, near Borley and the residents of that quiet hamlet; friends with feedback, including Jurij Senyshyn and Jon Harrison for reading and commenting on early drafts and help with historical accuracies; Owen Meredith, for his patience; my family, for their unfailing support and love; and my brother, James, whose feedback on the text was extremely helpful.

Large portions of this novel were written under the Umbrian sun at Giardinello. Thanks to Guy Black and Mark Boland for your endlessly flowing hospitality.

Contact

NEIL SPRING

f /neilspring.author

t @NeilSpring

www.neilspring.com